Eye of the Tempest

BY NICOLE PEELER

EYE OF THE TEMPEST

TEMPEST

Book Four of the Jane True novels

NICOLE PEELER

www.orbitbooks.net

ORBIT

First published in the United States in 2011 by Orbit

First published in Great Britain in 2011 by Orbit

Copyright © 2011 by Nicole Peeler

Excerpt from *Blood Rights* by Kristen Painter
Copyright © 2011 by Kristen Painter

The moral right of the author has been asserted.

A CIP catalogue record for this book
is available from the British Library.

ISBN 978-0-356-50050-8

Typeset in Times by Palimpsest Book Production Limited, Falkirk, Stirlingshire
Printed and bound in Great Britain by CPI Group (UK) Ltd, Croydon, CR0 4YY

Papers used by Orbit are from well-managed forests
and other responsible sources.

MIX
Paper from
responsible sources
FSC
www.fsc.org   FSC® C104740

Orbit
An imprint of
Little, Brown Book Group
100 Victoria Embankment
London EC4Y 0DY

An Hachette UK Company
www.hachette.co.uk

www.orbitbooks.net

To my friends.
You know who you are, and please know
you mean the world to me.

Chapter One

I awoke slowly, languorously, my still-mostly-sleeping brain registering surprise when my nose smooshed into soft leather rather than sheets. For a second I nearly panicked, before I realized I was nestled into a hugely over-stuffed cushion that was part of a leather sofa. The sofa and the shabby, homemade afghan in which I was cocooned smelled deliciously of lemon polish, cardamom, and just a hint of something more masculine. I knew, then, where I was. Not least because I was soon brushing a few stray dark dog hairs off my face as I rolled over and stretched.

And where is the man himself? I wondered, sitting up to peer around Anyan's dawn-infused living room.

It was only last night that we'd rolled into town from the Alfar Compound. For almost the past month, Anyan and I had been on a desperate hunt to find my mother's killers and shut down their pseudo-laboratories of torture, culminating in our finally outing Jarl as the menace he truly was. As tended to happen when I visited the Alfar Compound, a huge melee ensued, and the Alfar king, Orin, had been murdered by none other than his loving wife, Morrigan. Turns out the queen had been tupping her husband's second and brother, the even nastier than previously assumed Jarl.

During the chaos of the fight, Jarl and Morrigan escaped. So not only were the bad guys on the lam, but the Territory had been left leaderless until Anyan suggested they make like humans and vote on a new leader. Next thing I knew, my former lover, Ryu, and his favorite nemesis, Nyx, found themselves tied as interim leaders of their Territory.

Much to my delight, I also discovered that Anyan did *not* want to stay in the Compound. Instead, he wanted to return to Rockabill. With me.

Where I thought we would make sweaty monkey lovin', I groused, sighing as I stretched out legs tight from the previous night's ride back to Eastport on Anyan's motorcycle.

Instead, all my fantasies of playing 'hide the Milk-Bone' had been scuppered when, on the way home, we'd run into Blondie. The tattooed enigma had been shadowing me, saving my life quite a few times over the course of our recent shenanigans. We didn't know who she was, or what she wanted, but last night she'd let us know she was an Original: powerful, ancient, and supposedly a myth.

'And a total cock-blocker,' I grumbled to myself as I stood, slowly and stiffly, before shuffling off to dig my toiletries bag out of my duffel.

I'd been looking forward to having Anyan alone, finally, and I'd nearly done a backflip when he suggested I spend the night at his place. His excuse was that it made sense for me to wait for the morning, as I had all of Rockabill's supernatural community – plus Grizzie and Tracy – bunking down in my house for safety after Iris had been kidnapped. I knew, however, it was really because he wanted some patented Jane True sexor-cizing. But then Blondie showed up, all nekkid and pierced and tattooed and totally foxy. After which, the conversation between Dog-Boy and me went (roughly) as follows:

DB: 'OMG! Whatever could that woman want?'

JANE: 'I don't care! Let's go to your place! NOW.'

DB: 'No! I must be valorous and protect those under my care by investigating!'

JANE: 'Um, why don't you be valorous and protect those under your care AFTER we mambo horizontally. Then vertically. Then maybe to the Northwest.'

DB: 'I'm sorry, what?'

JANE: 'Nothing.'

So Anyan had tossed me through his front door with our luggage, telling me to 'make myself at home'. I'd flipped off the shutting door, reminding it loudly that I *had* been planning to make myself at home *on his face*. At which point the door was thrown open again, and Anyan had demanded, 'What?'

To which I'd replied, 'Nothing.'

So not only had we not had sex, but I'd also spent the night on the sofa, as I didn't feel comfortable invading Anyan's man space without express permission. Not to mention, my hormones probably would have forced me to do terrible things to myself in his bed, as he owned the raunchiest, Anyan-wrought, supernatural-Sutra headboard ever.

Still grumbling, I shambled over to Anyan's downstairs bathroom to go potty and clean myself up a little. Staring into my own eyes in the mirror as I brushed my teeth, I reminded myself that, while it sucked I had yet to molest the barghest, at least I was alive. There'd been more than a few times during the past weeks when my survival was anything but guaranteed. Not to mention, quite a few people – supernatural, human, and halfling – had died before we'd stopped Jarl and his crazy experiments.

Including my mother, I thought, my heart falling as I

remembered what I had to do today. My dad needed to know that the woman he still loved and still waited for, after all these years, was never going to come home. She'd been murdered by Jarl, her body one of the first to be discovered in an abandoned laboratory.

You didn't die for nothing, Mom, I thought, outmaneuvering the tears in my eyes by washing my face rather roughly. My mother's death had helped kick off the investigation that led to stopping Jarl. It wasn't much consolation, but it was something.

It'd be even better if Jarl were dead, I thought grimly, as I dried my face and hands. But at least he was on the run, his operations and people disbanded. *For now*.

Visibly shaking myself out of my depressing reverie, I tried to figure out what to do right then. Anyan must still have been out chasing Originals, and it was barely six o'clock in the morning. *I could go home, although no one will be awake. Or I could go for a swim . . .* Then I froze, a feeling of elation sweeping up from the soles of my feet as I put two and two together.

I'm in Anyan's cabin.

Anyan isn't here.

And Anyan did say to make myself at home, I thought, audibly purring. I'd been so curious about Anyan's life for so long, and now I had his cabin all to myself . . .

Which means there is nothing standing between me and his kitchen.

Like a flash I was out of the bathroom, all traces of sadness eradicated by my excitement. I peered around one last time to make sure I was alone, and then I darted toward what I knew was waiting for me. Every time I'd been here, it had taken pretty much every ounce of self-control I had not to go and hump the stove dominating Anyan's kitchen. I don't normally hump kitchen appliances, but this was no ordinary mod-con. It was something sublime. Something that transcended beauty, form, and function and could make an angel weep.

It was a Wolf Challenger Restaurant Range. And I loved it.

I skidded to a stop before my destiny, blinking as the ever-awakening sun gleamed off its brightly polished surfaces. Gliding a hand over its hard, proud, stainless-steel frame, I caressed its burners, prying one up just to see how unabashedly it opened itself to me. I thought of all the pots I could get on it, and how each one would simmer. Simmer just for me.

I dropped to my knees, pulling open the oven door. I could practically crawl inside. I wouldn't, because I'd (almost) seen firsthand what ovens can do to a body – albeit a goblin body – but I could if I wanted to. *And if I can get in here*, I thought as I peered inside greedily, *just think what else will fit . . .*

'Jane?' asked a voice. It was curiously nonchalant, considering I was half in, half out of an open oven door. But it still scared me enough that I started, whapping the top of my skull for my trouble.

Anyan sighed as he dropped down to haul me out of the Wolf's gaping maw. The barghest had a tendency to treat me like a sack of flour, and today was no exception. Without batting an eyelash, he lifted me up and set me on the counter, in order to look at the top of my head.

I was watching the little birdies fly in front of my eyes, so it took me a second to re-combobulate myself. In the meantime, he ran his fingers over my scalp, prodding until I winced, and then I felt a pulse of healing warmth filtering through my body.

'If we lived in a Road Runner cartoon,' his rough voice grumbled, 'I would come home one day to find your teeny-tiny arms and legs sprouting from underneath a gigantic Acme anvil.'

I gave him the stink eye.

'You are a disaster,' Anyan clarified, in case I didn't catch his drift. 'And are you all right?' he amended, treating my head to one last gentle prod, followed by another rush of healing magics.

Anyan's gray eyes sought mine but I ignored him, instead giving him a good once-over. Now that I could finally enjoy being around the barghest without all the stress of the investigation – not to mention the stress of not knowing whether or not he had any feelings for me – I felt like I hadn't actually *seen* Anyan in ages. Starting at the top, I noticed that he clearly needed a haircut. His thick curls were extra poufy, sticking out in barghestian afro-puffs shot through with grass and twigs from last night's Blondie hunt. Then my eyes raked downward, over his long nose and almost too wide mouth, loving the perfectly sensual imperfection of his features. His nose twitched at me, as if in response to my gaze, and I felt my own lips twitch in response. Traveling farther down, over clothes rumpled from undoubtedly being left to lie under a shrubbery somewhere while he ran about in dog form, I noticed he had a hole in his jeans, which rode low and sweet on his hips.

There's bones under that there denim, my libido reminded me, unhelpfully. *Bones for nibblin'* . . .

I told the libido to hush even as I felt my mouth water.

'Did you find Blondie?' I asked, as much to distract myself as to make conversation.

'Nope,' he grunted. 'Chased her to the edge of Nell's Territory, but then all scent of her faded, including magical. She must have holed up somewhere I couldn't get to. Underground, or in the water.'

'Do you think she can do thaaaaaaa—' I tried to ask, before my whole body turned to goop as Anyan's fingers started running through my long black hair. It was ridiculously erotic, until I winced as his fingers found a knot.

'Did you pack a brush?' the barghest chided.

'Did you raid a dog food convention to acquire your wardrobe?' I countered, jerking my hair out from underneath his hands in punishment.

After all, I thought with irritation, *I'm supposed to have sexy, postcoital bed head. Not 'I slept on your couch' head.*

His hands stilled in my hair as he looked down at his chest. His now filthy T-shirt sported an advert for Eukanuba. I'd already seen shirts for Alpo, Iams, and Purina, among many others.

'Okay, I admit, the joke got out of hand. But I'm not going to go out and buy myself a whole new wardrobe. These shirts are perfectly serviceable.'

I rolled my eyes. 'Serviceable? Anyan, I get it that you're utilitarian. If we were in the old country you'd write odes to factories. You'd sing the praises of the communal farm while you gnawed on a perfectly "serviceable" radish. But this is the new millennium. In America. Buy a button-up.'

The very tip of his crooked nose twitched, something that would never cease to amuse me. The hand on one knee shifted to pinch my outer-thigh fat, something that I found significantly less endearing.

'Jane, I'm a barghest, not a Stalinist. And what do you mean by "the old country"? I was born in this Territory, as you well know. And you should talk about writing odes to factories. You were practically committing sex acts on my range.'

I cast a long, lascivious gaze at the Wolf. Gods, it was gorgeous. I had to come clean.

'I can't help it, Anyan. I've never felt this way about a

machine. It's just so big . . .' My voice trailed off as my hot
eyes roved up from its sturdily planted legs to the boldly
flaring expanse of its saucy extractor fan.

'Jane, you are starting to creep *me* out. Someone who pees
on the local fauna in order to mark his Territory. That says
something.'

I eyed the Wolf, suddenly inspired.

'And no,' he added hastily. 'If you pee on it you do not
get to take it home.'

I pushed my bottom lip out in a pout, feeling a thrill up
my spine when I noticed Anyan stare like he wanted to bite.
His hands, resting right above my knees, squeezed lightly
and I was happily visualizing pulling him in tight to make
that bite a reality when he spoke.

'Speaking of home, do you still want to tell your father
today?'

And just like that, the libido crawled back into its hole. I'd
asked Anyan if he'd be with me when I told my dad about
my mother's death, mostly for support but also because the
barghest – even with sticks in his hair, like he had now – oozed
authority. I was going to have to tell my father a combination
of truths about my mom, Mari's, death and careful omission,
and I figured Anyan's presence would make the idea that I had
outside sources more credible.

But mostly you just want him there, reminded the part of
my brain that always insisted on being brutally honest. I
frowned, quashing the thought, unwilling to examine my
emotions regarding the barghest too closely.

'Yes,' I replied, finally, my chin dropping to my chest. 'I
need to get it over with.'

Anyan's big hand found its way under the heavy wing of
my long, black hair, stroking gently at my nape. It felt as
comforting as apple pie, and I marveled at how easily he

touched me now. My own hands itched to reciprocate, but I still had to get used to the idea that touches were okay. Anyan had been a fantasy for so long; it was going to take me some time to adjust to the reality.

'Come on, then. Let's clean up. You use my bathroom. I've a shower out in my workshop I can use.'

I raised my black eyes to meet Anyan's iron-gray gaze, letting all my anxiety shine through. The hand on my nape squeezed, gently, in response.

'It's going to be okay, Jane. We'll find a way to tell your father so he understands. You're doing the right thing. He can't live in ignorance and false hope for the rest of his life.'

I nodded, finally. Anyan stepped back so that I could hop down off the counter, and then we went our separate ways to clean up. I'd already used his upstairs bathroom once, so I knew where everything was located. The only thing that took a while was finding something clean(ish) in my duffel, but soon enough I came downstairs to find Anyan all spiffy, sitting on his sofa and waiting for me.

We walked outside to his motorcycle. I slung my arms through my duffel bag's straps, wearing it like a backpack, and then plunked the helmet Anyan held out to me on my head. I fiddled with the straps, watching as Anyan started to set his own helmet down over his still-wet hair.

I was just imagining the helmet head with which he was going to wind up when he suddenly lowered his arms, breathing deeply and looking around with confusion written across his expression.

'Why do I smell strange humans?' he asked, a split second before we were attacked.

Chapter Two

If whoever attacked us had given Anyan even a millisecond of warning, things would have turned out differently. Anyan's a warrior with battle-honed reflexes and a healthy dose of paranoia.

But there was no warning. One moment we were standing beside his motorcycle on his gravel driveway, and the next Anyan smelled humans. Then he was down, taken out by what sounded and looked, from the state he was in, like dozens of high-impact bullets.

Meanwhile, I was no longer the little rabbit heart that I'd been just months ago. So although I was too late to stop the bullets, as soon as Anyan hit the ground, I had full magical shields up and ready to protect both of us . . . from the supernatural attack that never came.

For instead of supes, I watched as half a dozen humans in very fancy SWAT gear emerged from the forests surrounding Anyan's house. I'd raised mage balls immediately, but I didn't let fire. Not least because I knew what the red laser beams trailing over both my own body and Anyan's meant. Plus, I knew damned well they could use those massive guns – while I sensed not a single iota of magic, the way they melted out of that thick green foliage was almost preternatural. These were professionals, even if they weren't magical, and they'd drop me with a bullet before I could take out more than one or two of them. So I let my mage ball fall to the ground and fizzle out, my mind racing for a way to incapacitate all of them without getting myself or Anyan killed in the process.

'Target is down,' I heard one of the men speak into his helmet's microphone. 'Secondary target is secure.'

I doubted even a full minute had passed.

The secondary target stood mute, my mind racing to figure out a way to save our skins. Meanwhile Anyan lay bleeding to death on his driveway.

Powerful supes, like the barghest, are tough to kill. They're hard to get a bead on in the first place, and they can also heal themselves as they take on damage. The only way to kill someone as strong as Anyan would be to ensure his heart or brain had stopped in that first attack, or to knock him unconscious when he was full of holes, so that he bled to death. My friend Daoud was nearly exsanguinated the time we were tracking the crazy halfling Conleth, and I never wanted to see that happen again. Especially to Anyan.

'I repeat, primary target is down,' the man said again as one of his cohorts strode over to where Anyan lay. The crunch of gravel under his boots seemed abnormally loud in the eerily quiet morning. I half expected the barghest to spring up and attack, revealing that it had all been a clever ruse.

But Anyan's body stayed where it was, red blood seeping under gray stone.

Meanwhile, there was only one thing I could think to do. I knew it was a risk, and I'd been told not to do it once before. But I could feel, in my gut, it was my only real option.

The man who had been speaking had a 'listening' face, after which he nodded and said, 'Yes, sir.' Then he looked at the man standing next to Anyan and said, 'Confirm the kill.'

The man raised his rifle to his chest, sighting down on where the barghest lay, undefended. He was aiming his massive rifle at Anyan's head. Taking a deep breath, but otherwise giving no outward indication, I sprang my trap.

Luckily for me, no one thinks I'm anything special. I'm a halfling, and everyone assumes – quite incorrectly, as with most racist stereotypes – that halflings are exactly what the name implies: half as good, half as strong, and half as necessary.

So while at least two of the men had their laser sites trained on me, they hadn't incapacitated me in any way. I was but a small woman, and only a little chit of a halfling.

Praise be to the god who invented underestimation, I thought, as I began to gather my power to me.

Running on adrenaline and instinct, I fell almost instant-aneously into the cocoon of magic I'd felt the other time Anyan had been hurt in front of me. It had been only weeks before, in Pittsburgh, that Phaedra had nixed Anyan's ambush by hurling him into a wall. He'd landed in a sickening heap, causing me to go all primeval and *reach* with my power. The only thing that had stopped me was Blondie's intervention and her warning that I should never, ever heed that siren's song to *pull*.

What I saw in my magical trance back then was just like what I saw now. Water, water everywhere, and all of it full of power. Water connected everything: hydrogen and oxygen atoms, tiny strings of pearls hung like billions of bead curtains across my vision. It was like being in the *Matrix*'s computer code, only instead of numbers there was water. And if you switched your perspective, it became obvious that just as the water droplets went up and down, they also went horizontally.

Connecting each and every one of us, I thought, as I went down deeper into my power, until I *was* my power . . .

And then I searched out the strings of beads connecting me to my attackers. Finding them, I reached, again . . .

And then, seeing no other alternative, I did exactly what I'd been told not to do. I pulled.

Focused on the man who was going to shoot out Anyan's brains, I only saw what I did to him. Despite the circumstances, and never regretting my actions, what I saw – what I did – still haunts me.

Apparently, people remember their first kill.

He was just setting his eye to his site when he jerked hard. Thankfully, he didn't have his finger on the trigger at that moment, or he may well have shot Anyan. Instead, his arm holding his assault rifle dropped uselessly to his side as he spasmed. I saw, in my peripheral vision, similar movements from his fellow attackers.

My assault lasted only seconds, but it felt like hours.

I called to the water in all the men's bodies, and it responded to me with the alacrity of a squadron of eager retrievers. I watched, cold, as the man upon whom my eyes were pinned began to shrivel, but I didn't stop. I didn't stop when he fell to his knees, and I didn't stop when he fell to the ground.

I didn't stop even when I saw that the fingers protruding from his leather half-gloves were desiccated like those of a long-dead mummy.

True guilt about my actions would never set in – I knew what I did was right. Those men made their choice when they took money to murder strangers, and – somewhere between the Alfar Compound and the Healer's mansion – I'd become hard enough by what I'd seen of evil to understand that fact. But visions of the bodies would still appear to me in random nightmares. At that moment, however, all I felt was *power* . . . The men's lives came to me through their bodies' water, and I tasted what it was to take another person's life by stealing, quite literally, their essence. . . .

The water in me answered the water in them, and I felt my magic's channels open wide, inviting, receiving, until I was as full as I've ever been of elemental force.

Still, I couldn't stop.

Full to bursting with magic, I kept soaking up more. It was like I'd opened up some internal pair of floodgates. I'd never felt so full, so strong . . . until it began to burn. Pain suddenly seared through my system hotter than a thousand suns.

Screaming, I fell to my own knees as the power stretched me to my limits. Just when I thought I'd pass out from the pain, the tide of my power turned. Just as all that elemental force had rushed into my open channels, it now all rushed out. I felt myself emptying, and suddenly I knew that what I'd hoped would save Anyan's life would probably end my own.

On the night I'd found my love Jason's body in the Old Sow, I was totally untrained and ignorant of my true magical inheritance. So I'd unwittingly used my magic – *all* of my magic – to pull him from the giant whirlpool off the coast of Rockabill. I'd almost died that night, so I knew that draining a supe of all of his magic killed him as effectively as draining him entirely of blood.

'Anyan,' I whispered, reaching out my hand toward the barghest. I was prostrate on my stomach, the gravel digging into my belly. Feeling my heart flutter, I figured I was done for. Everything seemed a bit hazy, however, and I now reckon that the only reason I wasn't panicked was that my brain wasn't entirely cognizant of what was happening. Instead I was quite calm; I just wanted to know Anyan was alive before I went.

Which is why I was so very, very pissed when someone had the audacity to roll me over like I was a side of beef. To be fair, Blondie looked almost as miffed as me when she finally settled me on my back.

'I told you not to go there, babydoll,' she mumbled, as her tattooed hands stroked down my face.

I wanted to protest, to tell her to see to Anyan before attending to me. But unconsciousness swamped me in darkness, and then I felt nothing.

The planet was dead all around. Nothing grew, nothing lived – except me, my siblings, and, somewhere out in the darkness, our cousins. I huddled with my brothers and sisters against the Earth, cradled by Water. So young, we were afraid to venture out of the sanctuary created by our parents. We were small, then. Unaware of our power and innocent in our play.

[*Everything is so young,* I marveled, remembering for just a moment that I was Jane True and that these images (memories?) couldn't be my own. But that moment faded, along with my humanity.]

Soon, however, we stretched our limbs and discovered they were long and strong. We flexed our power, realizing our potential. But born of Water and Earth – born of love – my siblings and I used that knowledge only for play – play that one day took us outside the safety of our nest. Unharmed, we looked at one another and felt joy.

[*I thought I had two eyes,* murmured she who had been Jane.]

Ever more confident, we strayed further afield, boiling the seas with the energy of our games. Our bodies grew along with our curiosity and soon we were almost too large to return to our sanctuary. To sleep, we had to press together in a tangle of limbs [*Too many limbs,* I thought, even if I wasn't sure who *I* was anymore]. And yet there was such comfort in those touches, knowing my siblings were always there, that I would never be alone.

Until the day our cousin, Fire's offspring, decided that he would like to play.

Born of ambition and rage, Fire's children were not curious or playful or kind. But they were strong. And the one that came to us that day was the oldest, the most powerful, of Fire's dangerous brood. At first it joined us in our games, and no one noticed when something changed. Until my sister's limbs [*So many limbs*] were floating past me, unattached, and the ocean ran red with blood.

I survived only because of my parents' intervention. Seizing upon Fire's child, they pulled him apart until even Fire itself couldn't rekindle him.

Returning to my cold nest, I huddled in the darkness, alone. [*So alone . . .*]

There was a war, then, between my parents and Fire. Air, as usual, remained neutral and I stayed hidden, at my parents' behest. The planet was nearly riven in two before Air interceded. A truce was made, in which Fire agreed that he would make no more children as powerful as the one who had killed my siblings. But he forced my parents to agree to the same.

Which meant I would be alone, forever.

That said, my parents, Air, and Fire could still create offspring, and they did. Creatures of less magnitude than my generation, but still powerful. Often too powerful. I watched as scenarios similar to the slaughter of my own family happened time and time again, until only the most wicked, the most powerful, or the most intelligent survived.

Time passed like water rushing over a fall, and eventually I noticed my parents were weary. Air had long since laid itself down to rest, tired of life and loss. Soon Fire joined Air, its passion turned cold and pointless. My parents held out longer, their love sustaining them. Yet, eventually, even they took to sleep.

I grieved the loss of Earth, Water, Fire, and Air, but I marveled at the glory of the world they had created. Their bodies merged to form a planet very different from the one

I had known, and their power combined generated something so beautiful I wept to see it: life.

The planet now teemed with life, life that I witnessed evolve from mere sparks to plants to animals and, finally, to humans. I saw the gleam of intelligence in their eyes, and I watched them love, live, and lose, and I felt my own loneliness driven home to me. [*So lonely . . . so lonely.*]

Soon enough, there was no place for me. Humans had spread across the globe, driving me from Territory to Territory. My size and power disrupted the planet, creating chaos.

Tsunami, I was called. *Earthquake. Volcano. Charybdis. Chaos. Kali. Ragnarok. Apocalypse.*

[*Never meant to hurt. Just so alone . . .*]

Wherever I went, Earth was shattered, or tidal waves rose from the depths. The Air grew furious and even Fire raged. As a creature of that first, misbegotten generation, I had become something too powerful.

I did not belong anywhere, anymore.

And so I, too, laid myself down to rest. To sleep. And as oblivion drifted over me, I set my protections . . .

Only to wake, gasping. A hand, holding mine, clutched my fingers tightly and I [*Jane True!* I remembered] turned to see the elated face of my father staring at me through eyes red with sleep deprivation. Tears streamed down his face and into his beard as he watched me as if afraid I'd disappear.

'Jane?' he asked, as I wondered when the hell he'd had time to grow a beard.

I tried to speak, but my voice wouldn't work. Instead, much to my consternation, I made a noise that sounded a bit like the braying of a donkey.

'Has our patient finally decided to join the land of the living?' came a cool voice from somewhere far below, just loud enough to hear. My father responded with an inarticulate shout of happiness. Nonplussed, my brain and my vision both a bit muzzy, I eventually managed to raise my head on a neck loose as a noodle. I looked around, blinking dazedly at a room lit only by the glow of a full moon shining through a skylight. Eventually, after my eyes adjusted to the gloom, I realized that I was in Anyan's loft bedroom, and in Anyan's bed.

How does my dad know Anyan? I thought. Followed quickly by, *Oh dear gods, Anyan*, as I suddenly recalled my very last memory.

But before I could say anything, I nearly fainted as an unglamoured goblin walked up the stairs to Anyan's loft, setting a green-scaled, black-clawed hand on my father's shoulder, his yolk-yellow eyes peering at me with an admittedly eggy combination of happiness and relief.

I wasn't surprised by the goblin – after all, they're the healers of the supernatural world. What I was surprised by was the fact that instead of freaking out as the nearly seven-foot-tall *unglamoured goblin* stood behind him, my dad merely squeezed my hand again as he reached up his other hand to clutch, in a clear gesture of gratitude, at the goblin's wickedly clawed mitt resting on his shoulder.

'She's awake. She's finally awake,' my dad sobbed, as I let my alarmingly heavy head flop back onto my pillow. I also got a glimpse of Anyan's naughty headboard and winced that my dad had seen it.

It's like the Wizard of Oz, only in reverse, I thought. *Dorothy's woken up to find that everything has gotten even weirder. Replete with dirty headboards.*

The goblin and my father beamed at me, and I wondered where to start.

I think I missed quite a bit while I was out.

Chapter Three

My father held the water to my lips while I drank, cradling my head in his hands. The goblin had given me a quick physical, removed all my various tubes – which I was more than surprised to see – and then left to grant us some privacy. I definitely needed his scaly green presence here (and my father's acceptance of his presence) explained, but I had more pressing matters to attend to. As soon as I could speak, I asked the question I'd been dreading.

'Anyan?' I queried, my voice beseeching.

'He's fine,' my dad responded, smiling soothingly. 'He's been here as much as he could, but he's also been busy with . . . other things.'

Unbelievable relief spread through me, even as my forehead rumpled, knowing that 'other things' could not be good. But before I could ask, my dad shook his head.

'Don't worry yourself, Jane. Not yet at least. You're awake. That's all that matters. I was so scared . . .'

At that admonition, my father's voice broke. So *I* nearly broke at the expression on his face, still so handsome, if a tad sad and careworn after all these years.

'Daddy,' I breathed. 'I'm so sorry . . .'

At that, he laughed, if hoarsely. 'Honey, please don't apologize. I can hardly blame you for being attacked.'

'Attacked . . .' I frowned. I was still under the influence of the dreams, and it seemed like everything else was very far away. Especially what had happened in Anyan's driveway.

I killed a man. I remembered, but without emotion. Then I also remembered that was inaccurate.

I'd killed quite a few men.

And yet I couldn't muster any guilt about that fact. All I could think of was Anyan lying there, bleeding, and, weirdly enough, about the 'doctors' Jarl had employed to staff his torture clinics.

Like the men who attacked us in the glade, those men were 'just doing a job', too.

They'd chosen to do evil for a paycheck, or because they enjoyed it, or both.

Comeuppance is a bitch.

'What happened?' I asked.

My father frowned. 'No one is sure. All we know is that you were attacked. And you saved yourself and you saved Anyan.'

I couldn't help but feel a prickle of pride at those words. Yes, I wished I'd never had to do what I did. But when the time was right, I'd womanned up and saved myself and Anyan.

'Your friend with the tattoos' – and here my dad made a series of bizarre sounds that I chalked up as my brain having a bit of a postcoma lapse – 'was able to bring Anyan right back with her healing skills. But you were another matter.'

Blondie's still here? I wondered. *Do I have some questions for her. Like what the hell she was doing following us in the first place. And, speaking of questions, my dad just said 'healing skills'.*

'Um, Dad?' I asked. 'How much do you know?'

His smile was small, but firm. 'I now know that your mother was a selkie. That she was magic. And I know that you're as much her daughter as mine. That you've got powers, too.'

I blinked back tears at the resolve in his voice. The resolve and the forgiveness.

'I'm so sorry I didn't tell you, Dad. About Mom. About me.'

'Pshaw,' he replied, shaking his head. 'I always knew how very special your mother was, and how very special you are. You have both been my greatest gifts. Now I just have more accurate words to describe why you're so special.'

And with those words the tears wouldn't be stopped, and he sat patiently while I cried.

'Still, I should have told you . . .' I said, as soon as the worst of my weeping had ceased.

'Yes, you should have. But I should also have asked. I knew about your mother's swimming, and about yours. I knew there was always something . . . different about both of you. But I couldn't begin to fathom . . . I've never been superstitious, or religious, so I had no idea what the answer could have been. I think I was frightened,' he finally admitted.

'Frightened?' I asked, my voice small.

'Frightened that what made you different was what made your mother leave. And that if I asked too much, or called attention to too much, you would leave, too.'

I rubbed my hand over my eyes, wiping away my tears. The thing was, my dad was actually right. My mom *had* left because she was different, and she would have taken me if she'd had the chance. I think she must have loved him, and me, in her own way. But her way of loving hadn't been the human way. And now she was dead.

'Dad, I have to tell you about Mom—'

'Shh, honey. I know everything.'

'You know? That she's—'

'That she's gone. Yes.'

I blinked at him. I couldn't believe we were even having this conversation, and part of me wished that I'd been the one to tell my dad about my supernatural life. But I wasn't sorry I'd missed out on telling him about my mother. I was still dealing with my own feelings, and was in no position to help him understand what had happened.

'Oh, Daddy, I'm so sorry . . .' I managed to choke out, eventually.

'Shh, baby girl,' he said, gathering me up in his arms for a fierce hug before he positioned me so he could look into my eyes as he talked.

'I had a lot of time to think about everything while you were out. And I'm okay. Your mother left us a lifetime ago, and I should have let her go a long time back. Almost losing you helped me see that. I loved her, and she gave me you. But you're what's important, and my being there for you.'

'You always were, Dad,' I said, hating the guilt I saw in his eyes.

'No, I wasn't. We should have left Rockabill after Jason died. You deserved a fresh start. And I didn't give that to you.'

I shook my head. 'I wouldn't forget Jason and what happened just because we moved. And everything worked out for the best—'

'You sorted yourself out, yes,' he interrupted. 'But at what price? I let you suffer because I wanted to be here if Mari came home. But she didn't, and now we know she won't . . .'

With that, my father's face fell and his eyes glazed with tears. He was putting a brave face on things, but he wasn't going to forget my mother, or deal with her loss, overnight. So I leaned forward in his hug in order to tuck my head under his chin, and I let my own tears join his.

We cried then, together, for my mom, for our family, for each other and our loss. As painful as it was to know she was gone, at that moment of sharing with my father, it felt like some very small part of my grief eased. Not all of it, but even that little bit felt like a lot.

I hoped he felt the same.

'How long *have* I been out?' I asked when we'd stopped snuffling. It had obviously been long enough for my dad to get over the shock of the supernatural world, have someone tell him about my mom's death, and grow a beard.

A week? Maybe two?

'A month,' he replied, to my horror.

'Good lord,' I whispered. 'A month?' No wonder my limbs felt all tingly and weird still. Feeling was coming back, but slowly.

'Yep. And we thought we were going to lose you quite a few times. Your power kept draining. Dr Sam says that if' – and here my dad again made that same series of bizarre sounds he'd made earlier.

'Gesundheit,' I interrupted.

'Sorry?'

'You sneezed.'

My dad laughed. 'No, that's your friend's name. With the tattoos.'

I blinked at him, and then it hit me. 'You mean Blondie? With the Mohawk?'

'Yes, that's not a sneeze. It's her name.'

'Hmmm,' I said, trying to figure out what he'd said and how he'd said it. 'I think I'll stick with Blondie.'

Especially since, although everyone keeps telling me she's my friend, I have yet to determine her status for myself.

For, while I'd once told the barghest I got a good vibe from the Original, that was before she showed up right before we were attacked in Anyan's driveway. Yeah, she'd saved me, but was it all just a clever trick to gain our trust?

Chuckling again, my dad shook his head ruefully. 'I had some time to practice while you were sleeping. Anyway, yeah, if she hadn't been here, you would be dead. It was her power that kept you going.'

'Hmm,' I said, wondering what the Original's motives were in keeping me alive. Not to mention, when had everyone become such chums? Last thing I'd known, Blondie was a stranger. And that's what she was to me, until I could talk to her myself.

In other words, Blondie and I needed to have a little chat.

'And Dr Sam is the . . .' My voice trailed off, still not able to say the word in front of my dad.

'The goblin?' he asked, his grin infectious. 'Yep. A friend of Anyan's. Both of them have been wonderful.' My dad started to make that funny combination of sounds, and then he stopped himself. 'Er, Blondie did most of the healing, but you needed to be kept fed and everything. Dr Sam also did things to keep your muscles from atrophying. You'll still be a little weak for a few days, but he said that if you woke up and had a swim, you'd be almost as good as new.'

My dad said '*if* you woke up' so casually that my heart broke. After everything he'd been through, he must have really thought I might die. He didn't deserve to worry like that; he didn't deserve that fear and pain.

I nearly started crying again, but he stopped me with what he said next.

'He healed me, Jane.'

'What?' I asked, confused. When had he gotten hurt? *If those motherfuckers hurt my dad . . .*

'My heart. It's as good as new. Like I was never sick a day in my life.'

My breath caught in my throat. My dad's condition had

been a part of our lives for so long that I couldn't imagine what it would be like to have him heart-whole and healthy.

'Really? Really healed?'

'Completely. And Anyan went with me to my doctor, so that he could . . . What do you call it? Glamour?'

I nodded.

'So he could glamour everyone, and he found someone to change everything in the system. Even followed me around so that all of Rockabill knows me as "Calvin True, that guy who has always been healthy". '

'Oh, Dad. That's marvelous—'

'It's been strange,' he interrupted, as if he didn't really want to discuss the issue. 'Such a blessing at such a terrible time.'

I nodded, knowing he would need a while to think through what had happened over the past month. I was, after all, something of an expert on getting over pretty big shocks to the system.

Before we could talk more about how he felt about his sudden return to health, the door to my room burst open as a girl with pearl-gray skin and hair the color and texture of seaweed entered.

'Jane!' Trill shouted, her voice as dark and eerie as an oil slick. But the smile that took up her strange, flat-featured face was so joyful that she was beautiful.

And just as instantaneously she was crowding past my father to wrap her arms around me – arms that smelled of brine. *My sea*, I thought, desire swamping over me as irresistibly as thirst or hunger.

'Don't smother her, kelpie,' came a gentle, grandmotherly voice from the other side of Anyan's massive bed. When I managed to extricate myself from Trill's grasp, I moved to greet the little woman I knew was waiting.

Nell Gnome's enormous gray bun floated above the

mattress, the rest of her plump, two-foot-tall little form revealing itself as I leaned over to the other side of the bed. When our eyes met, she smiled at me, illuminating her fairy godmother features. Features that all but disappeared in a thousand kindly crinkles.

'We thought we'd lost you, little halfling,' she said, as she levitated herself onto the bed to give me her own hug.

'I'm apparently not all that easy to kill,' I said to her, laughing as she patted me on the cheek as if to convince herself I was really there.

'No. You Trues are made of tough stuff. Calvin,' she said, nodding cordially toward my father.

'Nurse Ratched,' he intoned drily, twitching an eyebrow at me that caused me to blush. I'd left my father in Nell's care a few times, under a glamour that convinced him she was a nurse, rather than a gnome. A nurse I'd named Ratched, in a moment of pure insanity.

I made an *I'm sorry* face at him before turning to Nell.

'Okay. I need to know what happened.' Then I made a face as my bladder suddenly made itself known.

'Gottapeegottapeegottapee!' I chanted, moving over to the edge of the bed. Trill helped me stand on shaky legs, and then she practically carried me to Anyan's bathroom. Once she'd propped me up on the toilet, I shooed her away, but when I was finished, I only just managed to haul myself up by using the sink as leverage.

Staring at myself in the mirror as I washed my hands, I was greeted with quite a shock. My hair, first of all, was insane. For some reason it had grown exponentially, hanging down to my hips in undulating black waves.

Undulating is polite for greasy, I thought, making a face at my grubby self.

The hair was going to need to be cut stat, not least because my bangs were halfway down my face. And I was very thin, far thinner than I'd ever been in my life. The sweatpants and T-shirt I was dressed in draped off my frame like I was some jankie old hanger. As someone who enjoyed being curvy, I didn't like what I saw. Plus, I figured I lived enough of a knock-around life that I needed some padding.

I pulled down the sweatpants a little bit to poke at one of my hip bones in disbelief, unsure if I'd ever even known I had hip bones till that moment. Raising up my T-shirt, I realized I also had ribs! Sticking out from my middle!

Running my hands down my sides under the shirt, I decided I was not a fan of ribs on girls. At least, not on this girl.

When I returned to the bedroom, someone had rustled me up chips and a sandwich, which waited for me on a really cute breakfast tray table. *Anyan must be a fan of breakfast in bed*, I thought, an idea that pleased me on about four hundred levels.

Pausing before getting back into bed, I eyed the tray.

'Are you sure I can eat this?' I asked. I felt hungry, and my tummy was rumbling like an irate bear cub, but if I'd been asleep for a month . . .

'Doc Sam says you're good to go. If you feel like eating, you probably can. Just try to take it slow.'

I got back into bed and Trill laid the tray on my lap before sitting down next to it facing me. Nell echoed her position, her little legs kicking in the air. My father and Dr Sam must have gone downstairs, as I heard them talking about what I'd need, care-wise, in the coming weeks.

But what I need right now is this sandwich, I thought, as I proceeded to shove it into my face as if emulating a foie gras goose. *So much for taking it slow.*

At some point during tearing apart my meal like a rabid wolf, I'd mumbled at Nell that I still wanted catching up. The

gnome had backed away a step – probably nervous I'd finish
my sandwich and then start in on her – before filling me in.

'You were attacked by humans – mercenaries. They were
very, very professional and very, very expensive. And whoever
hired them was smart. I would have detected anything magical
coming into my Territory, unless they were ridiculously
strong, like your friend the Original, or one of the handful
of factions with powerful camouflaging powers, like the
nagas.'

I was too busy shoving food into my face to remind Nell
that Blondie was no friend of mine. Not yet, at least.

'And there aren't many nagas left,' Trill said, with a nasty
little grin.

'As I was saying,' Nell said, clearly admonishing her
seaweedy friend, 'whoever hired the humans was smart. Even
if a race can camouflage, the second they use magic I'd know
it. And it's hard for powerful beings not to use magic, especially in an attack. We can do it for a short time, like I know
you did when Anyan took you on that raid, but that was only
no-magic for about ten minutes. Most supes accidentally
break and do a little magic after a short while, and from what
we were able to determine, those soldiers were kicking around
Rockabill for at least a full day to enact that ambush. Not to
mention, if you have strong magical offensive skills, why on
earth would you practice such extensive, physical offensive
skills?'

'And to surprise someone like Anyan with any type of
offense, you have to be *really* good,' Trill added, as her
black-nailed fingers crept across my lap toward the potato
chips on my plate. She got a quick slap on the hand for her
pains as I finished the last of my sandwich.

I've got ribs to cover, I thought, unrepentant of my greed.

''Kay, but what about nagas and camouflaging?' I asked,

before starting in on my chips. If I were honest, I was already pretty full. But that had never stopped me before.

'Nagas and at least two other factions have abilities to camouflage their powers. They have to be very strong for it to be really effective, and they use up most of their power maintaining their camouflage. But it makes them effective spies, if they're successful.'

'How do you think Jimmu got into Nell's Territory?' Trill asked me, in a *duh* voice, as she eyed my ever-disappearing pile of Ruffles.

In return, I gave the kelpie my own patented *fuck-off* face. 'I was too stuck on the whole man-who-turns-into-a-snake-and-wants-to-kill-me thing to wonder much about the how-he-got-into-the-gnome's-Territory thing.' To conclude, I shoved about five chips into my mouth and then licked my fingers at her in revenge.

'So whoever hired the humans,' Nell said in a loud voice, obviously wanting our attention back on her, 'was smart, well connected, and wealthy. We do not use human servants. Ever.'

Just like you don't use human science, I thought sarcastically, remembering what everyone kept saying about Conleth and, later, Jarl's laboratories. *And speaking of my favorite evil Alfar . . .*

'Jarl?' I mumbled through my very full mouth, spitting out crumbs.

Nell shook her little head. 'How? His assets were frozen when he killed Orin. And yes, I'm sure he had money squirreled away,' she said in response to the face I pulled. 'And Jarl certainly had the contacts. But how could he have organized the attack?'

I frowned as I swallowed.

'Maybe he had it planned from a while ago?'

'How? You hadn't been in Rockabill for weeks. That team,

according to what Anyan's been able to find out, entered the
area the day you left the Compound, and they were hired
just before that. In other words, before Jarl needed to kill
you, and shortly before he began fleeing for his life.'

'He could have set it up beforehand and then just made
a single phone call,' I grumbled, completely convinced that
Jarl was responsible for everything nasty, up to and
including the flu, pigeons, and the relative inaccessibility
of the G-spot.

'He could have,' Nell intoned gently. 'And I'm not saying he
wouldn't have, or that he's not somehow involved. But what
we're thinking is that this goes even deeper than Jarl.'

My eyes widened, my chips forgotten despite my sudden
influx of ribs.

'Deeper? How?'

'This isn't the only Territory, Jane. There are Territories
all over the world, all of which are experiencing the same
population crises we are, and most of which have the same
tensions betweens halflings and purebloods. Some are more
forward-thinking than our Territory, but there are a lot that
are even less so.'

'So you think what?'

'Jarl can't be alone in this. Someone had to have informed
about your leaving – someone who was there to watch you
in the first place, since I know Anyan snuck you two out of
that Compound. Which is worrying enough, but we also have
to stop thinking just in terms of Jarl. Morrigan's obviously
been involved up to her eyeballs this whole time.'

'And she was the queen,' I said with a groan, beginning
to realize what Nell had already figured out.

'Yep. With lots of contact with other monarchs in other
Territories.'

Even Trill looked glum at that thought.

'Good lord. Do you think this is an international conspiracy?' I asked.

'Who knows? But I wouldn't rule it out,' Nell said, her normally relaxed features serious.

'Well, fuckerdoodles to *that*,' I said, my mind, at that moment, only capable of nibbling at the very edges of such a huge idea.

Trill giggled. 'Yes, fuckerdoodles to that. No more grim talk. Yay for Jane being awake! We need to celebrate! And I bet I know what you need.'

I looked at the kelpie, my eyes huge with longing.

'A swim,' Trill finished just as I'd hoped she would, causing Nell to nod sharply.

'It's still early in the evening, so a swim it is,' said the gnome. 'And since you're still shaky on your feet . . .'

And with that Nell grabbed my hand, along with Trill's. I felt my world spin as Nell used her borrowed Old Magic to apparate us both.

I would have protested the lack of warning, but all complaints dried up as I found myself right where I wanted to be:

Plopped, naked as a jaybird, directly into my ocean.

Chapter Four

Letting myself float in midwater, my long hair swirling around me as black as squid's ink, I opened myself to the Atlantic. As her power flooded through me, I trembled, but not as violently as I had initially. At first, the force of my element had hurt. Rusty from a combination of abuse and disuse, my magical channels balked against the encroaching power. It felt a little like alcohol over abraded flesh, or something forcing its way into too tight a space. But eventually, the power began to soothe until finally it just felt good.

Trill watched me, in pony form, from a short distance away. Her little black hooves were planted firmly in the sand, but her seaweed mane and tail tossed as she waited impatiently. I didn't let her rush me, however. Instead, I slowly – painfully – stretched my magical muscles, feeling them twinge and balk but finally accede to use. Eventually, when I was ready, I opened my eyes and grinned at her. Then I used my magic to dart away, looking back at the kelpie in a clear declaration of 'catch me if you can'.

I was moving slower than I ever had in the water, and sometimes my whole system would stutter like an old car's engine, but the more I used my mojo the easier it got and the better I felt. Trill followed at a short distance, allowing me to feel like we were really chasing one another even if she was clearly humoring me.

Swimming close to shore at first, to get the old sea legs back, I went through the sort of basic magical exercises with which I'd started out my training. Trill obliged me by sitting still when I worked up to lobbing mage balls (albeit underwater mage balls), but eventually she turned the tables. Giving chase, she pushed me to pull more on my power, limbering me up even further.

In the meantime, it felt like heaven to be back in the Atlantic. It was frigid, of course, but either magic or genetics, or a combination of both, kept me from really feeling how cold. All I knew was the water felt delicious against my skin.

Like the caress of a mother's soothing touch, I thought, poetically, until just a moment later that same soothing water smacked me down to the seabed.

In our play, Trill and I had wandered too close to the Old Sow. Her piglets were famous for springing up out of nowhere, whenever and wherever they felt like it, and one had caught me unawares. It didn't hurt when I landed, but it did knock my breath from me – a tricky situation when I was underwater. I had to calm my natural human reaction to suck in a breath and switch to my instinctual selkie brain to filter my oxygen through my magical connection with the water.

Not that I was in a hurry to pick myself up off the ocean floor anyway. The piglet whirled for a few more minutes nearby, rucking up water and sand and seaweed that rubbed against me in a pleasant exfoliation.

Who needs expensive salons? I thought, closing my eyes firmly against the firm chaff of the swirling grit.

Feels so good, I thought, turning over so that I was lying on my belly, my face toward the Sow. *So very good . . . And if this feels good, think how much better it would feel to be even closer.*

There was something about the way the water soothed against my flesh – undulating and gentle – that made me want to move forward. I wanted to feel more, to feel how it felt right over *there*. So, inching forward on my belly, I kept moving closer to that magnetic pull.

Until I saw rough, black-nailed hands grab me by my wrists and haul me backward till I was sitting quite a distance away.

What the hell were you doing? Trill mouthed at me. I'd gotten very good at reading lips underwater since I'd started swimming with the kelpie.

In response, all I did was blink at her in confusion. *What did she mean, what was I doing?* I thought. And then I felt the pain.

Looking down, I realized that I was covered in small cuts and bruises. What had, at the time, felt like the gentle exfoliation of a little grit must really have been the pummeling of decent-sized rocks.

Trill's hands on my shoulders shook me until I looked up at her face. *You were going right into the Sow,* she mouthed. *I had to shift underwater. What were you thinking?*

Trill hated shifting underwater; she must have been really worried about me. Which, in turn, made me worry about myself.

I don't know, I mouthed in response. And I didn't. I hadn't felt the pain of the rocks hitting me, hadn't felt anything but pleasure and curiosity.

Concern was etched all over Trill's features as she mouthed, *Let's go home.* I nodded, numb.

What the hell is up with me? I thought, as we turned back toward the shore of my cove. *It's like I was possessed or something.*

We swam together, Trill keeping me at arm's length while I tried to figure out what had just happened. On the one hand, I hadn't felt any overt magical influence. But, on the other hand, I'd learned that there were all sorts of magic out there, not all of which I recognized.

But whom have I met who has such power and *wants to hurt me?* Blondie was apparently an ally, as was Terk, the brownie who worked for Capitola's family back in the Borderlands. They were the only two beings with non-elemental magic, the type that my kind and I used, that I knew.

Which means we might have another new, unknown enemy, I thought with a mental sigh. I was being rather dramatic but, in my own defense, it *is* rather tiring having strangers constantly trying to kill my friends and me.

But before I could dwell on that thought, I felt Trill nudge me with her elbow and point forward. I peered through the water until I saw what she was showing me.

There, way ahead of us, stood a pair of legs standing waist high in the water. I squinted, swimming forward a bit more till I could see that the legs were big, bedenimed, and wearing motorcycle boots.

Anyan, I realized, and my whole body tingled at the thought. I looked at Trill, who rolled her eyes.

He's all yours, she mouthed, giving me a mocking salute before signaling I should swim ahead of her.

Where will you go? I asked her, trying not to smile when she motioned toward the beach quite a ways up the shore. After all, I didn't want her to think that I was abandoning her – hos before bros and all that – but I did want to ascertain that she'd be well away before I launched my vagoo at Anyan's face.

And speaking of my lady business, I am bare-assed naked, I thought, pondering that fact. Nell had – I assumed – apparated my clothes to their usual place in my cove, leaving one eminently fuckable (and, from what I could see, fully clothed) barghest standing between me and my modesty.

Luckily, I thought, shrugging for no one's benefit, *I've never been particularly attached to the concept of modesty.*

And then I swam as fast as I could toward those long, lovely legs. All the worry I'd been suppressing since waking up that I'd been too slow and that Anyan was dead urged me on. I'd been told he was fine, but being told something and seeing it for myself were two entirely different things. So I rushed toward him, needing to feel him – healthy and whole – against me.

At the last moment I kicked off the shallows, breaching the water with a tremendous splash. I landed, wetly, smack dab against Anyan's T-shirted chest, causing him to rock back on his heels before regaining his balance.

But his arms had wrapped around me immediately, and they never let go.

He held me there, partially in his embrace but also buoyed by a little surge of power from both of us, for what felt like hours but could only have been a handful of seconds. I was as limp as seaweed in his arms, my head cradled under his chin, my own arms draped around his neck. We were both breathing hard – in my case, from a combination of exertion, nerves, and desire.

I barely registered when Anyan started to move, although I did feel the retreat of the water from around our bodies as he walked the both of us up the beach. It was only when I felt him start to sit – presumably on my cove's resident ancient beached tree trunk – that I pulled my thighs upward, wrapping my legs about his waist so I could remain in his lap.

We stayed like that, me wrapped around him like a little leech, the only sounds that of our breathing and the steady drip of water from our ocean-drenched bodies. There were a thousand things I needed to ask him – a thousand things we needed to talk about. But all I cared about, at that moment, was the feel of his body against mine.

Everything else could wait.

'Thought we'd lost you,' he said, eventually. His voice rumbled through my body and I shivered. In response, he moved my hair aside and stroked a large, warm hand all the way down my back.

I shivered again, but for an entirely different reason.

'I thought I'd lost *you*,' I replied, feeling my voice hitch at the memory of him lying there, bleeding from everywhere.

Anyan left his one hand on the small of my back while the other knotted my hair in a rough queue, tugging my head back so that my face came away from his chest and I was looking into his eyes.

I gotta admit, it took everything I had not to moan. That hair-pulling thing he did really peeled my bananas.

'You saved my life again, little girl,' he said quietly, his eyes searching my face as if he were lost and I was his map. In response, my own throat worked uselessly, gone dry and tight from a combination of nerves and lust.

'Nothing you haven't done for me quite a few times,' I only just managed to croak out in a voice about four octaves lower than usual. I hoped the barghest found my sudden plunge into man-voice as sexy as I found his hair pulling, but I wasn't about to bet on it.

As if he knew what I was thinking, Anyan's reply was to pull my hair again. Only this time he tugged outward, rather than up, moving my chest away from his. I was still astride him, our hips flush, but he'd pulled my shoulders back so that my upper body was bared to him. Cradling my neck and the back of my head in his large hand, his eyes swept over said upper body, which I quickly remembered was very naked except for the two wings of crow-black hair that, having escaped his grip, fell alongside either side of my face and down over my breasts.

Thank the gods I currently resemble Cousin It, I thought, my face reddening under his scrutiny as that long, crooked nose twitched once, hard.

He ignored my embarrassment, stroking the hand that had been at the small of my back across my buttock and the outside of my thigh, raising goose bumps all over my flesh. His nose twitched again and lord and lady did I want to nibble the tip . . .

'You've hurt yourself, already,' he said as he harrumphed, his iron-gray eyes taking in the multitude of cuts and bruises I'd accumulated near the Sow.

I was about to spill the beans about my sort-of possession, and had even opened my mouth to do so. But all that came out was an only partially stifled groan as Anyan raised his free hand to run it down my cheek, to my neck, and down each arm, trailing healing warmth. His power pushed through my body – warm and strong – and I ground down on another groan. I also may have ground down on the barghest a bit, but under the circumstances, who could blame me?

Anyan, for his part, didn't seem to mind.

Instead, he grunted softly, his gray eyes spearing my black ones as his generous mouth pursed in concentration. At the same time, his hand on my hip clutched convulsively, squeezing nearly hard enough to hurt before his grip relaxed. Then that same hand reached up ever so slowly to insert itself under the hair on the left side of my face. Anyan spread his fingers, trailing his thumb across my jaw as he used his hand to push my concealing hair back away from the left side of my body. Without looking down, he reached across me to do the same thing to the hair covering my right side, leaving me naked before him. But he still kept his eyes on mine.

'Is this all right?' he asked, his voice husky with desire.

'All right?' I asked, wondering how on earth he could think it was anything but. Then I saw the concern on his face, like he was genuinely afraid I was about to say no. I immediately put his worries to bed.

'Of course it's all right,' I said. 'Unexpected, but all right.'

'Unexpected?' he asked, his turn to make me feel nervous.

I paused, unsure how to answer him. 'You're Anyan,' I replied, finally. A response that made perfect sense to me.

The barghest looked at me like I was speaking Flemish, but he started talking anyway. His hands were still where they rested on my forearms, but his eyes swept over me possessively.

'You lay there for weeks,' he said, 'and there was nothing I could do. I thought you were going to die, and there was nothing I could do. You were so small and still, and there was nothing I could do.'

With that, he stopped talking, and his eyes glistened suspiciously. The thought of Anyan tearing up, *and over me!*, nearly did me in. Without thinking about it, I flung myself forward, wrapping my arms around his neck and holding him tightly.

'I'm okay, now,' I murmured into his ear, his coarse jaw rasping against my cheek. 'And I'm here. I'm fine.'

Anyan's only response was to hold me tightly, his huge hands warm and strong where they gripped my flesh.

It felt wonderful. I felt safe, protected, and cared for. Nevertheless, I've always been greedy.

I wanted more.

So I pulled back from Anyan, just enough so that my nose

nuzzled against his gorgeously long schnoz, just as I'd fanta-
sized about doing so many times.

'Bad puppy,' I murmured, my voice husky.

His hand on my hip pulled my pelvis in snugly against his,
just as I leaned forward, my lips just brushing Anyan's . . .

'If I knew it was going to be this kind of party, I'd have
brought some towels,' came an oily voice from the crack in the
cove walls, causing me to yank Anyan's hair in surprise.

The barghest winced, and as I pulled away I growled,
'Trill!'

'Don't huff at me, Nell wanted you,' the kelpie chortled, as
she stepped from the shadows. She was again in her pony
form, and was prancing with mischief. Her pearlescent flesh
glimmered in the moonlight. 'How was I supposed to know
Anyan was planning on jumping your bones the minute you
woke up?'

'Leave them alone, Trill,' came Nell's kindly voice from
behind the kelpie. The little woman stepped up from behind
the sea-pony. She didn't seem at all discomfited by walking
up on us practically *in flagrante*.

'We're sorry to interrupt,' Nell said. 'But everyone's waiting
for you at the Sty.'

I gave Trill the traitor a sharp look. She should have warned
Nell that Anyan and I were, um, having a reunion. One with
no clothes, at least on my part. Trill just gave me her horrible
pony grin in response.

I gave her the finger.

'So if you're finished, we can get over there,' Nell said,
levitating my clothes a bit closer to where I straddled the
barghest. Then the gnome looked Anyan full in the face,
giving him her sweetest, most heartfelt grandma smile.

'We won't tell anyone we caught you jumping Jane's bones.'

Chapter Five

As I walked through the door of the Sty, I was hit with the familiar smell of the bar: beer and burgers, mixed together with a faint undertone of Pine-Sol. And there, around the large, square bar that jutted out onto the edge of the Sow's small dance floor, sat all of my Rockabill chums. They were clustered around Tracy – she and Grizzie were taller than any of my supernatural friends – and not paying any mind to the front door.

Nell and Trill, blanketed under the gnome's heaviest glamour, walked toward our group. For some reason, Trill had a hard time glamouring herself, especially if she interacted with humans at all. I think it was a concentration issue. So for the very, very occasional times she was away from her own kind, she kept her pony shape and let Nell glamour her to look like a wolfhound. If I let my gaze unfocus, I could see the large dog's shape padding over the clopping form of our little kelpie.

Before following Nell and Trill, I moved over to Anyan's side, peering up at him speculatively. I wasn't so slow that I didn't realize there was something happening between us, but that didn't mean I wasn't opposed to reassurance. After all, the last thing I remembered was that Anyan and I had been just a possibility. And while Anyan had had a month to think past those stumbling first steps – and leap all the way to bone-jumping, the ambitious sod – I was still lurking in a corner of square one.

The barghest, as if sensing my insecurities, reached out to cradle my jaw in his warm, dry palm. His skin was rough against my soft cheek, but that just turned me on even more.

'You have no idea how happy I am to see you upright,' Anyan's low voice growled. Then he leaned in to kiss my forehead, before moving his lips to my ear. What he whispered next made my poor, overtaxed libido nearly faint: 'But that doesn't mean I'm not going to want you flat on your back again as soon as possible.'

His teeth nipped my ear and I whimpered, a million Anyan-related fantasies suddenly swarming through my brain like overstimulated honey bees. When I didn't budge, my gaze turning inward to enjoy my own naughty thoughts, he chuckled before putting his hand on the nape of my neck to steer my dreamy ass away from the front door.

As we neared our friends, they turned away from Tracy to see us. When their eyes lit upon me, I felt my own prickle with tears at the joy on everyone's face.

As usual, Grizzie broke the silence. 'Jane!' came a shout, as over six feet of omnisexual goodness came darting toward me. For a second, I felt like a vole targeted by a peregrine, but then I realized that a mere falcon would never have the chutzpah to wear that tank top. It was white and sported, in effigy, a tanned body with huge boobs encased in a Confederate flag bikini.

Giggling, I allowed my friend to sweep me up in a dramatic hug. Anyan squeezed past us to get to the bar, and then the prickles turned to real tears as I felt a bunch of other arms around Griz and me. I felt like a rugby player in a scrum, but one made of love and acceptance. It was glorious.

'How was Belize?' Grizzie said, when everyone had moved a few steps back and I could breathe again.

'Um, Belize?' I frowned, looking around at the group.

Amy Nahual's normally placid, slightly stoned expression frowned as she nodded sharply, warning me to go along with Grizzie.

'Yeah, um, Belize was great. You know Belize,' I said, my brain scrambling to recall exactly where Belize was. 'Always hot?' I hazarded, smiling back at Grizzie when she grinned.

'That's great! Although you don't look tan at all.'

'Yes, well . . .' I started to say, but allowed myself to trail off with relief as Amy pulled me toward her for a hug.

'We told the humans, except for your dad, that you were in Belize. Just roll with it,' she whispered in my ear.

'Will do,' I replied, squeezing her tightly. 'You doing well?'

Amy chuckled her loose-throated, laid-back laugh. 'Always copacetic, sister. You know me! Glad to see you up and at 'em.'

Then she allowed me to be pulled away by first Marcus and then Sarah Vernon, the nahuals who owned the Sty. They each gave me a hug, Sarah promising to go right into the back and rustle me up the biggest burger with extra cheddar she could make. I didn't protest as Sarah rushed off to fulfill her promise.

My big shock came when Tracy, Grizzie's life partner, went to give me her own hug. Right before I left, Grizzie and Tracy had announced they were pregnant with twins. Tracy had already been pretty big for someone who was only three months gone, and now she was . . .

'Huuuuuuge,' I whispered, my wide eyes latched onto her belly, before clapping a hand over my mouth. Tracy's being so much bigger than the last time I saw her meant I finally realized I truly *had* been out for a month.

'I see Belize didn't improve your tact,' my friend replied,

drily, before pulling me as close as she could get me in a hug.

'Um, no. But I got you some baby clothes!' I blurted out, panicked by that evening's second mention of a country I couldn't quite place geographically.

Shit, where am I going to get baby clothes from Belize? I thought frantically, as Tracy's face lit up.

'How exciting!' she squealed, as I cursed at myself. Luckily, before I could dig myself any more holes, my attention was riveted to the figure standing awkwardly a few feet away, waiting to be noticed.

'Iris!' I shouted, nearly choking on my overflowing emotions. I was feeling things I didn't even know how to name. The last time I'd seen my succubus friend had been after relinquishing her to the care of strange healers. She'd been kidnapped by Jarl's minions both because she knew me and because, in her past, she'd given birth to a halfling son. I'd been made to believe she was dead, although she'd really been kept alive as insurance. That fact was a mixed blessing. I had been so happy she was still alive, but she'd endured horrific abuse before we'd rescued her from the evil Healer's mansion-prison.

So I loved seeing her, and I was happy that she looked much better than the emaciated, dead-eyed shell of Iris I'd left behind so many weeks ago. That said, she still didn't look anything like the sleek indoor cat she'd been before her kidnapping. My friend was still far too thin, and her eyes were still haunted. But most telling was the way she stood back, waiting to be noticed.

Iris used to shine so brightly that every eye in the room was riveted.

A hand from behind her touched her shoulder, as if to urge her forward, and I opened my arms. I almost dropped said arms, however, when I realized that the hand on her shoulder belonged to the satyr Caleb. He was huge, with the imposing chest of a muscle-bound human, but he was all goat from the waist down. Well, except for the very human genitalia on proud display. Goat haunches made finding pants difficult, but I would never understand what was so wrong about a loincloth. Anyway, Caleb was impressive as either a man or a goat, not least because of his craggily handsome face topped by his huge ram's horns. He was, however, also one of my former lover Ryu's deputies and I couldn't imagine what the satyr was doing here.

I looked around for Ryu as Iris came close, but he wasn't lurking anywhere. Then I was hugging my friend, and nothing else mattered.

'Iris,' I mumbled, almost incoherent. Sobs were her only response.

Everyone backed away, clearly giving us space. Grizzie and Tracy seemed confused by what must have appeared to them to be Iris's overly emotional response to my return from Belize. Little did they know that Iris and I had returned, together, from somewhere much further away: the hell that had been the Healer's grasp.

'How are you doing?' I asked, eventually, when she'd cried herself out. I pulled the sleeve of my T-shirt down over my palm to wipe away her tears. She wasn't wearing any make-up, making her look even younger and more vulnerable.

'Better,' she said, after sniffling for a bit. 'It's been hard. But I'm getting there.'

'You do look better,' I said, which was true.

'But I don't look good,' she said, sadly. This was also true.

'It's only been a month. Considering everything—'

'Yes,' she interrupted. 'Considering everything.'

We stood silently together, but it wasn't awkward. There simply weren't words that were suitable, so we didn't try to use any. Instead we hugged.

'Order up!' Sarah called, whisking past me with a plate full of burger, french fries, *and* fried cheese sticks. What can I say: my friends knew my vices.

For the first time since I'd clapped eyes on her this evening, Iris finally smiled at the look on my face.

'Some things never change,' she said, stroking an affectionate hand over my cheek. 'Go eat, Jane.'

We walked over to the bar, where everyone was sitting and chatting. Sarah had set my food down at an empty chair between Anyan and another empty chair next to Amy, which Iris took. Nell talked quietly with Marcus, who was petting Trill as if she really were the dog she pretended to be. Meanwhile, Sarah kept one eye on the bar as she chatted with Amy, Tracy, and Grizzie. I started in on my food, Iris watching me chow down as Caleb and the barghest talked, but I felt a thrill in my belly that had nothing (or at least mostly nothing) to do with cheese sticks when Anyan put a proprietary hand on the small of my back while I ate.

Granted, he also tried to steal a fry, earning him the same sharp slap on the hand that Trill had received earlier.

'Bad puppy,' I scolded.

Just because I wish to ravage you, doesn't mean you get to eat off my plate, I thought, staring down his shocked expression. *Not unless you like me with ribs.*

My libido whimpered at that thought. *Maybe he* does *like ribs?* it questioned, alarmed.

I looked between my half-eaten burger and the barghest.

Fuck that, I decided, picking up my burger and greedily dipping it in ketchup. But I did pass Anyan a fry, my expression conciliatory. Then I nearly jumped *his* bones when he raised the fry to my mouth, smiling sensuously at me as I ate it from his fingers.

Not a rib lover, my libido celebrated, noting how Anyan

watched my lips with a hungry expression – his own pursed
with wicked intentions. Then, using my lust as a distraction,
he swiped a cheese stick, the big bastard.

As I finished eating, Caleb and Anyan resumed talking.
They were discussing something that was happening around
Rockabill, but I was too busy wondering why the hell the satyr
was there to pay much attention. I was also too busy noticing
how Iris kept one eye on Caleb, even as she told me about
how far she'd come in the past weeks.

'But I owe most of it to him,' she said, as if she were
admitting something difficult. She gave Caleb an almost
beatific smile of affection, and I nearly choked on my burger.
Partly I reacted from shock, but partly from sheer joy at
seeing her eyes glow – if dimly – in that telltale succubus
way. I'd wondered if Iris's eyes would ever glow again, after
what she'd experienced.

Caleb and Iris? I thought, surprised despite my happiness
for her. The satyr was so solid and Iris had always been a
fairly typical succubus: flighty and a bit fluffy. The idea of
serious, calm Caleb with frivolous, excitable Iris was interesting, to say the least.

'Really?' I said, around a mouthful of food. I really needed
to stop talking with my mouth full.

'Yes. I know it probably seems strange. But he came down
with Ryu after you were attacked. And he ended up staying.'
Because of me was her unstated message.

'Wow,' I said, swallowing hastily.

Ryu was here? I thought. But I didn't say anything. This
was Iris's time to talk.

'What about, er, the mojo?' I asked hesitantly. The thing
was, succubi harvested essence from bodily fluids the same
as baobhan sith, like Ryu, harvested essence from blood.
Only difference was that any bodily fluid would do for succubi

and incubi, but they could feed only off lust – even if it was the sort of twisted, pain-filled pleasure preferred by Graeme, Phaedra's incubus minion. This reliance on essence meant that succubi, incubi, and baobhan sith couldn't be monogamous, long term, with another supernatural creature. Not if they wanted to keep their power. Instead, they needed to charge up with either humans or special halflings, like me, who created the right magical essence in their bodily fluids.

So what I was really asking Iris was 'Who are you boffing on the side?' After all, I could feel her using a small amount of glamour to keep the humans from noticing how unhealthy she still looked, and her usual succubus juju was beating, if very faintly, against my shields. If she could use magic, she was feeding from somebody.

The succubus's eyes glowed a bit brighter as she gave me a secret, sly smile, making Iris look like herself again.

'That's not a problem. Caleb's a terrible voyeur,' Iris said, pronouncing *terrible* in a way that let me know she found it anything but.

I blinked at her, sneaking a look at the satyr. His handsome, craggy face was as kind and as placid as ever. He looked like a sexy college professor in a movie, although the sandy-blond hair falling down into his eyes gave him a little-boy-lost appearance that was adorably innocent. Granted, he also had goat haunches and was naked as a jaybird, but I needed to stop seeing him through my human eyes, with their human values.

Finally turning back to Iris, I tried to reconcile my established image of Caleb as utterly respectable with my new image of Caleb peeping out of a closet at a couple screwing on the bed. I would have wagered Caleb had sex while wearing an ascot, not him being a certifiable kinkster. But you know what they say about judging a book by its cover . . .

And yet, considering the fact that Caleb's impressive man-janglies were one of the more startlingly prominent features of his cover, I guess I should have totally gone ahead and judged.

For a second, the human part of me worried about Iris. She seemed so smitten with Caleb, yet their relationship was hardly going to be the subject of a Hallmark made-for-TV movie.

But maybe it should be, my brain kicked in. *After all, look at her: he's made her comfortable enough to have the sex she needs to get strong. That couldn't have been easy after the abuse she endured. And the way they look at each other shows how much they care.*

Plus he's hung like a yak! chimed in my libido, which my brain ignored.

Instead, it touched on a subject I'd been confronted with innumerable times since joining my mother's world.

Hallmark movies deal with human lives and human relationships: short-lived love triangles, messy divorces, joyful reunions. All of which are played out in the course of a human life span. They don't deal with near-immortals. Or near-immortality.

And I finally admitted to myself what I'd begun to think about while dating Ryu, but had managed, mostly, to sublimate.

You only have human experience of relationships. And those last, what . . . fifty, sixty years at most? You have no idea what it would take to make a relationship last for generations of human lives.

I paled, my eyes drifting to Anyan's strong, tanned hand that was currently stealing more French fries from my plate. For a second, I got so depressed I didn't even want to slap it.

'Jane?' Iris asked, her voice concerned. Which made me feel like shit and also made me realize how ridiculous I was being.

Quit it, Jane. I thought. *Now is not the time to contemplate the exigencies of your supernatural existence.*

After all, everything was just about perfect. My friends were with me. My father was healthy. I had no secrets from (most of) the people I loved. Anyan had attempted to jump my bones (although, if I were honest, I had been the one literally to jump). That last thought made me feel a bit fuzzy and smug, and I placed my own small hand over the barghest's, where it lay on the table, thrilled that I could do so, before I turned to grin at Iris to dispel her concerns.

It's like I've woken up in heaven, I thought.

Until, that is, Stuart Gray shambled up. And I mean shambled. He looked odd, like he was wearing his own skin. I was reminded of the character Arnold Friend, from Joyce Carol Oates's famous story. Arnold Friend eventually appeared to be something not quite human, dressed in a man-suit.

I nearly fainted when Stuart's jaw ratcheted open.

'If it wakens death will come. If it wakens death will come. If it wakens death will come,' Stu began to chant, in an eerie singsong voice that was definitely not his own.

Belatedly, I knocked on the wood that was my forehead. Would I never learn?

Chapter Six

We all stood there, mouths agape, as Stu continued chanting: 'If it wakens death will come. If it wakens death will come. If it wakens . . .' Finally, Grizzie took matters into her own hand.

Smack went her palm against his cheek. 'Snap out of it, man!' she snarled. Stuart's eyes suddenly refocused and he raised his fingers to his face.

'Huh?' he asked, clearly dazed. Meanwhile, I belatedly realized I'd lost a chance at legitimately smacking the shit out of Stuart Gray.

Stu continued to look around, obviously confused over what he was doing with 'my' crew. Finally, he gathered himself and put his best asshole forward.

'Nice mange, True. Can't afford a haircut?' he said and sneered, before strutting off.

Anyan's human throat emitted a decidedly doggie growl, and I laid a hand on his knee. I appreciated his irritation at Stuart, but I was used to the idea that Stuart was, indeed, a fundamentally irritating person. What I was not used to was Stuart stumbling about like a zombie while making vague, apocalyptic threats.

'Bigger fish,' I mumbled at the barghest, as I turned to the others. We all huddled up around the bar to confab.

'What the hell was that?' I asked, watching as Amy whispered something to Tracy and Grizzie. The look of concern that had lit up their faces when Stuart shambled over was replaced by a placid smile, and then they got up and moved to a table in the Sty's restaurant half. I hated seeing them glamoured and sent away like children, but for their own safety (and sanity) they shouldn't be party to our conversation.

Amy's thin mouth bent into a frown. 'We don't know,' she replied. 'But it's been happening all over Rockabill.'

'Since when?'

'It started about a week after you and Anyan were attacked.'

I gave her my own frown. 'Do you think the two are connected?'

'In a way,' said Anyan. 'We're thinking the attack was a first attempt at gaining access to the Territory. Kill me, and kidnap you to use as leverage.'

'But why? Gain access to what? I mean, the Sty has great burgers, but I don't think it's enough to hire professional hit men.' Then I thought of something else. 'And what does Blondie have to do with all of this?'

'Blondie?' Iris asked, confused.

Anyan chuckled. 'It's what Jane called' – and here Anyan made that completely unpronounceable series of noises again – 'when we didn't know who she was.'

Iris grinned. 'I like "Blondie" better. Her real name hurts my jaw.'

Amy nodded. 'Hell, yeah. Blondie it is. Cuz that bitch can party!'

I looked at Amy, confused, till I figured it out. 'Do you mean *the* Blondie?' I breathed.

Amy nodded. 'We rocked the seventies,' was all she said, leaving me awestruck.

But Amy's former lifestyle wasn't the issue. *Our* Blondie, however, was.

'So what the hell was she doing here anyway? Why was she following us? And where is she now?' I probably sounded ungrateful toward someone who had apparently saved my life numerous times, but I didn't care. If someone shows up in my hometown, and then everyone appears to go a little bananas, that person was gonna be suspect in my mind.

All eyes turned toward Anyan.

'She's out gathering information. She was here the whole time you were in danger – she's the only one who could pump enough power into you to keep you going when you were bleeding out, magically.'

'And I'm grateful. But that still doesn't clarify what she was doing here.'

Anyan gestured to our seats, and all of the supes in attendance moved our barstools so that we could sit and see one another. Nell levitated herself to sit on the actual bar while Trill wiggled into the space between our circle of knees. This was going to take a while, as Anyan cleared his throat like he had to give a speech.

'A lot has been revealed while you were sleeping. It's all been going on for a while, but what we discovered about Jarl's operation here in our Territory brought things to a head. Basically, the schism we've seen here, between those who strive for purity and those who either ignore or encourage interaction with humans, is happening all over the world. Territories are either picking sides or splitting asunder from civil war. It's chaos, but with a focus. War is coming,' Anyan intoned.

Despite the fact that they had to know all of this already, everyone still looked almost as shocked as I did. Shocked and scared. I might have been hearing about this war for the first time, but prior knowledge obviously didn't make it sit any better with my friends. After all, it was one thing to know there was an evil renegade such as Jarl in a position of power, and another thing entirely to know that 'renegade' was anything but and was, instead, part of a power structure that could bring real war to our lives. Meanwhile, everyone was looking equally worried, not least because although my supernatural friends had undoubtedly been in their shares of fights and disputes, Anyan and Caleb were the only real warriors in the Sty that night.

'But what does this war have to do with Rockabill?' I asked, and then thought of a horrible answer to my own question. 'It's not going to be fought here, is it?'

Anyan shook his head no.

'The war definitely won't be here. To be honest, I don't know where it will be this time. It can't be the sort of war we've fought before. We have too much to lose, in terms of human discovery of our kind.' Anyan's brow creased in thought. 'It'll be a new kind of war – a modern war. But it will be just as bloody and just as violent.'

Way to sugarcoat it, I thought, taking a glum sip of my drink.

'So if the war isn't going to be here,' I said, after I'd swallowed, 'why is all this stuff happening here?'

'Something's hidden in Rockabill,' Nell said. 'Something powerful. Something that the other side wants.'

'What do you mean by "something" and by "wants"?' I asked.

'We don't know exact details yet,' Anyan told me. 'That's why Blondie's gone. Once you were stabilized, she went back out to try to find more information.'

'So what do you know?'

Anyan looked around at the other supes as if he were embarrassed.

'Well, Jane,' Iris said, 'to be honest, we're mostly going on conjecture. And by conjecture, I mean a nursery rhyme. An Alfar nursery rhyme.'

'A nursery rhyme,' I said, unimpressed.

Iris nodded and started in on what was obviously the little ditty in question:

'Four locks for power,

Four locks for force.

Four locks for the old one,

Whose time has run its course.'

As she spoke, my eyebrows rose steadily to meet my hairline. She registered my nonimpressed expression as she continued:

'Four locks to bring them all

And in the darkness bind them.'

My eyes widened and I nearly fell off my barstool until Anyan barked 'Iris!' – I'd been had.

The succubus giggled, looking so like her old self I nearly did a happy dance, but then she forced a look of contrition on her face.

'Sorry. Here's the real ending:

Unlock the crystals,

Unlock the land,

Unlock the water,

And with it take a stand.'

I frowned. 'That's it? From that you got Rockabill?'

Anyan shook his head. 'No, Jane. There's more to it than that. People have been looking for the source of this legend for centuries . . . It's like our Holy Grail, or Fountain of Youth.'

'Our Lost City of Gold,' Caleb rumbled, helpfully, in case my brain had fallen out while I had slept, and I could no longer understand analogies unless they were given in threes.

'But how did you land on Rockabill?' I asked.

'It makes sense that Rockabill has *something*,' Anyan replied. 'After all, why do you think this place has always drawn so many of our kind? And didn't you ever wonder why Nell is so powerful? Gnomes are strong, but Nell is ridiculously so.'

The others thought about that, as Sarah Nahual nodded.

'Both Marcus and I became stronger when we moved here. Not a huge amount, but enough that we both noticed. We thought it was our partnership.'

'And why did you move here?' Anyan asked. 'Why did any of you move here?'

Iris frowned. 'I dunno. I was passing through, and I felt I had to stay in the area. I just liked it here. I couldn't stay in Rockabill itself, as there weren't enough people to feed off . . . but I wanted to be close, for some reason.'

Both Sarah and Marcus nodded, as if Iris had summarized how they felt. Minus the people to feed off, obviously.

'Yeah, it's like I felt at *home* here. Even though it's nothing like where I grew up,' Amy replied. 'I only came out here to pick up some killer weed a friend had told me about, and I just knew I had to stay.'

As my friends talked, I started to get what they were saying.

'I was born here, because my mother showed up. But why Rockabill?' That question had always bothered me, ever since I'd been told my mother's true identity. Now it was starting to make sense. 'I mean, if she just wanted a . . . a mate, there are definitely better places to go. My dad was one of like five fertile men in all of Rockabill at the time. Everyone else was too old, too young, or too . . . problematic to have children by. So why not go to a place with more chances to find a baby daddy? Yet she came here.'

'Exactly,' Anyan said. 'There's power hidden in Rockabill – great power. It would be slightly masked by Nell's presence. And if it *is* the power from the nursery rhyme, it's a power so ancient, so foreign, we haven't truly recognized it. But still it calls to us, power to power.'

We all sat in silence for a few seconds, contemplating Anyan's words. It's not every day that you discover your 'choices' might have actually been made for you. Or, at least, helped along by forces outside of your control.

'So what's the power?' I asked, eventually.

Anyan shrugged. 'We don't know, exactly. But that nursery rhyme has been around forever. It's something old. Something strong. And something that shouldn't be found.'

'You couldn't have gotten all that from a nursery rhyme,' I said. 'Especially one so vague.'

'No,' Anyan said. 'Blondie's been chasing up this myth for centuries. And that's why she was following us. She wanted to use us as her invitation into Rockabill. She'd narrowed down her search to places *like* Rockabill – coastal cities with disproportionately large concentrations of supernaturals, and had been going down the list.'

I frowned, my brain *pinging* at the word 'list'.

'Why didn't she just introduce herself?' I wondered out loud.

'I asked her that. She said that she needed to know she could trust us before she told us what she wanted. If she'd just knocked on Nell's door, Nell would have booted her into Canada, as a powerful stranger. So Blondie wanted to suss us out, make sure we were on the level, tell us what she wanted, and then use our help figuring out if Rockabill really does house the power the nursery rhyme talks about. If she'd just told us, and we were both evil and really sitting on the right site, she'd have had a hard time getting through Nell to stop us finding it.'

I thought of the times Blondie had stepped in to save us while we were traveling. Yeah, she seemed on the level, and I could see that Anyan and my other friends clearly trusted her. But *why*?

Before I could air my suspicions, Iris interrupted my thoughts: 'But then you were attacked,' she said, solemnly.

'Yes. And Blondie thinks they're connected,' Caleb rumbled.

I looked up sharply. 'What?'

'Think about it,' Anyan said. 'Blondie's not the only person who was looking for that myth, and war is coming.'

'What does the war have to do with it?' I asked, confused.

'What does every war need?' Anyan asked, clearly rhetorically. I'd noticed that the barghest, while normally short-winded, did enjoy the occasional rousing speech. Unfortunately, he wasn't talking to a cabal of military strategists, and we liked to mess with him. So before he could finish his own question, we'd jumped in to 'help'.

'A punchy code name?' I hazarded.

'Fabulous uniforms!' Iris blurted out.

'Bulletproof jockstraps,' stated Caleb, getting into the spirit of things. Iris had obviously brought out the playful side of the normally serious satyr. No wonder he liked her so.

In the meantime, at his words, the entire group of us sitting in the circle – including the kelpie, with her eye-level pony view – all turned as one to look at the satyr's package. Undaunted, he reaffirmed his opinion.

'Definitely bulletproof jockstraps.'

'Yeah, um, *no*,' Anyan said. 'What every war needs is an *advantage*.'

'And an army,' I added, helpfully.

'And food. Don't armies march on their stomachs?' said Amy Nahual.

'Which means people to cook the food—' I agreed.

'Shut up!' Barked Anyan.

We shut up.

'In this instance, for the sake of this conversation, and before I beat the shit out of all of you, *every war needs an advantage*. Got it? Are we clear?'

We all nodded obediently, fearful that otherwise the barghest would snap and blast us into oblivion.

'Excellent. Good *gods*. Okay.' Anyan took a long breath, clearly counting to ten under his breath. 'So, wars need an advantage: something big, something powerful, something that will give one side an ultimate upper hand over the other side.'

'Whoever's King of the Mountain,' Caleb added, helpfully.

'Exactly,' Anyan said. 'So Blondie's people have been watching the other side, spying to see if they were mobilizing to get something that would give them such an advantage: a location, or a weapon, or a warrior. And that's how we got moved up Blondie's list – she discovered the enemy's interest in Rockabill.'

'Did Peter Jakes have anything to do with this?' I hazarded, seeing a hazy connection between this 'list of locations' and the halfling monitor who'd been cataloguing his own kind for Jarl and Morrigan, not knowing their true intention was to wipe out all non-full-blooded supernaturals.

'Yes,' Nell said. 'I, for one, am certain of that. I remember when he checked in, we had this really long conversation about how many supes were living in this area, and from far and wide. We talked about how very few were native, but most were passers-through who'd settled. He thought it was fascinating. I'm sure he passed on such information, even if he didn't know its implications.'

I shivered at that chilling thought. 'And when did the, er, possessions start?'

'Right after you were attacked,' Nell said. 'If we'd had any doubts about Blondie's story—'

'Wait,' I interrupted. 'I'm sorry, but can we stop there? I know I've been out of the loop for a month, but the last thing I knew, Blondie was some mysterious stranger we thought could be a renegade Alfar. Now we're all buddies? Are you sure we can trust her?'

Anyan smiled. 'Yes, Jane. I've done my homework on her, believe me. We needed her, obviously, when things were touch and go with you. So while she was playing nurse, I was doing some pretty thorough background checks. She's known by a number of aliases throughout the Territories as a friend to half-lings, and a rebel leader. Her reputation is solid: she wants change, but she's no terrorist or wacko. Everyone *does* think she's a renegade Alfar. Very few people know her true identity as an Original. But they do know her, and good people whom I trust have vouched for her.'

I frowned. I remembered Ryu telling me all those months ago, when we first met, that sometimes even supes who wanted to believe something enough could be glamoured. If a savior appears to fall from the sky, are you really going to be working overtime to discredit her?

Apparently Jane True would, my brain said.

'Like I was saying,' Nell continued, as if to drive Anyan's point home, 'if we *had* any doubts about Blondie's story before that, they were dispelled when the warnings started. There is definitely something lurking in Rockabill.'

'Is that what Stuart was doing? Was he warning us?' I asked, distracted from my thoughts about Blondie. There was so much going on, so much I'd missed out on, that I had to get caught up as quickly as possible.

'We think so,' Anyan replied. He had felt me shiver, and his hand rubbed along my shoulders comfortingly.

'But who's doing the warning?' I asked.

'We don't know. Whatever's hidden probably has a guard. Maybe an actual guard, maybe a magical alarm,' the barghest answered. 'These are some of the things Blondie's trying to find out.'

'So what's been happening? I saw Stuart, but what else has there been?'

'Lots of odd things,' Anyan replied. 'Lots of people acting like Stuart, and chanting that same phrase.'

'Or writing the phrase,' Caleb added.

Anyan nodded his agreement. 'As graffiti on buildings, or just over and over again on napkins or placemats or newspapers.'

'Tracy wrote it over and over in her crossword puzzle one day. It was freaky,' Amy said, and I got very pissed at the idea of someone using my pregnant friend as a passenger pigeon for a supernatural message.

'The Sow's also been acting up,' said Caleb.

'The Sow?' I asked sharply, thinking of what had happened to me earlier.

'Jana Henning lost her boat last week,' Marcus explained. 'A really strong piglet popped up right under her, way farther than any piglets should have been. The crew would have been drowned if it hadn't subsided just as quickly.'

'But the piglets have been acting up all over,' Sarah continued. 'It's like the Sow's expanding or something. Keeping everything away from her.'

'Well, that kind of goes against the experience that I had earlier,' I said, as all eyes turned to me.

'I was swimming with Trill. We were playing in the Sow, like we normally do. I got batted down by a piglet that sprang up, but that's not too out of the norm,' I insisted, as Caleb raised an eyebrow. 'But what was out of the norm was that I started to crawl toward the Sow. I don't know why. At the time, it felt good. It felt like . . . I dunno, like I was being massaged by the water. But when Trill hauled me back, I was covered in cuts and bruises.'

The little pony nodded where she stood among our knees.

'That's what happened to you?' Anyan asked, his face troubled. I nodded at him.

'She was really banged up,' he told everyone. 'I healed her,' he added, lamely, when Trill's pony form leered at him.

'Healing? Is that what's it's called?' she asked, clearly ribbing the barghest. I held back a giggle as he turned a rather intense shade of red. Iris gave me a look, arching an eyebrow at me in question. I responded with a cheeky wink that made her smile.

'And nothing like that's ever happened before with the Sow?' Caleb asked me.

'Never. I've always gotten a lot of power from her, but I've never lost myself like that.'

'We should keep the humans even farther away from the Sow for a while,' Marcus said. 'Just in case.'

Amy nodded. 'And we should put our heads together and try to remember when and where all the possessions occurred. And catalog any new ones.'

'I can make one of those maps with the pushpins like they have on CSI,' Iris gushed, sounding excited about the idea. To be honest, after all the drama she had experienced, I was surprised she wanted to be involved in more. But I could see how she might feel good being proactive, rather than merely defensive.

'Not a bad idea,' Amy replied, giving Iris a warm smile.

'Yeah, but what does all of this tell us?' I cut in, still not quite sure what was going on after my long hiatus in coma land. 'I mean, what do we actually know about what is happening?'

'Well, we know that humans as well as some of us are being possessed,' Nell responded to me. 'Most of the possessions take the form of warnings. But yours seemed to be leading you into the Sow.'

'Maybe that was just a more aggressive form of warning?' Anyan wondered aloud, as he tried to figure out why the possessions would change style. 'Maybe whatever's out there is trying to show us its power. Show us what it can do.'

Sarah shrugged. 'Maybe. Or maybe the Sow's just reacting to all the power that's shooting around. Natural habitats can be influenced by our hoodoo.'

'The voodoo that you do so well,' I intoned solemnly, if randomly. I was ignored. And yet I persevered. 'So we know that there are possessions taking place and that they consist of some type of warning. But warning about what? I'm asking, basically, what do we really *know*, rather than what are we guessing?'

'There has to be something here, in Rockabill. It's the only explanation for the possessions, and us getting attacked the way we were,' Anyan said. 'I'm the strongest power here, besides Nell. And she's well nigh unstoppable. So they wanted to get me out of the picture and use you as leverage, probably against Nell. So they could enter the Territory.'

'But Jane got 'em, instead,' Iris said, her voice proud.

'What else have they tried?' I said, realizing that couldn't have been the bad guy's only attempt in a whole month. 'That can't have been their only attack.'

'It wasn't,' Caleb agreed. 'There are all sorts of little things happening. Probes at Nell's boundaries; things sneaking in, obviously looking for something, before running off; "tourist" humans who act funny, but not in a possessed way. After what happened to you and Anyan, we've been watching the humans as carefully as our own kind. And Nell's been kept very busy watching her boundaries.'

'There have also been creatures sniffing around Iris's, as well as some of the other beings that are outside Nell's immediate protection,' Caleb said, his voice gone cold and hard. Iris put a hand on his, gently as if to calm him. But I think she was also reminding herself he was there to protect her.

'So lots of little intrusions. Any ideas who's doing it?' I asked.

'There have been a few reports. Harpies . . . and some humans glimpsed something like a giant,' Anyan replied.

'Or a spriggan,' I spat. 'Phaedra's crew.'

'We think so. But there are other helpers. It has to be a fairly large operation,' Nell said. 'And there are reports of similar problems elsewhere. Other places that might house something, or someone, of value.'

'Grim's been busy in Borealis,' Anyan added, as if to affirm what Nell was saying.

'The Grim? The one Cappie told us about?' I asked. Grim was a friend of Anyan's who lived in, and guarded, the little suburb of Chicago called Borealis, where halflings had made themselves a very cool home. Other than that, and the fact that he was seriously powerful, I knew nothing about Grim. He wanted to remain a mystery wrapped in an enigma, and Anyan respected his friend's wishes.

'Yep. He guards something strong, and someone's been trying for it. Using very similar strategies,' the barghest said.

'So, what we know is that war is coming. The bad guys are looking for things that will give them an advantage. And one of those things happens to be here, in Rockabill, but we don't know what it is, or where,' I summarized, suddenly feeling immensely tired both physically and emotionally.

'Well, we know it's locked. And that there are four locks,' Iris said, still managing to look on the bright side despite everything she'd gone through. I saw Caleb stroke her blond head after she'd spoken, and my heart went pitter-patter. He so *got* her, I realized – he was rewarding her for a bravery, a strength of spirit, that he would only recognize as either of those things because he really *understood* Iris – who she'd been, what she'd suffered through, and how she was fighting to regain the part of herself she'd lost in that mansion.

'Like what kind of locks? What do they look like?'

'That we're not so sure about,' Anyan admitted. 'But they're here. Somewhere. Probably.'

'But we're not really sure what they contain?' I said, just to be clear.

'Er, no,' was all Anyan could say.

We all sat around the bar at the Sty, not meeting each others' eyes. Although we weren't talking, I knew everyone was thinking the same thing I was, or at least a close approximation.

Oh, fuckerdoodles.

Chapter Seven

My morning swim was a combination of my usual outing and a new kind of reconnaissance. I swam in and around the piglets, Trill keeping watch, trying to see if I'd go all *Exorcist* and try climbing into the whirlpool again.

But nothing happened, and I kept my usual respectful distance from the Sow. She swirled about in front of us, silent and inscrutable, while Trill and I circled like not-very-fearsome sharks.

After my swim, I went home to shower and then got ready for work. It was my first day back in my normal routine in a very long time. I'd been traveling for weeks before the attack that had left me comatose for a month, so I was incredibly lucky I had such understanding (and slightly glamoured) employers. I was also more than ready to get back into the swing of things, especially since I was really feeling my oats. The night before, shortly after we'd had our run-in with Stu, I'd nearly fallen asleep sitting up. I'd had a busy day for someone who'd been asleep for so long. Anyan looked a bit disappointed when Nell offered to apparate me home, but I took her up on the offer. I didn't think I could stand up for much longer, so any hanky-panky with the barghest was going to have to wait.

Which meant that I began my long walk to work well

rested and feeling good – almost entirely normal. Or as normal as I could feel, given the circumstances.

Because, once I entered our little village, I saw that things were definitely odd in Rockabill. Nothing a stranger would have picked up on, but I could feel it. It wasn't all the people about – there was always a lot of foot traffic in Rockabill. Except when it was raining or snowing, people would drive into the town center, but then they'd park to do most of their errands on foot. This was partly due to how small our little village was, but it was also because it was an ideal way to socialize. Everyone would walk around, coffee in hand, chatting about who had done what to whom. In a place like Rockabill, there were no secrets and, except for the tourists, no strangers. Anyone who planted him- or herself here for longer than a single summer was fair game for the outrageously generous acts of kindness, the sometimes cruel gossip, and the ceaseless *interest* that was life in a very small community.

And for better or worse, I was a Rockabillian. So the tension that had sprung up while I was sleeping grated at me like nails on a chalkboard. Everyone was walking around like they expected something to jump out at them. Which I supposed was understandable if your friends, loved ones, and neighbors could start yelling weird threats randomly and for no obvious reason.

Or start writing on the walls, I thought, seeing evidence of badly painted-over graffiti on the outside of Tanner's Bakery; our little supermarket, McKinley's; the Trough, our diner; as well as some of the sidewalks and benches. Underneath the fresh paint, I could clearly see the words 'Rises', 'Death', and 'Come' defacing the brick or shingle sides of our downtown buildings. I wasn't opposed to things 'rising' or 'coming', but having 'death' sandwiched between the two words was a bit of a buzz-kill.

It's not just that everyone's on edge, I observed, as I walked through our little town center. *It's like they don't trust themselves.*

It *would* be pretty weird, however, to discover yourself defacing public property when you've never so much as spat on the sidewalk. The whole point of why we were so up in each others' business is that Rockabill *wasn't* San Francisco or Seattle. Rockabill wasn't known for attracting eccentrics, crazy geniuses, and the simply crazy. Yes, we had our fair share of oddities, but for the most part we were all pretty 'normal' people. Every once in a while someone would do something like run off with a tourist, or invest in alpacas, or begin selling paintings of their own vagina on Etsy, but that was rare. Most of us were nice and bourgeois, so to have people in our community acting out like this (and with no memory of how or why) was really terrifying.

Which explains why everyone is walking on eggshells, I thought, watching as Marge Tanner – returning to her bakery after delivering pastries to Read It and Weep for our bakery case – gave Gus Little – who bagged groceries at McKinley's but was really a stone spirit – a nervous nod. The idea that someone might be nervous around *Gus* illustrated how badly Rockabill nerves were frayed.

I'd grown up thinking Gus was mentally a bit slow, when in reality he was sort of like a dryad, only instead of bound to a tree he was bound to a rock somewhere right outside town. Like their namesakes, stone spirits were often unflappable and a bit obtuse, meaning that Gus had never done anything to raise eyebrows in his life. Unless being someone who never raised eyebrows did, indeed, raise eyebrows.

Things are bad, I realized, grimly, as Marge gave me my own wary greeting, as if to assess whether I'd freak out on her, before stopping to chat. We exchanged some pleasantries about Belize and about the bakery, giving Gus time to walk into McKinley's. After I'd said goodbye to Mrs Tanner, I walked past McKinley's, glad Gus was inside so I didn't have to force a conversation with him. Even my knowing his true nature and sharing his supernatural world with him didn't make socializing with the stone spirit any easier.

I ducked into the bookstore and was immediately ambushed. 'Oof,' was my awesomely articulate response to being shoved, face first, into Grizzie's surgically enhanced bosoms the second I was through the door.

'My dahlink,' she purred. 'Where have you been all my life? How could you abandon me for Belize?'

'Ahm thowwy,' I mumbled into her cleavage.

'Fickle bitch,' she replied, finally releasing me. 'Now, tell me everything. And when did you start hanging around with Juan Besonegro?'

'Um . . . who?'

'Juan! The artist! Since when did you guys know each other?'

'Do you mean An . . . wan? The big guy?' I asked, finally putting together that Grizzie meant Anyan.

'Ooooh, is he big? I thought he would be.'

I blinked at her.

'Yes,' she said and sighed, disappointed. 'The big guy, from the other night. The way you two were looking at each other, I figured you'd know each other's names, at least. And maybe each other's ticklish spots.'

'Yeah, sorry, I do know . . . Juan. I'm just out of it today . . .'

'So, where *is* his ticklish spot? And can I have a go?' Grizzie asked, raising her hands to scritch her fingernails in the air, a gesture that I found alarming, to say the least.

'His ticklish spot is right next to your pregnant girlfriend, you slattern,' I replied, backing away from her talons, painted a lurid shade of neon green to match her black wraparound dress with its neon-green-winged lapels, hem, and French cuffs.

'Ugh, don't remind me,' Grizzie sighed, mock seriously. 'I'm totally ball-and-chained. I'll be forced to start wearing housecoats. Actually, I would rock a house coat,' Grizzie said, as she struck a dramatic vamp pose with one arm in the air and one foot out to the side, toes pointed.

'You totally would,' I said, heading toward the back so I could drop off my stuff before starting work. I knew Griz would follow.

'Seriously, though, how do you know Juan?' she asked, her curiosity obviously very piqued.

'How do *you* know Juan?' I countered, trying to figure out what I needed to know of Anyan's human persona before answering.

'Who *doesn't* know Juan?' Grizzie asked, rolling her eyes and leaning against the doorframe as I set down my bag and jean jacket on the table in the back room. 'He's totally famous, totally mysterious, and a total all-in-one sausagefest.'

'Classy, Griz,' I said, giggling.

'What, it's true!' she replied, poking a fingernail into the side of her long, black French braid to scratch her scalp. 'He's hotter than candy on a stick. Huckleberry, cherry, *or* lime.'

'He is definitely hot—' I started to say, before Grizzie interrupted me with some more Juan worship.

'I mean, he's not pretty, by any means. Not like Ryu. Whatever happened to Ryu, anyway?' I started to reply, but she didn't let me. Grizzie was on a roll. 'Who cares, he was pretty, but too fancy. Who wants fancy? Our Jane needs someone stable . . . someone grounded . . . someone more domestic . . .'

I blushed, realizing that Anyan *was* all of these things.

Yes, he was a dangerous-ninja-dog-man, but he was also everything Grizzie was describing.

'Someone who'll throw you down on the bed and show you how it's done . . . Someone who'll tie you up and let you know what it is to be a woman . . . Someone who'll spank that little—'

'Grizzie!' I barked, bringing her sexual tirade to a halt, and just in the nick of time. She'd gone all glassy-eyed and drooling.

'Oh, sorry. I get carried away.'

'Oh, do you, now?' was my sarcasm-laden response.

'Anyway, he's hot and I'll bet he'll spank you.'

My only rejoinder was a throaty whimper, my mouth gone dry.

'So, you know him how?' Grizzie said, interrupting me before I could plunge too deeply into my own Anyan-spanking fantasy.

'Um . . . we met . . . hiking. He has a cabin in the woods.'

'You? Hiking?' It was Grizzie's turn to make free and easy with the sarcasm. She had a point.

'It was more . . . strolling,' I clarified, lying my pants off. 'By the beach. You know I like to walk by the beach.'

'But you've been in Belize.'

Shit! I thought, my brain shuffling away.

'We met a while ago, while I was strolling. Then we . . . uh . . . we saw each other on the plane.'

'To Belize?' Grizzie asked, clearly not believing me.

'No, that would be ridiculous, obviously,' I said, although that was totally what I'd been going to say. 'On the connecting flight. Back to Eastport.'

'Ohhhh, okay. And you guys talked? Reconnected? Maybe joined the mile-high club?'

'We talked. There's been no . . . joining, as of yet,' replied Jane True, Ms. Suddenly Shy.

'Awww, you're blushing!' Grizzie cried out, excitedly. 'You like him! You like Juan!'

I couldn't deny it, so I just blushed redder.

Grizzie stopped giggling. 'You really like him,' she said, suddenly serious. 'You do, don't you?'

I didn't know it was possible, but I think I managed an even brighter shade of tomato. 'Yeah, I like him. But, I mean, it is what it is,' I said. 'He's a lot older than me. And he's really famous,' I said, knowing that Grizzie thought I meant Anyan was famous as the artist apparently known as Juan Besonegro.

'So?' Grizzie asked, all combative.

'So, he's out of my league,' I started, stopping when Grizzie held up both hands, palms facing outward.

'Whoa, whoa, whoa, Jane. I saw the way he looks at you. He was staring like he wanted to get right the hell *in* your league, in front of all of us, at the bar.'

I nodded. 'Yeah, I know we're attracted to each other. And I know it'll probably go a lot further, and soon. But it's gotta be different for him. He's been *around*, Griz. I'm some girl who fell in love with her high school sweetheart and hasn't ever left home. I doubt we think the same way about stuff.'

'What do you mean, "think the same way about stuff"?'

'I mean . . .' Pausing to gather my thoughts, I turned around so I could half sit, half lean on our break table.

What *did* I mean? I realized that I wasn't entirely sure, so I started talking: 'I mean that he's already lived a lot. He's probably been in love dozens of times, gone on hundreds of first dates, gotten all dramatic about different people, and then realized he was silly. Eventually, it's gotta stop, doesn't it? It all has to get a bit . . . pointless?' Grizzie made a face, so I pulled back. 'Okay, not pointless. But less *big*, right? I mean, how many times can you fall head over heels in love before you start to wonder if love really exists?'

'Dude, was there a puddle of cynicism waiting on your wrong side of the bed this morning?' Grizzie asked, her expression clearly horrified. 'Life is always *big*. It's your *life*.'

But what if you've lived a hundred lifetimes? I asked silently, thinking of the preternatural calm of the Alfar. *Is it still 'life', then? Or something a lot less lively?*

'Take me as an example,' Grizzie was saying. 'If you want to talk about life experience, I've ratcheted up quite a bit in my time. I've done lots of crazy, extreme things. I've not only been around the block, but I've burned the block down. At least twice.'

I couldn't help but agree. Grizzie had lived a very crazy life.

'And I'm still enjoying life, Jane. Cuz that's how I choose to be. I think that you're mistaking certain people – people who have this "been there, done that" attitude to everything – with people who've experienced a lot of stuff. They're not the same thing. I bet the people who walk around acting like they've already done everything twice were walking around like that before they did *anything*. It's just who they are. People who *want* to live? They live.'

Bizarrely enough, the person I thought about as Grizzie finished speaking was Morrigan. She'd convinced everyone she was everything Alfar immortality represented: something cold and detached, like a living zombie.

But Morrigan fooled us all, I thought, realizing that what Grizzie said had a lot of merit. Yeah, Morrigan was clearly a conniving, evil bitch. But while those weren't the best character traits, they were definitely a choice she made and they were definitely anything but cold and detached. She'd chosen to live as a cheating, murderous, purist monster, but she'd definitely chosen to live.

But that doesn't mean you, Jane True, can compete with all of Anyan's life experience, my brain cut in, rather rudely. My libido gave it a raspberry, but it was still too caught up in its own spanking fantasy to formulate any kind of real argument against my pessimistic logic.

'You don't look convinced,' Grizzie said, frowning.

'No, I think you're totally right about what you were saying,' I replied, shaking my head. 'I think you're right about choosing to live versus just living.'

'But?'

'But . . . that doesn't change the fact that he's lived a lot. And I haven't.'

Grizzie's wide mouth frowned even more, and she walked toward me until she was perched next to me on the break table, one arm around my waist.

'Are you saying that you think he's too good for you, Jane True?'

My silence was my only answer.

Grizzie sighed, clearly at a loss. 'That's just . . . stupid,' she replied, eventually.

I couldn't help but laugh. Grizzie laughed too, but without a lot of humor.

'I don't really know what to say, honey. You know I think you're amazing and perfect and gorgeous. And I know Juan wants you and he'd be silly to pass up the opportunity you represent. But who knows what another person's priorities are? Some people still think Tracy was crazy for taking up with me, or that I'm crazy for staying with Tracy.'

I frowned at her: my turn to protest.

'I know you're not one of them,' Griz said, squeezing me closer. 'What I'm saying is that people never make any sense.

Who knows what the hell they're thinking half the time. But there was something about you and Juan together that was . . . comfortable. Sexy and sparky, and all of that . . . but also comfortable. You look like you fit. Fit for what, I dunno. Maybe just for a few months of jungle sex, maybe for a lengthy future culminating in an old age full of tons of grandkids and a smattering of broken hips. Who knows? But in the meantime, give yourself a fucking break. You're a catch, for anybody's net.'

I strained upward to kiss Grizzie on the cheek. I wasn't so sure about my being a catch, but she was right about the other stuff: I didn't know anything about what was going on between Anyan and me, because there was nothing yet to know. I needed to stop worrying about it and let things play out.

Hopefully with added jungle sex and little or no hip breakage, I thought, wondering for the trillionth time in our friendship at Grizzie's propensity for terrifying imagery.

'Enough about me,' I said. 'I want to hear all about you, Tracy, and the babies.'

Grizzie grinned, and her happiness was so dazzling that it made her earlier ball-and-chain jokes all the funnier.

'Well, Tracy's being a total cow and pooh-poohing all my baby names. I mean, there's nothing wrong with Lesbia! It was a perfectly acceptable name to the Romans.'

Chapter Eight

Walking toward Anyan's that night, I was still giggling over Grizzie and Tracy's Great Baby Name Debacle. For a girl, Tracy was leaning toward Christie, Loren, and Abigail, while Grizzie was adamant that Lesbia, Sappho, or an unpronounceable Goddess symbol were totally the way to go. It got even worse with boys' names. Tracy had suggested Wyatt, James, or Thomas, but Grizzie was gunning for Rock A. Billy or the completely inexplicable choice of Manchego.

The thing with Grizzie is you could never *really* be sure when she was serious.

Manchego's gotta be a joke, I thought, keeping my focus on the hilarity of the afternoon's events rather than on the fact that I was walking toward Anyan's. If I *had* stopped to think about it, however, my thoughts might have gone something like this:

VIRTUE: You're just going to train with Nell, as usual. Don't get all crazy.

LIBIDO: I'll give Anyan a training!

VIRTUE: You'll do no such thing. (A) He is undoubtedly the one who will do the training, both inside and outside of the bedroom. (B) This is the time for *magical* training. Not the naughty kind!

LIBIDO: Mmm. Naughty.
VIRTUE: Focus!
LIBIDO: I'll give Anyan a focus!
VIRTUE: I hate you.

After that little exchange, both my virtue and my libido quieted. Then I noticed how sweet and crisp the air was scented by the ocean and the first hints of spring. In other words, I was really enjoying the long walk back to Anyan's when my cell phone rang. I dug it out of my purse, and then frowned when I saw who was calling.

'Hey, Ryu,' I said, after taking the call.

'Jane!' Ryu said, practically shouting. 'It's so good to hear your voice!'

I paused before speaking. In my memory, it had been only a little bit ago that we'd had our final spat outside the Healer's mansion. But for him, I'd been comatose for a month. During which he'd apparently come and visited me a few times and helped to investigate the humans who had attacked us. In other words, he'd had a month to act as a good friend, rather than the angry ex he'd been after he'd again found me with Anyan.

'Thank you, Ryu. And thanks for coming to Rockabill and helping out.'

'Oh, no, it was the least I could do. How are you feeling?'

'Totally fine. Ridiculously well, actually. Although we've still got a lot going on here.'

'Yeah, I know. I've been talking with Caleb about it. Do you need me up there?'

The question was a loaded one, if ever I'd heard it.

'You know what?' I said, carefully. 'I don't think so. But if we do, you know we'll call you right away.'

He paused, with relief or disappointment, I don't know. I

couldn't assume either reaction – after all, I know he had cared for me, but he was also Ryu. And a month was a long time for someone like him, despite his longevity. He was a mover and a shaker, not a waiter-arounder.

After that we made some small talk for about ten minutes. We discussed Caleb and Iris, and we talked about my dad having been healed. We did *not* talk about Anyan. Eventually, Ryu was the one to wrap up the conversation, reminding me that all I had to do was call and he'd be there in a snap.

I thanked him, and I meant it. Then he hung up. And then I waited.

Only to discover that nothing happened. I didn't feel any unrequited lust, or any anger, or any grief. I felt the pleasant feeling one feels when they've talked to someone who is important to them, and the conversation had gone well. I felt like . . . Ryu and I could be friends.

And that felt good.

Less good, however, was the other thing I suddenly both felt and heard: an explosion from somewhere to my right.

What the fuck? I thought, as the rest of the forest went silent.

I was about halfway between the edge of town and my house, so basically in the middle of nowhere, which meant it couldn't have been a car backfiring. Plus, it had been strong enough to be felt, and not just heard, so that meant some kind of explosion. And as most of our locals avoided hunting with grenades, an explosion had to be something nefarious.

Another huge boom rocked toward me again, but this time I was ready. Putting out my feelers, I recognized a clear undercurrent of magic.

Without thinking, I raised shields and a mage ball and ran toward the sound. Well, scrabbled is more accurate, as the underbrush was pretty dense. When I did start thinking, my first emotion was pride that I had, finally, learned some reflexes that sent me *toward* danger rather than *from* it. My second emotion was to worry about what the fuck I was getting myself into.

But I didn't let my fear stop me. Instead, I put a little magic into my run, pushing forward with my shields to clear the ground in front of me so I could move faster. I backed off on my magic only when I knew I was getting near the commotion. I could hear what sounded like pretty intense fighting from right up in front of me.

Hoping to sneak up on whatever was making all the racket, I shut down the mojo as I crept toward what had to be a glade. In the dim evening light, I could see stars twinkling from a space free of canopy . . . and a fuck ton of magic being thrown about like it was D-day here in Boofookey, Maine.

When I neared the clearing – hunkering down to stay behind a cover of undergrowth – I nearly gave myself away by swearing.

For standing directly in front of me – less than a yard away – was the unmistakable tree-trunk legs of a spriggan. And since I could clearly see the now rather melty face of Graeme, the rapist incubus, standing on my right-hand side of the glade, I knew that spriggan had to be my favorite shit-for-brains thug, Fugwat.

What the fuck are they doing here? And where is Nell? There was no way the gnome could be unaware of such explosive trespassing.

I got lower, so I could peer between the spriggan's spraddled legs to see what he and Graeme were attacking. What I saw made my blood boil.

Pinned by enemy fire against an enormous boulder, his arms spread as if protecting something precious, stood Gus.

His bald pate gleamed with sweat and his glasses hung off one ear as he bravely defended his rock.

Or are the rocks defending him? I wondered, as I watched various stones – some mere pebbles, some as large as my fist – unearth themselves from the ground and go winging toward Graeme and Fugwat.

I stood, quietly, ready to attack Fugwat from behind and make my way to Gus, when a series of shrieks pierced the air.

And where goeth Tweedledee and Tweedledum, there followeth the damned air brigade, I thought as, sure enough, Kaya and Kaori (whichever was which) came streaking downward, harrying Gus away from his rock. My rescue plans were put on hold as I tried to figure out a way to save Gus from four baddies without getting both of us killed. I was also trying to figure out what, exactly, Phaedra's lot was doing in the first place.

It's like they want Gus's boulder, I realized, even though I couldn't, for the life of me, figure out why anyone but Gus would want the stone spirit's rock.

Then again, I can't really understand why anyone would want Gus, either. I'm sure he was a very nice stone spirit and all, but *man* he was hard work.

Speaking of which, I thought, as the harpies' attack on Gus intensified. The poor little guy was obviously struggling, and I was hiding in the bushes.

No fucking way, I thought, remembering that moment when Anyan was attacked and I just stood there. *Not this time.*

Inhaling deeply, I stood up right behind Fugwat, who'd moved forward a few feet toward Gus's boulder. Conjuring the biggest, baddest mage ball I could muster, I held the swirling iron-gray orb in my hand as I used my outdoor voice.

'Fugwat! Duck!' I shouted, praying that my plan worked.

And it did. Fugwat dropped like he'd been shot, leaving Graeme's flank totally undefended. I let fly my mage ball, which smashed through the incubus's token side-shields and into the side of his head with a crunching noise that was music to my ears.

It's not that Graeme was more of a threat than the spriggan, really. I just liked him even less.

By the time Fugwat had raised his rather empty head to see what had happened, I was across the clearing and running to Gus's side. He'd seen me and was reaching out a plump hand when the lean, dun-colored shape of Kaya (or Kaori) came streaking down from the sky, landing a solid blow across the stone spirit's forehead.

Blood gushed from Gus's wound and I cried out, extending my hand and my shield toward him as I solidified the latter using a combination of power woven through the water saturating the air. The second harpy, Kaori (or Kaya), bounced off my impromptu shield with a *thud* before she could strike Gus.

Squawking painfully, she tumbled to the ground. While I wouldn't normally kick a person when she was down, I was more than willing to kick any of Phaedra's murderous lot. So I dropped my shields, funneling my force into another large mage ball. Instead of throwing this one, however, I bowled it at where the harpy lay, hooting piteously. Her sister snatched her up from the ground just a second before the mage ball could strike.

They spoil all my fun, I thought, as I finally gained Gus's side.

The stone spirit was weaving on his feet, clearly wounded. As I had absolutely no healing skills (another huge gap in my education), there was nothing I could do but try to keep him from getting hurt any worse until Nell finally arrived.

And where the hell is that gnome? I thought, as I watched
Kaya (or Kaori) land her sister Kaori (or Kaya) a few feet
from where Graeme lay. I think the rapist incubus was smol-
dering, which pleased me to no end.

The mobile harpy sent a blast of healing energy at Graeme,
even as Fugwat finally cottoned on to the fact that he'd been
tricked and insinuated both his sizeable bulk and his even
more formidable shields between me and his cronies.

Gus's hand clutched at mine as he pulled me toward him
to get my attention.

'Save her!' he pleaded with me. 'They want her! I don't
know why, but they want her!' It took me a second to put
two and two together, and then I realized that the 'her' in
question was Gus's boulder.

I was about to tell him that I'd try when we both fell silent
under an onslaught of incubus magic so dark, so violently
sexual, and so terrifying that both Gus and I turned as one.

Graeme stood there, his waxen face even odder than before.
The incubus had been gorgeous once: an Apollonian delight
of perfectly symmetrical, golden male beauty. But such beauty
had only barely masked the monster peering out of those
sky-blue eyes. When Conleth – the ifrit halfling – had melted
Graeme's original face, the subsequent healings had left the
incubus with a weird, waxen parody of his former glory. In
other words, he now looked on the outside like the horror he
was on the inside.

Graeme stepped forward, waving his cohorts behind him.
The look in his eyes froze my blood; he wasn't any more of
a fan of me than I was of him.

'Jane, you stupid little cunt,' he articulated in a tone that
was paradoxically friendly and light. 'What on earth do you
think you're doing?' Graeme backed up his words with a
wave of juju poured directly at me. It was so strong that I

staggered, whimpering as visions of sex and pain crowded into my brain on a wave of magic.

Focus, Jane, I scolded myself, bracing myself both physically and with my power. Trying to keep my shields up and intact, I pulled Gus closer to me. I wasn't sure if I was trying to protect him or to remind myself that I wasn't alone with Graeme.

'You're not meant to be here fighting like this,' Graeme's voice floated toward me, and with those words came more images, more suggestions. I shook my head violently as my shields wavered.

What the hell is this? I thought, frantically. I'd never dealt with anything like what Graeme was doing. Physical assaults, sure. But mental? *I didn't even know that was possible.*

'Jane's not a fighter,' came that voice, again, the words searing into my mind. 'Jane's meant to be tied up . . . fucked . . . like the little slut she is.'

I'm not a slut! my brain insisted, that word jarring me enough that I managed not only to solidify my shields, but also to raise a mage ball that I lobbed at Graeme's head.

And what's wrong with being a slut, anyway? grumbled my libido, as Graeme's shields absorbed the impact of my missile. But he did step back a few paces, giving me some breathing room.

'I think you mean some other Jane,' I yelled, hiding my growing fear behind bravado. ''Cause this Jane's gonna kick your ass!'

Okay, it sounded a bit lame, even to me. And Graeme's only response was a chuckle so evil it raised the hair on my arms another inch. I must have looked like a scared cat or a porcupine, at that point.

'Slut,' Graeme hissed. 'Just a little slut, built for your pain, my pleasure.'

I growled, lobbing another couple of mage balls that I pulled out of the air with practiced ease. Anger was making me strong, but I needed to watch my power levels.

Unfortunately, Graeme was able to deflect my barrage and keep talking. Behind him, the spriggan had backpedalled toward the boulder, where he was doing something I couldn't quite make out. It was a testament to how badly Gus was hurt that he didn't even seem to notice his rock was being man-handled.

'Don't act like I'm lying, little Jane,' Graeme said loudly, trying to refocus my attention on him. And succeeding at it. 'I know it's what you want, what you crave . . .'

Again, images assaulted my mind: bodies bent, chained, whipped, bruised, cut . . . blood and semen dripping across lacerated flesh and I moaned.

'That's it, Jane . . . open your mind . . . drop the inhibitions that fetter you . . . let . . . me . . . in.'

And with those words, Graeme's magic rolled across me so powerfully that I fell to my knees, my head feeling as if someone were forcing a chisel into my skull.

I groaned, putting my hands up to my ears to block out his voice . . . but the voice was *inside my head* . . . It was Graeme . . . *but he was inside* . . . and I had to block him out, but the more I tried the more I realized . . . *the voice is yours, Jane.*

The voice was mine. And I did want it . . . I was his slut, his fuck toy, to be used and discarded, and only his pleasure mattered because his pleasure was my pleasure was his pleasure . . .

Graeme's searingly cold blue eyes were right in front of me, so I crawled forward, toward him . . . *your lover . . .*

. . . my lover . . .

And then his hands were in my hair as he jerked my head

up so that I knelt in front of him. Gus's small fists pummeled at my lover's torso, but they were ignored until, with a negligible flick of his wrist, Graeme flung the stone spirit away with his power.

In that second, his power divided by Gus's assault, Graeme's hold on me broke just enough that I struggled, hard, suddenly remembering who and where I was. And that Graeme was anything but my lover.

In that split second, two things happened.

The first was that Graeme grinned evilly as he hauled me up to my feet and toward him. But instead of biting me, as I'd expected, he only whispered in my ear.

The second was that Nell's power blossomed through the glade like a mushroom cloud. The force of her mojo shook all of us to our bones as she stood atop Gus's boulder, peering around to get a bead on the situation.

Then, with another huge outpouring of power, she apparated all of the bad guys out of her Territory and, hopefully, straight to the moon.

Once I knew Gus and I were safe, I used all my remaining energy to stay upright.

'What happened?' Nell demanded, levitating over to check on me and the stone spirit.

Raising my head wearily, I looked the gnome in the eyes.

'Something tells me we just found the first lock,' I said, feeling my knees buckle.

Without Graeme's hand in my hair, I was in no shape to keep myself upright. So I tumbled to the side, where I was caught at the last second by large, strong hands.

Anyan's face was more than a little worried when he turned me over, asking how I was. 'He was in my *mind*,' I babbled.

'In my head, like he was me. Telling me what I wanted, who I was—'

'Shhh, Jane. I know. He can do that,' Anyan said, stroking his hand across my cheek. I had to remind myself that it was Anyan's hands, not Graeme's. Then I remembered what Graeme had said, and I shuddered, pulling away from the barghest.

Sitting up, I drew my jean jacket tighter around me. 'Why didn't you tell me he could do that? Why didn't I know?'

'I'm sorry,' Anyan replied, letting me move away from him. 'There was so much to teach you, and so little time.'

'Why did he never do that before?' I asked.

'Um . . .' Anyan said, clearly trying to figure out what to say. 'He didn't really have to before,' the big man finally said, sounding embarrassed. It took me a second, and then I cottoned to what he was saying.

I'd been so weak before that Graeme didn't need to pull out his big guns.

I bit my tongue on the nasty retort I had waiting. I was letting Graeme get to me, and taking it out on the barghest.

But what Graeme said . . . came an insidious thought that, try as I might, kept worming deeper into my consciousness.

Shivering, I looked toward where Nell knelt over Gus. What I really wanted to do was take a scrub brush and Lysol my brain. But if I couldn't do that, I wanted a distraction. No more thinking about Graeme.

'Is Gus all right?' I asked, even as I forced myself to take a deep breath. But I couldn't stop thinking about what Graeme had said to me.

Anyan is Anyan. Graeme is Graeme. And a liar, I reminded myself, even as I focused on Nell.

'He's hurt. Anyan's stabilized him, but I think we should get him to Caleb or Dr Sam,' answered the gnome.

'Can you apparate us?' I asked, wanting to get right the fuck out of this glen so I could think straight. I felt like I was wearing Graeme residue, and I needed to get away, to where I was only me again.

'Yes. You both ready?' she asked.

I nodded and stood, as Anyan moved toward me. I tensed, but didn't let myself move away.

It's Anyan, I told myself, trying to get Graeme out of my head. *It's Anyan. Don't let that monster get to you.*

So I held still as Anyan walked to my side. I held still as the barghest raised his hand. I didn't flinch when he took my chin between his fingers.

'Are you okay?' he asked.

I forced myself to nod, and I forced myself to say, 'I'll be all right. Just really freaked out.'

Anyan nodded to me and then nodded to Nell.

'We're ready to go.'

It was only when Nell's magic surrounded me that I allowed the long, rolling shudder to work its way up and through my body. For every time Anyan touched me, I heard Graeme whispering again.

Don't act innocent, slut. I know that's just how your barghest likes it.

Chapter Nine

'I think Dr Sam is stoned,' I whispered to Trill, who nodded gravely.

'He was with Amy,' she whispered back, and I grimaced. That would explain the red eyes. And the fact that the goblin was wearing only boxer shorts and a few multi-colored leis.

'Is Gus going to be okay?' I asked, from where I sat next to the kelpie. She'd taken Anyan's overstuffed chair, and I was perched on the arm. Gus was stretched out on Anyan's sofa as Caleb and Dr Sam attended to the little stone spirit.

'He'll be fine by tomorrow. He got quite a knock to the head, but we got to him before his brain could swell too much,' Caleb's deep voice rumbled.

I grimaced as Dr Sam giggled delightedly and totally inappropriately.

'Why on earth did they attack Gus?' Anyan asked. He was sitting on his fireplace ledge across the room from me.

'Who knows?' Nell replied, rocking away in the little rocker she apparated everywhere with her. 'But it was definitely a coordinated attack. Phaedra got my attention and kept Anyan and me busy while her entourage went after Gus.'

'They weren't after Gus,' I interrupted. 'They were interested in his rock.'

'His rock?' Anyan asked. 'Why on earth would they want Gus's rock?'

'Why on earth would they want Gus?' Trill countered, voicing what we were all secretly thinking.

'A great big fucking Zen garden?' Dr Sam questioned the universe.

'Maybe,' I conceded to our stoned doctor's wisdom. 'Or maybe there's something on or inside that rock we've never noticed. I'm betting it is, or it houses, one of the locks. We need to check it out, carefully.'

Caleb nodded. 'Definitely. But how about in the morning? We're all tired, and it's not going anywhere. Plus, I left Iris alone.'

None of us missed the plaintive note in his voice, and Nell smiled at him.

'Home you go, Caleb. Thank you for your help.'

Caleb's magic gathered as he gave Gus one last once-over before saying his goodbyes. After which Nell apparated him back to Iris in a burst of magic, tousled-blond hair, and enormous schlong.

Lucky Iris, my libido sighed, jealously.

Then I nearly jumped out of my skin as a hand brushed beneath my hair to grip my nape gently. Anyan (*to whom*, I reminded myself for about the twentieth time, *I need to attach a bell*) tilted my head away from him to reveal the vulnerable shell of my ear, just a little, as he leaned down toward me. My whole body shivered.

And not in a way that has anything to do with Graeme, my libido purred, although my brain was still swirling around discontentedly.

'Don't leave with the others,' Anyan growled into my ear. 'I want to know what happened.'

Trill got up from the chair, giving us some space as she

gave me a cheeky side-eye. Then she went and whispered to
Nell.

'Can we leave Gus here for the night?' the gnome asked,
nodding at Trill's words as she stood up from her rocking chair.
She walked over to the stone spirit, placing a small hand on
his forehead. 'I could apparate him, but he's so peaceful. And
I'm not entirely sure where he sleeps.'

'It's fine, Nell. Let him rest,' Anyan said as his hand began
to massage the back of my neck in a way that neither my over-
active brain nor libido could argue with. My eyes closed as
my body relaxed. His touch was so strong and possessive, and I
felt almost hypnotized by my desire to submit . . .

Just like Graeme made me feel.

I sat bolt upright, dislodging Anyan's hand with the force
of my movement. He cast me an iron look just as we heard
a thud.

Dr Sam, giggling, had ended up ass over teakettle from
where he'd tried to sit in Nell's rocking chair. His long, scaly
green limbs waved in the air as he chortled, his lei tangled
around his head.

Nell sighed and wiggled her fingers. Dr Sam poofed out,
no doubt apparated back to Amy and her famous five-foot
glass bong. Then the little woman nodded her goodbyes to
us and poofed away herself and the kelpie.

Leaving me alone with Anyan.

I raised my eyes, slowly, to meet his. He wasn't looking
at me like he was angry. Instead, his face betrayed a hint of
confusion but also a stubborn look like he just wasn't having
any of what I was dishing out.

And since what I was dishing out were undoubtedly the
lies of a known psychopath, I couldn't blame him.

'Outside?' he asked, inclining his head toward where
Gus slept. The little stone spirit had had enough drama

for the day. He didn't need to be involved in our little Graeme-inspired soap opera.

I nodded, and we headed toward Anyan's front porch. Once there, he took one corner of the railing to perch on, and I took the opposite side. Our knees were almost touching, and we could see each other's faces, but otherwise we had space.

'What's going on, Jane?'

Anyan was never one to beat around the bush.

'I'm just skeeved out from my run-in with Graeme, earlier. He was in my head. I still feel . . . dirty.'

'Tomorrow we'll work on some mental shields for you. Graeme's talent is rare, but dangerous. Now that he's in the picture again, we'll get you protected.'

I nodded, avoiding his eyes. 'Well, I always wondered how he did it. I mean, how he fed on the women he tortured, since incubi aren't supposed to be able to feed on pain.'

Despite my logical tone of voice, I shuddered. Knowing that Graeme had *literally* made his victims 'want it' totally skeeved me out, on so many levels. It was an ultimate act of victimization that made me hate the incubus even more, if that were possible.

'Now,' Anyan said, his voice low, 'what else is going on?'

I hugged myself tighter, unsure of what to say.

'Spill it, Jane. I can hear those brains of yours crunching all the way over here. You're obviously upset, and with me. Tell me what I did.'

Shaking my head, I finally met his eyes. 'You didn't do anything. I promise. It's just that Graeme said something. About you. Being like him.'

'And you believe him?' Anyan's voice, considering the fact I'd just compared him to a vicious sexual predator, was remarkably calm.

'Of course not,' I replied. 'I mean, I know you're not like him.'

'But?' Anyan asked, playing our old game, now gone horribly less fun.

'But . . .' I paused to think, and then decided thinking wasn't going to work. Sometimes, the best way to come at an issue was by babbling it into submission. 'But you scare me, to be honest. Not the way Graeme does. I do know you're nothing like him. But you're still . . . still a lot. A lot to handle. I don't mean your junk, obviously, as we've not gotten to the fondling-bits stage yet. And I can't believe I just talked about your junk. Anyway, I'm not saying you're *not* a lot to handle, in the junk department, but I meant "a lot" more as in, like, "you". You're a lot. Just . . . a lot.'

I finally stuck a cork in it, amazed, once again, at how much absolute shite could fall out of my own face.

Anyan frowned at me for a second. It wasn't a look of anger, more of concentration as his brain scrambled to tease apart my word snarl. Then he smiled.

Why's he smiling? my brain wondered as I dropped my eyes downward, unable to meet the intensity of his gaze.

Who cares? Lick him! my libido answered.

Meanwhile, I sat with my hands in my lap, again feeling a bit like a bunny rabbit in the sights of a hunter.

Only I kind of like it when it's Anyan, I realized. So I forced myself to look back up at him. His eyes had grown hot, and I knew things were going to come to a head.

You thought that on purpose, my virtue chided, as my libido chortled.

Mmm. Head, was its only reply.

'You know I would never hurt you,' he said. His voice was rough with lust, and it made my spine quiver.

'Of course,' I replied, forcing my eyes to stay on his.

'But you're afraid of me?'

'That's not it, really. It's just . . . It's more like . . . I'm just . . .' *Scared shitless of this whole thing*, I thought, not wanting to admit it.

'So you're not really afraid of me. But you're afraid of something involving me?'

I frowned. 'Obviously, but that doesn't mean . . .'

'Are you afraid of how you feel? Of how I make you feel?' With those words, Anyan stood his long frame up from where he'd been sitting on his verandah railing and came to stand in front of me. He towered over me, of course.

'Stop it. You always do that. You get up in my space and I feel . . . crowded.'

Instead of moving back, he moved a step closer.

'Is that all you feel?' he asked, doing his best imitation of Socrates. 'Crowded?'

Gagagagagaga, my libido supplied, helpfully. It also sent my blood skittering to all the organs my blood shouldn't be in, if I wanted to think. And I did want to think, damn it.

Thinking bad. Railing sex goooood, was my libido's only response to my complaints.

The feel of the barghest's big hands on my thighs, right above my knees, jolted me back into awareness. My eyes traveled to Anyan's wide mouth, his lips pursed in concentration.

'Answer me, Jane,' he commanded, making me shiver again.

'Stop telling me to do things,' I replied, sharply. He only smiled.

'I like telling you to do things.'

'Quit it. I'm not a little girl.'

'No, you're not. I know that. And you know I know that.'

I kept schtum, unsure where this was heading.

'You know that I think you're brilliant. And brave. And strong,' he said, stepping even closer as his hands spread my thighs, just a little, to accommodate him. 'You know I respect you, utterly. Which is why you like it, despite yourself, when I do things like this . . .'

And with those words, his hand reached behind me and did that knotting trick, where he gathered all my hair up in a rough queue, before tugging my head back, not quite gently. As if prompted to do so, my breathing deepened and lust poured through my veins.

'Because you know it's a game,' Anyan said, as his teeth bit gently into my neck, a lovely sensation that had nothing to do with Graeme's cruelty and everything to do with pleasure, shared. His tongue licked at the spot his teeth had been, as if my skin were as sweet as ice cream.

'A game?' I mumbled, unsure whether we were actually having a conversation or if we really were about to have railing sex.

Railing sex! my libido exulted.

'Mmm-hmmm,' the barghest purred, the sound muffled as he moved his mouth to bite the other side of my neck, a bit harder this time. The sting was delicious, as was the hand he moved to cup the bit of my bottom overhanging the railing. The grunt I gave at the feel of his teeth on my flesh gave way to a soft moan as his tongue again licked, taking away the sting.

'A game,' he repeated, withdrawing his mouth so he could look me in the face. His eyes were latched on my mouth, his own still pursed a little in concentration, as if he were busy mentally enumerating all the filthy things he could do to me.

I've got 150 . . . more if we can source a goat, my libido challenged his, silently. My virtue warned that Anyan was probably more than up to such a provocation.

And just like that, he moved his hips in tighter to mine, his body opening my legs farther until he was hard up against me and I could feel just how 'up' for the challenge he really was.

'What kind of game?' I squeaked, in lieu of humping him like a Maltese in heat. His big hands pulled me forward as his eyes went to mine. The look of desire I saw there took my own lust and magnified it a thousand times. The sight nearly took my breath away, and at that moment I wanted Anyan more than I'd ever wanted any man. Even Jason.

'A game where you let me be the boss, in the bedroom. You let me take control. You let me show you just how much I want you. You let me take that sweet little body and make it *feel*.'

Where do I sign? my libido asked, completely sold.

'And then?' my brain forced me to ask, unsure whether it wanted to be anybody's love slave, no matter how tempting the offer.

'And then we can switch,' Anyan said, his lips twitching in a smile. 'And I'll be all yours.'

I couldn't help but smile back, and then giggle at the images that raced through my head: *Anyan in a French maid's uniform . . . Anyan wearing a saddle . . . Anyan in lederhosen, wielding an enormous sausage . . .*

'Just be gentle,' he warned. 'I'm delicate.'

'Delicate my ass,' I said, laughing outright.

But all laughter ceased as his hands found my hair. One went to the nape of my neck, while the other got a firm grip on my hair. Then Anyan tugged my head back, so that my spine had to arch over his forearm, my face upturned to the evening sky. I knew he was giving me a taste of what he wanted from me – a kind of submissiveness that both excited and scared me.

To be entirely honest, though, I was mostly excited.

My heart crashed against my ribcage and I was barely able to breathe through my nervousness. All I could see was the moon hanging plump and ripe in the center of my vision. My hands moved to Anyan's wide shoulders, my nails digging into his shirt as my fists clenched. I'd never felt so vulnerable.

Which is why, when Anyan's big hand moved my shirt up my body, I gasped. His calloused hands rasped deliciously against the soft skin covering my ribs, and then his fingers moved over the thin material of my bra – an admittedly rather serviceable cotton jobbie. I moaned, feeling my nipples harden, but still, when his mouth found my left breast, I nearly jumped out of my skin. First of all, it was patently unfair of him to go diving straight for my nipples. We'd never even kissed properly, and there he was, skipping entire bases. Second, I'd never before been touched the way Anyan touched me. His mouth on my flesh was hard, persistent, even through the thin material of my bra. Calloused fingers that squeezed around my breast accompanied his mouth as if he were taking possession of my body, as if he owned me.

I'd only really been touched by two men in my life. And, while I know it's not right to compare, I couldn't help it. Jason had been all tender solicitude, and Ryu had camouflaged his delightfully filthy nature under the guise of being a gentleman. But Anyan's touch was demanding, insistent – almost frightening, if I was honest. His mouth and his hands promised he was never going to back down, never going to yield, until he'd taken what he wanted.

When he nipped at my breast, none too gently, I felt a rush of heat flush through my body. Then, after sucking away the sting, he moved his shaggy head over to latch that wide mouth onto my right nipple, but not before roughly pulling down the fabric of my bra, so that his lips found my bare skin. I thought I saw stars as I wondered, belatedly, whether we were gonna need a safety word.

It'll be Geronimooooooooo . . . 'Oooooooh,' I said, before my feeble attempt at self-preservation dissolved into a throaty moan as Anyan released my hair to wrap his arms around me, pulling me forward as he suckled hungrily at my breast. I raised my head as I twined my own fingers in his hair, taking back a modicum of control by grinding my hips against his and causing him to release my flesh with a gasp.

Then I was the one tugging on hair, as I pulled *his* head back. His eyes were closed, his lips parted. Zeroing in on his mouth, I moved forward to kiss him.

If we are going to do this, we're going to do it in the correct order, I reprimanded him mentally, as I stopped just short of a smooch to nuzzle my own nose against his. I couldn't help it. I felt the tip twitch against mine, making me giggle. But my laughter ceased at the hungry look in his eyes.

'Bad, *bad* puppy,' I murmured.

Then his lips found mine. The first few seconds of our first real kiss were hardly movie quality: I had my mouth open, so our teeth clanged against each other like gongs. Then we had to figure out how my small mouth would fit against his wide one, which took a few moments.

But then it all fell into place, and his kiss sent my world tumbling in a gyre.

His mouth was hard, insistent, daring me to pull away. So I met his ferocity with my own, suddenly wanting to eat him up like pie. I was the first one to bring tongues into play, licking gently at his lower lip until his mouth opened to mine. Our tongues met on his turf, swirling against each other, his following mine back into my own mouth. I sucked at his tongue hungrily, suddenly desperately wanting to be filled by him, wanting to taste him, just wanting . . .

And Anyan was happy to oblige. His body rubbed against mine as he pulled me closer. I wasn't sure if I was even on the railing anymore, or if he was holding me to him. My legs twined around his waist, pressing the heat at my center against his hard abdomen, my heart thumping in my chest.

Our kiss deepened, impossibly. It felt like I was feeding from him even as I fed him a bit of myself. I was losing myself in Anyan's mouth, but my body was ready to move on. My own hand in Anyan's hair pulled him back from me just enough so that I could reach to pull my plain, long-sleeved black tee all the way off. I felt the railing under my butt, again, as he put me down so his hands could move to fumble at my bra strap. While he worked, I placed my palms on either side of his face, as I feathered kisses over his eyelids and forehead, finally dropping down to suck just the tip of that ridiculously sexy nose.

'Shit,' Anyan swore, under his breath. He was having trouble with my bra strap, which amused me no end.

Who's the dominant one here now, Mr Let Me Take Control? I thought smugly, until the barghest resolved the issue by taking a firm hold of either side of my bra's clasp and pulling till I heard a *snap*.

Shit, it was my turn to swear.

But before I could think any further on the demise of my delicates, Anyan's hands were at my bare breasts. His fingers squeezed my nipples while his palms cupped and I nearly swooned at the sensations.

He used the opportunity of my head-thrown-back moan to find my neck again, kissing and biting his way down the left side until his shaggy curls tickled my chest. Then he kept kissing downward, working his way left till I felt his warm breath on my bare nipple.

At least we have run the bases properly this time, my virtue acceded, completely overwhelmed by lust, along with all the rest of my systems.

Then Anyan's hot mouth suckled, and I thought I might overload on the pleasure of it.

My right hand braced myself on the railing as my left found its way into his hair. Running my fingers through his curls as he suckled me, I looked down at him, feeling a curious mixture of possession and pride. I knew that part of my pleasure was from knowing that this was Anyan at my breast. I'd wanted him for so long, and was as elated at having him, finally, as I was terrified.

He came up for air only long enough to steal a quick, hard kiss before attending to my other nipple. One couldn't accuse this shapeshifting man-dog of not being thorough, bless him.

While I was enjoying the barghest's attentions immensely, however, I also wanted to do my own exploring. So I tugged, tentatively, on his hair. As if in approbation, Anyan bit the soft underside of my breast sharply, making me gasp. But he also moved his head back and up so he was, once again, towering over me.

'I want to touch you, too,' I breathed, causing his lips to quirk either with a smile or desire, or both. I reached my hand under the bottom of his shirt, running my fingertips over his abdomen as he went to pull off the pesky bit of material separating me from my barghest chest.

Which is when we heard the polite cough from the doorway.

Anyan and I froze, both of our eyes wide. You'd think after being attacked, together, we'd have learned not to let our guard down.

Or our brassieres.

Anyan turned around, carefully shielding me with his wide shoulders as I peered about for my shirt. I didn't see it anywhere, of course, and presumed the naughty barghest had kiestered it when I wasn't looking.

Meanwhile, I could see, over Anyan's shoulder, Gus standing just inside the front door. His bald little head gleamed, but not as brightly as the porch light shining off his Coke-bottle glasses.

'Do you have any milk?' the stone spirit asked, absolutely oblivious to the fact that he'd just ruined a moment that had promised railing sex. 'I'm very thirsty,' he concluded, as if ordering from a waiter at a restaurant.

'Um . . . milk. Yes, I believe I do have milk. In the fridge,' Anyan replied, remarkably cordial for someone who'd just been cock-blocked by Dr Bunsen Honeydew.

Instead of helping himself, as Anyan had implied, Gus just continued to stand there. Staring.

Anyan sighed and turned to face me. I shrugged my shoulders.

'Go help your guest,' I said, running my index finger over that wide mouth.

'Want my shirt?' he asked, nipping gently at my finger.

'I'm pretty sure I could do a naked cancan and Gus would be none the wiser.'

'You're probably right,' he said, with a sigh. 'I'll get him his milk then.'

'And then tuck him back into bed on your couch?' I asked, really wanting to know if there was any chance of getting our rumpy-pumpy back on tonight.

'And then tuck him back into bed on my couch,' Anyan said. Meaning, *Not unless we kill and eat the stone spirit.*

'Damn,' I said.

'Damn,' he agreed.

'Well, I will see you tomorrow, then.' My voice was heavy with disappointment, and I thought my libido might shrivel up and die at the horror of not getting laid that night. 'And I'll also see you tomorrow night?' I asked, hoping to give my poor, tortured sex drive something to live for.

'Unless the sky falls down, I plan on shagging you silly as soon as possible.'

I giggled. 'I like that. I'll write it in my calendar.'

'Put some hearts around it. So I know you're not just using me for sex,' was Anyan's only response. Then – to my utmost pleasure – the barghest gave me the softest, sweetest kiss on my lips before he turned around to attend to Gus.

Who exhibited not the slightest awareness I was hanging out, half naked, on Anyan's railing. Bless.

Chapter Ten

'Looks like a rock to me,' I said, as I kicked my boot against Gus's boulder. In the bright morning light, Gus's glade was lovely. Quiet and peaceful, when it wasn't being attacked by Alfar purists, the boulder dominated the small open space surrounded by trees.

'Stop kicking it. It's like his girlfriend, or something,' Iris chided, pulling me away by the elbow.

'It's a rock,' I reminded her.

'Don't judge. I'm schtupping a goat and you seem to be falling for Man's Best Friend.'

I frowned, turning to where Anyan and Caleb were deep in conversation, also trying to figure out what secrets the huge hunk of stone in front of us could reveal. The four of us were trying to figure out where, and how, Gus's rock could contain some kind of magical lock. Meanwhile, Nell and Trill were off, partly trying to track down Phaedra, but mostly working sentry duty to make sure the Alfar couldn't enter our turf again.

'It *is* sort of humiliating,' I admitted to Iris about Anyan's other identity. 'I mean, he is a really *big* dog. But why a dog? Why can't he be something more respectable . . . like a wolf. I could say, quite proudly, "I'm shagging a werewolf!" Instead, I'll say, "Yes, he's a dog . . . but a great big dog! Really huge!

And fierce! And he wubs it when you scratch his belly,"' I concluded, gently scratching at Iris's tummy as I did so.

She laughed, wiggling away from my tickles. 'Oooo, so you're shagging, are you?'

I winced, realizing what I'd said too late. 'Not exactly. But we've done our best. We keep getting interrupted . . . invading evil, and all.'

'It happens,' she said drily, carefully trying not to put too much emphasis on her words. I'd realized quite quickly that Iris didn't want to dwell on what had happened to her. Yeah, it was an elephant in the room, but she wanted us all to act as normal as we could about that elephant. For her sake, we tried.

We both clammed up, giving the men a *totally not talking about either of you* stare as they walked in our direction and then past us to examine the other side of the rock.

'I gotta say, you and Caleb are pretty adorable together,' I whispered, once the coast was clear.

'Yeah,' she said and smiled, her eyes glowing gently as she hunkered close when the satyr and the barghest teamed up their magic and began blasting the rock with various probes. 'He was totally unexpected. I sort of wondered if I'd ever feel like this again. Then, with what happened, I was pretty sure I never wanted to feel *anything* again. Till out of the blue Caleb showed up. And it was . . . it was like everything became new again.'

'Wow. That's amazing,' I said, and she nodded, a small smile gracing her lips.

'And he's hung like a yak,' I heard myself adding, much to my own horror.

'That helps, too,' she giggled, wrapping an arm around me. 'Should we go see what the boys are up to?'

I nodded, and we strolled over to Anyan and Caleb, who

were doing something that felt like trying to crack the boulder in two.

'Whoa, whoa, whoa,' Iris hollered, racing over and standing up on her toes to flick both idiots in their earlobes. 'What do you think you're doing? That's Gus's *rock*. Think about his feelings if you turned it into playground pebbles.'

Both men stopped, looking at each other guiltily. Caleb shifted on his haunches, his hooves clomping nervously, and I wondered what it was like sleeping next to him. Talk about cold feet.

'So, no destroying the rock, yes?' Iris demanded. Both men nodded their heads, sheepishly.

'Good,' Iris continued. 'So, what have you big dicks discovered?' We all looked at her, a bit shocked.

'Dick as in detectives, duh,' she said, rolling her eyes. Iris acted so young, and so contemporary, that it was easy to forget she'd been alive when people could still say 'dick' – either for 'Richard' or for 'detectives' – without giggling. 'What's up with this rock?'

'Um, well, we've tried to strip it of any glamours, in case something's written on it, but there don't seem to be any. We've tried to probe it, to see if there's something inside, but it seems solid,' Caleb replied.

'You tried to crack it in half, because you're asshats,' I added, helpfully. Anyan used his power to poke me in the belly, and I *oofed* in response before strengthening the shields I'd let go weak around my friends.

'It seems to be just that: a rock. Nothing carved on it, nothing in it. It's not giving off any power of its own, except some residual Gus juice,' Anyan concluded, causing both Iris and me to shudder at that last image.

'So, it's a rock,' I said, before going poetic. 'And not a lock.'

'Yes. It appears that way,' Caleb answered me, his voice dissatisfied.

We all backed up a step to stare at it. There had to be something here, or Phaedra wouldn't have risked her best people. Unless Phaedra wasn't the diversion . . .

Maybe Phaedra's entourage was the diversion, I thought, my brain thrilling at my genius. But right before I could speak, Iris beat me to the chase.

'So, like, have y'all tried *under* the rock?'

We all blinked at her, as my purported genius flew out of my ear to join all the other vapid ideas floating about the air above our heads.

'I mean, maybe there's something under it. Maybe they weren't trying to do anything to the actual rock besides move it,' my succubus friend clarified, as we all shook our heads at our own obtuseness.

'Of course,' Caleb breathed. 'Iris, what a great idea.'

Iris flushed almost purple, her eyes shining. I don't think I'd ever seen her look so pleased with a compliment, and I knew she had entire volumes of poetry written to her beauty by enraptured humans and supernaturals alike.

'Never thought to look under the rock,' Anyan said, obviously feeling foolish.

'It's my fault,' I said. 'I was sure they were trying to steal it. I never thought they might be trying to *move* it.'

'Well, we can't be sure I'm right till we get it up and over,' Iris reminded us. 'You don't think Gus will care if we move it, do you?'

'We can put it back. He'll be none the wiser,' Anyan said, as I felt him rev up his magical engines. Caleb added his own strength to Anyan's, and as they were both earth elementals, their power was uniquely suited to moving stones around. That said, it was a massive stone, heavy enough to give the strongest single-elemental (or double-elemental, in Anyan's case) trouble.

So I wove my power through theirs. They'd been trying to lift and carry the stone with their magic, which was silly. We didn't have to move it to Eastport. We just needed a peek underneath.

'Let me, guys,' I said, interrupting their attempts to lift it out of the way. 'Just funnel your power through me . . .'

And they did, the odd feel of their earth magic making my spine tingle. I couldn't do much with their power besides channel it, but that's all I needed.

I created a wedge with my own power, directing it toward the base of Gus's rock. Then I rammed it home with Anyan and Caleb's power. Exerting more pressure as I widened my wedge, the boulder began to shift, slowly. By then, the boys realized what I was doing and the three of us poured our magic into upsetting the boulder. Finally, it wobbled, began to tip, and then it slowly toppled to its side.

'I was right!' Iris exclaimed, as if not quite believing it herself.

And she was. For lurking underneath Gus's boulder was a hole, just about wide across for the biggest of us to get through. Where it went, nobody knew. But I was pretty sure we were about to find out.

'It's like something from Zelda,' Anyan said and frowned. I know I felt a bit weak from all the magic we'd poured into moving the rock. I'm sure he did, too. Only difference was, I could already feel him pulling strength from the ground he stood on. I was going to have to wait for a swim to recharge.

We all gathered around the hole, peering down into the darkness.

'We should call Nell and Trill,' Caleb intoned. 'They'll want to be here.'

'Tell them to bring ropes,' Anyan said in agreement.

'Lucy,' Iris said, giggling. 'We got some spelunking to do!'

I sighed. That should have been my line.

'Careful, Jane. Not too fast . . . let out a little more rope . . . there you go . . . I got you,' Anyan coached, until I felt his hand on my hips.

It was dark in the cave, despite the mage light Anyan had already set aflame. He didn't want to go too crazy with the magic until we knew what was down in the cave. A lot of supernatural alarms were set only to magic, so as not to blow up random passing humans or animals. This also explained why Anyan and I had gone down the hard way, instead of apparating. Who knew what was waiting for us under Gus's rock? But if it *was* something old and powerful, as Blondie and Anyan suggested, it might not take kindly to a display of powerful magic.

Iris, Caleb, Nell, and Trill all peered down at us from above, waiting to get the all clear for Nell to apparate them in.

I created my own mage light, keeping it weak. Anyan claimed his own tiny light, and together we started reconnoitering. But not before we set one last weak light by the rope for us to follow if we got lost.

'Let's see what we have here,' Anyan said, pacing forward. I followed him, about a step behind, guarding our backs but also giving my sight a chance to adjust to the darkness. I guess my underwater-strong eyesight was better than Anyan's because after a few moments I could see just about everything the little cave offered. And when I did, I gasped.

'What?' Anyan asked sharply, no doubt afraid I'd hurt myself or had heard something dangerous.

'The room, it's . . . it's . . .' I peered around carefully,

making sure that I was really seeing what I thought. 'It's
beautiful,' I said, going ahead and beefing up my mage lights
as I lit a few more to float over my head.

Light spilled through the cavern, reflecting on the multitude
of crystals stuck in the earth walls. That light bounced, reflected,
and refracted, creating a chaotic rainbow that danced along the
floors, ceiling, walls, and our own flesh.

'Whoa,' Anyan breathed, stepping next to me and taking
my hand. It felt good to see this with him, both of us enjoying
the beauty. And the feel of his big hand clasping mine just
made it that much better.

'I think we can tell the others to come down now,' I said.
He only nodded, so I went ahead and walked back to our
rope, regretting that I'd had to let go of the barghest's hand
to do so.

'It's safe!' I called up, and a few seconds later I heard
various *poofs* as my friends were apparated nearby. Then I
heard an almost simultaneous gasp as each of them took in
the beauty of the room.

'So pretty,' Iris breathed, walking toward a wall to touch
one of the crystals. Caleb and I followed her. As her fingertips
met the crystal, it sang a sweet song, causing the both of us
to jump toward her.

But the note faded, and no harm was done to anyone. I
heard us all let out the breaths we'd been holding, as one.

'Do they all do that?' Iris asked, reaching for another
crystal. And it sang, as well, at the touch of her fingers,
although this note was lower.

'How curious,' Caleb said, reaching his own hand out. As
his fingertips brushed against a patch of crystals cropping
up from the floor to about waist height, they all sang for him,
each a different note.

We all stepped toward a wall and began touching. The

room buzzed with sound. We laughed, together, until Anyan shouted.

'Wait!' he said, pointing to the middle of the room as it went quiet but for a faint echo of dying notes. 'Look.'

Smack dab in the center of the cavern, right near where our rope still dangled, it looked like something was trying to come up from the soft dirt of the cave floor.

'It's kind of like the base of a pedestal or something,' Trill said, her oil-slick voice nervous as she tiptoed toward the disturbed floor.

'It's gotta be the lock,' I said. 'Or the crystals are the lock. Something is a lock for sure.'

'Where did it come from?' Iris asked.

'You were touching the crystals and it just . . . started to come out,' intoned Caleb.

'Like a red rocket?' I conjectured. Anyan gave me the stink eye. He was obviously sensitive about the red rocket issue, being part dog and all.

'Was it the noise that made it come out?' Nell wondered, strumming her hand along a row of crystals. As if to prove her wrong, the small outcropping in the floor retreated back to wherever it had sprung from.

'How bizarre,' I said. Then I had a thought. 'Okay, this is totally *Goonies*, but what if we have to play the right notes?'

'Right notes?' asked Nell. 'Like a song?'

'Probably not. Unless you guys see any sheet music anywhere. I'm thinking a resonance . . . either a scale or a group of one note together.'

Anyan was facing me, but his eyes were closed and his head tilted. It was like he was listening or remembering . . . or both.

'Yes,' he interrupted. 'Right as the ground moved you'd all played a same note . . . It was sort of like . . .' And then the barghest sang out a clear, beautiful tone. I had no idea he could sing, leaving me floored.

'Now we have to figure out which crystal plays what,' Iris said, already touching the crystals around her. I was still watching Anyan, trying to wrap my mind around the fact that the man could *sing*, too, when he nodded sharply.

'That was it. Whatever you just touched . . .'

Iris reached out a hand again and touched a crystal. It cried out in the glittering cavern, pure and sweet.

'So how do we find out which one to play?' Trill asked. 'They're not exactly marked.'

'It's the size,' Caleb rumbled. 'They're different notes for different sizes. Iris's note is . . . about as long as her forearm.'

We each looked around, using our own forearms, with an inch or two either added or subtracted depending on how long our arms were, until we each found a few crystals that were about right. Then we took turns strumming them, trying to find the ones with exactly the right pitch. Finally, all six of us had found our exact crystals, but we were still unsure of what to do.

'So, should we just all play them?' I asked. Everyone nodded, and we all obediently touched our crystals. They sang out, but nothing happened.

'No, it was a bigger sound than that. Everyone was going nuts right when the floor moved. Lots and lots of sound, played really furiously. We're gonna have to do more than just touch 'em,' Anyan said.

'Are you trying to get us to stroke our crystals for you, Mr Barghest?' Iris said, sweetly, and I rejoiced at the sight of her flirting so openly, even if it was with my own man-dog.

'I've been trying to get you to stroke my crystal for years, Iris,' Anyan bantered back. 'Now let's all stroke together . . . On three, two, one . . .'

And with that we all started strumming away at our crystals. We began by attempting to be decorous: either whacking at or playing the crystal like one would a tether ball or a guitar. But the sound wasn't quite cacophonous enough, and eventually we all gave up and stood there, openly jerking our crystals in a more than vaguely masturbatory manner. Whoever had invented this lock should get credit for inspiring the Shake Weight.

As the brilliant sound of the note crashed through the cavern, the floor began to shiver exactly where it had earlier. We kept stroking, any embarrassment at our motions quashed by seeing results. So we stroked harder, faster, watching as the floor rose into the shape of a steep pyramid, about three and a half feet tall. Then all the music ceased, and our crystals were dead in our hands.

Ouch, chafing, I thought, letting go of my crystal and stretching out my hand before shaking it a bit. Everyone else was making similar motions. *That much stroking is hard on a body*, I thought, wondering how Alexander Portnoy had done it.

I also wondered who in the hell had created this 'lock', and whether they were totally clueless or had a great sense of humor. Knowing the often emotionless Alfar of today, unless things had changed dramatically since the ancient Alfar walked the earth, I figured it was the former.

Together, we walked toward the pyramid, stopping to form a circle a few feet away from it.

'What is it?' Iris asked. Caleb shrugged, clearly stumped. And it didn't look like any of the rest of us had a clue.

'Let me see,' Nell said, and I felt her give the pyramid a gentle probing. As if on cue, more crystals sprang from the sides of the pyramid.

We frowned at each other, wondering what to do next, when Iris reached forward.

'Makes sense that what we did before should work now, too,' she said. Before we could stop her, she'd reached out and touched a crystal that looked the same as the one we'd just been group-fondling before.

The now familiar sound zoomed out through the room, and the previously exhausted crystals all began not only to sing with the pyramid's crystal but to glow, faintly. We all took a step back as the glowing increased, eventually blinding us with its brightness. Shielding my eyes, I, for one, was figuring we were done for, when suddenly the light ceased, leaving the cavern in darkness again.

Blinded by the light, our eyes took a few seconds to adjust. But when they finally did, we saw that it was only our abused vision that had assumed it was entirely dark again. For floating a few inches above the tip of the central pyramid hung what looked like a mirror, its surface showing a series of sinuous shapes that changed with every second. Frowning in confusion, we all took a step forward.

'What is it?' I breathed.

Nell sighed from where she stood next to me. I hadn't noticed the gnome's expression, as she was so much shorter than me.

'It's an ancient Alfar hieroglyph,' she informed us. 'A sigil.'

'Great!' Iris replied. 'You know what it is. Can you read it?'

'Of course I can,' the gnome replied, her kindly voice gone bizarrely irritable for someone who was telling us everything was going to be okay.

'But not this one,' Nell concluded, to our regret. 'It's gotta be not only *the* lock, but it also *is* locked. And until it's unlocked, it's unreadable.'

It took me a moment to think my way through that, but eventually I nodded to myself. The lock was locked. Or something.

Iris asked the question we all were thinking: 'Well, can you unlock it?'

'I have no idea,' Nell replied, staring at the hieroglyph in contemplation. 'But there's only one way to find out,' she finished, as she stepped toward the pedestal.

Chapter Eleven

We braced ourselves as the first waves of magic crashed through the cavern. The force of Nell's power pushed us back, until Caleb, Iris, Anyan, and I were all pressed against the walls, trying to avoid being shish-kebabed by the decorating scheme of priapic crystals. Meanwhile, the grandmotherly little gnome stood facing the pillar in the middle of the cave, forcing her power upward toward the dangling mirrored surface with its ever-changing sigils.

She pushed and she pushed and she pushed . . . and nothing happened.

Lowering her arms, she swore a blue streak. I'd first noticed when Conleth had attacked us in Rockabill, all those months ago, that Nell became Pirate Nell, Swearer of the High Seas, whenever she got frustrated with something magical. And today was no exception.

After she'd finished reveling in her theories regarding the probable connection between the ancient Alfar and people who enjoy sexual congress with their own mothers, she lowered her little arms. And then raised them again only to yell, 'Motherfuckers!' one last time, before finally lowering them to her side.

She took a long, deep breath before she finally turned around to face us.

'Anyan,' she said, very politely for someone who'd just made even my jaded ears turn purple. 'Could you help me, please?'

He grinned and walked toward Nell.

Iris, Caleb, Trill, and I just gave each other sideways looks as we settled ourselves firmly against our safe, relatively crystal-free patches of wall.

Nell's power had felt strong enough to level mountains. But combined with Anyan's formidable strength, I wasn't sure we wouldn't be crushed. So I quickly threw up the strongest shields I could muster around the four of us against the wall, and I soon felt the others join their own power with mine.

In the center of the room, dust and small chunks of crystal were swirling through the air as Anyan and Nell really poured on the juice. As for the sigil, it had continued its wild changing, but now that I was watching it closely again I could see that every once and a while the permutations would stutter, as if it were starting to wind down.

'Something's happening!' I called, pointing at the mirror-like surface.

Anyan's sharp ears picked up on my shout, and he peered upward before he nodded, letting me know he saw it, too. Then he nudged Nell, gesturing for her to look. When she'd seen what we'd seen, the two of them bombarded the sigil with even more power.

That's when it started to glow.

I amped up the shields I'd thrown around my friends, knowing I'd need a swim very soon. But I was also beginning to get a bad feeling about all this. Nell had seemed pretty confident she knew how to unlock that sigil so we could read it, but what they were doing felt more like the magical version of kicking in a door. Whoever created that mirror obviously didn't want it to be read easily, so what else had they done to protect it besides making it hard to find?

The air in the cavern was really getting stuffy as all of Anyan and Nell's mojo blew the dust around. It was also getting dark as our mage lights winked out, all of our magic channeling into either unlocking the sigil or protecting each other from the unlocking of the sigil. Only that mirrorlike surface floating in the center of the room glowed eerily, until its light began to pulse. I squinted upward, trying to see through the gloom and grit.

It's not pulsing, I realized, as I blinked away the grime from the eyes. *It's spinning*.

Sure enough, the mirrorlike oval was spinning like a top, moving faster the more Anyan and Nell sent their mojo winging its way. Then, suddenly, its light went supernova and became tinged with pink as the mirror began to glow an angry red.

I was just about to scream for them to stop when it exploded. Despite having thrown so much of my power into our shields, we were still badly shaken. I had moved a little bit forward, about to yell, so I had enough space between me and the wall that when I was flung back, I hit my head pretty hard. I didn't pass out, but it was touch and go there for a second, as I felt myself slide to the floor with a *plop*.

Blinking in the darkness, all I could hear was coughing, barking and a . . . baby crying?

Why is a baby crying? I wondered, trying to shake the ringing from my ears. I sat up, weakly, and then flopped down again with a splitting headache.

'Eww, gross, stop licking me, Anyan,' I heard Iris say, from a few feet away. Then I heard a doggie whine, which explained both the barking and why Anyan was licking Iris. Sort of.

Once I no longer felt like a chisel was being driven through my brain, I lit a weak mage light, although I didn't try to sit up again just yet. As soon as the light went up into the darkness, it was blocked out by a big hairy beast lapping at my face.

'Anyan, dude, what the hell?' I said, swatting his big dog's head away. Even though he looked like a giant puppy, he was still Anyan inside of there. And while I definitely wouldn't mind a thorough licking from man-Anyan, it was decidedly weird coming from dog-Anyan.

The barghest whined again, sitting back on his haunches to scratch at his ear with his back leg. Then he stopped and sat, staring at me, till I finally raised myself up on my elbows.

'What is *wrong* with you?' I asked him. 'Go help the others.'

Anyan whined again before he hunched over to his left side in order to nip at an itchy place on his hindquarters.

I was about to ask him if he'd also gotten hit in the head when I heard it again: the distinctive wail of a baby's cry.

I stood, shakily, to find Caleb helping Iris to her own feet. Trill was standing, dusting herself off just to my left. We all lit more mage balls to find the cavern a wreck. Most of the crystals had broken off the walls and were heaped about the room. The pillar still sprang from the dirt, and above it still hung the mirrored oval, showing off its ever-changing sigils. But it had stopped spinning and was no longer glowing with its own light.

'Did you guys hear a—' I began, just as Iris pointed to my right, her eyes wide. I peered over, sending a mage ball trailing in the direction of her finger.

'Nell!' I cried, as my eyes lit upon the gnome's large, gray bun. She must have been lying with her head pointed toward me, for that was all I could see of her.

We all hurried over to Nell, Anyan bounding in front of us, barking and wagging his tail maniacally. I couldn't begin to understand why he was acting like that, and it was driving me nuts. In fact, I was just about to yell at him as he scampered about our feet when I heard Iris cry out.

'Holy shit!' I exclaimed, staring down at Nell's bun . . . and the baby attached to it. For where there should have been the grandmotherly, if tiny, shape of our local Territory's guardian, there was a baby, swaddled in Nell's little homespun dress.

Trill's voice swore behind me, as she echoed my shock. We all stood there, staring at each other with wide eyes. All of us except for Anyan, who was thoroughly laving his fuzzie doggie balls with his tongue.

'What the hell is wrong with you?' I shouted at the barghest, what little decorum I had left snapping like a twig. 'Nell's a . . . baby! We need your help!' I waited for that gravelly voice I knew so well to speak from the barghest's throat. But instead he only panted at me, and then went back to his tongue bath.

Dread washed over me as a horrible thought raced through my head, but before I could pursue it, the baby started wailing. Iris and I looked at each other, and then walked forward. She picked it up, cradling it gently against her chest just as I felt a very foreign, yet distinctly familiar magic shimmer through the cavern.

With a very loud *pop*, Blondie appeared in the middle of the space. Her hair was still in a Mohawk, still tipped pink, and her tattoos glimmered in the light shining from the few forgotten mage lights we still had strewn about the cavern. She wore low-cut jeans, and a tight white wifebeater displayed her lithe, muscular form.

'What the hell happened?' the Original demanded, her magic sparking off her like enraged fireflies. 'Is Nell dead?'

All of us in the cavern still standing on our own two feet looked at each other, not quite sure what to tell Blondie. It was like we were saying to each other, with our eyes, *What we think happened couldn't have happened, right?*

'Because her Territory is now unprotected,' Blondie snapped, causing us all to freeze. I gulped, looking at the baby in Iris's arms.

In that case, I thought, thinking of Blondie's assumption that Nell had to be dead, *I hope my worst fears are actually correct.* Then I looked at Anyan, who'd moved on from his testicles and was now contentedly lapping at his own anus.

Or maybe not.

'Nothing's happening!' I shouted for about the fourth time, the panic rising in my voice. Anyan was sitting, drooling on the floor and patiently waiting while Blondie tried various things to get him back into man-shape.

Since returning to Anyan's cabin, and having gotten over the initial shock of what happened in the cavern and Blondie's sudden appearance, I'd remembered the million things I wanted to ask the Original. But getting our friends back definitely took priority.

'I know,' she growled, throwing some more mojo into her attempts. I went to stand by her, offering her my own power. I felt Blondie funnel my force into her own and out toward Anyan, but still nothing happened.

'This can't be happening,' I repeated, also for about the fourth time. Having Anyan trapped as a dog – a real dog! – was probably the scariest thing I'd ever seen.

'Shit,' Blondie said, lowering her arms and releasing my magic. 'Nothing's working.'

I looked at her, my face gone white, before turning to the others.

'So Nell is now a baby,' Iris said in her turn to repeat herself, for about the fifth time. 'And Anyan is a dog.'

Blondie sighed and scratched at the exposed skin on the side of her head; it looked like she'd freshly shaved around her Mohawk that morning. Then she went and sat down by the fire Trill had built in his fireplace. I think the kelpie was just trying to keep busy – she hadn't said anything since the cavern. She was probably even more freaked out than me, if that were possible.

Not that we weren't all upset, so we'd returned to Anyan's to regroup after what happened. Only to discover Gus had managed to lock himself in one of Anyan's cupboards. The stone spirit was currently in Anyan's kitchens, making himself a peanut butter, banana, and potato chip sandwich, a combo I found bold and intriguing, although everyone else seemed to think it was disgusting.

'What else could have happened?' the Original responded to Iris, stretching out her long legs. 'We have one baby whose power signature reads "immature gnome", and a dog instead of a barghest.'

'But that doesn't make any *sense*,' I pleaded, my voice a little hysterical. 'How could this have even happened? And why a baby and a dog? It's illogical!'

Blondie narrowed her eyes at me, as if she were thinking hard. Then a look came over her face like she might have figured something out, but her next words answered nothing.

'Sometimes there are too many players,' she said, cryptically, before staring off into the fire as if communing with herself.

I watched as Iris shifted the baby Nell on her lap. Anyan, meanwhile, went and curled up to sleep on the floor next to Blondie's feet, soaking up the heat of the flames. Even as a dog he seemed to trust her. I, however, wasn't so sure.

'It must have been an ancient Alfar trap,' Caleb's deep voice intoned. 'The sigil was set in a mirror, and the whole thing locked with very ancient magic.'

'But it's still not logical! Why a *baby* and a *dog*?' I repeated, still refusing to believe that the man I'd just made out with was a for-real dog, while our resident Yoda was now crapping in diapers. As if he knew we were talking about him, Anyan raised his sleepy head, his tail wagging distractedly. He was clearly exhausted from the past hour of licking his own genitals.

'Think about it, Jane,' Caleb replied. As always, he was calm. 'It's an ancient spell, set with ancient magic. You know your human folklore. Think of your Celtic mythology, your Arabian tales, your Norse and Native American trickster figures: what's the one thing you can rely on about magic in all of those mythologies?'

I thought about it for a minute, even though I already knew the answer. 'You can't,' I eventually replied, miserably. 'You can't rely on it.'

'Exactly,' Blondie said, snapping out of her daydream. 'It's precocious. Magic, even in your modern, watered-down fairy tales, has a mind of its own. If you ask the genie in a bottle for everlasting life, he'll turn you into a spring breeze. If you steal a staff enchanted with speed from a fairy prince, it will turn you into a greyhound.'

'But why a baby and a dog?' I whined, still unable to believe that the only genitals Anyan would be licking for quite some time were his own. Or maybe some of the neighborhood bitches', and for once I didn't mean Linda Allen.

'Realistically, the spell was originally enchanted to incapacitate anyone who toyed with the sigil,' Caleb rumbled from where he sat next to Iris. 'Over time it probably morphed. Developed a . . . sense of humor.'

'How is this funny?' Trill asked, from where she sat near Anyan. It was the first time she'd spoken. The kelpie seemed in shock, watching the flames dance in the fireplace.

'It probably killed whoever fucked with it originally,' Blondie stated, starting to lose patience. 'Now it's changed so it's doing things to them that aren't death . . . but that just as effectively knock an opponent out of the game.'

'You said "changed". Do you think something interfered with it?' I asked.

Blondie shrugged, but I could have sworn she looked guilty. Like she wasn't telling us something.

'Who knows,' she said. 'Maybe it just morphed on its own, like Caleb suggested.'

I watched her warily. *She and I are going to have a talk, soon*, I decided. *Like, before we leave this house.*

'So Anyan's really a dog,' I said, instead. 'An honest-to-god dog.'

'Yep,' said Blondie.

'And you can't change him back? Not even with all your power? What I felt you do in Pittsburgh, to Phaedra . . .' I was referring to the enormous feats of magical strength that Blondie had committed while she was following us.

Blondie shook her head. 'I can do that sort of thing only if I don't want to do much again for the next week. I also had some help – a couple of talismans I'd poured some excess power into. It's an old trick . . . but I haven't had the time or the extra power to make any since then.'

I frowned. I hadn't seen Blondie wearing anything, besides her piercings, when she was following us. And she'd gotten nekkid enough that I was pretty confident about that fact.

Not that you've ever even heard of talismans, I thought. *So they could have been the piercings, for all you know.*

'But why is Nell a baby?' Trill interrupted my worries, her voice gritty as if she were just waking up from her shock.

'Because it's the weakest thing she can be,' Blondie said, her voice gentling for the obviously upset kelpie. 'She can't bond with the earth at that age. Even very young gnomes, if they can bond, can be led by the earth to protect itself. Now she's just a squalling infant. Leaving the Territory—'

'What in tarnation have you done with my aunt?' yelled a voice from Anyan's driveway.

'Undefended,' Blondie finished, drily, just as Miss Carrol came swinging through the cabin's front door.

'If you've hurt her, you tattooed hussy, you are going to see the back of my . . .' Miss Carrol's words trailed off as her eyes took in the sight of Nell's enormous bun attached to the baby in Iris's arms.

'What in the Sam Hill is going on?' Miss Carrol demanded. 'Why has that baby got my aunt's hair? And why is Anyan licking himself in ways improper to either man or barghest?'

I sighed, looking over to find that Anyan was indeed getting frisky with himself. Again.

'Miss Carrol,' I said, trying to keep the immature gnome in check. 'There's been an accident, as you can see. Anyan and Nell were . . . what? Regressed?'

'Regressed?' Miss Carrol repeated.

'She's a baby and he's a dog,' Iris replied, helpfully.

'I can see that, sugar.' Miss Carrol's voice dripped syrupy venom. 'But *how* did this happen?'

'I'm sure you know Gus was attacked last night,' I explained. 'We went to investigate this morning and found a hole underneath his boulder. In it was a cavern full of crystals. If you touched them the right way, they made this sigil thing pop up out of the ground.'

'But it was locked,' Iris added.

'Yeah, so Nell and Anyan threw all this power at it and . . . bam! One baby and one doggie, at your service,' I finished.

'Well, ain't that a bitch,' Miss Carrol swore. 'How are you gonna turn 'em back?'

Blondie sighed. 'I have no idea. I've tried everything I know. I'll send out some requests for help to see if anyone has ever seen anything like this before. But in the meantime, they're just going to have to stay that way.'

'They can't stay that way,' I said, my voice shrill.

We haven't had sex yet! my libido keened, unable to believe the object of its affections had managed to give 'doggie-style' a completely pejorative connotation.

'Well, they're going to have to,' Blondie said, grimly. 'Either we come up with something ourselves, or we learn something through figuring out what's going on here in Rockabill. Maybe whatever is making these people talk is responsible for what happened to Nell and Anyan. We have to get to the bottom of everything.'

'Now,' I added, helpfully.

'Sugar, we need to have figured this here problem out about ten minutes ago,' Miss Carrol said, shaking her head.

'Mmm-hmmm,' Iris and I hummed, lured by the siren's song of the immature gnome's inexplicable Southern accent into thinking we, too, could sound like Miss Scarlett.

'You know what you need to do,' Blondie told Miss Carrol, her voice solemn. I looked between the two of them, not sure what was going on.

'I can't,' Miss Carrol said, pleadingly. 'It ain't right. I can't just take it from her.'

'I don't think you have a choice,' was Blondie's only reply.

Shit, I thought, finally realizing what was happening. *Miss Carrol might have to take over Nell's Territory.*

And while that sounded like an ideal answer to our problems, it was anything but. For if Miss Carrol bonded with the land, it would be hers until something happened to rip it away from her. Usually, and except with the interference of ancient Alfar magics, that happened with death.

In other words, Miss Carrol couldn't just bond with Nell's land and then give it back to her when her aunt grew up or we reversed the curse. If Miss Carrol took Nell's land, it was hers until she died. Leaving Nell with nothing.

'There has to be another way,' Trill said, panic edging her voice.

Blondie looked at the kelpie sympathetically, but her voice was steel. 'Nell's Territory is under attack and now it's unprotected. The weaker creatures here,' she began, waving in Gus's direction. The stone spirit had peanut butter slathered over most of his chin. 'The weaker creatures here will be completely vulnerable without Nell's protections. You've got to step in.'

Miss Carrol shook her head. 'I can't just take it from her like that. This is her home.'

'She might not live to remember how much she loves it if you don't protect her,' Blondie said, her voice sharpening incrementally.

'Wait,' I said. 'This isn't fair to any of us, especially Nell. There has to be another way. What are the stages you go through to bond with the land, Miss Carrol? Or do you just . . . bond?'

'No, there are stages, sugar. It doesn't happen all at once.'

'And are there stages where you can still withdraw?' I asked.

'Why sure. Up until you're fully bonded, you can always opt out.'

Blondie looked at me, warningly. 'Miss Carrol *can* start

the process, Jane, but if she doesn't finish it she's not going
to have any real power.'

'Okay. But what *will* she have?' Iris asked, equally eager to
keep Nell's Territory free to be given back to her in the future.

'I'll be like a . . . squatter. And like any squatter, that
means I have some rights. I don't own the place, but it's sort
of almost mine. And anyone looking at the Territory from
afar might not realize it's unoccupied.'

'Will that fool Phaedra?' I asked Blondie.

'I have no idea,' she said, clearly unhappy even to be talking
this way. 'It might. It might not. But if she has or does figure
out that Nell's out of the picture . . . we're screwed.'

We all looked at each other and I suddenly really, really
wanted Anyan. He was always the one who came in at such
moments and told us all what to do. I hadn't realized how
much he was our leader until right then. Someone else was
going to have to step up.

'Okay,' I said, before clearing my throat. 'Here's what we'll
do. For now, Miss Carrol will begin the process and . . . squat.
The rest of us will take patrols, trying to make sure nothing
happens in the Territory. If it does, we call for Blondie. Do
you have a cell phone?' I asked the Original, who nodded.
'Great. Hopefully no one will notice that Nell's not actually
appearing anywhere. In the meantime, we need to be ready
to act if something gets too big. That means, Miss Carrol,
you have to be ready to take that last step, if we need you to.
We can't risk everyone's lives, including Nell's, just to save
her place here.' At that, Trill made a funny noise that I assumed
was protesting my giving Miss Carrol such a command.

'And what will we do?' Iris asked. 'Besides patrol?' Trill
made another strange sound. Maybe she was crying. Or she
was really pissed.

'We'll work on changing these two back,' I said. 'We'll

work on figuring out what the hell is going on in Rockabill. We'll work on—'

At that, Trill stood up. I was expecting her to argue with me. But my friend's flat-featured face was oddly empty, as if the proverbial lights were on but everyone had snuck out back to the shed.

'The Signs protect destruction!' a voice very unlike Trill's boomed out from the kelpie's body. 'The Signs protect destruction! The Signs protect destruction! The Signs protect . . .'

We all looked at each other, totally freaked out. But just as the Original took a step toward Trill, the whole cabin shook as if a missile had hit it. We grabbed onto the furniture around us while the ground shook and Anyan began barking like he was being pestered by rabid groundhogs.

When the shaking stopped, we all looked around to make sure our friends were unhurt. And we were – the only damage to the cabin a few books fallen off shelves or paintings off walls. Trill, meanwhile, was still muttering, 'The Signs protect destruction,' but when Caleb went and shook her gently, she came back to herself.

But Miss Carrol looked spooked. She was obviously afraid this meant an attack that would force her to bond with Nell's Territory. And as I looked around, relief turned to fear on all my friends' faces. None of us wanted to be a party to stealing Nell's home.

All of us except for Anyan, of course.

He was chewing on one of his own paws.

Chapter Twelve

'Yeah, Jane. I'm sure you do want to talk, and we definitely have a lot of catching up to do. But now?' Blondie asked. I squinted at her, the low-lying light of the late-afternoon sun right in my eyes.

'Yes, now. It'll take five minutes,' I answered, using my Resolved Voice.

'Um, sure. Fine.' Blondie peered around, as if to verify our privacy. Trill was inside, making Nell a bottle from supplies Amy had run over just a few minutes ago on her break from the Trough. When Amy left, she'd taken Gus with her into town so he could work his shift at McKinley's. In the driveway, Anyan danced around Iris and Caleb, who were trying to load the big dog into Caleb's SUV. Anyan was having none of it.

That left Blondie and me on the big wraparound porch, in relative seclusion.

'So what's up?' she asked.

I thought about how to approach my questions, and then decided that diving right in was the way to go.

'I know I owe you my life. Everyone's told me that, about a million times. But why should I trust you?'

The Original blinked at me. 'Don't beat around the bush, babydoll,' she said.

'I'm sorry,' I said. 'I probably seem ungrateful. But everyone else has had a month to get to talk to you, to get to know you. Last thing I remember, you were a mystery to us. Now everyone's best friends, but I need to know why.'

'Can't the fact that your friends trust me be enough?' she asked.

'Frankly, no. After all,' I replied, 'they needed you to keep me alive. That was a need you could take advantage of . . . either through magic or through good, old-fashioned manipulation.'

Instead of looking offended, Blondie grinned.

'That's a solidly distrusting attitude to have, babydoll. You're learning. How about we start from the beginning?'

'From the beginning?' I asked, unsure of her meaning.

'Yep,' she said, sticking out her hand for me to shake. 'Nice to meet you. I'm—' and here, she said that totally unpronounceable string of bendy sounds, grunts, and clicks.

I blinked at her and then took her hand and said hello before trying my damndest to imitate that string of noises she'd just made.

Blondie made a face, before repeating her name.

I tried again. Her grimace deepened.

'That's terrible. You have a tin ear. How about a nickname?' she asked.

I nodded, knowing it would take me a good year, at least, to pronounce her true name.

'Sometimes my friends call me—' she started, and then, I swear to the gods, she said what could only be spelled 'Xctvbivobi.' I stared at her for a second, before giving her name the old college try.

'Yeesh,' was her only response. 'That's even worse. Can you do Cviciaoozozo?'

I tried. I failed.

'You've lived a long time,' I pleaded. 'You have to have had human names. Can't we use one of those?'

Blondie frowned. 'Those names are my history, and they're dead and buried. Plus, some of them are still on various wanted lists.'

I responded by tentatively trying her real name one more time.

She made a cat's-anus face.

'Tell you what,' she said. 'What would you like to call me?'

I shifted on my feet. 'I sort of had a nickname for you before.'

'Great,' she said. 'What is it? As long as it's not Bitch-Faced Monster, we can roll with it.'

'Um,' I said. 'I called you Blondie.'

Blondie grinned. 'That's perfect. I fucking love Blondie. That bitch can party.'

I sighed, thinking of Amy. 'So I've heard,' I said.

'Blondie it is. At least until I can get that tongue of yours whipped into shape,' the Original said, giving me a bawdy wink and taking a step toward me.

I blushed, feeling a little twinge of heat in my belly. The fact is, the Original was not only super hot, but she had that Tilda Swinton, David Bowie, or TAFKAP style androgynous pansexuality. The kind where *everyone*, regardless of gender or sexual orientation, kinda wanted to boff them.

But you're smitten with a dog, I reminded myself, turning away from Blondie to watch as Anyan barked, did that doggie-playful-bow thing – with his ass in the air and his tail wagging – and then raced away just as Caleb and Iris got close enough to grab him.

'Well, Blondie,' I said, turning back to the Original. 'It's nice to meet you. I'm Jane.'

We shook hands, pseudo-solemnly.

'So, now that we've been introduced, what do you want to know?' she asked.

'I was told you were here because you're searching for something in Rockabill. Some kind of power. And it's hidden away, according to a nursery rhyme, and protected by four locks.'

Blondie nodded as I spoke.

'So,' I continued. 'You followed Anyan and me around the country, instead of coming straight here and dealing with Nell. You say you did that because you wanted to see what we were like, but you never approached us, just followed us. And then we get attacked, but you're right there to "help out". Can you see why I'm a little suspicious?'

Blondie sighed. 'Yes, I can. And to be frank, I haven't been completely honest.'

I stiffened, unsure of where this was going to go. If Blondie decided to admit to being allied with Jarl and his cronies, we were fucked, what with Nell *and* Anyan out for the count.

'Don't get all uptight,' the Original chided. 'I'm not a bad guy. I just know a little more than I told the others.'

I frowned and she shook her head.

'They weren't secrets you had to know, and you'll understand why I had to keep them if you'll just let me finish.' When I stayed quiet, clearly indicating she should talk, she continued.

'The fact is, there's more to the nursery rhyme than most people know. I've found the original version, which is more of a harsh warning than a nursery rhyme. It's written in ancient Alfar, so there are only a handful of people around today who can read it.

'It says the same stuff as our nursery rhyme version, about something ancient being locked away. But it goes on to talk about how the creature – and this version specifies that it's a creature – will not only destroy a lot of stuff upon waking, but that it also has the power to create for itself a champion.'

'A champion?' I questioned.

'Yep. It has the power to gift its own strength to someone. Anyway, there are a number of things we don't know, but we know the creature has the power to *give* power – and that's power that a lot of people want.'

'But if not many people can read ancient Alfar—' I began.

'Unfortunately,' she interrupted, '"not many" does not mean "only me". The bad guys know everything I do.'

'And who, exactly, are the bad guys?' I asked, remembering Nell's fear that this problem wasn't just national but international.

'People just like Jarl, all over the world. It's the same war that we've fought a million times, or so it feels like.'

'Those who want to live with humans versus those who want to subjugate them?'

'It's more than that,' Blondie replied, raising her tight white wifebeater just enough to scratch lazily at the piercing in her belly button. 'It's about how we live. One side wants strict hierarchies – strict laws about who can and cannot lead, and how we live our lives. The other understands the idea of choices, and how we must be free to make them. Part of that is how we live with humans. Some of us want no contact, and for humans to be, basically, our slaves. Others understand we need humans . . . that we'd be lost without them.'

'Okay,' I said, remembering to focus on my original questions and not go off in a tangent that could be Blondie-induced. 'So why were you following Anyan and me, instead of working with Nell to get access to the Territory to find the creature?'

Blondie pursed her lips, obviously gathering her thoughts.

'I really did need an invite into the Territory. Nell isn't trusting, especially of someone with my powers.'

'And?' I prompted, knowing there was more.

'And,' she said, slowly and carefully, 'I was interested in the two of you.'

I frowned. Why would she be interested in me and Anyan? Anyan was the only one worth following . . . And then it all fell into place.

'You think Anyan could be the champion,' I stated, knowing I had to be right. It made sense: why else would someone like Anyan feel he needed to make a home here? Maybe he was *called* by the power. And who better to take on some mysterious championship (if that's what it was called) than someone who was already a badass?

Blondie was watching me with a furrowed brow, which smoothed out as I talked. Undoubtedly, she was relieved that I had guessed her secret.

'Well, let's say I *thought* Anyan was the champion,' she intoned, nodding her head toward where both Caleb and Iris were *still* trying to shove Anyan's recalcitrant ass into the back of the SUV.

'Oh,' I said, realizing what she was saying. 'Doggies don't make good champions?'

'No,' she replied, drily.

'Do you really think we'll be able to change them back?' I asked, worry cutting through my other Blondie-related anxieties.

'I know we will,' she answered. 'We just have to find those locks. With the power the creature contains, we can fix both Nell and Anyan.'

'Are you sure?' I asked.

'Positive. But we have to go. As soon as we check out

whatever that explosion was, we'll head straight over to Gus's rock.'

I nodded, and then had a thought.

'Why can't you be the champion?' I asked.

She was about to answer when she stopped and got a funny, faraway expression on her face.

'Well,' Blondie agreed, eventually. 'Both Nell and Anyan are out of the picture.'

'It makes sense. You have the most power. And you were drawn to Rockabill, like everyone else.'

'Drawn to Rockabill?'

'Yeah,' I said. 'We figured that's why there's all the supes here. Power draws power.'

'Is that why you're here?' she said, grinning.

I laughed. 'Nope, I was born here. So, are we going to tell the others?'

She frowned. 'The fewer people who know the truth, the safer we all are. If one of us falls into enemy hands, or even just babbles the truth, everyone would be looking for the creature and its power, not just the few people who already know the legend.'

I thought about what she had told me, and whether either Caleb or Iris or the others really *needed* to know it. Finally, I nodded, agreeing with her estimation that I needn't tell anyone what she'd just told me. Yet.

'So do you trust me, Jane?' Blondie asked, suddenly serious.

Not answering her for a moment, I watched as Iris and Caleb finally managed to shove Anyan into the car and shut the door. Suddenly, I made my decision.

'Sure,' I said, smiling at her. 'I trust you.'

She returned my smile, obviously relieved.

'Good,' the Original said, moving in for a hug.

Her arms went around me and I gave her my own hug. She felt lean and long against me, and I felt my libido cock a (bi)curious eyebrow. Telling it to hush, I waited till she'd released me.

''Bout ready to go?' she asked.

'Absolutely,' I replied. 'I just have to text someone, and then make a quick call.'

As she walked away, I readied my phone. I waited, my fingers crossed that my plan would work, as Blondie talked with Caleb, her back to me. Then I hurriedly snapped a photo of her profile as she turned to talk to Iris. When she turned to cast a glance back at me, I snapped a full-on photo of her while pretending to text. The picture wasn't great, with the sun behind her, but it would have to do.

Then I made my phone call.

'Hello?' came Ryu's familiar voice.

'Hi, Ryu. It's Jane,' I said, knowing he already knew that from his cell phone display screen, but saying it anyway.

'Is everything okay?' he asked, his voice worried.

'Sort of,' I said. 'Actually, not really. Nell's been turned into a baby, and Anyan into a dog. A real dog.'

'What?' he asked. 'How?'

'Some ancient Alfar booby trap.'

'Do you need me to come there?'

'No,' I replied. 'Actually, you'd better stay away. If there's any more of these traps and we get taken out, we'll need someone to come finish this. But if you're here, we might lose you, too.'

'Okay,' he said, but he didn't sound happy about it. 'So, what do you need?'

'Caleb said you came here when I was in the coma?'

'Yes,' he said. I didn't ask him why, or thank him. The others were all looking at me from where they stood by the car chatting, and I needed to make this quick.

'Did you meet Blondie when you were here?'

'Who?' he asked.

'The Original.'

'No,' he replied. 'I was only there for a few hours, and she was off doing something when I was there. But I heard all about her.'

'I need you to check up on her. I doubt anyone else knows what she really is, so don't go that route. Just ask around, as if she were any other suspect. Do your usual thing, but try the oldest beings you know, as well as the usual. I'm texting you a couple pictures of her.'

'What do you want to know?'

'Anything. I have to know we can trust her. Everyone else does, but there's something odd. I can't put my finger on it. I want to trust her, but I know there's more than she's telling us.'

'Are you sure? Anyan's not exactly easy to fool,' Ryu warned.

'I know. But apparently she was the one basically keeping me alive. That's a good way to gain trust, quickly, without deserving it,' I replied.

There was silence from the other end of the line, and then Ryu's voice.

'True,' he said. 'I'll ask around. Just send me the pictures.'

'Thanks,' I said. 'Call me as soon as you find out anything.'

'I will. But you're sure you don't need me?'

'No,' I said. 'But I need this information more. And we need you safe, in the wings, in case we fail.'

Or in case Blondie really deserves my suspicions, I thought, as Iris waved to me to hurry as she and Caleb climbed into the front seats and Blondie climbed into the back with Anyan.

She had to use her magic to keep the big dog from bolting past her to freedom.

'But I gotta go,' I said. 'Call me?'

'Of course,' Ryu said. 'I'll get right on this.'

'Thanks, Ryu. Talk soon. Bye.'

'Bye. Take care.'

And with that, he hung up. I took a few seconds to attach the pictures to a message and send them to Ryu, and then I walked over to the car.

I really hope we can trust you, I thought at Blondie, as I felt her use just a smidgen of her huge strength to hold Anyan still as I climbed into the back seat.

Because otherwise we are totally fucked.

Chapter Thirteen

Although Anyan had hated getting in the car, he changed his tune when we started moving. He looked very happy sticking his head out the window over my shoulder, from where we'd coaxed him to jump into the very back of Caleb's SUV. His soft fur against my cheek should have been comforting, but any such emotions were mitigated by the fact that he was panting, long ropes of saliva dripping from his mouth, and occasionally barking at passing street signs.

In other words, everything he did reminded me that the man I'd come to rely on was no longer lurking inside that dog. There was only kibble and slobber. Lots and lots of slobber.

As if on cue, from the seat beside me, Blondie apparated a handful of tissue and passed them over. She'd already apparated herself a long-sleeved T-shirt to wear over her wife-beater, undoubtedly not wanting to turn mortal heads. It was still well chilly here in Maine, despite spring nipping at Rockabill's heels.

'Thanks,' I mumbled, as she gave me one of her disconcerting winks.

'Where should we head?' Caleb asked, his massive ram's horns raking the ceiling of the SUV as he turned to look at Iris. She had her hand in her lover's lap, something I normally wouldn't have noticed.

But normally people wear pants when they're driving, I thought, wiping a stray rivulet of Anyan's spit off my earlobe as I replied to Caleb.

'Go to the town square. Everyone will already be there,' I told him.

We didn't know where to head, as all we'd felt was a big boom. Nell would have been able to pinpoint the noise, but she was sucking down formula at the moment. So instead of relying on the gnome, we had to rely on Rockabill. Meanwhile, Iris tittered at my response, knowing small-town life as well as I did. And sure enough, when we arrived at Rockabill's town square, there were already quite a few people milling about.

Caleb pulled rakishly across a few parking spots, and I was jumping out of the car before it had even completely stopped. Anyan followed me, scrabbling over the back seat and undoubtedly putting a few scratches in Caleb's upholstery.

'Hi, Mr Tanner! Mrs Tanner!' I shouted across the square at our local baker and his wife. He waved back in return, but I also noticed Bob and Marge exchanging slightly panicked looks.

'What's happening? What was that explosion?' I said, panting from running across the square.

'We're not really too sure, yet,' Mr Tanner started, looking to his wife for help. 'We were having breakfast in the Trough—'

'All we know is we heard the bang,' Mrs Tanner interrupted, nervously.

'And then Sheila and Herbert both got calls on their cell phones, and they raced out of the Trough going toward the B & B.'

I felt my stomach clench. Ever since Sheila and Herbert had taken over the Black and White B & B – Nick and Nan's little pun on Gray – it hadn't been the same. Nick and Nan had been Jason's grandparents, who'd raised him after he'd been abandoned by his own mother, a drug addict. I'd grown up running between my house and Jason's, and the B & B had been as much my home as Jason's. When Jason died, and Nick and Nan had passed away shortly after, the house had passed on to the nastier side of the family, Jason's yuppie aunt and uncle, Sheila and Herbert, and their darling son Stuart. Otherwise known as the Bane of My Existence.

The New Grays, as they were still called after all these years, gutted the B & B. What had once been shabby, inviting, and comfortable was done over to reflect a colder, more corporate if elegant feeling. Unfortunately, what the Grays hadn't considered was the fact that people don't come to Maine looking for chrome and glass, softened only by the occasional Louis Quinze replica armchair. They want quilts, warm fires, and clapboard.

The Black and White B & B sank like a stone, making Stuart's already unpleasant family even less friendly.

'What's up?' Iris asked. My friends had come up behind me while I was thinking of Jason, his grandparents, and what had once been a home to me.

'It sounds like it came from the Grays' place,' I said, after thanking my fellow Rockabillians and turning to face my friends.

'Where's that?' Caleb asked. Iris's eyes were watching me, undoubtedly aware of my feelings.

'It's pretty close behind mine,' I answered the satyr, carefully keeping my voice neutral. 'But you have to take a different road. I know the way.'

And Understatement of the Year goes to . . . Jane True! my brain said, snidely. The truth was, even now, after so many years, I still dreamed of that walk to and from Jason's house. I knew that if I had to, I could easily have found my way to his place in the dark, in a snow storm, whatever.

It was a route carved into my heart, grooves of memory made permanent through both love and heartbreak.

We all trotted back across the square and loaded into Caleb's SUV. We realized we'd forgotten doggie-Anyan only after we'd left the square. After turning around, we found him getting his ears scratched by Mr Allen, Linda's much nicer father. I threw open the door, and he jumped onto our laps in a miasma of flying fur and dog breath.

Why do you have to be a dog, you asshole? I thought. I knew it was unfair to blame Anyan for getting caught up in ancient Alfar booby traps, but I was still pissed off. I had a funny feeling I was going to need a hug pretty soon, and I wished very fervently it could have been Anyan's arms administering said treatment.

Heading back up our route once we got the non-ghest barghest shoved into the back of the car, Caleb met my eyes in the rearview.

'What do you know about these Grays?' he asked. 'Any connections to magic or anything?' As he finished talking, he hissed in a breath. Iris had her hand in his lap again, and I think she must have been squeezing his scrotum in warning.

Which is why pants are a plus, my virtue thought smugly, a statement my libido heartily disavowed.

'No,' I said. 'It's okay, Iris. I can talk about it.' The succubus looked back at me, concern etched on her features. Caleb's face, which I could see in his rearview, looked confused.

'The Grays are the aunt and uncle of my . . . friend, Jason. The one who died.'

Caleb's lips parted as he made an *eep* face, thinking he'd put his foot (or rather, hoof) straight in it.

'Jason and his grandparents were extraordinary people, and

they were Wiccans. But they weren't supernatural at all.' *Unless kindness isn't really human, which I've sometimes thought might be the case.* 'As for the people who live there now, these Grays are definitely not supernatural. They're assholes, but they're not supernatural. It makes no more sense that they'd be attacked than it made sense Gus was attacked.'

'So maybe it's not them but their land,' Blondie said. 'Maybe they're sitting on top of something like we found at Gus's.' We sat in silence, mulling that over for a bit.

'If I'm turned into a goat, I'm going to be very irate,' Caleb rumbled from the front seat. It was such an unexpectedly flippant comment coming from the usually sober satyr that we all sat in shock for a few seconds before tittering like school kids.

'If Jane becomes a seal, I'm gonna club her and make a hat,' Blondie added, making us all giggle harder. My laughter choked off, however, when she punctuated her joke by raking her nails over the top of my thigh.

'You're just jealous because you're an Original. You can't get any more devolved,' I jibed, trying to recover my equilibrium as I poked the Mohawked woman in the ribs with a finger. She squirmed, and then poked me back.

'But what would I become?' Iris whined from the front. We all thought about that for a second.

'Vagina dentata?' Blondie hazarded. It didn't make sense, but it didn't matter. We were all laughing hilariously as we made our way to my once-and-former home.

I, for one, was grateful for the distraction.

Everybody got out of the car except for me. Caleb and Iris walked hand in hand together up to the edge of where Jason's house had once stood. I simply stared, in horror.

I also noticed, with that weird attention to random detail

that characterizes traumatic events, that the swishing of Iris's hips beat almost in time with the flicking of Caleb's goat tail.

Meanwhile, Anyan went to pee on some trees and then sniff at his own urine. Then Caleb moved to where Sheila, Herbert, and Stuart all stood, staring down at their house. Caleb pulled Sheila and Herbert aside, while Iris talked to Stuart. Blondie stood outside of the car for a moment, before noticing I hadn't gotten out. She climbed back in to confront me.

'What's up, babydoll?' she asked. 'Something's wrong. C'mon, spill.'

I turned to face her and, to my horror, tears welled up in my eyes and flowed down my cheeks. It was stupid to cry in front of someone I was having investigated, but I couldn't help it.

Blondie leaned over to close her open car door, and then turned back to me. Next thing I knew she was hugging me, her arms like steel despite their slenderness. But she was warm, and her long-sleeved shirt was soft. I accepted the hug gratefully.

'Cry it out, babycakes,' she purred. So I did. Then I cried some more. And then I kept crying, until even I was beginning to think it was a little bit ridiculous.

It's just that seeing Jason's house *gone* had shaken me up, badly. So badly, in fact, that it had taken a few moments to register.

'What h-h-h-happened?' I finally managed to choke out, my voice snotty.

'I dunno. You lost your shit before I could find out,' Blondie said, her smile taking the harsh edge off her words.

'It's *gone*,' I said, finally iterating what had been going through my head since we drove up Jason's former driveway.

'The house? Yep, it appears to be. Now are you going to tell me whose house it really was?'

I sat back rubbing my face on my sleeves until Blondie

handed me a tissue she found in Caleb's glove compartment. Blowing my nose noisily, I tried to think of where to begin.

'The house used to be owned by my boyfriend,' I said, finally. 'Well, by his grandparents. His name was Jason. And we grew up together.'

How lame does that sound? I thought, hating having to tell this story. Because it always sounded lame: a bad episode of a bad teen drama. *Girl and boy love each other, like, for real, yo! But then they, like, lose each other and it's wicked sad. Seriously. Cut to awesome new song! Rock out!*

'So what happened?' Blondie prompted.

'You have to understand. We were . . . we were everything to each other. I don't know if I can explain it . . .'

'You were lovers?'

'Yes. But also siblings. Gods, that sounds creepy. But it's true. We were together pretty much all the time, from the moment Jason moved here to when he . . . when he died.'

Blondie grimaced, putting an arm around me so we were cuddling side-by-side like necking teenagers.

'When did he die?'

'Years ago. I was just eighteen. We were still in high school. It was an accident, but also my fault.' Even now I couldn't believe how easily I said that, and how I could say it and know it without feeling like I needed to go bury myself alive in order to repent.

'How was it your fault, if it was an accident?'

'He caught me swimming. I'd kept it a secret, even from him. Everyone growing up around here knows you can't swim in our waters, let alone anywhere near the Sow. But he saw my clothes. And he went in after me.'

Blondie and I were silent for a long while.

'Wow,' she said, eventually.

'Yes,' I replied.

'You do know it wasn't really—'

'My fault?' I finished for her. 'Yes, I understand, now, that I didn't cause Jason's death, in the sense that I didn't push him in. I had no idea he'd find me. But it doesn't change the fact that he died that night, and it was because he found my clothes on that beach.'

She frowned at me, and I sighed.

'I *do* understand that it's not entirely my fault, now. I've come to terms with that. But his death and the circumstances aren't something I'm gonna forget either.'

'That's intense, babydoll. I'm sorry.'

'Thank you.'

'And you still have a connection to the family? The house?'

'The family, no. His grandparents died pretty soon after Jason did. Their hearts were broken: it's like all the life went out of them. The people who took it over are Grays, but they're not family. At least not to me. But the house . . .' I trailed off, unable to finish.

'The house was something,' she said, her turn to finish my sentence.

'Exactly. It feels sometimes like Jason's been wiped off the face of Rockabill. Nobody talks about him anymore. Nobody seems to remember. I know people do, and most of them are avoiding the subject because they're trying to be nice to me. But it feels like he never existed, sometimes.' Blondie nodded, letting me talk. 'And sometimes, when that feeling got really bad, I'd drive by here. Or walk from my house, just like I used to when I would meet him. It was . . . something,' I said, echoing Blondie's words.

'Those "somethings" are important,' she said, squeezing me gently with the arm she'd wrapped around me. I nestled closer, instinctively, before remembering I wasn't supposed to trust her.

She's either a master con artist or she is *trustworthy*, I thought.

We sat for a few moments, looking at where Jason's house used to stand. I was grateful for Blondie's silence, and for her being there. I still believed she was up to something, but I had to admit I *felt* I could trust her, deep in my bones. Meanwhile, her sitting with me right then, so patiently, made me want to believe that instinct rather than question it.

'Well,' I said, after scrubbing my hands over my face, 'it looks like I'll have to find me a new "something". In the meantime, we need to find out what happened.' And with that, I pushed gently away from Blondie and got out of the car. I didn't regret losing it like that, it was bound to happen with anything involving Jason, but the clock was ticking.

Blondie got out with me and together we walked forward to where Caleb was questioning Sheila and Herbert Gray. As we got closer, we could see that the house was still there, sort of. It had just fallen through the ground into what appeared to be an absolutely enormous sinkhole.

I didn't think they came that big in nature, I thought, grimly. *At least not around here.*

Sinkholes were common around Rockabill, but nothing so large it would swallow a house whole.

As for the Grays, they'd been responding eagerly to the satyr's questions. Undoubtedly Caleb had glamoured them to believe he was a journalist or a policeman, but when they saw me they clammed up. A look like she was sniffing vinegar passed over Sheila's face.

'I bet you're pleased to see this,' said Sheila. I rocked back on my heels, unable to believe either her words or the spite with which she spoke them.

'What are you talking about?' I replied. 'Why on earth would I—'

'You always hated us taking over the Black and White. You hated what we did to it. We know you told tourists at that bookstore not to stay with us.'

I did no such thing, I thought as I stood there, mouth gaping. Sheila used my shocked silence to wind up for one last swing.

'Well, now it's in the ground, with your precious Jason.'

At those words, Blondie's hand shot out and smacked Sheila across the face. Her head whipped around, the crack of Blondie's hand on Sheila's face like that of a firecracker.

Herbert Gray took a few discreet steps back, obviously unwilling to come to his wife's aid. To be honest, upon thinking about it, I'd never actually seen him speak unless spoken to.

But Sheila still had her defenders. Iris had led Stuart away from his parents, undoubtedly using a sprinkling of succubus magics to lure him where she wanted. But he came charging back at the sight of his mother getting slapped, bellowing like a bull.

Caleb reached out a hoof and tripped Stu, who fell flat on his face, still hollering the whole way down.

'We don't have time for this,' I snapped. 'Thank you for sticking up for me,' I said to the fuming Original at my side. 'I appreciate it. But right now we need to know what happened. So . . . undo all this and let's start from the beginning.'

Even I was a little shocked at the authority in my voice, but everyone snapped to pretty quickly. Caleb hauled Stu up, Iris steered Mr Gray toward us by the scruff of the neck, and Blondie reached forward to manhandle Mrs Gray into cooperating.

Then I felt Blondie's power wash over the humans. She whispered to them that we'd only just arrived, they wanted to cooperate with us, and that they really, really wanted to be nice to Jane.

I smiled at that last bit, as Blondie used another surge of power to keep the Grays in place. Then we rearranged ourselves together opposite them to appear as innocent as Girl Scouts selling delicious cookies door-to-door.

When Blondie drew back her magic, Mr and Mrs Gray were smiling, absurdly happy for two people whose house had been gobbled up by the earth. Only Stu looked like he wasn't sold on Blondie's glamouring. He'd always had an odd resistance to magic, which explained why my 'be nice to Jane' that had worked great on Linda never quite stuck with Stu.

'Like we were just telling the nice men from the insurance company,' Mrs Gray gushed, 'we have no idea how this could have happened! Right, honey?' Mrs Gray then turned to her husband, who looked almost as happy as she did that they weren't sure how their house had disappeared.

'No, sweetheart! I have no idea how this could have happened! In fact, we were at dinner when it did!' Mr Gray was equally excited. I could practically *see* the exclamation marks bubbling from his lips.

'Wait, wait, back up,' I said. 'What nice men from the insurance agency?' While the supes I was with probably had never dealt with human insurance companies, I knew damned well there was no way any agency could get someone out to Rockabill that quickly.

'The nice men! Who came right away! They were fast!' Mrs Gray was practically singing her responses at this point.

'What did they look like, these agents?' Caleb asked.

'They were so kind! And so professional! And so kind!' Mrs Gray went ahead and sang.

'They were weird,' Stuart said, his never-pleasant voice

gone particularly petulant. 'Despite what my mom says, they weren't professional. They were weird.'

I elbowed Blondie. I knew if I asked a question, Stu would react badly, glamour or no glamour.

'Um, weird how?' the Original asked, taking the hint.

'The one dude was huge, first of all. Like circus-freak huge. And the second guy was creepy. And they didn't help us at all. They just talked to my parents for like four seconds and then jumped into the hole and came out again like fifteen minutes later. They were fucking weird.'

'Lang-uage!' Mrs Gray sang. Stuart rolled his eyes.

'Whatever, Mom. Seriously, they weren't right.' Stuart stopped talking, and then eyed my friends for a second, blinking as if he couldn't quite focus his vision. 'Kinda like you guys . . .'

'All right then,' Caleb said, hastily. 'You three should head into town. Check yourselves into a hotel.' He paused when I gave him a Look, realizing the B & B *was* the hotel. 'Um, check yourselves into those cabins Mr Allen owns. Make your calls from there. Call your insurance agents . . . I know they were just here, but you'll want to call them again.'

I smiled at the satyr's kind use of his magic. I would have let the Grays sit, thinking their insurance claims were being processed. But I was a bitch and Caleb was just the sort of goat-man you wanted to bring home to mama.

The Grays shuffled away, Stuart less pleased about leaving but not wanting to let his parents wander off alone. Once they were gone, we all turned to the ginormous hole through which the very roof of the Grays' house still peeped. I knew what was coming next.

So much spelunking . . . so little time.

Chapter Fourteen

I dangled above Blondie while she made rude comments about my ass. Caleb and Iris were staying aboveground, well out of the way. If we tripped another Alfar booby trap, something that took us out like the other had Nell and Anyan, they were supposed to call Ryu.

So once again, I found myself descending into the earth, a position I wasn't entirely comfortable with on a number of levels. Not least because of the one-woman peanut gallery below me.

'It's like a gumdrop, but an ass,' the Original was saying. 'I've always been more of a breast girl, but now I get it. You're a woman and yet you offer all the comforts of a recliner.'

'Will you just help me down,' I chided, having had enough of Blondie's flirtatious yammerings. I wasn't sure if the Original was serious, but I did know most of the older supes were switch-hitters. Yet right now we needed to be applying our brains and our bodies to solving the mysteries cropping up around Rockabill, not seducing one another.

Not to mention, even *my* libido couldn't rouse itself at the sight of my last real link to Jason sunk into the earth.

'All work and no play makes Jane a dull girl, gumdrop ass and all,' Blondie muttered, helping me land beside her but insisting on pinching said ass at the same time. I *meeped*, pulling away.

'That hurt. And I'm not exactly in the mood for games,' I said, pointedly staring at where Jason's former home leaned precariously next to us.

The sinkhole it had fallen into was enormous, big enough that there was room for Blondie and me to walk abreast of each other around the entire house. Meanwhile, the B & B looked almost entirely intact, even though it was leaning alarmingly. Part of me wanted to climb into that house and act like none of this had ever happened, starting with Jason's death and moving onward.

But that's not an option, I thought, straightening my shoulders and looking away from what had been one of my last surviving connections to Jason.

'Where should we start?' I asked. 'What are we looking for?'

'Beats me. Let's just hope that what we're looking for isn't in the house.'

'Or that it didn't fall on top of it,' I added.

We both grimaced at each other, and then started walking around the perimeter of the sinkhole. We'd gone only a little way around the house before we came across a few tunnels in the wall.

'I don't suppose you know if we should take one of these?' I asked, eyeing the three holes I could see from our current position next to the Grays' now-sagging front porch.

'Hmmm,' she said. 'This is gonna require some investigation,' and with that, she began to strip off her clothes. Her body was as lithe and muscular as I remembered, every inch covered with tattoos that ranged from the very primitive to more traditional tribal tats, from pirate tats to sailor tats, and finally a smattering of more refined, modern-looking tattoos. A crazy mixture of ink splashed along her skin almost as if her flesh embodied the history of the tattoo. It should have looked a mess, but somehow it didn't.

And besides, I realized, *she's lived so long she probably* does *embody the history of the tattoo.*

But the wink she gave me when she handed me her clothes was anything but antiquarian, and I felt my cheeks flush in response.

She reminds me of Ryu, my libido purred. *Always ready for pleasure.*

Pleasure we don't have time for, my virtue chastised, trying to figure out where to stash the Original's clothing. I finally laid the little bundle on the Grays' front porch, hoping the house didn't collapse on it. When I turned back to Blondie, she had her eyes shut as if she were concentrating.

'What we need is something with a keen sense of smell . . . but more than that . . . something that can *sense*—'

And with that, and a terrific outpouring of magic, the Original was gone and a large moth fluttered where her head had been. I walked forward, my hand extended toward the marvel. The moth landed on my fingers, its wings of brown and dun – with splashes of white, red, and indigo – brushing my fingers as it found purchase on my skin.

'How can you *do* that?' I asked, wondering again at the constant violation of every physical law I'd grown up with that was my new supernatural existence.

As if fluttering away my questions, the moth alighted from my hand to sky-amble lazily toward one of the openings. There it hovered, for a handful of seconds, before making its way to the other tunnel, and then the other. Finally, it returned to the middle tunnel, fluttering its way a few feet inward. Then with another wash of magic, a nekkid lady crouched, shivering, in place of the moth.

After grabbing Blondie's clothes, I rushed them over to her. She was shaking so hard, however, that I had to help her.

'Flying's h-h-hard,' she said through chattering teeth, as I pulled her shirt over her head, carefully avoiding touching her naked frame. I swear her nipple rings winked at me in the darkness.

'I bet,' I said. 'Are you okay?'

'Yeah. I just need a moment . . .' And with that, I felt a tremendous surge of power as Blondie drew strength from . . . somewhere. With others of my kind – the Alfar-derived, I guess you'd call us – I could feel their elements answering them as water answered to me. But with Blondie, there was that four-elemental surge that said 'Alfar', but there was more . . . a bit like the surge I felt around Nell or Terk, Capitola's little brownie, who both used old magic.

But that's not quite it, either, I thought, my senses unable to pin down exactly what I'd just felt. *Whatever it is, though, it's* strong.

Blondie, meanwhile, looked decidedly healthier. She stretched her lithe form – and I felt the twinge of jealousy I always feel when already-long people make themselves even longer – then looked at me.

'C'mon, babydoll. There's something down this way that's calling to me.'

'Calling to you?'

'Well, I actually felt something that's warning me away. But in this case—'

'We'll consider that an invite,' I said, drily, wondering when I'd become that white person in Eddie Murphy's stand-up routine who goes inside the obviously haunted house – despite the house whispering, 'Stay out! Stay out!'

Together, we set off down the winding tunnel. Luckily, the ceiling was high and I didn't feel very hemmed in. But as we continued, the floor began to slope downward, as if the ceiling was struggling to meet it. Soon enough we were stooping, the tunnel continually narrowing as we pushed forward.

'Keep breathing, Jane,' Blondie warned. 'This is just the first test.'

'Test?' I asked, admittedly rather breathless from feeling the weight of the walls around me.

'Yep. This is the first thing that makes you want to give up and go home. It's just a tunnel. We'll get through it.'

There was wisdom in her words, but they didn't make me feel less hemmed in or nervous. Which only got worse when the tunnel suddenly grew even narrower and we had to crawl. The dirt beneath my hands, though, felt soft and cool and clean, and I focused on that feeling rather than the darkness behind me or the walls at my flanks.

Until, that is, something skittered out from underneath my right palm as I set my weight on it.

Shuddering, I *meeped*, and then began a series of 'ews'.

'Almost there,' Blondie soothed. 'I can feel the air changing . . .'

And sure enough, soon we were pushing through a ridiculously narrow hole into a larger cavern. As I pushed my shoulders through, wriggling to extricate myself, I knew how a newborn baby must feel.

I have been reborn, I thought as I got my shoulders through the hole, but I got caught on my bottom half. *And I shall henceforth be known as Hips-Got-Stuck.*

Blondie grabbed me underneath the armpits and helped pull me through, dusting me off a little too thoroughly when she had me upright. I was so distracted by the cavern we were in that I let her manhandle me as I unleashed a series of softly lit mage lights to float around the dark space.

Unlike the crystal cave from earlier, this one was made up of unadorned rock. But it was no less impressive: naturally vaulted ceilings of variously hued granite arched above us, jutting craggily, as if carved by rough hands.

Or rough magic, I thought, peering around the cavern for evidence of anything untoward.

'There,' Blondie hissed, nudging me in the ribs with her elbow and pointing with her chin. Sure enough, embedded in the stone to our very far left, we could see in the wavering light of our mage balls just the outer edge of a mirror thingy similar to the one under Gus's rock. I gestured, and one of my closer mage lights moved just enough to reveal the mirror's smooth surface.

Just like the one I'd found before, this mirror held some sort of ancient Alfar sigil. But instead of full glimpses of different sigils popping in and out, this one snaked. A serpentlike dark line traced around sinuously to create new forms, never stopping long enough to identify what – if anything – it read.

Blondie and I approached the mirrored surface slowly, our magics pushed out enough to sense anything lurking but not enough, hopefully, to trip any booby traps. When we were finally standing in front of it, I was confronted with the exact same mystery from the crystal cavern, only this time I knew how dangerous our fiddling could be.

'Well, obviously we shouldn't blast at it,' I said.

'No. That ended badly,' Blondie replied, wryly.

'To be honest, I don't even want to touch it with magic,' I said. My own words made me pause. 'Maybe that's it,' I said, after a few moments. 'Maybe it's not about magic at all. Maybe it's like in a mystery . . . There's always a knothole in the tree, or a special book in the bookcase . . .'

And with that, I began groping around my side of the mirror. Blondie watched me cup, pull, fondle, and basically harass the rock face it was housed in, before she interrupted me.

'What on earth are you doing? Why would the Alfar use a physical trigger when they had all that magic?'

Because it works in Clue! I wanted to snap, but I didn't.

'Think about it,' I said. 'It sorta makes sense. If they're living before the other species evolved, then all their cohorts are really powerful: they're other ancient Alfar, Originals like you, and first-magic creatures like Brownies. So why would you use magic to defend something when everyone has powerful magic? It's a good defense now, cuz there's not as many creatures with that much juice. But back then?'

Blondie frowned, and then pulled up her shirt sleeves to well above her elbows as if getting ready to duke it out. I hope she wasn't planning on duking it out with me – she'd win.

'It's good logic, Jane. But it's wrong. This is a glyph,' she said, as if that should mean something to me.

'I know,' I said, remembering what Nell had told me. 'An ancient Alfar hieroglyph.'

'No, it's a *glyph*,' Blondie said. Obviously dropping the 'hiero' meant something to her, but it meant diddly-squat to me.

'Lucy,' I said, wearily. 'Please 'splain.'

'Glyphs are interactive locking devices.'

'Wha?'

'They're interactive, meaning we have to do something to the glyph itself. And they're locks.'

'Locks are good,' I said, thinking of the nursery rhyme. 'We want locks.'

'Yep. Now we just have to figure out how to interact with it.'

'With magic?' I said, looking at it warily. All joking aside, I really did *not* want to end up a seal, or worse.

'Well, you're actually half-right in this one. These *will* probably work with touch,' Blondie said.

'Like an ancient version of an iPad?' I asked.

'No, not like that at all. Are you ready?'

'Ready for what?'

'We gotta get in there and touch it,' she replied.

I gave her a Look, but moved up to face the glyph with her.

She gave me a look that read, '*You touch it*,' just as I gave her a similar one. We frowned at each other. Then we both reached forward at the same time. Before I could stop my hand from moving forward, my fingertips landed squarely on one of the tats on her forearm, one that appeared to be of a very ancient tribal nature . . .

Suddenly I was in a different cave, squatting next to a smoking fire. The cave smelled overpoweringly of human sweat and rotten meat, but the smell was familiar rather than off-putting. I was cutting up a kill with my sister – a young buck – and we were carefully hanging the meat to dry. With such successful hunts, our clan's winter wouldn't be so hard. She smiled at me, her mouth and chin smeared with blood from the delicate organs we'd snacked on as we worked, and I smiled back, content as I'd ever been . . .

'What the hell?' I shouted, as I found myself plummeted back into my body, Blondie looming above me. I'd somehow ended up flat on my back. 'I was you!' I accused her. 'In a cave! What the fuck just happened?' I demanded, sitting up as she sank down next to me.

'Didn't I tell you about my tats?' she asked, running a hand up her arm and shivering, her eyes closing to slits for a second.

'Yeah, um, no,' I said, watching her touching her tattoos, feeling my face flush with heat.

'They're not just ink,' she said. 'They're my memories.'

'What does that mean?'

'I imbued them with my memories. So that I wouldn't forget things from my past, no matter how long I lived.'

I blinked at her. 'Wow . . . why?'

She snorted a laugh, and then moved so we were sitting side-by-side, her muscular forearm close to mine. I resisted the urge to touch another tattoo.

'You've seen what happens to the really ancient. Eventually they stop living and just survive.'

'So, to combat that, you put all your best memories in your tats?'

'Not just my best. Some of my worst, too. And not just anything I enjoyed or hated. I tried to choose memories that made me who I am. The memories that really made me feel.'

I looked up into her clear blue eyes. 'That's amazing. Did it work?'

'You tell me. You've seen enough Alfar. Am I like them?'

I couldn't help but smile, thinking of her energy – her life. 'No. You're not like them.'

'You can touch, if you want,' she said, her voice soft, inviting.

'But they're your memories. Isn't that . . . too much?'

'Not for you. I know you're coming to our world late. I've seen what can happen to people like you who don't know what they're in for. I've no doubt you've noticed things that give you pause, because you're someone who watches and thinks. But still. Near-immortality isn't all it's cracked up to be.'

I thought of the cold Alfar and their preternatural calm; the sadism of creatures like Graeme, bored over the millennia into monsters; hell, even the kindly selfishness of Ryu I saw as an extension of his long life. Although short by Alfar standards, he'd lived long enough to become set in his ways, while being entirely unaware that he'd become so.

So I reached my fingers toward Blondie, not knowing where to start. When I paused, she drew herself up to pull her shirt over her head. Then she guided my fingers to her naked abdomen, laying my hand over her muscular stomach. When my palm came into contact with the small skull and crossbones lurking right beside her navel, I was suddenly standing onboard a ship plunging through rough waters, foam and water all about me as a storm formed overhead.

I was shouting commands, my Spanish perfect, as my crew hustled around me, preparing for the storm . . . but not just for the storm. For we knew the English merchant ship was only a few miles off our starboard bow, and that she'd be floundering in such seas even worse than we . . .

'You were a pirate?' I gasped, coming to myself as Blondie withdrew my hand.

'Among many other trades,' she replied, smirking. I wanted to ask her more, but soon enough she'd moved my hand to where a woman's head, her hair bobbed like a flapper, stared out from over Blondie's left hipbone.

Her stomach pressed against mine as we kissed, our tongues entwined. Her breast moved beneath my questing fingers and she moaned sharply when they found her nipple roughly. My own body grew wetter at the sound of her pleasure. I loved her, even knowing she didn't feel the same for me. I'd learned it didn't matter. For, love or no love, they all died and left me alone . . .

Tears pricked my own eyes as I met Blondie's blue ones, but she was already moving my hand to her left shoulder. My fingertips grazed over what looked suspiciously like a . . .

I stood, unable to contain my awe at the marvel before me. Shining wood and gleaming white porcelain combined in such a way that I would have thought it art had I not already had its function explained to me. Unable to believe it really did what my hosts said, I reached out a hand toward

*the wooden handle hanging from its chain and I pulled . . .
and to my delight the water did, indeed, swirl away . . .*

'You tattooed the invention of toilets?' I asked, only to see
Blondie shrug.

'It changed everything. It really did. I've got the invention
of toothpaste on my right calf,' she said, but instead she
moved my hand to her right shoulder and a large, tattered
flag.

*Her first real battle; her first real war. No longer mere
skirmishes between the upstarts calling themselves Alfar and
her people. We weren't different races, the idiots, and yet
they were so intent on subjugating everything different from
them to their will that they can't see what's obvious . . .*

'The Alfar,' I said and gasped. 'Not a different species?'
And this time my hand moved on its own, seeking across
Blondie's flesh for answers.

*I saw the end of the battle of the Black Flag. The Alfar had
brought with them something old; something foul. They'd raised
it from its sleep, and it had laid waste to everything in its path.
It went after those Alfar that had awoken it, first, then had
moved on to the rest of the Alfar on the field of battle. But we
did not rejoice at the fall of our enemies, for we knew the creature wouldn't stop there. We also knew if we attacked, we would
suffer terrible losses.*

*And we knew that the Alfar generals – sitting miles away
on a distant hilltop – had planned this all along.*

*My people charged, and when it was over, nearly everyone
who'd fought that day was dead, our side, and their's. But those
who fought on my side didn't keep ourselves back on mountains
and let others do our fighting. Indeed, I was one of the only
warriors of my kind to leave that place alive; but the Alfar had
hundreds held back on that mountain. I knew, then, they would
harry us to extinction . . .*

My hand moved down Blondie's arm, wanting more.

Images of women, children, things . . . a sea of emotion flooded over me . . . fighting, loving, quiet moments with friends, the deaths and births of so many loved ones . . .

Blondie moved my hands to her back, all new sensations and images pouring through me as she lifted my shirt, gently, letting my skin press against hers.

An assault of images, sensations, a jumble being processed slowly – too slowly – by this brain . . . so much experienced, so much learned . . . so many terrible fashions endured . . . Weeping, I called out for those who were gone as, laughing, I relived that first time we drank together, or joked together, only to have that person fade in time and space, my only constants were my loneliness, my mission, and my tattoos . . .

So hungry for her kisses, the pretty thing, so sad and so alone for so long . . . but now I've got you, don't I, pretty . . . hands searching, hers finding, yes, sweet thing, yes, harder, yes, lips so small, yes, her taste, yesyesyesyes . . .

Only then did I realize that I had my hand on a tattoo of a splay-legged woman, her thighs spread across Blondie's pubic bone. My mouth was on the Original's, and I didn't know whose pleasure I was experiencing – mine or hers, with the woman who inspired the tat. I'm also pretty sure I wasn't supposed to be making out with the woman underneath me.

Anyan's a dog for one night and you've already got your hands down someone else's pants, my virtue clucked.

My libido took a bow.

Chapter Fifteen

Overwhelmed by sensations, I pulled away from Blondie, sitting up. I discovered I was straddling her, my shirt rucked up nearly to my neck from where I'd been pressing myself against her. She had her hands on my ass, and didn't look too upset about the contact.

'I'm sorry,' I said, throwing my leg over her so that I was sitting on the ground instead of on top of her. 'That was intense.'

'I've lived a long time,' was her only reply, her lips twitching in a little smirk as she sat up and then reached for her shirt and pulled it back on.

'Still, I shouldn't have . . . Did we make out?'

'Well . . . sort of,' she said, winking at me. 'But don't worry, I won't tell. Unless you want me to. And it was just because of the tats . . . People sometimes have strong reactions.'

'They're . . .' I began, reaching out my fingers to stroke over a little bit of tattoo tracing out of Blondie's sleeve. But I stopped myself. 'Amazing,' I finished.

'And chicks dig 'em,' she quipped.

'No, seriously,' I insisted, trying to worm past her defenses. I'd been immersed in her, nearly literally, and I knew she wasn't merely the lovable rogue she pretended to be. All thoughts of mistrusting Blondie fled. 'They're amazing. And you're amazing. The life you've lived . . . and then to do what you did, with the tattoos. To include those particular memories. So clever.' I wasn't quite up to full brain power, all my blood and attention having been spread out to other areas.

'You're pretty incredible yourself,' she said, sitting forward and kissing me boldly on the lips. For a second, I responded, still wrapped up in her memories and the feel of her against me.

But then I drew back. Anyan was still inside that damned dog, hopefully. And now was not the time.

'I can't,' I said. 'I'm sorry.' I realized I meant it as I said it.

'Not feeling the "another woman" thing?' she asked.

'Um, no. That's definitely not it,' I admitted. 'But there's Anyan. And there's . . .' I motioned toward the glyph in my best Vanna White impression.

'Mmm, yes. There is that. As for Anyan . . . maybe he likes to share.' With that, Blondie turned back to our mirrored mystery.

Sharing is caring! chimed my libido. I stored that thought away to ponder later. And by ponder, I meant fantasize. But for right now . . .

''Kay, we still have to touch this thing,' Blondie said.

'Agreed,' I said, going along with her change of subject. 'Who wants to do it?'

Blondie pursed her lips and scratched at her tattooed neck. For a second, I itched to touch those tats one more time . . .

Instead, I sighed. 'I'll do it.'

It made sense. She was stronger than me, and she was the only one who could beat Phaedra to become the champion. If anyone was expendable, it was me.

My fingers trembling, I reached toward the sigil. Blondie watched me, a small smile on her lips as if she'd won something.

'If it does turn me into a seal,' I warned her smug expression, 'I'm coming after you. Slowly, and ponderously, but I am coming after you.'

She grinned in reply, and I reached forward. Then we both jumped away as the glyph flared with my finger's brief contact. For a second, it glowed as if lit by the sun. My heart was pounding in my chest and I knew I was grinning maniacally in sheer panic . . . only to watch as nothing happened and the glyph went cold and dead before us. So I reached forward again, to touch the sigil once more . . . And again it flared, power flooding the cavern. This time I was ready for it, however, and I kept my hand where it was.

Only the sigil *still* faded, despite my holding my fingers in place. It did the same thing when I touched it again, and again – flaring to life, but then dying.

'Okay,' Blondie said. 'It liked the touch. But then it must want you to do something.'

'Like what?'

'I dunno. But it's as though it gets bored when you stand there.'

I started pressing random places on the sigil, but everywhere I touched just made it do the exact same thing – flare, and then go out. Meanwhile, it never stopped changing shape, each sinuous form flowing into the next, led by that line's serpentlike head . . .

Led by the head . . . my brain echoed as a chill ran down my spine. Concentrating on the sigil I watched as it morphed, trying to get a bead on what I wanted . . .

Darting my hand forward, I touched exactly what I'd wanted to touch – the head of the snake. My body jolted as I made contact and the sigil flared again, but this time a thrill of power arced through my body.

'That's it,' I said. 'It's the sigil . . . it wants us to . . .'

'What?' Blondie said, as if urging me on. I flicked my eyes at the tone of her voice. 'Wants us to what?'

Frankly, I wasn't sure, so I reached out my fingers to try to touch that snaking serpent's head again. The sigil flared; I felt the same shock. But this time I tried to keep pace with it. As long as I did so, the sigil continued to flare, and power continued to surge up my arm. There was just one problem . . .

'Shit! It's too fast!' I kicked the wall in frustration. 'Motherfucker!'

'Here, let me,' Blondie said, taking my forearm in a firm grip.

Then she started to move my arm. Her own movements were quick and sure and confident. In fact, they were very confident.

A little too confident, I thought.

Her grip strong on my arm, Blondie piloted my hand like she was Helen Keller reading Braille. There was nothing hesitant about her movements, and my heart sank.

I trusted her, I thought, fearing once again that my trust had been for naught. *But what about everything I saw in her tattoos?* I questioned. I felt like I'd seen into her soul, and it was a good one.

She does *know more than she's telling us*, I thought. *But that doesn't mean she's evil.* With that, I squashed down my doubts and just went with her movements. I had to ride this bronco to the end and see where it took me.

Meanwhile, my Blondie-guided fingers flew across the sigil as the light grew brighter and brighter. But I was touching only the right side of the mirror, totally avoiding the left. Finally, it settled into half of an ornate shape that would have looked a bit like a stylized Celtic version of a Christmas wreath, had the other side been filled in. Meanwhile, the glow increased, and for a very uncomfortable moment I was reminded of the light right before the crystal cave's glyph exploded. Just as my heart really started to pound in fear, Blondie completed exactly half, and the sigil went supernova as the Original's free hand shot forward to grab mine.

* * *

'Where the hell are we?' I asked, coughing on the wet air surrounding us. Thick mist walled us in, seemingly as solid as the cavern in which we'd just been standing.

'Beats me,' Blondie said, her eyes squinting as she tried to peer through the murk.

But before I could ask any more stupid questions, or some of the very *not*-stupid questions I needed to ask Blondie, the mist before us parted like the curtains of a stage, revealing four translucent figures.

They looked like ghosts, or like fake holograms in movies. There was no attempt to make them seem 'real', and yet I had no doubt that the four people had once existed.

'Melichor,' Blondie spat, pointing at the tall, imperiously bearded man standing on the far left. 'An Alfar king famous for his power and his lack of emotion.' Despite being pointed at and discussed like a villain in a movie, Melichor gave no indication he could hear us.

'Tatiana, his consort,' Blondie said, pointing at the woman of medium height and build standing next to the cruel king. 'Equally powerful, but her cruelty took the form of expedience. She'd do anything to win.'

I couldn't help but think of Orin and Morrigan. *Some things never change.*

'Beside them are their respective second-in-commands: Glynda, a woman whom you never wanted to cross. She hid her passion for cruelty behind a mask of steel. And Straif. Not too bright, but insanely strong, he'd do his mistress's bidding no matter what she asked of him.'

'And these are all Alfar?' I whispered, waiting for the illusions to move, or blast us into oblivion, or something. But nothing happened.

'Ancient Alfar. From just after the Schism.'

'You mean just after the different factions were created?'

'Yes.'

'And what I saw in your tattoo . . . Before that they were like you?'

'Yes. Before that, there were only us. Hence the title "Original".'

'But how did they change? What was the Schism, exactly?' I asked, feeling like I'd learned more substantive information about my new world in this past day than I had in the past six months.

She looked down at me, her face curiously blank. 'You'll touch that tattoo soon enough, babydoll,' she said, as her fingers found what looked like a large bull's horn right below her left ear. 'But for now, let's figure out what the hell is going on.'

'Speaking of which,' I said, confident I could ask what I needed to ask since we'd been standing there gabbing and so far absolutely nothing had happened. 'We need to talk.'

'Again?' Blondie asked.

'Again,' I said, diving right into the truth. 'The way you traced over that glyph . . . you knew what it was supposed to be, didn't you?'

Blondie paused. 'Um . . . I haven't been entirely honest with you,' she began.

I interrupted her with a frustrated sigh. 'That's the second time you've said that,' I said, testily. 'I was really starting to feel like I knew you, and now this. How can I trust you if you hide things from me? And why do I sound like I'm the love interest in a bad made-for-TV movie?'

'I know,' Blondie said. 'And I'm sorry. I'm not used to working with other people.'

'It isn't hard,' I interrupted her, huffily. '*You* tell *us* what you know about the problem, and then we all conquer it together. Rather than doling out information like dog treats. Now, what is it you didn't tell me *this* time?'

'There's not a lot. It's just that I know the glyph.' With that she stopped, as if my curiosity would be satisfied with such a total nonanswer.

'So *how* do you know the glyph?' I prompted.

'It's common?' she offered. I just stared. 'It's complicated,' Blondie said, eventually. 'But I swear to you, it's not that I'm hiding something that puts you in danger. I have a source.'

'So, who is it?' I asked.

'It's someone I can't talk about. Someone very old. Someone I'm not supposed to have contact with.'

I frowned. 'Why? Is it like a double agent?'

After a pause, Blondie nodded. 'In a way, yes. You could definitely say that . . . a double agent.'

I wasn't entirely satisfied, but at the same time I kept remembering touching her tattoos. I *trusted* her, damn it. I felt I'd seen what she was made of. And I also really liked her.

I want to trust her, I realized. *For better or worse, I want her to be a friend.*

So instead of arguing, or pursuing more answers, I merely nodded.

Blondie smiled at me, clearly relieved. But I shook my finger at her.

'You had better be telling me everything. I'm sick of being one step behind you. If there's something I need to know, I wanna know now.'

'I know,' she said. 'And I'm sorry.'

I nodded my head, accepting her apology. Then, as one, we turned back toward the silent, ghostlike figures. Blondie took my hand, again, and together we stepped forward. As if we'd flipped a switch, the four figures before us started to move.

There was no sound, but there didn't need to be. The mist behind the huge statues took shape to create a translucent, sinister landscape. Behind the figures, swirls of mist came together to become a giant beast, which looked like the love child of an angler fish and a giant squid. Tentacles and teeth and weird dangling eyes were everywhere as the monster churned in front of us, a writhing mass of fog-hued flesh.

Calmly, majestically, the translucent figures of the long-dead Alfar confronted the beast, and we watched as they bested it after what had to be a vastly abridged version of a fight. While the creature, lashing and gyrating, fought what looked like itself, the Alfar calmly dispatched spell after spell. Eventually, one of the ghosts laid down, obviously slain in the battle, but it was done in the same way one lays down to begin doing crunches at the gym. Shortly thereafter, the creature also stopped moving, as if its strings had been cut. It slowly settled to earth, but its tentacles were wrapped around a glowing sphere, as if it were dragging the sphere down with it to its grave. The Alfar tried to wrest the sphere away from the creature's limbs, but to no avail. Eventually, they gave up and used their combined power to bury the creature and its sphere in the sea, before covering it all up with land. Upon this natural prison, they set locks . . . the very sigils we'd found here and beneath Gus's house. We watched as four sigils floated up into the air above where the creature was bested, and then flew down to nestle in various places on an otherwise unreconizable landscape that appeared under them. Then the four Alfar figures turned to face us, again, raising their arms with their palms facing outward.

'No trespassing,' Blondie whispered, translating.

'Or you're all fucked,' I added. My own little spin on the sitch.

We studied the four figures, one still fallen, standing in front of us.

'So they captured the creature and locked it away, along with its power. They tried to get the power from the creature, but it didn't work and they gave up. I'm assuming that's the power that can make a champion?' I asked, making sure I'd gotten everything. When Blondie nodded, I continued. 'But what was it? It looks like a kraken.'

'Krakens are smaller, with more eyes,' Blondie said, and I got a weird feeling of déjà vu at her mention of eyes. Before I could explore that sensation, the Original kept talking. 'But it *is* something very ancient. Probably the most ancient thing here besides the Earth herself. Very big, very powerful, and very prone to destruction.'

'So what happens if it wakes up?' I asked, pretty sure I didn't want to know the answer.

'Well, first of all, we'll lose much of what it's sleeping under.'

'Which is?'

'A large chunk of the Eastern Seaboard.'

I gulped, staring at her. 'And?'

'Isn't that enough?'

'I meant, like, is it evil? Will it destroy even more stuff than just where it's sleeping?'

Blondie frowned. 'Evil doesn't matter in this case. It's just too big for this world.'

'So how do we destroy it if it wakes up?'

'I dunno. I dunno if it *can* be destroyed. If all that lot could do was contain it . . .' she said, pointing at the ghostly ancient Alfar.

'Shit,' I repeated.

'Yep. But if it makes you feel any better, we know how to unlock the actual locks,' Blondie said.

'Great, because that's what we need. To unlock them.'

She gave me the stink eye. I sighed.

'Seriously,' I said. 'Do you really think it's the best idea to unlock the sigils?'

'If one of Phaedra's lot does it, and gets all that power . . .' Blondie replied, her expression grim.

'Yes, I know,' I said. 'Champion, shmampion. "There will be only one." Yadda, yadda, yadda. So how do we unlock them?'

'Finish the sigil, obviously. At the halfway point we got the handy-dandy instructional video. The full glyph must open it up for us. Ready to try it?'

'No,' I said.

'Good,' she said. 'Let's go up there and unlock us some Alfar glyph action.'

I gave her a long look.

'You sure about this?'

'Sometimes we have to confront things head-on, Jane.' The way she'd said that again made it sound like she knew more than she said she did . . . like she was trying to warn me of something.

I sighed. 'Did your double agent tell you this?'

'Nope. Everyone knows that sometimes the bull needs to be grabbed by the horns,' Blondie said. Then she laughed, a little maniacally.

My brain wasn't convinced still, but I could see that Blondie thought she knew what she was doing. And there was something else: even though my brain disagreed with the present course of action, my gut felt like it was the right thing to do.

Just like your gut trusts the Original, my brain responded sourly, not at all happy at being trumped by my instincts.

'Fine. On yer head be it,' I said, in my best pirate voice, before backing up a step to give Blondie room to work. But instead of stepping up to finish the sigil, she motioned me forward.

'It has to be your hand,' she said. When I frowned, she pulled a face. ''Cuz you did the first half, dork.'

I shrugged, and raised my arm. She grasped my wrist again,

right where she had before, and began tracing the other half of the sigil. It took her a while to get the knack of it again, but soon her finger was twisting over the glyph. Power flared, died, and flared again – this time illuminating the full wreath shape of the ancient Alfar lock – but still nothing happened.

'What the hell?' she said, her turn to kick the wall. 'I know I'm doing it right, but it won't work!'

'Maybe it's a different key,' I said, soothingly. 'Maybe that's not the way it's done.'

'Or,' she said, as the color drained from her face, 'it's already unlocked.'

I felt my own face fall. 'Shit. Graeme and Fugwat.'

'The Grays said they came down here.'

'But for fifteen minutes. We've been down here well over an hour and we've just figured the thing out. How the hell could they have done it so quickly?'

'Cuz they knew, babydoll. They've known all along. I've got my own memories, and some very old friends, but they have access to Alfar knowledge that we don't. Now put your game face on and up shields,' she said, putting her hand out toward me.

'Why?' I asked. But I raised defenses anyway, and then grabbed her fingers in mine.

'Because I think we're about to be in the middle of a showdown.' And with that, Blondie apparated us into another dark space. Before I could get my bearings, a powerful mage ball clipped the edge of my shields, shoving me toward the Original.

'I said your game face, not your Girl Scout face,' she warned, spinning me around to face our opponent.

Phaedra didn't look at all happy to see us.

Chapter Sixteen

We were in the crystal cavern beneath where Gus's rock had stood, but everything had changed. The crystals were cold and dead, and the mirrorlike glyph surface was static now, showing the same fully traced Celtic-knot-wreathlike pattern that we'd last seen underneath Jason's former home. Phaedra had her full contingent with her: the two harpies, Kaya and Kaori; Graeme, her rapist incubus; and Fugwat. The spriggan was picking his slablike teeth with a broken-off crystal.

For about five seconds, there was quiet as Phaedra and her lot stood gaping at us. When I suddenly felt her power swell to match Blondie's, I resisted the urge to fall face first on the floor. Instead, I swiftly wove my shields through the Original's. Her odd power signature made it more difficult than with other elementals, but it just took a little more nudging. Once our shields were set, I started surging power through them, and not a second too soon.

Blondie, that impetuous scamp, was the first to fire: a barrage of mage balls so fierce I could actually feel heat coming off them. Phaedra's lot pulled in tight, reinforcing each other's defenses as their leader launched her own attack.

On the one hand, watching an Alfar and an Original hammer at each other was interesting. The amount of power was breathtaking, as was the creativity of their pummeling.

But on the other hand, it was just that: pummeling. And raw strength versus raw strength – while awe-inspiring at first – gets a mite boring after a while. Even though I had no doubt the Original was stronger than Phaedra, the bald little Alfar had enough of her people with her to negate most of her weakness. Numbers helped make us evenly matched, which meant witnessing this fight was a bit like watching those plastic robots box, without the promise of one of their little plastic robot heads ever popping up.

In other words, this could take forever. And I hadn't brought any snacks.

On second thought, I realized, looking around. *Phaedra and Blondie might have the stamina to make this last forever . . . but I don't think the cave does.*

Between the Alfar and the Original, enough force was flying about that the walls of the cave were starting to shake. I used my own power to increase the mass of the shields over our heads, so that falling crystals wouldn't drill through our skulls.

That would be uncomfortable, I thought as a huge crystal bounced off the shields right above my forehead and hit the ground a few feet away. *Probably as uncomfortable as getting completely crushed*, I added, as more crystals came raining down as the cave walls shook harder.

The two fighters had noticed the effect they were having on the cavern as well. In a game of supernatural chicken, they met each other's eyes as they forced their power toward one another. That power crashed together and then streamed upward, causing a crack to form in the ceiling of the cave. Neither one would relent, however, and the power forced that crack up and open. Daylight shone through as I used my own power, as did Phaedra's cronies, to shore up the earth around the crack before it could collapse in on us.

I felt a rise in my belly – that familiar feeling of resentment at always using my own energies to clean up the messes made by more powerful creatures. Luckily, however, I wasn't the only creature who had had enough.

'You're too late!' Phaedra was shouting behind the wall of magic her people had erected in front of her. 'I've already unlocked the second glyph, and the next two will fall shortly! I *will* claim the prize!'

'If you can find 'em,' Blondie grunted, forcing even more magic toward Phaedra as I pulled frantically at my own power to keep the walls around us from coming down.

'It's only a matter of time,' Phaedra said, unwittingly admitting that she did not, indeed, know where the other two sigils were. 'We have resources you cannot imagine,' the evil little Alfar cackled. 'And soon you'll know what it is to suffer.'

Been there, done that, I thought, as Blondie frowned.

'Who's "we", anyway, elf?' the Original asked, using the Alfar's most hated term after 'halfling'.

Phaedra laughed even more maniacally, as the two harpies sidled behind their group.

'Wouldn't you like to know?' the Alfar asked, quite rhetorically.

'Yes, we would,' I muttered, keeping an eye on Kaya and Kaori.

'Um, duh?' Blondie said, loud enough for Phaedra's ears. 'We *do* want to know. That's why I asked.' And with that she winged a few more mage balls at the Alfar, as if in punishment for asking stupid questions.

'All you need to know is that you should be glad Rockabill will not exist for much longer. For when our forces rise, you will all be slaves.' Phaedra's blood-red eyes – extra large underneath her shaved pate – met mine. 'Well, except for those of you we kill for being stains,' she finished.

'I like to consider myself more of a smudge,' I called back, lobbing a few mage balls of my own to punctuate my sentences. Just because I was letting the Original do her thing didn't mean I was weak anymore. And I looked forward to teaching Phaedra that particular lesson.

'You are something to be wiped clean, and I will enjoy being that dishcloth,' Phaedra hissed at me, her posture menacing.

'What the hell are you *talking* about?' I asked. 'You just called yourself a dishcloth, you idiot. That was the worst villainous threat I've ever heard.'

Blondie chortled. Phaedra fumed.

'It's not a threat!' the Alfar shouted. 'It is your fate! To be crushed!'

'And lemme guess . . . You're the rolled-up newspaper that will do the crushing?' I said.

'Or the big dirty boot?' suggested Blondie. 'The boot in the face? The brute, brute heart of a brute like you?'

Clearly not having read her Sylvia Plath, Phaedra could only fume.

'That's enough,' came Graeme's voice through the darkness. 'While we'd love to stay and play,' he said, touching the edge of my shields with that dark mind, 'we have things to do.' And then the incubus unleashed his thoughts: a paradoxically gentle touch of darkness that made me break out in a cold sweat.

The touch spoke more clearly than words: *I can get to you anywhere.*

Keeping their shields with them, Phaedra and Graeme let the two harpies launch them into the air. I watched them go, Graeme's eyes stayed on mine as they flew through the huge crack in the cavern's ceiling. I shuddered when I could finally look away.

'We need to work on your emotional shields,' Blondie said,

in a distractingly conversational tone that I appreciated. 'And we will, very shortly. But right now, we've got a playdate.'

Fugwat stared at us, stupid and abandoned, from his corner of the cavern.

It sucks to be the henchman no one cares about, I mused, wondering just what Blondie would do to him first.

'I don't know anything!' the spriggan sobbed, for about the fortieth time. And, once again, I heard that horrible crunching sound come from underneath Blondie's boot.

'Tell me everything you know, or I'll break even more,' my sadistic friend shouted, raising her foot in the air menacingly above where Fugwat crouched.

When he only whimpered, she went ahead and crushed another of the beautiful crystals she'd apparated for the spriggan's benefit.

Who knew Fugwat torture would cost the lives of so much bling? I mused, watching as Blondie melted down a cluster of sparkly bangles with a wisp of her fierce power.

The spriggan sobbed at the sight, but didn't change his tune.

'I don't think this canary is going to sing,' I suggested, gently. 'And somewhere there's a Claire's whose stock is seriously being depleted.'

'Fuck,' said Blondie, kicking the wall against which the spriggan leaned. Then she turned to me. 'Do you think he's telling the truth?' she asked. I considered the question. On the one hand, Fugwat had been really shaken up after being left by his gang. He obviously hadn't assumed he was as expendable as Phaedra thought him to be. And if Phaedra thought he was expendable, he probably didn't know anything. On the other hand, Fugwat might not know what he knew. In other words, he might have picked up on things, or overheard things, that would make sense to us, if not him.

'I have no idea,' I said, finally. 'I don't know a lot about interrogating prisoners, to be honest. I took the elective in creative writing that semester, instead of Torture 101.'

'Shit,' she swore, again. 'I really don't want to have to go in—'

'Go in?' I asked, sharply. While the bling torture had been amusing, I wanted no part of actual torture.

'Mentally,' she replied, grimly.

'Oh,' I said. 'Like what—'

'Graeme does? Yes.'

'You can do that?'

'I can. But unlike Graeme, I'm really good at it. So I can do what I did to you in that soda shop.'

I nodded, remembering. The first time I'd met Blondie she'd made me see all sorts of vines and stuff grow out of the darkness. All when, in reality, I'd been standing in a brightly lit ice-cream parlor.

'Which is not invasive at all,' she finished, as I nodded again. For what she'd done to me had felt outside of my mind, rather than in it. I knew she hadn't been party to my thoughts, or anything like that.

'But you can do more than that?' I prompted.

'Oh, yeah. Like I said, I can do what I did to you, which is basically a party trick. Or I can go in. Way in. I can pull whatever I want out of your mind. But that's more like what Graeme does. That's more like—'

'A violation,' I said, for her.

'Yes,' she replied. 'And not something I like doing.'

'I can understand that,' I said, fulfilling my requirement for Understatement of the Week.

'But if Fugwat knows something, and we don't get it out of him, and this whole part of the country gets wiped out—'

'Then we'll be responsible.'

'Yep.'

I came up beside her and took her hand in mine. 'You'll have to do it,' I said, hating to put that on her, hating to make her responsible. But she's the only one who could be sure Fugwat was telling the truth.

'I know,' she said, and I felt her squeeze my fingers with her own. 'But it sucks. Sometimes I wish I could go back to hunting and gathering. Life was simpler back then.'

'Betcha it wasn't,' I said, resisting the urge to tweak her wee button nose. 'Life is usually difficult. It's just about keepin' on, keepin' on. For which we will need the Eastern Seaboard.'

She snorted. 'True, Ms True. Very true. Now stand aside. This could get ugly.'

'Nope,' I said, keeping my grip on her fingers. 'I'm with you for this. We're doing it together.'

The smile she gave me at hearing my words warmed the cockles of my heart, and also made my palms sweat a little. It suddenly occurred to me that, secret keeping or no, I was well on my way to developing a girl crush. Of which the makers of Selkies Gone Wild would, undoubtedly, be happy to hear.

After she took a few deep breaths, I felt the Original's power ripple out, but not in the way I was used to. This wasn't physical power; this was something totally different. That said, I couldn't really describe it, as it was so intangible. Instead, it was like a disturbance, but one that rippled my mind and my emotions rather than my hair or clothes. In other words, my physical senses weren't registering anything, but it was like a fan was blowing over my brain or my heart.

'Wow,' I breathed, opening up my senses and letting my magic touch Blondie's. On the one hand, it was interesting.

But, on the other, more devious hand, I could *almost* feel how she was doing it.

And if I can feel how she does it, I can stop Graeme in the future, I thought.

Letting my magical senses pick up everything they could, I tuned back into the scene in front of me.

If Blondie's power was wafting in on a gentle breeze over my brain, it was obviously blowing against Fugwat's like a typhoon. His face was pinched shut, his every muscle straining as if trying to physically keep out the Original's mind. But it was no use.

Suddenly, his eyes snapped open to reveal what appeared to be a vacancy, just as his face and body slumped slackly.

'Tell us what we want to know, Fugwat Spriggan, and your mind is yours again.' Blondie sounded weary, both emotionally and physically. If doing the mind mojo burned up that much of an Original's power, no wonder Graeme employed it only as a last resort.

'I told you,' the spriggan whimpered. 'I know nothing. The other two marks are still hidden.'

'How did you find the first two?' she asked.

'They were recorded. Alfar histories said where to find them. It was just a matter of getting past the gnome.'

Blondie looked at me, warning me with a small shake of her head not to let our big gnome-is-now-a-baby secret out of the bag. As if.

'You've already opened this glyph?' Blondie asked, although, by its static appearance, I was pretty sure we knew the answer.

'Yes,' was Fugwat's only response.

'And where else is Phaedra looking?' I asked, instead. Fugwat didn't answer, however, until Blondie repeated my question.

'She's got no idea,' he said. 'She's looking everywhere. But she thinks one has to be in the sea somewhere.'

'Why do you want to awaken the creature?' Blondie asked.

Fugwat whimpered, but he didn't speak. I felt the Original exert more mental force.

'Tell me. Why do you want to awaken the creature?' she repeated, brutally forcing her own mind into Fugwat's.

This time the spriggan was no match. He slumped forward even more, his eyes staring glassily. 'The dragons are awake,' he murmured. 'The white king and the red queen are mustering their forces. Phaedra says we bring the fall of Man.'

At his words, Blondie went stock still, her own eyes growing large and distant.

The dragons? I thought. *What the hell? And who are the white king and the red queen? Maybe Jarl and Morrigan? He is awfully pale, and she's got the blood of Orin on her hands.*

But before I could speculate more, I felt Blondie withdraw her power from Fugwat. She still looked discomfited, but she was obviously doing her best to appear like all was normal.

'Well, that wasn't useless,' she said. 'We know that Phaedra's as stuck as we are, at least. So that gives us an advantage.'

'Who're the white king and red queen?' I blurted out, too curious to wait.

She frowned. 'That's not something we can discuss here. And I have to do some checking into things . . . What's happening can't be happening. I need to do some research. Can you be patient with me, Jane?'

I considered the question. I hated being left in the dark, but I did trust Blondie.

'Sure, I can be patient. As long as you promise to tell me when you find out something,' I said.

'I will. I promise. But right now, we have to take care of the here and now, in Rockabill,' Blondie said. I frowned.

'Are you sure we need to pursue this champion thing?' I asked. 'Why can't we just bury all of this?'

'What do you mean?'

'Well, if Phaedra's the issue . . . we can always just take out her and her gang.'

'I'm assuming you mean "take out" as in "dead",' not as in "Chinese food"?' she asked. I nodded, surprised at my own bloodthirstiness.

'I've considered it,' she admitted. But now we know someone is behind these attacks . . . so they'll just send more people. At least we know Phaedra, and know some of her weaknesses.'

Blondie had a good point. Even if Phaedra and her gang weren't around, it didn't make Rockabill any safer from other beings sent by the enemy.

'What if we find and destroy the glyphs? So they can't be awakened, and no one gets to be champion?' I asked.

'I don't think they want to be destroyed, as our friends learned the hard way. We could end up like Anyan and Nell. Or worse.'

'What if we don't open them, but find them and guard them?'

'For the rest of our lives? No matter what they send along to take *us* out?'

I sighed. Blondie was right. We had to find the creature and let her get the power it offered, and then she could do something about it. Which raised an interesting question.

'What will you do when you're champion?' I asked.

'What?'

'What will you do with all that power?'

She frowned. 'I dunno. I hadn't thought about it. What would you do, Jane?' Her eyes had a faraway look when she asked that question, as if she were thinking hard.

'I dunno,' I said. 'Keep it safe, I guess.' Then I frowned. 'But something has to be done about the creature, doesn't it? If it makes a champion, it's still big and buried, right? Can it still be awakened?'

'Yes, it could still be awakened. Would you kill it?'

I frowned. 'Why would I kill it? It's this ancient thing. That would be like steamrolling Pompeii.'

Blondie's eyes refocused, and she smiled at me. 'We will have to deal with that issue, but let's deal with everything else first. I like to do things by the seat of my pants: too many plans make for too many things to go wrong.'

'And we still have to locate the missing glyphs,' I started, before I was interrupted.

'The signs protect destruction,' Fugwat called from the floor in front of us. Blondie and I frowned at each other before we both looked toward him.

'The signs protect destruction,' he repeated. 'The signs protect . . .'

He continued on like that, his eyes closed and his mouth hanging, barely moving as he spoke.

'I don't think Fugwat's in the driver's seat,' I said.

'Nope.'

'The sign protects destruction,' the spriggan added, helpfully. Blondie took a step toward him, but I stopped her. I wanted to try something different from the 'smack now, ask questions later' everyone seemed to favor these days.

Instead, I moved forward to crouch in front of the spriggan.

'We know the signs protect destruction,' I said, in my calmest, most soothing voice.

'The signs protect destruction,' Fugwat replied.

'Yes,' I said. 'We got that, but—'

'The signs protect destructions.'

'Okay, but—'

'The signs protect destruction.' Clearly, Fugwat's possessor was not one to be sidetracked. The spriggan was rocking faster now, repeating 'the signs protect destruction' at an even more rapid rate. I tried to interrupt him a few more times, but it was useless. Frustrated, I grabbed Fugwat by the shoulders.

'Fine! We get it!' I shouted. 'But where are the damned signs?'

Fugwat's still-vacant gaze flicked to mine, as if something were using his eyes to study me. I resisted the urge to back away, instead meeting that blank stare with my own black eyes.

'That which is closest to your heart,' came a deep voice that sounded nothing like the spriggan's normal tones, before he collapsed in a heap at my feet.

'What?' I asked, partially of the spriggan and partially of Blondie. 'What does he mean "closest to my heart"? Why *my* heart?'

Blondie wandered over, toeing the spriggan with the tip of her boot. I was too in shock to do anything but blink as she apparated him out of the cavern with a powerful burst of magic.

'I dunno, sugarpants,' she said, her eyes shifty. 'Add that to our list of mysteries.'

'Where'd you send him?' I asked, inspired by the part of my brain not reeling at what Fugwat's possessor had just said.

'Abu Dhabi,' she replied.

'Really?'

'Yep.'

'Huh. Maybe he can hang out with Nermal or Odie,' I said.

'While I appreciate that we're on the same page with the Garfield references,' she said, taking me by the shoulders and turning me to face her, 'right now we've got to dig down deep and find out what's closest to that pretty little heart of yours. Before Phaedra's lot does it with a spoon.'

Thanks for that image, I thought, shuddering. *Too bad I've got no idea what that thing meant.*

Chapter Seventeen

For the first time ever, five people were sitting around my battered old kitchen table and *not* playing poker. My father, the usual poker culprit, was out with his own friends, having a 'man's night' down at the Sty. Nowadays that meant sitting around the table with cheeseburgers as they discussed their latest medical ailments. I still couldn't get over my relief that my dad now had only typical, age-related joint aches to complain about, rather than a genetically flawed heart.

Unfortunately, I still hadn't had a chance to celebrate with him. Blondie had apparated us directly from the cavern underneath Gus's rock to my cove, where I'd had a quick swim to recharge, and then to my house, where we'd rounded up the troops. Currently sitting around my kitchen table were Trill – cradling baby Nell – Caleb, Iris, Blondie, and me. Oh, and Anyan, who was underneath the table, trying to sniff everyone's crotch.

What I wouldn't give for a rolled-up newspaper, I thought, suppressing a yawn. We'd been going for almost a day at this point, and I was starting to feel it. *But at least someone had the good sense to make bacon*. I licked at a few greasy crumbs of a bacon sandwich still clinging to my fingers. *All war efforts need the warming effects of salty pork fat to keep their wheels turning*.

'Um, Earth to Jane. Are you with us?' Blondie's sharp voice cut through my reverie.

I looked at her, and then dropped my eyes pointedly at the uneaten strip of bacon on her plate. She sighed, and then pushed her plate toward me. I quickly began eating her bribe before she could change her mind. Or give it to the dog.

Who gives away bacon*?* I wondered. *Originals are weird.*

'Selkies,' I heard her mumble, before taking a deep breath. 'Anyway, we were asking you if there were any other places that were close to your heart, Jane.'

'Where've you checked, again?' I asked. After my swim, I just might have fallen asleep for an hour on my ratty old couch while we waited on everyone to arrive. Blondie had been busy checking out the places I could list for her off the top of my head, so I enjoyed a wee catnap. Only to awake to the non-ghest barghest licking my face like I had Alpo hidden in my cheeks.

Blondie sighed. 'We've checked where Jason, Nick, and Nan have their memorial stones, and where their ashes were buried. We've probed the hell out of your house, and Anyan's. We've tried your friends' houses, and we've even tried Read It and Weep.'

'And you got nothing?'

'We got nothing.'

Hmmm, I puzzled, as my brain yawned. *I wish I had more bacon . . .* Then I thought of the most obvious thing ever.

'Did you check the cove?' I asked. Clearly that was the place closest to my heart.

'That was the first place I looked,' Blondie replied. 'While you were swimming.'

Iris nodded. 'Everyone knows your obsession with the cove.'

'It's not an obsession . . . It's a healthy relationship. The cove gives me pleasure. I keep her sand combed. It works for everyone.'

'Uh-huh,' Iris said, patting my hand.

'There's one thing that makes no sense,' said Caleb. 'Jane's been alive for only a few decades. Surely her interests can't have dictated where these sigils are buried.'

'No, it's got to be something that's a coincidence. Something that Jane happens to like and that's also where one of the glyphs is buried,' Blondie said.

'How do we even know to trust this voice?' Iris interrupted. 'I mean, all it's done is warn us, in a way that's really scary.'

'Is there a friendly way to warn about the destruction of a big chunk of the continent?' asked Trill.

'I think what Iris is saying,' said Caleb, always the peace-maker, 'is that those "warnings" could just as well have been threats, or bait. Maybe whoever is doing them is leading us on a wild goose chase.'

Blondie frowned. 'Were any of the other places close to your heart?' she asked me.

'I've never even been to Gus's rock, but obviously Jason's house was very close to my heart,' I answered.

'So we have one connection and one nonconnection,' Blondie said. 'Which leaves us with nothing.'

'Are there any other things that connect the two places?' I asked.

'Well . . . they were both homes,' Iris said.

'Both built *under* homes,' I said.

'Actually, had houses built over them,' Blondie corrected.

I chewed my lower lip as I thought. This whole conversation was starting to sound very familiar . . .

'But one was the house of a mortal family. The other was the rock of a stone spirit. Both homes, but still very different,' Blondie argued.

'Actually, Nell and I lived where that house stood, too,' Trill said, still rocking the baby in her arms.

'When?' Blondie asked, sharply.

'Hundreds of years ago. Right before Nell bonded to this land. And come to think of it, so did Russ.'

'Who's Russ?' Blondie asked.

'He's a really old nahual,' I answered. 'He's been retired for a few years as a family pet. A dachshund.'

'Why isn't he around? Why haven't I met him?' she demanded. Apparently She Who Keeps Secrets didn't like being left in the dark about something.

Iris sighed. 'Poor Russie isn't doing well these days. He rarely goes outside anymore.'

'But he lived where the Grays did?'

'He definitely built the house that stood on the property, prior to this last one being built. And, actually, I think he might have built that second house, too,' Trill answered, thinking. 'No, he definitely built that one, as well. He's the one who sold it to Nick and Nan. There were some other folks interested, including quite a few of our kind. But Russ wanted to keep the sale within Rockabill, to Rockabill folk. He's lived here since the town was built.'

'I think that's it,' I said, starting to put it all together. 'Trill, why did you and Nell live on that spot?'

'I dunno. It was just . . . home.'

'And did other people want to live there?'

'Sure, lots. It was nice property. Easily defended, back in the day. And scenic, what with it being built on the bluff.'

'But Russ got it?' I asked.

'He was there right after us, and then Nell helped him defend his claim once she'd bonded with her Territory,' said Trill.

'Defend it from whom?' I continued.

'All sorts . . . It was like everyone wanted to live on that spot. Mostly supernaturals, but some humans, too.'

'And how did Gus find his rock? Are stone spirits born with their rocks, or what?' I asked.

'No, they find them and bond with them. Just like Nell did, only they have about one-gajillionth of a gnome's power,' Iris said.

'So Gus was drawn to his rock, just like all these creatures have been drawn to the Grays. Remember what we were talking about earlier?' I asked.

'Why Rockabill?' Blondie said, apprehension dawning.

'Exactly. Why Rockabill? We agreed something drew supes here . . . Now we're finding more specific places within Rockabill that are doing the drawing.'

'So the place that's close to your heart must be somewhere that's close to everyone's heart,' Blondie concluded.

'And that can only be one place,' I said. All faces turned toward me expectantly.

'I know you've already searched there, but it has to be the cove.' Blondie frowned at my words, but I continued. 'Think about it. My mother took me there as a child. She was drawn to it. All these years, Nell kept it glamoured. She said it was to keep out local kids, but why did she even care in the first place? She was obviously drawn to it.'

'I love it as much as Jane does,' Trill said in her oil-slick voice.

'See? We're all drawn to it. Even Anyan hangs out there.' I felt a cold nose press against my foot from where doggie-Anyan lay under the table. 'It's gotta be the place.'

'But there's nothing under it,' protested Blondie.

'So it's not underneath. It's somewhere else,' I insisted.

'But you've never seen anything, Jane. And you're there all the time,' she pointed out.

'I was never *looking*. Take me back there. I promise you we'll find the glyph.'

Blondie sighed. 'C'mon then. It's no skin off my back. And I do hope you're right.'

I made sure to grab my cell phone and slip it into my back pocket at Blondie's words. Then I felt the now-familiar gut-wrenching sensation of apparation, a second before I felt cold sand under my bare feet.

Caleb and Iris were scouring the north wall while Blondie and I scoured the south. We'd left Trill at home, as it was feeding time. As for Anyan, he was having a great time peeing on things, and then sniffing appreciatively at the wet spot.

I'm never kissing him again after this, I thought, and then fruitlessly tried not to wonder if my only opportunities to kiss Anyan again would forever be doggie kisses. *We'll find a way to change him back*, I told myself. *Even if it takes the rest of my life.*

Not that he'll live that long, my brain interjected. *As a dog, he's not using his magic. Without his magic, he'll age. And a big dog like that will live, what, twelve years if he's lucky?*

I felt my anxieties settle into grim resolve. My life was littered with too many losses. There was no way I was losing Anyan.

Confident that Anyan's cure was tied up in our victory, I searched the cove with new determination. We were all peering under rocks and into crevices. Iris sat on Caleb's shoulders so she could look higher up the walls. We backed away from each surface to try to get a big-picture view, in case there was something we could have missed.

But we found bubkes.

Swearing, I flopped down in my sand. 'I *know* it's gotta be here,' I said and groaned. 'It has to be.'

'Babydoll, I see nothing,' Iris said, squatting down next to me.

'Nor I,' said Caleb, taking a seat on the giant driftwood tree. Shaking her head to indicate her own lack of success, Iris perched next to the satyr. Anyan busied himself with peeing on the free end of the tree.

We nearly made out right there, I thought, *in that exact spot. And now it's your toilet.*

I felt like that moment encapsulated all of my pent-up frustration, and I buried my head back in the sand to glare accusingly at the stars swirling above me.

But as soon as I did so, the cool sand sucked at all my previous get-up-and-go, and though my mind was still whirling, I felt my body relaxing. The cove always had that effect on me.

The others discussed where else to look while I stewed.

It has to be here, I thought. *It has to be . . .*

Sleep now, and dream, whispered the cove, as it had in the past. *Sleep now, and dream.*

I was back with my sisters and brothers again, their peace my peace – and together we played. [*Wait, I have no sisters, no brothers . . .*] I was so happy, and they were so happy. We dreamed together and then woke to the bright blaze of the stars [*I see the stars, too*, Jane thought through half-lidded eyes, before wondering who 'Jane' was]. The stars danced into patterns that we followed with delight, until, entwined together, we fell into sleep.

[*Deep in her own mind, Jane stirred, recognizing that fall of limbs. She knew it meant comfort, a nightly ritual, but deep down she knew it wasn't her comfort, nor her ritual. But still, looking up at the sky that mimicked what lay below, she knew that pattern . . .*]

'Earth to Jane!' Blondie's sharp voice broke through my reverie. She had stood and was looming over me menacingly.

'Hmmm?' was my sleepy response.

'What are you, a narcoleptic? We need your help, so sit up and fucking pay attention,' the Original snapped at me.

Part of me bristled at her harsh tone, but the majority of me was still half asleep, almost hypnotized by my dream. I stretched in the sand, feeling my ocean call to me for a swim. And feeling an equally strong pull from the sky above.

'Jane, I said sit up,' Blondie repeated, her voice grown cold.

I stayed right where I was, peering up at the stars. 'You seem to think I'm falling asleep on the job,' I said, putting one arm behind my head like a pillow. 'But I'm not. In fact, I've solved our riddle.'

'You have?' she asked, skeptically. 'Was the answer written on the inside of your eyelids?'

'Nope,' I replied, letting her stew.

'Then where?' she said, through gritted teeth.

'The answer,' I drawled, letting her steam, 'is up there.' And with that, I pointed to the heavens.

'Up there?' she echoed, looking from the sky, down at me, and then back up at the sky as if to ask *And what have you been smoking?*

'Yep. We've been looking from the wrong angle,' I said, as I finally sat up. 'Can you grow wings big enough for two?'

'Um . . . yes? But why?'

'Because, *babydoll*, we are going for a little flight. Now come on . . . pay attention . . . Do what you need to do to get us flying.'

I watched her strip off her long-sleeved shirt, only just managing not to wink back at her nipple rings reflecting the light from our mage lights. Around her, the air shimmered with power as a set of lustrous white wings sprouted from her tattooed back. They looked as comfy and clean as two big, soft duvets, making me crave a nap even more.

She's like the love child of an angel and a drunken merchant marine, I thought, marveling at the sight. Anyan must have appreciated it too because he barked so hard at Blondie's metamorphosis that I think he choked on his own tongue.

Distracted by doggie-Anyan's shenanigans, it took me a moment, when I looked back at the Original, to realize that I was marveling at her boots as she launched herself up in the air. Without me.

Oooo she's a bitch, said my brain.

I'm so in love, thought my libido. At this point, I wasn't sure if I wanted to *be* Blondie or make out with her. *Or both*, I wondered, in what would be my philosophical conundrum of the decade.

We all watched her soar up into the heavens and then hover on a cloud of magic as her white wings scythed through the air in slow, powerful sweeps. She was up there for only a few minutes when she began flying hither and thither.

She's opening the glyph, I thought, as she must have finished, only to hover above us again.

But nothing happened. So she did it again. And then again.

Then she was landing beside me, swearing like a she-devil between hoarse pants.

'It's not fucking working!' she cursed. 'If those fucking harpies got here first, I am going to rip off their beaks and shove them up their—'

'Take me up,' I interrupted calmly. 'Let me see.'

What I didn't tell her was that every time she'd flown her complicated pattern, I'd felt a kick, but not from below us.

It came from the ocean.

For a second, it looked like she was going to turn her

tongue on me – and not in the nice way. But at the last second she paused, and then held out her arms. While Anyan bounced around us barking, I walked over to where Blondie stood.

'Caleb, Iris, you need to take Anyan and get somewhere safe,' I said, turning to where the satyr and succubus stood watching us. 'I'm not sure if this is going to work, or if we'll just set off another trap like we did before. But I think this is going to be it, and if we lose – or if we get incapacitated in any way – it's going to be up to you two to call in the Mounties.'

Caleb shuffled his hooves, and Iris looked at me, concerned. 'Are you sure?' she asked, looking to Blondie as if hoping the Original would contradict me.

'Jane's right. This is something we need to do alone.'

I frowned, looking at Blondie. *That wasn't what I said, at all*, I thought, again feeling like Blondie was talking about something I wasn't necessarily clued in to.

Iris was still frowning, but she'd taken Caleb's hand and grabbed Anyan by the scruff of his neck. Blondie's power flowed around us as she apparated my friends somewhere safe.

And then I finally experienced the stuff about which songs are written: Blondie Supermanned this ho.

Scooping me up underneath my armpits, she used a combination of her powerful wings and even stronger magics to lift us both into the night air. I resisted the urge to squeal and hide my face in her neck, à la Lois Lane. I also concentrated on not peeing myself in terror. Flying without a plane is *very scary*.

After what felt like an eternity but was really just a handful of magic-laden wing beats, we were hovering well above the cove.

And then I saw it. The intricate sigil that we'd been chasing and tracing, carved from my cove. The wreath was part of the top of the walls, with the soft sand upon which I'd lain, loved, and grieved making up the wreath's center. I'd always known the cove's walls were very thick, but because they were also very, very tall, I'd never seen them from above. In fact, when I thought about it now, the mere existence of my cove didn't make any sense. It was more like a rock fence than a normal cove. I realized we'd all been duped, and I didn't know if it was Nell's glamour, the powerful magics that must have formed the cove, or a combination of both that had made what was really a completely unnatural structure seem normal.

'Ready?' Blondie yelled in my ear, the volume carried off by all the empty space around us.

I nodded.

And with that she swept me away, tracing the sigil with the tips of her fingers or her wings, whichever was easiest. But just as before, nothing happened. At least nothing where Blondie was looking, which was beneath us.

I couldn't help but laugh as I saw the real culprit. *It's always been about you, hasn't it?* I thought.

'Do it again!' I shouted. Before she could protest and say that it was a waste of time, I continued. 'And this time, look over there!'

I was pointing at the Old Sow.

This time, as she flew her pattern, we both kept our eyes on the Atlantic. And we both saw it – piglets lit up like underwater flares in a pattern that could only be one thing.

The last glyph.

When Blondie stopped flying, they stayed lit for about ten seconds, and then they went out.

'Fuck,' she said. 'It's a double lock. Yeah, there are four glyphs, but the third unlocks the presence of the fourth. Goddamn Alfar,' she panted.

'Are you going to be okay?' I shouted, remembering what she'd said about flying. 'You'll have to make a few more circuits so I can see to unlock the last glyph!'

'I'll fly, keeping them lit,' she replied grimly, winging me over to the water. 'And you swim.' I nodded, understanding that I was the obvious choice for this mission.

And then she dropped me, clothes and all, into my ocean.

Chapter Eighteen

It was one thing to see the pattern of lit-up piglets from above, but it was another thing to be among them, at ocean level. At that moment, I knew what it felt like to be that apocryphal squirrel in the Christmas tree: lights all around me, turning randomly on and off.

Only this Christmas tree has swirling branches that will kill you if you get too close.

Even on the outer edge of the Sow, where I was treading water, I could feel her power. I'd been told that the whirlpool had been tempestuous lately, and people hadn't exaggerated. Normally I enjoyed my jaunts through the piglets, but even at this outer edge I had to keep my shields toward maximum to keep from getting sucked up into one like a dust bunny by a Hoover.

And I'm going to have to go way farther in, I thought, watching as a piglet placed alarmingly close to the Sow herself blazed at me briefly.

Thankfully, as I didn't really fancy getting pulled apart by my favorite water feature, I had no idea where to start. Unfortunately, however, I also knew that Blondie's flying a repeated pattern above the Cove would attract attention. Either she was unglamoured and being seen by everyone, including the bad guys, *or* she was glamouring the shit out of herself and attracting the attention of anything remotely magical in a fifteen-mile radius.

Which means time is of the essence, and I have to try something, I thought, swimming toward one of the lights. I felt a surge of power coming from it, but it ebbed before I could reach it, and I didn't see the next light pop up till I turned around. But by then it was too late.

I waited till another piglet lit up close to me, and then I used my mojo to propel me forward. Again, I felt that pull of magic, but again I was too late.

There has to be a better way to do this, I thought. Just then the piglet next to me blazed, along with that same signature pulse of power. Suddenly, I knew what I had to do.

Well, libido, said my brain to its most exasperating enemy, *you've always favored things that pulse. Now is your time to shine.*

My libido bowed to its sensei, and I closed my eyes as I put out my magical feelers.

Left, I felt, as I moved toward the power tracking over my skin. It was more than a little crazy to be swimming around the fifth largest whirlpool in the world with my eyes closed, but – similar to Peter Parker – I had to trust my selkie senses. That didn't mitigate the buffeting I was getting, though, as I neared the source of that magical pulsing.

Right, came the next set of instructions borne to me on the ocean current, just before the buffeting became too much. This one was close. *Then left . . .* far away this time . . . *have to motor . . .*

The power called and I answered, zigzagging across the periphery of the Sow, weaving and darting. Sometimes I wasn't fast enough and I'd have to start over, this time putting more mojo into my swimming. I drew from the ocean even as I did so, and the very pulses of power that I followed crept under my skin. Their force was so potent that, despite the amount of energy I was expending, my reserves were more than full.

Straight ahead . . . now left . . . now right . . . back, and hurry . . . back again . . . right . . . As I got better at the game, the pulses grew faster, more powerful, letting me know I was on the right track.

The game was also drawing me closer and closer to the Sow. Every pattern we'd traced was an intricate wreath, weaving inward into a final, central point. But while sticking your finger, or your wing, into the middle of an empty circle was easy, I'd come to realize that the circle I was currently swimming had the Old Sow herself at its epicenter.

Not so easy, that.

Meanwhile, although I was doing my favorite trick of ignoring the pertinent facts of a given situation, the ocean wasn't making that easy. Despite the pull of the power bursts, the ocean herself was battling my every move. Currents pushed and pulled me, slowing me down considerably.

I'm not gonna make it like this, I realized, trying to think of a way around the water.

But then I thought about that underwater battle between Trill and that evil kappa, when we'd been investigating Iris's disappearance. That night, Trill had taught me to *use* the ocean, rather than submit to her.

It's like a metaphor for my life, I realized, as I stopped to tread water and think about the problem. *I'm always trying to work with everything, go with everything . . . I don't like to shake things up or fight or assert myself. But being submissive is a luxury I can't afford. Not right now.*

Right now, I need to take what I need, without apologies.

And with that thought, I shut my eyes again. But when I felt a pulse of power from my left, I didn't pull myself through the water.

This time, I told the water to take me.

Guzzling up all the swirling energies around me, I expended an equally large force, *demanding* from the water, rather than asking it – forcing it to do my bidding.

And grudgingly, eventually, the Atlantic obeyed. This time, when I sensed a target, I moved so quickly through the water it stung. The energy I was using was tremendous, and under normal circumstances even the swirling power of the Old Sow wouldn't have been enough to power me. But it was like the whirlpool had suddenly gone supernova. So much so that I could still keep my own reserves topped up while throwing around so much mojo.

Scything through the water, I felt the pace of the appearing symbols become more frenetic as I drew the sigil. Meanwhile, the spiral pulled me tighter in toward the Sow. Strengthening my shields beyond anything I'd ever done before, I could still feel the press of the water all around me. Indeed, 'pressure' was the word of the day. There was the pressure of the situation – knowing Rockabill would be destroyed if I failed; that I'd lose everyone I loved, including my father and Anyan, who would die a dog. There were the literal pressures of all that magic forcing itself into me as I forced it back out again, plus that of the ocean and the buffeting currents of the Sow and her piglets. The part of me that only ever wanted to be normal and quiet and grounded whispered to me to give up . . . to let other, more powerful and more capable beings handle the situation.

For a fraction of a second I slowed. For a fraction of a second I wanted to be the old Jane again, the one who didn't have to save the world, or at least a sizable chunk of it. Instead, I wanted that world to be normal again.

Um, Jane? asked my virtue, which was having no truck with my little pity party. *When were you ever normal?*

I almost laughed, then. I thought of my life: the losses, the joys, the secrets, the lies, the love, and the connections.

My life has never *been normal*, I realized. *And the world has never been normal. It's never been good, or just, or clear. But that doesn't mean Phaedra gets to destroy it.*

And with that thought, I took off swimming again.

This time I didn't let myself think or slow down. I didn't even allow myself to feel – I made myself into a bullet, cutting through the water toward my goal. When I got to the point I had stopped last time – near enough to the Sow to feel her strength – this time, I continued.

That last complicated loop was a challenge made nearly impossible by the push and pull of the powerful currents near the Sow's epicenter. But again I demanded from the ocean, and again she eventually acceded, although the struggle was fierce. When I finally reached the last lit-up piglet, I knew what was coming.

But that didn't mean my heart wasn't in my throat as I felt one final pulse of power from my left. Right in the center of the Sow herself.

What I did next was my patented combination of both the logical and absurd. I imagined myself in a powerful shield that resembled a hamster ball, and I rolled myself toward the heart of the whirlpool. It took everything I had in me to push my shields forward, the Sow dancing and swirling like a column of light before me. Turning and turning in the gyre of the Sow, all I could think of was Yeats's 'Second Coming'. Anarchy was threatening; monsters like Phaedra and Graeme had been loosed upon my world. I thought of Yeats's warning: *The best lack all conviction, while the worst / Are full of passionate intensity.*

I might not be the best, my virtue thought, panting as I strained forward, both my physical and magical muscles pushed to their limits, *but I'll show that damned Alfar a thing or two about conviction.*

And hopefully not about drowning, my libido added, just as my little hamster ball of shields butted itself up directly against the Sow. If I thought I'd faced opposition before, nothing could compare to that edge of the Sow. It felt like I'd butted up against a brick wall. I threw my magic into high gear, chanting Yeats's first stanza to myself like a litany while imagining Phaedra's face – so definitely the worst, with her passionate capacity for hate – as my target, smack dab in the middle of the whirlpool. After a strangled moment, in which my every nerve – both physical and magical – felt like it had gone up in flame, the wall began to give under my onslaught. Pushing harder, I forced my hamster ball forward until the wall crumbled before me. The blazing core of the Sow rose to meet me.

Reaching my hand forward, I parted my magic to touch that pulsing glow.

Magic boomed around me, so strong and fast that it took me a moment to realize my shields were dissolving despite me. I tried to throw them back up, but the Sow reached for me before I could.

Well fuckerdoodles, I thought, ridiculously calmly, considering. *I am going to die.*

But I didn't die, because the Sow wasn't trying to kill me. Instead, she pulled me in and cradled me. The water swirling just a few feet in front of me was powerful enough to rip me limb from limb. But where she held me, she was gentle. Then I felt the Sow's primordial power push through my feet toward my head, arcing up and out of me. I couldn't understand what she was doing, until I felt the waters part around me.

She's using me as some kind of catalyst, I realized. *I'm like a magic wand made of Jane.*

Sure enough, I could feel the power pulsing out of me, pushing aside the water. The water was swirling around me again, but this time in the opposite direction, creating an inverse whirlpool. That said, I didn't realize exactly why that was happening until I felt my feet touch the ground. I'd been floating midway up the Sow, but now I was on land. Dry land.

Well, okay, it was wet, muddy land. But it was definitely the seafloor, and the water was parting above me – up and up – until finally the sun peeped through. It was like standing in an elevator shaft made of water, one that continued to get wider.

I blinked as the sky momentarily darkened, and then Blondie crashed down next to me with a *whoosh*. She crouched on the ground, panting, as I watched her wings dissolve.

'Christ, Jane, could you have taken any longer?' she said and groaned, huffing like an asthmatic as she drew power from the still-supercharged air around her.

'Dude, this was hard. You try reversing the laws of physics,' I said, as I gestured toward the walls of water around us. Then I realized what I'd done.

'I totally pulled a Moses,' I marveled, inordinately proud of myself.

She stood up, windmilling her arms to stretch out shoulders undoubtedly gone tight with flying.

'Yes, well, your results *are* impressive,' she conceded. 'But I thought I was going to die up there.'

Hi, Pot, I thought. *Meet Kettle! I swam into a huge fucking whirlpool!* But I kept my mouth shut.

'Yeah, well, now the last two glyphs are opened. What's next?'

'Um, there's gotta be something underneath here, cuz there's nothing above us,' was her helpful response, as we both peered around, trying to discern anything in the muck of the seafloor.

We began pacing back and forth, kicking aside seaweed and other debris. We each thought we saw something a few times, shouting in excitement and then quickly apologizing. Finally, I hit the jackpot.

'There's a hole!' I shouted. It was hard to see in the dark mud, but there it was. Big enough for a person to fit through, if they didn't mind getting muddy.

Blondie ran over, and we both peered into the opening.

''Kay,' she said, and I felt her magic *pop* as she apparated her climbing rope and harness. 'I'll lower you down. You tell me if it's clear, and then I'll apparate using your voice.'

She helped me get into the harness, and within minutes she was using her magically strengthened muscles to lower me down into the hole. When I was only a few feet in, I lit the puniest of mage lights, waiting to see if it set off any magical booby traps. Not feeling anything, I went ahead and strengthened the light till I could see the cavern.

It was another nondescript gray hole, just like the one underneath the Grays' B & B. Only this one pulsed with an insane amount of magic.

When I was on the ground, I lit a few more mage balls. When nothing happened, I shouted up to Blondie that it was safe. I felt the rope go slack when she dropped it, and then it fell to the earth in a serpentine coil while I busied myself getting out of the harness. Meanwhile, she apparated herself next to me.

'So, what do we have here?' she asked, looking around the dark cave. She lit a few more mage lights, but it didn't help much except to reveal that the ceiling above us was domed, with the now tiny-appearing hole at its apex.

'Can you feel that magic?' Blondie breathed, shutting her

eyes as if enjoying a tune only she could hear. A shudder racked her body, and she clenched a hand over her belly.

'I can feel it,' I said, but I could also see that I wasn't *feeling* it the way she was. She kinda looked like she might come in her pants. I just felt power.

But then I felt a whole different type of power altogether.

'Shit,' I swore, pulling Blondie back toward one of the cavern walls.

'Huh?' she said, woozily, as if drunk off whatever she was sensing.

'We've got company!' I shouted, pointing at the hole just as one dun figure darted through, to be followed swiftly by another. The harpies swirled around the hole as Phaedra appeared, lowering herself down on a column of earth magic.

Fucking Phaedra, I thought, as Blondie and I set up shields.

Once the Alfar was on the ground, one of the harpies darted back up through, only to appear again towing Graeme. Fugwat must still have been on enforced vacation in Abu Dhabi. Phaedra's entourage fanned out behind her, the harpies together on one flank and Graeme defending Phaedra's other flank.

'I would ask you why you were doing my job for me,' the bald little woman drawled, her face split by that wretched little moue of a smile that I'd come to loathe so much. 'But, frankly, I could care less.'

'Do you really think you can take me?' Blondie asked, her question wonderfully rhetorical as she stepped forward and simultaneously lit herself up with mage fire.

Meanwhile, my eyes darted around the cave, trying to discern where there was a tunnel, or another hole, or something that would get us through to another room. Because while the cavern had suddenly gotten rather crowded, it wasn't with anything we wanted to find.

Just evil Alfar and their sadistic cronies, I thought, as Graeme eyed me from behind Phaedra. I felt that squicky mental power of his reaching out, but this time I was able to use what I'd learned from studying Blondie work on Fugwat to shut down the incubus. It wasn't elegant, and it wasn't controlled, but I squished his mental power flat with a well-deserved pummeling of force. At which Graeme blinked and shook his head slightly, as if it had hurt him.

If I can use those channels to hurt him, maybe I can use them to get in his *head, too?* Unfortunately, Graeme was no fool. He wasn't going to let himself be walloped again that easily, and I felt his mental probes reverse backward into the safety of his own shields.

And that's when the fight really started. Just like last time, Blondie and Phaedra blasted at each other while the Alfar's entourage pumped power into her shields.

Only this time, I didn't take a back seat. Instead, I went on the offensive. The ocean was right above me, after all, pumping its power through the cavern ceiling, as well as trickling in on the rivulets of water that swirled around our feet. I was also still ridiculously revved from my time in the Sow. Unworried about getting depleted, I let rip with my own fierce barrage of mage balls. Only I ignored Phaedra completely.

Instead, I concentrated on her people. After all, if they were putting all their power into shielding Phaedra, they couldn't be shielding themselves very well.

I let rip a maniacal cackle as I saw my mage balls buckle Kaya and Kaori's weakened shields, and then felt them scramble to pump their magic back into their own shields at the expense of Phaedra's. In response, the little Alfar's blood-red eyes grew wide, and Blondie responded with an even fiercer barrage. I kept the pressure on the harpies, which did weaken Phaedra. But the two bird-women were too experienced and were still able to send some power to Phaedra. Plus, Graeme was completely free to act as Phaedra's personal shield generator.

Strategizing as I stepped closer to Blondie, I kept lobbing mage balls at the harpies, even as I switched the majority of my firepower to Graeme. Because I was no match for the incubus yet, offensively, that shouldn't have made much difference. But I wasn't really trying to get to Graeme. I wanted his girlfriend.

Just like I thought she'd do, Kaya (or Kaori – I still had no idea which was which) went all squishy at the sight of her boyfriend getting attacked and threw some extra strength at Graeme. That meant Phaedra was one minion down. And when I turned all my force away from the harpies and blasted at Graeme full strength, I soon felt Graeme's girlfriend further decrease her own shields. I kept blasting at Graeme, letting her think I'd forgotten about her and her sister in favor of bigger prey, until she dropped her shields entirely. Leaving her easy pickings.

Keeping smaller mage balls firing on Graeme while I created a bigger mage ball behind me, I waited till Kaya (or Kaori) took a sympathetic step toward her boyfriend. Unprotected by anything – even the edges of her sister's shields – she fell like a nerd for a hot chick dressed as Harlequin when my mage ball hit. Her sister cried out while her lovable beau barely even cast a glance in her direction.

Why do *women date assholes?* I wondered, as the ambulant harpy withdrew all of her shields from Phaedra in order to beef up her own. Then she retreated to kneel next to her sister, healing her as she did so.

Not wanting either harpy back in the game quickly, I transferred all my firepower back to them. As some of my shots were either deflected or went wide, they lit up the back wall of the cavern. That's when I saw it. On the far side from us, about twenty paces behind where Phaedra's people were making their stand, there was what looked like the entrance to a very small tunnel.

'I see a tunnel!' I shouted at Blondie, above the din of our magics.

'Where?' she asked.

'Other side of the cave. Behind the bad guys.'

'Of course,' she replied, doing a very fancy mage ball that split into three at the last second, blasting at the harpies, Phaedra, and Graeme simultaneously.

'We need to get over there!' I said, as I thought up ways to get Phaedra and her group to reverse their position.

'Nope, *you* need to get over there,' was the Original's only response, as she blocked a wave of fire with which Phaedra was trying to incinerate us.

'Huh?' I inquired, stupidly.

'There's something I need to tell you,' she began. I sighed. *This can't be good.*

Chapter Nineteen

'You know how you asked me if I was telling you everything?' Blondie asked. My skin prickled at her words, but Phaedra had moved a few steps closer in the seconds Blondie and I had talked. The Original went back to pummeling the Alfar, a fierce look on her face, and I waited patiently for her to drop whatever bomb she had waiting for me. Meanwhile, I kept lobbing random missiles at Graeme, just to keep him on his toes.

And then I felt my ass buzz. I had no idea what it was, till I realized I'd stashed my phone in my back pocket before leaving Anyan's.

How the hell is it still working? I thought, marveling at the modern cell phone. *And who the fuck is calling me?*

I pulled out the phone with one hand, as I sent mage balls with the other. It was Ryu. He'd left a voice message.

'Hi babe,' he said, using his 'cryptic casual' tone I knew so well from his dealings with the Alfar. 'Did some checking up on that issue you called me about. Didn't get anything from anyone Anyan hadn't already talked to, so I dug deeper. Found a very old contact – someone who's been around forever. She told me she never knew your subject personally, but that she knew *of* her. She didn't have too much to say, but she did say one thing that makes me nervous. Turns out your girl has a nickname. It's "Oathbreaker".' At Ryu's words, my heart dropped.

Has she betrayed us? I wondered, stepping away from Blondie carefully.

'So I'd watch my step,' continued Ryu's incongruously friendly voice. 'Be in touch if you need anything. I'll keep asking around.'

I moved a little farther away from the Original, carefully erecting my shields between us. Meanwhile, Blondie had pushed Phaedra back to her starting point, when Blondie turned just a little bit toward me, still keeping one eye on our enemies.

'Like I said,' she started, and then realized I'd backed away and put up my shields. 'Jane?'

'Oathbreaker?' was my only reply.

Blondie sighed. 'Oh, don't freak out. I'm not working for Jarl. Any oathbreaking I did was a long time ago,' she explained, taking a step toward me even as she scoured the ground in front of Phaedra's lot with a wall of fire.

I backed up another step to maintain my distance, lobbing a missile at Graeme as he tried to move away from Phaedra.

'Shit, this is ridiculous. Hold on a second.' With that, Blondie unleashed a crescendo of magic that wasn't physical. It was the mental magic she'd used before, on Fugwat.

Time stood still, and it was like we were standing alone in an entirely dark space – so dark it was as if we were surrounded by black ink.

'How did you do that?' I breathed. 'Did you . . . freeze time?'

'This isn't *Charmed*,' she said, rolling her eyes. 'I just put us all in our own little black boxes. Unfortunately, I have to be in one, too, or I'd just leave them there as we went on our merry way. But that's not the point.'

'No,' I said. 'It's not. The point is you telling me why you're called Oathbreaker.'

'I know. And I'll get to that. I've got a lot to tell you.'

'So start,' I snapped. I'd had more than enough of her secrets.

'The thing is, I know more about what's under Rockabill than I've let on. And so do you.'

'Huh?' I said, confused by this turn of events. Unlike her, everything I knew I had spilled.

'The creature and you have a connection. It's watched you, since you were little. It's known you all your life.'

'What the hell are you talking about?'

'Your dreams,' she said. 'After you were attacked. You need to remember them.'

Her words held power, and I felt her mind nudge mine. And with that, I remembered *everything*.

'Oh my gods,' I said. 'The creature . . . I was the creature.'

'And that's not the first time,' she prompted again.

Suddenly, I knew she was right. I'd often been the creature in my dreams – as a child, growing up, when I was in the hospital.

'And it's been with you, too,' Blondie said, reacting to the expression of recognition on my face.

I looked at her, my eyes wide. 'How do you *know* all this?'

She returned my gaze, her expression conciliatory. 'That's what I haven't been honest about,' she replied. 'It's been talking with me. We've been . . . I guess you could say, working together.'

'What?' I demanded. 'Why didn't you tell us?'

'Because it didn't want you to know,' she said, her voice soothing but her words anything but. 'It's got plans for you . . . I was just facilitating those plans. You'll understand when you talk to it.'

'What are you *talking* about?' I demanded, furious. 'How can you stand there and tell me that you've been manipulating this whole situation and expect me to trust you? And what the hell do you mean *talk* to it? And how do you even *know* this thing, anyway?'

Her smile, at that, was grim.

'I told you you'd soon be touching that tat,' she said. Then she pulled the neck of her shirt down and tipped her head to the side so that the large black bull's horn gleamed at me.

I blinked, my mind racing. 'So this has to do with the Schism?' I asked, remembering she'd connected the Schism and that particular tat when we'd rolled around together in the second cavern.

'Yes,' she said, beckoning me with her free hand to come touch the ink decorating her graceful neck.

I moved forward slowly, and then stretched out a finger to make contact with her dark-stained flesh . . .

I was so full of rage, and hurt, and a desire to see ourselves freed of those that hated us. I thought of everyone I had lost: my sister, killed by our own clan because she shared my blood; so many of my friends, picked off one by one when they were weak because the humans feared us; my people, so powerful and yet forced to live as animals by those we had the strength to control, had we but the will . . .

And so I raised the horn, channeling my power . . . It ripped through me, the pain agonizing. Yet even more agonizing was feeling what the horn was doing – not strengthening us, as I'd thought it would, but changing *us. Its magic warped by time, it created of us what it would, focusing certain powers of each individual until they were utterly different than what they had been. Only I remain untouched . . . I knew instantly I would never live down what I had done. The oaths I had broken to my people, to our magic . . .*

'Oathbreaker,' I breathed.

'Yes,' she acknowledged. 'I'm the one who changed us. I used a power beyond my control because I was like Jarl – I wanted humans to die. For us to rule. And I was punished for my hubris.'

'But what does the creature have to do with this?' I wanted to ask her so many questions, but I was also aware we still had things to do, and that somewhere in the darkness, Phaedra was still waiting.

'It will explain. It wants to talk.'

'That's what I have to do? Go . . . talk to it?'

'Yes. It's already opening up to you, in your dreams. It likes you, in its way.'

'Why?' I asked, totally confused.

She shrugged. 'Who knows? But it sees something in you. It's chosen you.'

I felt my skin grow clammy with fear.

'What the hell do you mean, it's chosen me?' I demanded.

'It's always been aware of you, as it slept. It always thought you'd be important. When it woke, it called me to follow you – to recruit you. You would have gotten dragged in eventually, but it saw more in you than just a foot soldier.'

I frowned. 'Go on.'

'It's always wanted you. But when you were attacked – which it had nothing to do with, by the way – it communed with you even more deeply. Became even more certain it wanted you.'

'For what? What the hell would it want me for?'

'The creature has been watching us, Jane. It knows what's going on. The reason I really followed you is because it told me to, because it wants to take a side. It wants to take our side, and it's ready to choose a champion. That champion is you.'

I blinked at her. Then I couldn't help it.

I laughed.

'What the hell are you talking about?' I asked, between slightly hysterical, choked giggles. '*You* are the champion!'

'It could never be me, babydoll,' she said, sadly. 'I'm the cause of all this mess.'

Rather selfishly, I was too focused on my own panic to acknowledge her sadness.

'You do recognize that this is *absurd*?' I asked, my voice rising shrilly. Panic was setting in, not least because Blondie hadn't yet cracked a smile. 'I'm not a warrior! I'm a selkie! A *half*-selkie! I'm not a champion!'

'There are many ways to fight, Jane,' the Original intoned, her voice lower than usual, her spine straighter than she normally carried herself. For a second I glimpsed the ancient being behind my neo-punk friend, and I shivered. 'And there are many weapons with which to do so. Strength of arms is only one weapon out of many, and oftentimes the first to fall.'

'But why me?' I asked, my voice small and, admittedly, scared.

'We do not choose our destinies,' Blondie said, shrinking back down to become my friend again. Her voice was soothing and her hand gently reached out to rub up and down the top of my arm. 'Sometimes they choose us. And you were chosen for great things, Jane.'

'I still don't understand,' I repeated, trying to wrap my brains around what she was saying. 'You were told to come to me? By the creature?'

'Yes.'

'So it's aware?'

'Yes. Physically, it's been asleep, but mentally, it's always been aware and free.'

'And it knows me?'

'Since you were born. This is its home, and you have spent much time dreaming.'

I remembered napping in the sun with Jason, as a child. We were like lapdogs, always snoozing when we had the chance.

Or like seals, I realized, with a sad little smile.

And then there was all that time in the hospital, I remembered, *spent dreaming under the influence of prescription drugs*.

'But why would it choose *me*? Are you sure that's what it said? You weren't misunderstanding it?' I was practically begging, but at that point, my dignity was my last concern.

'As I said, it likes you. It sees goodness in you, as well as strength. It saw, during its dreaming, the coming storm. And it knew its power was needed. So it woke itself, and instructed me to facilitate your meeting. But that doesn't mean this is over; you're still going to have to prove yourself. A champion always has to run a gauntlet, Jane – this is just the beginning of your work for tonight.'

I knew what a gauntlet was – I'd seen a bloated Richard Gere huff and puff his way through one in that horrible movie he did where Sean Connery could have kicked his ass at any minute but had to play the weaker Arthur to Gere's Lancelot.

'Am I going to have to, like, literally jump through hoops?' I asked, pointing at my nether bits in an attempt to remind Blondie of my new identity as Hips-Got-Stuck.

'What? I doubt it. But you do have to go into that tunnel and face whatever's waiting. Are you ready?' she asked.

'No,' I replied, wondering whether I would cry. I kinda wanted to, if I were honest.

'Good. I'm gonna release the bubbles. You take out the

harpies and the incubus. I'll take care of that Alfar. Once we're close to the tunnels, you run like a cheetah.'

I blanched at her suggestions.

Take out the harpies? And Graeme? I was confident I could take out the trash, or a checking account, but Phaedra's minions?

And she's on crack if she thinks I can run like a house cat, let alone a cheetah.

'Yep. C'mon,' and with that, I felt a tremendous pull of power as Blondie pulled one of those shining swords of light out of the air in front of her. That said, hers was different – I could see a solid form inside it, and I wasn't entirely sure if it was made of steel or raw power, or a combination of both.

Twirling the sword like a ninja warrior, she hewed the air in front of her. The blade cut through the air with a whistle, but as we got closer to Phaedra, I realized what else it cut through.

She's cutting through their shields, I thought, as I watched Phaedra's eyes widen in panic. Scampering a pace or two behind Blondie, I readied mage balls as we neared our enemies.

The harpies were the first to go. I don't mean 'go' as in 'dead' as in 'I killed them'. I mean they up and went. Kaya (or Kaori) watched us coming toward her and her wounded sister, and then she did the smartest thing I've ever seen either of those two birdbrains do. She gathered Kaori (or Kaya) up in her arms and winged her way through the hole in the cavern ceiling.

Phaedra watched her two minions leave with a look of such rage on her face that I hoped, for the harpies' sake, Blondie took no mercy on the Alfar. Otherwise, there was bound to be negative-two harpy ladies flying the skies after this evening.

Despite the defection of Kaya and Kaori, I wasn't feeling any more confident about fighting Graeme. There was something so evil about the incubus. He was a creature made of fear for me, something that haunted my nightmares to this day. Blondie telling me to take him on was like her telling me to go up against the boogeyman.

But she left me no option. We were nearly across the expanse of the cavern, her fiery sword lighting our path toward Phaedra and Graeme. Graeme took up a flanking position on Phaedra, but his eyes were on me. Again, I felt those magical probes of his tickle the edges of my shields, but carefully this time. No doubt uncertain about whether what I'd done last time was fluke or skill, he wasn't going to forego his most powerful weapon that easily.

Swinging her sword harder as she scythed through Phaedra and Graeme's ever-increasing shields, Blondie claimed another step toward our enemy, and then another.

Gritting my teeth, I allowed Graeme to make his own inroads. His hesitant mental probe turned into an increasingly more confident touch against my mind. My every reflex screamed at me to smack away his touch, but I held myself steady.

He has to believe he has me, I told myself. *You can do this, Jane . . .*

Again I thought of Yeats, using his words to ground me: *The blood-dimmed tide is loosed, and everywhere/ The ceremony of innocence is drowned . . .*

Not gonna let this *blood-dimmed tide drown my friends*, I thought, bolstering my strength.

Graeme's mental touch grew bolder yet, as it whispered to me of bodies bound – one in pain to the other's pleasure – and I allowed myself to react the way I knew he'd like. My eyes grew large, my hands shook . . . I took an involuntary step back from him, which only made him push harder with that dark mind.

Meanwhile, Blondie had nearly closed with Phaedra. I could feel the Original pulling hard from the charged air around us as she expended a terrific amount of energy cutting through the Alfar's shields. At the same time, Phaedra was doing everything in her power to keep those shields intact, but they were parting like butter before Blondie's glowing weapon.

Her eyes undoubtedly as wide as mine, I watched as Phaedra scrambled away from Graeme, pulling her shields with her. Dashing away from us in an undignified little sprint, the Alfar picked the worst place to run. I groaned, inwardly, as she made her away directly toward the one part of the cavern we didn't want her to see: the part with the little tunnel. Blondie swore, taking off after our favorite nemesis while throwing mage balls by the dozen in an attempt to get Phaedra to turn back around and meet Blondie's charge.

Graeme, for his part, had dealt with his mistress's abandonment with aplomb. At first he'd hesitated when she'd run off, as if unsure whether to follow her. I'd like to think he was afraid of taking me alone, but that's highly unlikely considering how often – and how thoroughly – he'd trounced me in the past.

Meanwhile, I kept tight rein on my expression. I didn't want to give away the trap, so I didn't overbait it by doing anything too dramatic, like faking a swoon. But when his next hesitant probe touched my shield I visibly cringed and backed away just the slightest step.

Most likely realizing that the same bad luck that had taken his great protector away had also taken mine, he grew bolder. Smirking, he strode forward, pushing at my mental shields more firmly. I kept up a modicum of the sort of shield I'd

formed before, when I'd slammed his down, but I purpose-
fully kept it weak.

The nice thing about Graeme was that he could be counted
on for two things: sadism and arrogance. So it wasn't very
surprising when, feeling my vulnerable defenses, he went
ahead and slammed into them with everything he had – all
that gruesome mojo, filled with the pained screams of his
long life's many victims.

Bracing myself, I allowed my shields to recede before
him. But that was the key word: recede. What probably felt
like crumbling to him was really just me pulling them in,
as close as they would go, until I think they were actually
under the surface of my skin.

The important fact, however, was that they still stood. So
when Graeme opened his own channels to blast at me with
everything he had, I was ready.

Focusing my power into the narrowest stream I could make
it, I waited till after Graeme had finished. To him, it felt like
he was hitting me full blast. And to me, it felt like he was
painting me in nightmares, but none of them got under my
skin.

I'd taken a big risk. If he'd figured out what I'd done, he
could have walked up to me and simply torn my head off,
something I would never have survived no matter how quickly
Blondie intervened. But I knew that Graeme got off more on
making his victims collude with him on their destruction than
he did on the actual destroying. Not that he didn't enjoy the
pain-infliction part, but I knew he *really* enjoyed the fact
that he could make his victims beg him to torture them.

So the only magic he leveled at me was mind magic. And
when he was done, it was my turn.

Ramming forward with the thin shafts of power I'd created,
imagining an ice pick as I did so, I pushed as fast and hard

as I could. I knew I had only moments before Graeme realized what I'd done and he closed off his channels.

So I struck like a serpent, thrusting myself forward, physically, with the strength of my magical *push*. Graeme's eyes widened as he felt what I'd done, but he was too late. My power burrowed through his channels, straight past his own defenses, buried as it was in his own mental probes. Quick as one of the incubus's own leering winks, my power was blasting into his brainpan.

Graeme's body spasmed, his waxen face grimacing in a rictus of pain. Unlike him, however, I took no pleasure in his obvious torment. But I knew we needed Graeme out of this fight, so I pushed even more power through our connection, despite feeling sullied through contact with his depraved mind.

Luckily, the contact was short-lived, for Graeme quickly crumpled to the ground. He lay on the ground, twitching, his eyes rolled back into his head. Before I could let any pity for that monster filter through my system, I hit him with a mage ball to the head, and another, until he was still.

I wasn't sure if he was dead, but he was definitely still. And I'd seen way too many movies where the girl goes to check if the bad guy is actually dead and gets her ankle grabbed in return. So instead I hit him with one more mage ball and then wove the water around him tight in a binding spell. I put enough juice in it to last a few hours.

Phaedra, meanwhile, was currently battling with Blondie. The Original had caught up with the Alfar well before the entrance to the tunnel, and they were having a good, old-fashioned bash-off. Blondie's weapon was that same glowing sword, and Phaedra had created two short swords of her own, but her weapons were purely made of power. Unfortunately, Phaedra's swords were no use against Blondie's fierce, real-steel-and-magic version, and they kept dissipating at inopportune moments. Phaedra nearly lost her head, and at least one ear, a few times, although she kept managing to roll away or create another weapon at just the last second.

I had to give it to the bald little Alfar: she was nothing if not a fighter.

'Enjoying the view?' Blondie shouted from where she was bashing at Phaedra.

I didn't answer, but tried to get closer to the Original.

'Never mind me!' she called. 'I'll keep this one busy. You go on up ahead! Fulfill your destiny!'

I gulped. She made all this sound like an episode of *Highlander*, what with all the destiny talk. I was someone who had issues, not destinies. I also didn't really enjoy the whole 'go it alone' aspect of today's activities. I'd been pretty sure that, when I'd taken down Graeme, Blondie would make short work of Phaedra, and we could discover, together, whatever was hidden under Rockabill.

I preferred the buddy system to the 'Jane has a destiny' system.

'Go on, Jane! I'll be right behind you!' Blondie called, just as Phaedra swung at her, hard, with a combo of magic-laser-sword and pure mojo. Blondie *oofed* as her shields buckled, and she listed to the side.

'Goddammit, Phaedra,' she said, irritably, as she righted herself and her shields. 'What part of "just give up" are you not understanding?' And with that, the Alfar and the Original went back to bashing at each other, leaving me to do as Blondie commanded and go off to change both Rockabill's fate and mine.

Oh fuckerdoodles, I thought, sidling toward the tunnel. *Oh fuckerdoodles*, I thought again, more emphatically, when I saw Graeme's still form shift just the slightest bit. I prayed my bindings would hold.

What have I done to deserve this? I thought, as I scrambled toward the tunnel entrance.

All this trouble, when all I ever wanted was to bask on a warm, flat rock.

The tunnel before me was dark as I entered, and darker still as I made my way in. I was just about to light a mage light when the ground dropped out from under me.

The echoes of my screams were all I heard until the next sound: that of my body hitting the floor, hard.

Chapter Twenty

I'm not sure if I passed out or had the wind knocked out of me or what. But I was definitely out of it for at least a few minutes.

Stretching my limbs slowly, I felt aches but no real pain. Nothing seemed to be broken.

I let myself lie on the cool ground for a moment, gathering my thoughts – and my magic – about me. The atmosphere in these caverns was so damp it felt more like the ocean than it did air, and that went for elemental power, as well. It was like I was lying with my body in the shallows of a beach, everything was so saturated with the sea's power. So I went ahead and recharged, not taking the power around me for granted.

When I finally sat up, I carefully sent out some short probes while lighting a tiny mage light. When nothing reacted badly, I made the mage light bigger till I could see.

I was sitting on a cold floor that was way too pristine and way too white to be natural. It looked like a solid sheet of marble and stretched as far I could see.

Liberace would love this, I thought, gathering my legs under me and standing, slowly.

When I was on my feet, I peered around the darkness, trying to figure out where on earth I could be. I did, after all, know where I was supposed to be – somewhere under the Sow – but marble flooring was really not what I expected for under-Sow decor.

My mage light rose over my head as I looked around, and I let more magic pulse into it. Too late, I realized that my actions weren't going unnoticed. My light got brighter and brighter, despite my no longer pumping magic into it, and that's when I realized that more lights were coming up, all around the room. None of the lights were attached to walls; they all floated, in what seemed to be a long oval, with me at one end. At the other end, I could very faintly make out the shape of either a door or a mirror.

Well, I thought. *It's fairly obvious where I'm supposed to go.*

I looked around the darkness for another option, but there wasn't any. *Besides*, I thought, *when in search of Wonderland, one plays by the rabbit's rules . . .*

Walking forward, I kept my magics flared out around me, both shields and probes working overtime.

Ouch, I thought, as pain started registering up through my feet. *I must have hurt myself when I fell.* But it was an odd pain, not from my arch or from my ankle as I would have assumed. It felt like it was coming upward through the soles of my feet. *Weird.*

But I kept trudging forward, despite the pain in my feet never letting up. When I was a little closer to the fixture at the other end of the oval, I still wasn't sure what, exactly, it was.

A mirror? A door? A portrait?

For there did seem to be images dancing over its surface, but they weren't standing still, and they didn't seem to be my reflection.

It looks sorta like the mirrors the glyphs are set in, I thought, pausing my strides to attempt to stretch out my feet – pointing and flexing my arch – to try to work out whatever cramp was getting the better of me.

It feels fine, now, I thought, irritably, as I worked my left
foot around. Nothing hurt, although my right had begun to
ache as if the pain had been transferred. And as soon as I
put my left foot back down on the ground, pain again flared
up through both my legs.

I frowned, putting my weight on my left foot, as I strode
forward onto my right. Again, the pain receded, and then flared,
as each foot lost and then regained contact with the floor.

Shit, I thought. *It's the floor.* A memory flashed through
my mind of the Little Mermaid: the 'real' Brothers Grimm version
of the story and not the Disney version. In that tale, after her
deal with the Sea Witch gave the mermaid legs, every step felt
as if knives were being driven into her feet. So that when she
danced with her prince, later in the story, and everyone lauds
her grace and skill, they should really have been praising her
sheer masochism.

I shuffled forward, the pain increasing. After checking the
soles of my shoes to make sure they weren't ripped open, I
tried a few more steps. But still the pain increased. I swore,
but persevered a little more forward, cursing out loud this
time.

'Shit!' I shouted, as my next step felt like a long, needlelike
lance shooting up through the heel of my foot.

I continued to swear, creatively and with great vigor, as I
looked up toward the mirror in front of me. My pained steps
had shuffled me close enough that I could finally see what
the mirror or portrait or door contained.

Iris? I thought, wondering what the succubus was doing at
the end of the hall. *Why on earth is Iris . . .* But just as I finished
that thought, Iris shifted to become Anyan, the man. I almost
cried out with relief to see him outside of his doggie shape,
until I remembered that this mirror wasn't showing reality. I
shuffled painfully forward, anyway, towards Anyan. But then

the mirror changed, again, and there was my dad, smiling at me and looking – finally – so healthy and hale.

It's everything I have to live for, I realized, as I took another painful step forward. *This is a test. To see what I'll do for the people I love.*

More images appeared with each stumbling step: Caleb and that unit I'd come to ignore so well; Grizzie inexplicably wearing Western gear, including some very tight chaps; Tracy patting her enormously pregnant belly.

I finally know what those crazy people who walk on spikes feel, I thought, trying to make light of the fact I was in absolute agony. *And I'm only halfway there.*

A few more steps and it didn't feel like knives on my feet anymore. Instead, it felt like fire – a burning sensation that compounded with my already sore feet to make walking murder. I tried everything to mitigate the pain: I bit my tongue and clenched my fists so tightly my nails bit into my skin, all in an attempt to use differently placed pain to distract the foot pain. But every step I took just made it worse.

Another picture flashed on the mirrored surface in front of me. This time, it was Miss Carrol. Then she was replaced by the Tanners, who owned our local bakery.

I screwed my courage to my sticking place and took one huge step forward . . . only to land in a crumpled heap. I'd heard of crippling pain but had no idea what it meant till now.

'Fuckfuckfuckfuckfuck,' I gibbered, collapsed in a heap over my aching feet. While I was down there, I pulled off my shoe and then pulled up my pant leg to check my flesh. But it was totally unmarred. And yet, any part of my body that touched that floor eventually began to prickle, and soon enough I was standing again. There still stood a huge gulf between me and the end of the oval.

You have to do this, Jane. Suck it up and go.

And with that, I strode forward. Unfortunately, the bigger my strides, the more the pain hit. But smaller steps meant only a constant, nattering pain. I did my best impression of Lamaze breaths as I strode forward, only to nearly pass out before I realized I was only ever inhaling. As I learned later in life at yoga, it hurt more on the exhale.

When I was about a third of the way to the mirror I stopped, panting. Sweat had broken out over my whole body, drenching my skin. I felt like I'd had a bucket of mucky water thrown on me. My long-sleeved tee clung uncomfortably, and my comfy old camo pants were stiff with mud.

Feeling tired and gross and beaten down, I looked to the mirror for inspiration. Only to be met with Graeme's leering expression.

'What the fuck?' I asked, very rhetorically, to the empty room.

The incubus only smiled with more malice, reaching into his pants to pull out his already engorged penis. Only biologically correct terms worked to describe what he did; there was nothing sexy about the way he stroked himself, watching me. His masturbating was less like a sex act and more like a militant feeling up his gun before shooting a civilian in the head.

Soon enough, however, Graeme disappeared, only to be replaced by Ryu's cousin, Nyx. While I didn't think Nyx was as evil as Graeme, I couldn't actually be sure. She had, after all, brought a human – her 'sack lunch' – to her supernatural compound, only to ignore him when a huge battle took place. She didn't even notice when he was killed.

I took a hesitant step forward, not exactly liking what I saw before me. It was one thing to think that my friends' safety waited for me behind that glossy surface, but to think about all the people I loathed in the same context . . .

Fugwat flashed across the mirror, and then Kaya and Kaori.

Together, of course, since I didn't think they could actually exist apart. When Morrigan appeared in the mirror, and then Jarl, I'd already ground to a halt. The mirror lingered, then, on the oafish, bullying face of Stuart Gray.

And therein lies the test, I realized. It was one thing to walk over hot coals – quite literally – for the people you loved. But another thing entirely to endure such torture for enemies and idiots.

But I don't get to judge, I realized. Not in that way. *If someone attacks me, I have the right to fight back. But I don't get to allow some force to wipe out everyone – good and bad – as if I'm a god.*

I'd never liked Job's whirlwind. And that's what would happen if I allowed Phaedra to win. She'd rouse the creature, destroying the East Coast. And then she'd destroy even more with the power she won.

So I walked forward. The pain was brutal, but I gritted my teeth and I endured. I knew it wasn't 'real' pain – no marks were on my feet or legs. I'd survive this test, but Rockabill itself wouldn't survive if I failed.

Finally, I made it to the sigil. Graeme was back up, leering and whacking off at me, but I ignored him as I pushed at the mirror. Okay, in all honesty I sort of fell forward onto it, but it worked.

Swinging the door open, the room around me winked out into darkness as I once again plunged forward into nothingness.

This time, I didn't even bother testing a mage light. I just flung my arm out into the darkness and lit up my surroundings like it was a beach wedding.

I was still on my hands and knees where I'd landed. Hard. There were definitely going to be some interesting bruises decorating my body after today.

For some reason, that thought made me think of Anyan, still trapped as a dog. He was the one who always healed me . . . The thought of those big hands rubbing over my body made me miss him fiercely.

We have to reverse that spell. Then I thought of what Blondie had said. *We need the creature's power.*

Stumbling to my feet, I got my bearings. This new room was just as stark, white, and unnatural as the other one had been. Although, instead of an oval of lights, this room was dotted by four enormous statues set up to form a square. The figures stood so tall – I barely made it to their knees – that it took me a moment to realize what I was seeing.

It's those ancient Alfar, I realized. Melichor and Tatiana stood on one side of the square, looking as forbidding as their ghostly shapes had before. Across from them, forever their seconds, stood Glynda and Straif.

As I walked into the room, I felt magic swirl around me. The statues all turned, as one, to look down. I froze, blinking in their gaze like a deer in the proverbial headlights, but they didn't move again. Their eyes seemed still to be unseeing stone, but one never knew.

Once the statues had finished moving, a light shone down from above to land smack in the middle of the square made by the statues. Within that light floated what looked like a pedestal.

I moved forward slowly, carefully, imagining Straif's huge hand reaching down to smoosh me like a bug. When I got to where the pedestal stood, I stared in confusion.

It wasn't really a pedestal. Instead, a thin, gilt rapier floated horizontally, looking from the side like the pedestal top. And under that floated a vertical scabbard. It didn't take a rocket scientist to figure out that this test must be about sticking the rapier into the scabbard.

The problem was that lying prone over the scabbard's mouth was a white dove, its wings outstretched like some sort of feathery crucifixion character.

'Shit,' I swore, under my breath, as I stared at the conundrum. Meanwhile, the dove watched me back, its beady little eyes rolling as its breast fluttered in panic.

First things first, I thought, studying the sword. The rapier looked razor sharp, and so very thin, but I knew the damage it would do to that white breast. I moved around it, trying to see how it was floating, but it was obviously magic.

When I reached for the pommel, I couldn't help but emit a low chuckle. The rapier's grip was surrounded by a large, circular shield that was the same shape as the sigil we'd just chased all over Rockabill. Grasping the sword, I pulled, nearly falling back on my ass when it came to me with no resistance whatsoever.

I stood there, sword in hand, staring down at the bird. The bird stared back.

What kind of test is this? I wondered. *Is it testing my resolve? My cruelty? My willingness to sacrifice? Or is it the complete opposite? Do they want to see my mercy, my kindness?*

I studied the faces of the statues around me for some clue as to the true nature of this test. Because if I got it wrong, my little corner of the world was doomed.

What would they have honored? I wondered, scrutinizing the ancient Alfar's enigmatic stone expressions. *The Alfar I've known are either distant or monstrous. Either they wouldn't care that I murdered what amounts to a fancy pigeon or they wouldn't even notice.*

What had Blondie said about these ancient Alfar? I remembered her mentioning something about power, and about cruelty. But certainly there had to have been wisdom, too, for the Alfar not only to have thrived but, in their own way, to have flourished?

I walked around the scabbard again, feeling the weight of the rapier in my hand. The bird was still shuddering in fear, its lovely white breast feathering up and down.

Besides the fact that I wasn't a huge fan of animal cruelty, I had no idea what I was supposed to do. Kill the bird? Try to free it? Do a tap dance with it on my head?

And what right did these ancient Alfar have to test me in the first place?

It was then I realized what they would have wanted. Any being that would muck about, so, with others, wouldn't want mercy or kindness. They'd want strength – of arms and of purpose.

'I hate that you're making me do this,' I told the statues, as I stood up from where I'd been kneeling. 'I hate that you're making me kill this little bird just to prove I-don't-even-know-what to your long-dead asses.'

Clutching the pommel of the sword, I readied myself to place the tip of the sword right at the bird's breast. Part of me knew that it had to be a fake; no bird could have survived underground like this, for thousands of years. And yet it didn't look fake. It looked alive, and terrified of me. So it took me a while to work up the nerve to actually do it. The bird kept watching, the whole time, like it knew. Finally, however, I forced myself to place that point right where it would cut through to find its scabbard.

I don't want to fuck this up, I thought. If I did it too slow, or did it wrong, the bird, fake or not, would suffer more than it had to. *This is so evil. What if they'd put a baby here, instead?* I shuddered, and then stilled myself, including mentally. I didn't want my stray thoughts giving the magical tests any ideas.

Then I pushed down, hard.

A burst of bright blood marred the perfect white of the dove's breast. 'I'm sorry,' I whispered, as those panicked black eyes popped in pain and fear.

'I'm sorry,' I whispered again, as I kept pushing through the bird's body, until the rapier was firmly sheathed in its scabbard. Bizarrely enough, I would remember killing that bird better than I would remember killing the humans who had attacked us at Anyan's. One had been a desperate act done in the heat of the moment; this was done with calculation. At that moment, I hated the Alfar more than I ever had. They'd made me ruthless.

My 'I'm sorry' then began to echo through the chamber, making a mockery of my whispered sentiments. I'd still killed the bird, after all.

'I'm sorry, I'm sorry, I'm sorry,' boomed through the white hall as I stepped back from the sword. The pigeon, scabbard, and sword all disappeared in a puff of magic, and I saw a pair of white doors appear where they'd once stood. But the doors were sealed shut.

'I'm sorry, I'm sorry, I'm sorry,' continued the echo, till I put my hands over my ears to quiet it. That's when the door began to tremble, as if it were being forced open from the other side. I took another step back, unsure of what would happen when it finally burst open.

Or what will burst through, I thought, raising my shields and a mage ball, to be on the safe side.

But when the door finally ratcheted itself open, only darkness waited for me.

I lofted my mage ball and stepped through into liminal space.

Chapter Twenty-One

This room, unlike all the others, was inhabited. And not only with magic so powerful that my knees nearly buckled when I walked through the door.

Upon first entering, my mage lights had revealed what I first thought were enormous tree roots. Trained to think of the supernatural world as one in which our myths were almost-right, my brain jumped immediately to Norse legend.

'The World-Tree?' I wondered aloud. *Was this what Phaedra had planned? Some old-fashioned Ragnarok action?*

[Not the World-Tree, child,] an amused voice rang in my head. [Look closer.]

Upon first hearing that voice, loud and clear but definitely not verbalized, I acted as bravely and with as much dignity as I always did. Dropping flat to the floor, I glared around with wild eyes, trying to figure out who the fuck was in my *mind*. Unlike Graeme, however, these were just words. I felt no presence, so it didn't feel nearly as squicky. Just *weird*.

The mental voice chuckled. At me. Awesome.

Way to keep the enemy on their toes, I thought as I picked myself up off the ground.

'Who are you?' I called into the darkness.

The voice kept chuckling: a warm, gentle sound that matched the rich, if curiously nongendered tones of its speech.

[You know me, little one,] it said, eventually.

'So I've been told. But it doesn't feel that way,' I replied, uncertainly.

[You do. In fact, we've spent quite a bit of time together.]

Now that I was standing, I lit a few more lights and took a few steps farther into the room.

Not tree trunks, I realized, staring at what I'd thought had been knotted lumber in front of me.

It's only lumber if lumber is green. And kinda wet. With suction pads.

Cthulhu, I thought.

[A distant cousin,] the voice answered, in all seriousness.

I could only stand and blink, open mouthed.

What I was staring at, after all, was a pile of tentacles that filled the back wall of the enormous cavern in which I stood. And yet, they appeared to consist of mostly the tips.

If those are just the tips, I thought, *how big is the rest of this thing?*

[Big,] said the voice, chuckling again.

It was no fun having a conversation with something that could read your mind. *Especially*, I realized with horror, *when at least a third of your mind is almost always thinking about either sex or food, or both.*

That amused chuckle pushed through my brain, again.

Mortified, I took another step closer. 'Who are you?'

[I lived before names,] it said. [But I am what I am.]

'Like Popeye?' I blurted out, before I could stop myself.

A tentacle lifted itself, causing me to skitter back. But all it did was flex, like it was a bicep. It was my turn to giggle.

[Do you know what you're here for, little Jane?] the creature asked then.

'Blondie told me you chose me,' I said. 'But I think you're crazy.'

[Crazy?]

'You can't be serious about me,' I told it, trying to make it understand the truth. 'I'm not a fighter. I'm not anything. I work at a bookstore.'

[You've done quite a bit more than work at a bookstore, this past year,] the creature reminded me.

'But not by choice,' I said. 'I didn't want any of this.'

[Perhaps that's why you're perfect as a champion.]

'I don't understand,' I said, meaning everything about this situation.

[Not all heroes are born, Jane. Some are made. And those bring with them a different insight. It is such insight – the insight of the person who has been outside, who has been, as you say, nothing – that is sorely needed right now.]

'But I don't want this . . .'

[Perhaps you think so. But you must make your choice. And undoubtedly there are things that will sway you. Everyone has a weakness. Should we experiment?]

With that, one of the creature's tentacles moved, slithering toward me. Knowing it could crush me with any of its many, many limbs, I tried to keep still and look brave. I think all I managed was to look terrified, but in the same place.

The thick, mottled tentacle tip flipped itself over with the paradoxical elegance of a hand model to reveal a large, flat sucker probably the length of my whole arm. Or one of my legs. But I had short legs, so that wasn't saying much.

[What are your weaknesses, Jane True?] the creature asked.

At that question, two answers popped into my head, simultaneously. The first was: foot rubs. The second was: pastry. I kept both to myself.

'Is this a test?' I asked, 'Like those tests you created that I went through outside?'

[I did not create any tests,] it answered, with a non answer.

'So you had nothing to do with those tests?'

[That's not what I said. Now answer my question, Jane. What would seduce you? What would make you turn your back on your friends? Your family?]

I frowned. 'What do you mean, turn my back?'

[I mean leave me be. Then Phaedra and her friends will have the opportunity to force my prison open. To 'free' me. Unfortunately, my prison is vast. And built under much of your North America.]

'Well, then there's not a lot you can offer me, if "turning my back" means letting everyone I know and love be destroyed.'

[Ah,] it thought. [Are you sure?]

And with that, another one of those flat, mirrorlike sigil surface thingies appeared, floating over the creature's enormous sucker.

[I can give you anything,] the creature purred. [How about wealth?]

And with that, the mirror's surface showed an image of what I could only describe as the love child of Jane True and Paris Hilton. It was me, but so very, very not me. 'I' was dressed in all designer gear, sitting in a limo and playing with a little dog that was dripping in as much bling as 'I' was.

It was my turn to laugh. *Seriously?* I thought.

'If I wanted stuff, I would have just stayed with Ryu,' I told the tentacle.

[Ah,] it said. [Ryu. What if you could have a Ryu who wanted what you did? Rockabill, and a family, and domestic bliss?]

And with that the image shifted from Paris-Jane to an equally ridiculous image: Ryu, wearing carpenter-fit jeans and a flannel shirt, holding not one but two babies.

I laughed even harder. *That's not how things work*, I thought, not bothering to try to control my laughter enough to speak. *You can't just change people into what you want them to be.*

I didn't comment on the fact that that's exactly what Ryu had wanted to do with me.

[Very wise, young one,] said the creature. [But there are things I can change.]

And with that, the mirror showed Anyan as a dog. He was sitting, glaring at his own tail as if it might spring to sentient life and take off with his butt, when he suddenly sat up with what appeared to be an embarrassed look on his face. Then he was engulfed in a circle of green light, and then he was standing, a man again. And naked as a jaybird.

I admit it: I ogled. I ogled hard.

[I could give you your lover back,] the creature whispered, letting its magic surge to let me know just how powerful he was.

It was tempting to say yes, I admit. The thought of Anyan safe and sound was a powerful draw.

But he'd only be human and whole long enough to die with the rest of us.

'As much as I want Anyan back the way he was, I can't take your offer,' I said, knowing I was doing the right thing but still wanting to kick myself all the same.

[How good you are,] the creature said, its voice arch. I snorted.

'Not good, just realistic. We'll get Anyan back the way he was, when all of this is settled.'

[What about death?] was the creature's next, unexpected answer.

'Sorry?' I asked, not understanding the question.

[What about death?] it repeated. [What if I could bring,

say, your mother back from the dead?] And with that, the mirror showed me Mari, my mom, laughing. She was wearing her red wrap-dress, the hand-me-down that I still wore. She had my eyes, my figure. I noticed, however, that my nose was my father's, for he had joined her in the mirror. Obviously, he was older than her now, but – because of the goblin healer's intervention – still healthy. He embraced my mom, his arms tight around her, as she hugged him back. They stayed like that, frozen in the tableau that had been my greatest child-hood fantasy.

'You can't do that,' I whispered.

[Can't I?] the creature asked. And this time, the wave of power it unleashed actually did bring me to my knees. I went ahead and stayed kneeling.

I had to admit, it was tempting. The sight of my father's face was what did it: he looked so happy, and I knew he would *be* that happy.

But for how long? asked my rude, ever-practical brain. *Even if this thing can bring you back your real mother, the point is it'll be your* mother. *And she will leave, again. She can't stay with you on land. She couldn't the first time, and she wouldn't the second.*

What if she's brought back different, so she won't leave? whispered an ugly, selfish part of my brain.

Then she won't really be your mom, the rest of me replied, knowing it was true even as I thought it. *And you don't get to bring back somebody already dead, mourned, and* survived, *at the expense of so many living.*

My dad had survived the knowledge of my mom's death, but he wouldn't survive knowing bringing her back had killed so many others. He was a good man.

I also knew the creature had been party to my little mental conversation, so I didn't bother replying when I looked back up to the mirror to watch my happy fake-parents swirl away like ghosts. Sitting back on my heels, I hung my head.

[So strong you are,] the voice whispered. I couldn't tell if it was mocking me or not.

'No,' I replied. 'Just practical.'

[Is that it?] the creature asked. [Even practicality breaks . . .]

And that's when the creature pulled its sucker punch.

'Jason,' I breathed, feeling my body tense as I stared into the mirror.

For Jason stared back. Not Jason as I'd last seen him, as an eighteen-year-old boy, but Jason as he should be now, had he lived.

Had you not been the death of him, whispered that tiny, traitorous sliver of my mind. It had been quieted, but never completely silenced.

The handsome, golden boy I'd known had become an even more attractive man. He'd have been only twenty-seven, but already crow's feet wrinkled the corners of his eyes.

He always did spend too much time in the sun, and too much time laughing, I thought. Then I shook myself. That's not Jason. Jason is dead. He never got to earn crow's feet, or anything else.

Certainly not those sun streaks in his blond hair, or that filled-out body that had grown thicker and manlier. He looked like a young lion when he smiled at me with that same easy, happy smile I'd known so well. I took a step forward.

I couldn't help it.

'That's not fair,' I said.

[Has the world ever been fair?] it asked. [Especially to you?]

'Quit trying to manipulate me like this. You can't *do* any of these things. They're impossible. I don't know what game this is you're playing, but it's over.'

[What about what you want, Jane?] it asked, as if I'd never spoken. [It's never about what you want. Why not take something for yourself, for once?]

'I only want to stop Phaedra. I want to keep everyone safe.'

[Such a martyr. And a liar. I know you want things . . . You needn't lie to me. To yourself.]

'What would you have me do?' I shouted, frustrated. 'What we want doesn't always matter! Who do you think you are?'

[I'm someone who can give you back your love,] the voice whispered. And then Jason stepped out of the mirror.

He walked toward me. I was rooted in place, shock filtering through my system like a thousand lightning bolts.

When he reached out to touch me, I was glad to be already sitting on the ground because I would have crumpled like a marionette with its strings cut. Jason only crouched down to my level, a patient expression on his face. His hand on my shoulder was gentle as those achingly familiar blue eyes searched my face.

I waited for the questions I thought he'd ask: *Where was I? What happened? What was going on?* But Jason only stayed crouching, smiling.

'Jason?' I asked. His smile broadened, his eyes twinkled.

I reached out tentative fingers to touch his chin. Rough, warm skin met my fingers and I shuddered. 'Is it really you?'

His only response was to move his chin downward so he could kiss the tips of my fingers. His lips felt like they always had.

For a split second, I imagined launching myself into Jason's arms. I knew they'd be warm, and solid, and they'd feel just like Jason's.

But they weren't really his.

'He's not real,' I said, although I allowed myself to stroke a hand over Jason's rough cheek, so achingly familiar yet so strange – a combination of memory and fantasy.

[Why would you say that?] asked the creature.

'Jason was always the talker,' I said, smiling sadly. 'I was the quiet one. If he'd been in the ground for ten years, he'd be yammering like a skipping CD right now.'

[You're right. But I can give his shell all of your memories,] the creature crooned, his mental voice seductive. [He'll be the Jason you remember, down to the last detail.]

'But they're *my* details,' I said, standing up and brushing myself off. Jason's body echoed my movements, still smiling sweetly at me. 'That's not the same as the real Jason. I loved him partly because he was always surprising me. He'd never surprise me again if I made him up. Besides, the real Jason would still be dead.'

[You wouldn't have to remember that fact,] said the creature.

'What do you mean?'

[I could wipe your memories. Put you back where you were before Jason died. Take you far away from this place, set you up as a family. You'd remember only life and love, and you'd be together.]

While the creature was talking, Jason's body had moved along beside me and put an arm around me. Meanwhile, the creature played out his offer using that damned mirror. Jason's body held me while I watched the creature's promises play out in front of us. I felt like I was in a bizarre, supernatural version of *The Price Is Right*.

In the mirror, Jane sat at a small table on the verandah of a log cabin. Interestingly, it looked mighty similar to Anyan's. Jason soon joined her, carrying a big platter of something. He set it down in front of Jane, calling into the house as he did so. Two little girls, one dark and one light, came carrying their own smaller plates out to join their parents. They all sat down together, Jason eating off Jane's plate as he almost always had in life, while the four talked animatedly, if silently.

In my heart of hearts, if I was honest, I knew I would have given anything for that picture to have been a reality.

But instead I shook my head, stepping away from the warm, strong arm of Jason's body.

'It's not real,' I said. 'And it can't be real. I would have loved for that to have come true, but it didn't. Jason died, and I'm a different person now.' Almost as if to prove my point, the figures wavered and then disappeared, leaving only the replica of Anyan's cabin sitting alone in the mirror.

[But it could be real. I can make it real, for you,] came that seductive whisper.

'Only by destroying me,' I said, almost sadly. 'I'm not that Jane anymore. And, to be honest, I don't know if I'd want to be her. She was sweet, but she wasn't able to cope with things. I like being who I've become,' I said, realizing that fact for myself only as I said it for the first time.

I really do like who I've become, I thought, much to my evident surprise.

'And again,' I said quickly, before the creature could up his ante any more, 'I don't get to choose my happiness over others' lives. That's not my right. Nothing you can offer me will change that fact.'

First, Jason disappeared. For all my brave words, my heart wrenched at the sight of him fading away. Then, the mirror disappeared from above the creature's enormous sucker, and its tentacle slithered away. Finally, all the tentacles began slithering. Left and right they went, untangling themselves to reveal another door in the opposite wall.

This door was black, not white, and it was carved with all sorts of Alfar symbols.

Exit all hope, ye who enter here, I conjectured upon their translation. They stayed shut as I neared, and I had to push my way through them. They were heavy, but I managed to push them open by putting all my weight into it.

Call that service? I griped, mentally, only to come to a halt as soon as I'd crossed the threshold.

For I'd come face to cornea with one enormous fucking eyeball.

Chapter Twenty-Two

The eye blinked at me. I blinked back.

Like my own, the eye was jet black. Unlike my own round orb, however, this one was more a horizontal slit – like an enormous subtraction sign. And it *was* huge: the eye itself, along with the round, slightly protruding socket in which it was housed, was larger than the entire length of my body. The skin around the socket was green-gray, but then it flashed orange, and then brown.

Like a chameleon, I thought as it blinked at me again, and I blinked back. *Or an enormous octopus.*

[Come around, Jane,] said that warm, sonorous voice in my mind. [Come around and see my home.]

I sidled past the eye, which watched my progress. Only then did I realize it had been moved around in its socket, and that I'd come in through some sort of side entrance.

Once I'd walked in front of it, I peered around the room. It had once been white marble, like the others I'd just been in, but it was now streaked with algae, lime, salt, and sand. Partially that was because there was a lot more water here than there had been. Water ran down the rock walls, like natural fountains, spilling into pools here and there, or dripping out onto the floor. All that water made it look a lot more like a natural cave than those other overly white spaces had.

Similar to that last room, however, this one also had tentacles piled around, here and there. They pulsed and twitched occasionally, but were otherwise still.

Also like those other rooms, this one heaved with power. Yet the power was slightly different, somehow. The other rooms had been Alfar, laced with something else . . . Here, I just felt that 'something else'. It felt a little like Terk's brownie magic, or Nell's power when she tapped into the old magics, but more concentrated. More like Blondie's power, actually, but still not exactly that.

[It's the wild magic,] the voice said. [Older than old, it's the first magic. Tapping into the elements themselves, not just the elements' radiated force.]

I turned back to the eye. 'I guess that would make sense, since you're so ancient. So's your power.'

The creature chuckled in my head, and I had the odd experience of watching the mottled green-gray skin around the creature's eye crinkle in amusement and flash brown, until the laughter in my head ceased.

[You are a practical little creature, little one. And so calm.]

I shrugged. 'This past year has been all about the surprises. I've learned to roll with change.'

[Aren't you frightened?] it asked.

'Of course,' I admitted. 'But you could have killed me at any point, couldn't you, since I've been in your home. Plus,' I hazarded, having formed a hunch from having the creature in my mind for these past few hours, 'you were the one possessing everyone, weren't you?'

There pulsed a feeling of agreement in my head – less language and more a sense of affirmation.

'I thought so. So, if you'd wanted to kill me, you could have just possessed me and made me dash my brains against a cave wall, or used that sword to kill myself instead of that bird. Which was a dastardly little trick, that bird.'

[Not my trick,] the creature interrupted. [That was put there by those who built this prison.]

'The Alfar?' I asked.

[Yes, that is what you call them.]

'That makes sense. Although I'm surprised I passed any test that they created.'

[You didn't,] the creature intoned, in my mind. [You failed.]

'But the door . . .'

[I opened the door. The test was meant to test resolve. Your apology, plus the time you took to make the decision and the fact you paused at killing another creature, meant you failed.]

'Huh,' I replied. 'Well, I never was very good at standard-ized testing—'

[Why did you pause?] the creature interrupted. [It was only a bird, after all.]

'It *was* only a bird,' I acknowledged. 'But it was the principle. Whoever set that test up was being cruel, and expecting me to do something equally cruel. It's one thing to kill a bird for food or because it's . . . I dunno, attacking your babies. But the way it was just put there, like that . . .'

[And yet you did kill it.]

I hung my head. 'If I didn't, it'd be dead anyway. And so would a lot of other people, and animals.'

[How did making that decision make you feel?]

I thought about that before answering. 'It made me feel used. Out of control. Like I don't get to live my life the way I want to, but the way other people dictate.'

[You've felt like that for a while, no?]

Yes, I admitted, although only in my thoughts. I knew it

was useless to lie to the creature, since it could be in my mind so easily. And yet I felt like I wanted to talk to it for some reason. It felt good to be so honest – I felt like I *could* be honest with myself, in a way that was never easy.

[Since when?] the creature asked.

'Since all of this started. Since I learned about my mom and her world, my life's been exciting, but not necessarily mine. I love it, too,' I insisted, knowing that my feelings for my new life were complicated. 'But sometimes I wish I had more control over the way I live.'

[And yet I gave you choices, and you refused them.]

I smiled, sadly. 'They weren't really choices. They were fantasies.'

The creature seemed to be thinking about what I'd said. When it finally spoke, its voice was grave.

[Would you like to hear my story?] the creature asked. [For I, too, have felt acted upon. My life has not been my own. And yet, I have learned to accept that fact. Even to embrace it.]

Realistically, I knew that I had no choice in the matter. The creature clearly wanted something from me, and whatever it wanted involved me knowing its life. But I appreciated it giving me a choice.

'I would be honored,' I said, meaning it. I had no idea what I was getting myself into, but I knew it would be interesting.

[Come forward, little Jane,] it intoned. [Come forward and open your mind . . .]

I stepped forward, letting my shields drop away, picturing my mind as an opened Tupperware container. Partly, I figured that the creature could probably take what it wanted, anyway, so I should play along. But, I was also interested.

And while the Tupperware imagery wasn't the most elegant of visions, it clearly worked . . .

For suddenly I was plunged into the sea, the water roiling with my siblings' play as we twined in and out of each other, making knots of our limbs for the pleasure of feeling each other's touch and the equal pleasure that was the challenge of unknotting ourselves.

The sea was our home and our mother, and in her embrace we played. At night, we took shelter in our father's arms, a large cave that barely contained our intertwined, sleeping forms.

I've been here, Jane True realized. *I remember this. You were with me when I slept.*

[Yes,] the creature acknowledged. [It was easy to reach you then. But you thought it was all a dream . . .]

Your sisters and brothers, I realized, horrified at the knowledge that this gentle mind, touching mine, had suffered such loss.

[Yes,] was all the creature replied, and even after all these millennia its thoughts harbored immense grief.

For despite the ages that had passed, I could feel the love and the comfort in that cave of intertwined tentacles. *To have had so much, and then lost it all.*

'Who killed them?' I asked.

[A cousin. A creature of Fire. It was killed, in return, but that brought me no comfort.]

No, I thought. *It wouldn't.*

'Why did it attack you and your family?' I asked.

[Because it could. Because it was its parent's creature – mercurial and so hungry.]

'And your parents?'

[Water and Earth, who lay down together to form the world. We were born of love.]

'And yet you destroyed so much . . . your memories are full of death . . .'

[Yes,] it replied sadly. [But I was created for a world that ceased to exist. In that world, our play was harmless. Later, the world was no longer ours and I no longer fit.]

'And so you were imprisoned?'

I felt the creature smile in my mind, but it was a sad smile that countered the sense of peace I was still living, nestled in among my (long-dead) siblings. We were still communing in its memories, and it felt like we were narrating one film over another.

[I have things to show you, child. Things that will help you to understand not only your own world and your place in it, but also what you must do next. For I am not the only thing of power left on this planet, nor am I the most dangerous. War is coming, little one. And we must all choose a side.]

And with that I was pulled out of the nest and into what felt like a stream of memories. I was living them, but it was like they were running in fast forward. Senses, impressions, and sights all streamed into me, through me, but I lived each for every second it took to pass through.

I watched as the world went from the ocean it had been, with a cluster of earth in the center, to a place of continents. Once my kind – for I, Jane True, was still living through this great, elemental being – were mostly eradicated either by accident or design, the elements bonded together one last time. Earth gave matter, water gave substance, air gave breath, and fire gave its spark so that life could once again flare into existence. This life, however, was tiny, embryonic. It stirred around me and I held my very breath for fear of destroying it. Soon, however, it thrived, and developed, ever evolving until the embryo became a multitude of shapes and forms. And then it continued changing and growing.

Eventually the seas could no longer contain its multitudes, so life went looking for more space on land. There it thrived, as well, and soon both earth and water contained a plethora of beings so amazing in their variety and splendor that I was happy merely to observe and study.

The land creatures were the most interesting. I'd never forget the development of feathers, nor the first time an ape walked on two legs and had thoughts beyond its next meal or shelter. I rejoiced at mankind, for I could watch them through their dreams, and later, as I developed my powers, through their very own eyes. They were so complex and intelligent. But despite their potential, I knew that fire was in their veins – along with earth, air, and water – and that it was in fire's nature to flare up and destroy.

When that first human felt my presence in her mind and asked me what I was, I was as shocked as she was. I went deeper and felt her connection to her progenitors: the elements. We were not the same; where I was elemental, she was in touch with the elements, but still she was some-thing *more*. The next step in human evolution, I taught her to use her connection to the elements to manipulate her world. She could create fire with a touch, shield herself from harm with the air, call to water so that she never remained thirsty, even create shelter out of the barest envir-onment for herself and her family. Finally, I was able to teach her to change her shape, until she swam with me as a porpoise.

The part of me that was still Jane True nearly shat itself at these revelations. *Are we all really just humans?* I thought. *Could all the Alfar mythologies about being a different species be lies?*

I also realized something else. *Oh my gods, that's Blondie!* I thought, watching the young human woman change herself into a porpoise, and back. *Is she* that *old?*

Others were born like that first elemental girl, the one Jane True knew as Blondie. It wasn't a common mutation, but it happened often enough that I was able to manipulate them to help them find each other. Some, however, lived so far away that I had to teach them myself. I'd learned to guide their powers and their training in their dreams, so they never learned of my existence. But I still loved them, as a parent loves a child, which is why the first one to be murdered hurt so much.

He was only a boy. The first time he called forth fire to warm his freezing family, his father called him evil and slit his throat.

The killings were more common after that. Some of my children were able to create places for themselves in their clans as shamans, or even as demigods, but most were abused, cast out, or killed. I guided the survivors and the exiles together, creating safe havens where they could live together in peace.

I blamed fire for the other humans' inability to understand my children. But I'd forgotten that fire lived in their veins, as well.

I'd also forgotten that while I was *one* of the last of the ancient elements left on earth, I wasn't *the* last.

It started out as a whisper in the dreams of my most powerful children. In their waking life, they were shielded from me. But sleeping, they were more open. And while I never searched their minds, such sleeping whispers would sometimes intrude upon me.

Their dreams revealed some who wanted more power. More important, they wanted power in order to seek revenge upon those who had cast them out, or hurt them, or killed others like them.

These ones banded together, practicing their magics not to make their lives better and easier, but so they could use their power as a weapon.

Soon enough, this attracted the attention of one of Fire's only surviving children. He was young – hardly older than humanity – and Fire had made him deliberately weak in an attempt to create something that could survive itself.

On his own, Fire's progeny could do little. He was just a whisper of flame – but just as a single match could start a blaze that burned down half a continent given the right conditions, he knew he'd found the perfect kindling in my children.

He whispered to them of an artifact: a child of earth who had laid down to rest in its parent's bosom, and had died there. Reabsorbed, its corpse had added to the power that now fed my little elementals. But it had left part of itself behind.

'. . . a single horn, like that of a bull,' Fire's child whispered. 'With which you can magnify your power beyond your imagination. You can become as gods . . .'

Some of my children left in the night, guided by the flame that led them, like a will-o-the-wisp, to their doom.

The horn was found and brought back. Its magic was unleashed . . .

Suddenly the memory I was living slowed, until I was in the moment again, watching everything unfold from the creature's viewpoint behind one of its children's eyes.

I watched as a young woman stepped forward, holding aloft a bull's horn the length of her forearm. Her tattooed forearms . . .

Blondie, I realized, my heart thudding in my chest. *She was there, at the beginning, and here, as well?*

My friend was obviously making a speech, gesticulating vehemently with both her free hand and the horn. Around me, some of the other people's faces reflected agreement, others concern, others confusion, and a few anger.

One of the angry-faced beings – a young man, who looked very similar to Blondie – stepped forward, confronting the Original. They were up in each other's faces, while panic shot through our host's system. He was obviously terrified by the proceedings, and feeling his panic made watching the scene a whole other level of experience.

Blondie backed away from the man, shouting something as she held the horn aloft in both hands. And with that we felt her power swell and surge through the horn.

Fire's child had been right. Blondie's already-strong power was, indeed, magnified. I watched, trapped by my host's mute horror, as wave after wave of knee-buckling force pulsed out of Blondie. Inside my host, magics realigned themselves as he lost contact with three of the four elements, and he felt his bones shift into that of his favorite fishing shape: a seal.

Around me other creatures were either in different shapes or still morphing when Blondie's power finally used itself up and she collapsed. There were a handful of creatures prescient enough to throw up shields and powerful enough to hold them during the horn's onslaught, but even they'd lost some of their power. They were still standing, however, and together they moved to secure the horn and Blondie.

My host changed himself back into human form, realizing as he did so that he'd been cut off from all elements but water. He tried other tricks: creating fire, pulling force from the earth, flying with air. All of these attempts failed. Finally, he tried to change into something other than a seal. That was unsuccessful as well.

Everyone standing in that clearing looked around at one another, obviously at a loss over what had just happened, or how to proceed.

'That was the Great Schism,' I breathed, closing down my mind so I could open my eyes and be just me, Jane True, again. 'I knew she did it, but I only saw her memories. They were brief.'

[It was a very traumatic event,] the creature said.

'What was the bull's horn?' I asked.

[It was a horn, but not that of a bull. Nor was it really from a child of Earth. In reality, it belonged to one of Fire's most violent children. When the child was destroyed, only the horn and another artifact, a hoof, were left. Both held tremendous power, but the horn remained at large.]

'Where's the hoof?' I asked.

[Protected,] was all the creature would say. I knew I wasn't getting any more on that subject.

'So let me get this straight,' I began. What I was learning this week went against *everything* I'd ever been told about the Alfar, their origins, and the supernatural world. The Alfar had obviously had a great time inventing their own mythology, with themselves on top. 'Blondie found the horn with the help of another of Fire's children – a voice that told her where to go.' I felt assent in my mind, the creature's version of a nod. 'She brought it back and used it. I felt her anger when I touched her tat . . . she wanted to get rid of humans?'

[So many of her kind had suffered abuse. She was full of hate.]

'But the horn actually created the Schism?'

[Yes. It picked out one aspect of the various beings' magics – those individual beings most favored. Or it just assigned them an identity arbitrarily. It's hard to say, with magic as old and foul as the horn's was. Once each faction, as they are now called, was locked into place, their magics were locked into place. And as long as they bred with another of their faction, they would breed true. If they were successful, that is.]

'And she was the only one unaffected?' I asked.

[She's the only one who retained her power.]

'She must have been so hated,' I said, marveling at her audacity even as I pitied her.

[And yet she's the reason her people survived,] the creature informed me. [Fire always destroys, but oftentimes from that destruction comes life. This was no exception. Extreme exposure to elemental magic kills humanity's ability to breed, over time. If my children had stayed as powerful as they were, there would have been maybe two more generations, each with fewer progeny. And then there would have been none.]

'I knew it,' I said. 'I knew it had to do with the magic. So the weaker the faction—'

[The greater their chances of breeding.]

No wonder there are so many nahuals, and so few Alfar, I thought.

[Exactly,] the creature responded.

'But you helped them,' I said. 'They would never have known what to do with their power if it weren't for you. Why did they imprison you?'

[Open your mind, and I'll show you this imprisonment,] the creature replied, amusement tinting his response.

I did, and felt myself whooshed back into the creature's memories. The loneliness and grief was unbearable; so many years alone, and now my children disbanded into factions that hated one another. Everything had fallen apart.

So I decided to sleep.

I found a place to nest, building up the land around me so that I was part of both Earth and Water. At least I could be with my parents as I slept.

And with that I took my leave, falling into a sleep so profound as to echo death, although my great mind continued to sweep through the sleeping brains of animals and people alike.

That's when the Alfar found me. And they made my nest into a death trap.

I watched as King Melichor and Queen Tatiana, along with their seconds Glynda and Straif, re-rigged the land around my sleeping form. They assumed I was a weapon and that, were I to awaken, I'd destroy everything. On the one hand, they wanted access to this weapon, but on the other hand, they wanted to deny access to others.

Part of the traps they set was the magnitude of my waking. In order to free me, my nest would have to be dissolved. Including everything that stood upon it.

'You're not a weapon,' I said, already knowing that but wanting to get it out there. 'You're not even evil. You've just been built on.'

[Yes. But if my prison is destroyed, so is everything that rests upon it.]

'So if Phaedra does manage to release you, even if you don't want to, you'll destroy the Eastern Seaboard?'

[Precisely.]

'Good grief,' I said, marveling at just how anarchical the little Alfar truly was. Then I thought of something. 'But what do *you* want?'

[I'm sorry?] the creature asked, its voice surprised.

'What do you want? Do you want to be free?'

The creature paused before responding. [Would you let me be released, if it meant so much destruction?]

I snorted. 'I don't think I'm in a position to allow anything. I'm just asking.'

[You are kind, little one. But no. I do not need to be 'free'. Freedom is a relative term. My mind is free, and I experience so much through people like you, who are open to me. Meanwhile, my body was never for this world. Let it lie here and rest.]

Phew, cuz that would have sucked, I thought, before I could stop myself. Then I forced myself to say, 'If you're sure.'

The creature merely chuckled.

'So what are we going to do?' I asked. 'I know you don't want to, but technically you're still capable of destroying a big chunk of the world. And there's this nonsense about me being a champion . . .'

[Well, first things first,] came the creature's calm voice in my head. [I think you should probably deal with what's behind you.]

I cocked my head in confusion, before twirling around on my heel.

There stood Phaedra, looking as muddy and bruised as me, but also very, very pissed.

Chapter Twenty-Three

'Hey, Phaedra,' I said, effecting calm. 'What's up?'

It was her turn to blink at me.

'You look like you've been through the wars. How'd you get past Blondie?' I asked, suddenly alarmed for my friend.

Is she our friend? I thought, suddenly remembering Blondie's heretofore unmentioned role in the Great Schism. *Is this all her attempt to make things up?*

'Cavern collapsed,' Phaedra snarled. 'The bitch apparated herself out without a scratch.' With that, Phaedra spat out a mouthful of what looked like blood.

'Huh,' I said, taking in the little Alfar's condition. *Why isn't she healing herself?*

'But she's not going to be able to find her way back in so easily,' Phaedra said and leered, and then I felt a little bit of pull from the earth and water around me as the Alfar visibly started to heal.

'Oh, no?' I asked, keeping Phaedra occupied while I tried to pinpoint the alarm bells going off in my head. They weren't negative alarm bells; they were positive ones, like I was 'hot' on something that would make a big difference, if I could only figure out what it was.

'The whole tunnel system collapsed behind me,' said Phaedra with a smirk, as she kept drawing weakly from around her. It was like she didn't want me to feel what she was doing. 'She wouldn't know where to apparate herself to find us. You're trapped down here with me.'

And you're trapped down here with us, I thought, for the creature's benefit. 'How'd you make it through?' I asked, not having to feign the quaver in my voice. To be honest, I was more scared of the idea of being trapped than I was at the idea of being trapped with Phaedra. There was something about the Alfar that was off.

'Speed and shields,' she replied, healing the last of her wounds. But she still looked funny – pallid and not her usual sprightly, if evil, self.

Only then did the Alfar raise shields, pulling hard on the elements around her to form them.

Just the elements around her, my brain realized, beginning to understand the little Alfar's predicament. Despite my forming ideas, I kept my face carefully neutral and took a step backward as if intimidated by the bald little woman in front of me.

I could hear the wet *snick* of the eye blinking behind me.

'You know, we don't have to do this,' I said, as she raised a mage ball and I pulled up my own shields, encompassing the eyeball to be on the safe side. I was pretty sure the creature could take care of itself, but still. The thought of a mage ball in my own eye made me squicky.

'Of course we do,' Phaedra replied, pulsing magic into her mage ball.

'But we don't. The creature isn't even a weapon. It's actually really nice,' I said, realizing how inappropriate that sounded as soon as it was out of my mouth.

Well, nice in a 'destroy a big chunk of the world despite itself' kind of way, I thought.

'Of course it is a weapon. Either it wipes out you and your allies like a scourge, or it gives me its power. Either way, I will destroy you and everyone like you,' Phaedra said, as she volleyed mage balls at my shields. I absorbed them without effort. *Her balls aren't nearly as full as they normally are*, I thought, to my libido's vast amusement.

'But it's not evil,' I repeated. 'It's not even really imprisoned. I mean, it is, but that's because the Alfar made it look that way.'

She blasted away at my shields for a bit, before coming up for air to regroup. Once again I felt her pull at the elements. I knew, then, what was wrong.

'I know, idiot halfling,' she said, clearly fed up. If she was smarter, or a better actress, she wouldn't act so put out about not having been able to take me down already. But luckily she was Phaedra – evil and cunning, yes, but not the most diabolical devil in Hell, by any means.

'You know?' I asked, trying to keep her talking as I figured out my strategy.

'The stupid thing blasted its thoughts into every supernatural in Rockabill. We all saw its lies,' she said, her face a mask of rage.

'Really?' I asked, surprised that the creature had made common the truth it had shown me. 'It showed everyone everything?'

'Yes,' she said, obviously fuming. 'Although I am sure very little of it can be believed.'

'Really?' I repeated, stupidly. 'You mean the *whole* thing? With the creation of the earth? And the supernaturals really being mutant humans? And the Great Schism? All of it?'

'Yes!' she growled, her face spasming with rage each time I adumbrated.

It sucks when your ideology turns out to be false, I

thought, understanding her anger for what it really was –
fear.

'If you experienced what I did, then you felt what it felt.
More important, you felt what its host, the man who became
a selkie, felt. You know it can't be lies,' I needled.

'Anything can be a lie,' Phaedra insisted, almost shouting.
'Anything can be created. Nothing can be believed, and that
was lies.'

'If nothing can be believed, then why does the creature
have to be the one lying? Why can't what you've been taught
about your origins be the lies?'

I realized how hard this had to be for Phaedra. Yes, she
was a nut, but she'd been taught that the Alfar were far
superior (and unrelated) to both humans and other supes. The
creature's version of things went against everything Phaedra
had ever been told and what she'd based her whole life upon.

She actually turned purple at my words. It was an interesting
choice of complexion, considering her blood-red eyes.

'We are not humans!' she snarled, and I felt her magic
blast at me as she pounded against my shields with both force
and well-aimed mage balls.

Gotcha, I thought, feeling her pull once again, and despite
her having lost her temper, at only earth and water.

'You should really calm down, Phaedra,' I said, once she'd
spent herself and had to recharge. Like me, she could pull
water from the air, cocooned as we were by water in this
ocean cave. Water that also kept out most air-elementals.
What there had been, she'd probably already hoovered up.
'Being human's not that bad.'

She snarled again, her face a mask of inhuman rage.

'And besides,' I said, before she could answer back with
either mage balls or words, 'you're going to burn yourself
out.'

'I am Alfar, you stupid bitch. I will burn *you* out!' she yelled back at me, eyes manic with hate.

'No,' I replied, calmly. 'You won't. You can't burn anything, not down here. You're surrounded by water, dampening out your fire. And you're cut off from air, as we've not had a fresh gust of anything but your own gaseous bellowing since we came down here.'

'I still have earth, and I still have water,' she said, but more quietly. She'd gone on the defensive, not that it mattered.

'No, you have only earth,' I said, and then I struck.

Using the same trick I'd learned from Trill and the kappa, I pulled the ocean over to my side. It was like playing string with a kitten: every time Phaedra reached – expending power – I drew the water's power back to me, out of her grasp.

Ever the Alfar, meanwhile, Phaedra wasn't able to accept that I could best her with my own element. And instead of backing down and using her remaining element, like a sensible person, she just kept reaching.

And I kept shutting her down, till she was panting, her shields severely weakened. Only then did she back away and pull from the earth at her feet.

'There you go,' I said, smiling sweetly at her. 'That's a good girl. Now you know what it's like to be one of us, with only one element.'

She growled something incomprehensible but almost certainly obscene as she pulled and pulled and pulled . . .

'You're so slow,' I said, elegantly pulling my own water mojo around me like a cloak. 'Not used to just having the one, are you?'

She snarled, lobbing a rather ineffectual green mage ball at me. It reminded me of Anyan, and I felt my own flare of temper.

'And so weak,' I jibed, trying to keep her off balance. But

I was also telling the truth. I knew she wasn't the strongest Alfar, but being able to pull from and combine all four clementals made her far more powerful than the majority of us single-elementals. Now she had only earth, and it didn't appear as if she could hold too much of the element's power at one time.

She's got small earth pockets, I mused. *While my own dear water pockets are generous.*

'Are you going to talk at me all night, or are we going to fight?' the little woman asked finally, pulling herself upright.

She called that one, I thought, having fully intended to talk at her for as long as possible. But she didn't need to know that.

'Oh, we're going to fight, all right,' I said, baring my teeth in what I hoped was a predatory smile but I feared might look like I was requesting a spot spinach-check. And then I started pummeling her.

[Good, Jane, nice form,] the creature's voice spoke in my mind, nearly causing me to lose my concentration. I'd almost forgotten about it, lurking behind me.

Thanks, I thought, as I kept pulling water-elementals away from Phaedra whenever she tried to reach, using them to recharge even as I launched barrage after barrage of mage balls. Phaedra's shields were absorbing them, but she was weakening.

[What you need is a weapon,] the creature stated, and I thought of Blondie's killer (literally) sword. The creature chuckled.

[No, you'll not be able to create that sword. That's a real weapon, forged by my surviving child. That's part of her magic as much as it is the physical world. You need something different. Something made for you.]

Like what? I thought, as I kept Phaedra busy with a fresh volley of zinging mage balls.

[How about . . . this,] the creature said, as in front of me appeared a two-headed ax.

'An ax?' I said aloud, my voice unable to hide my scorn. *Me with an ax? That'll be like an episode of outtakes from the ill-fated Jane the Barbarian.*

[Actually a labrys,] the creature informed me.

'See, I don't even know my axes. That's exactly why you need a different champion,' I said, nearly nicking Phaedra with a mage ball. She'd been distracted by an ax appearing in front of me, out of nowhere.

[Just take it. See how it feels,] the creature said. I think I was trying its patience.

'Fine,' I said. 'But if I chop off my own leg, I'm hopping after you.'

The creature stayed silent as I reached out my hand. As soon as my fingers made contact with the haft, all my nerves – and my magic – sang. It felt like the ax had been made for me. The wood felt perfect against my skin, but it's also like I *recognized* the weapon, on some primeval level.

Holy shit, I marveled, as my hand closed around the ax's handle. Power surged through me and the wood of the handle seemed to mold itself to my hand.

What is this thing? I marveled.

I drew my arm back, taking the ax from where it hung in the air before me. But instead of falling to the ground with a *thunk* as my arm lost to its weight, like I thought would happen, the ax seemed to weigh nothing at all.

[Now give it some power,] said the creature. [Make it yours.]

I concentrated, somehow knowing exactly what the creature meant for me to do. It was like the weapon itself was whispering to me. I shut my eyes, letting my shields absorb Phaedra's attacks, as I opened myself to both my power and the labrys . . .

Voila, I thought, as I opened my eyes to discover that I held in front of me a weapon made of both pure energy and steel – something to rival Blondie's own fearsome sword.

Phaedra's attacks stopped, and she looked at me with horror.

I took a few admittedly awkward swipes with the ax. I remembered Ryu elegantly dueling with Jimmu, the naga prince, at the Alfar Compound.

I'm not quite that elegant, I thought, as I chopped away with my new toy. The good news was that Phaedra, at least, was looking even more vexed than I was.

'I'm full of surprises,' I informed the little Alfar, as I took a step toward her, brandishing my new weapon. 'Which you should keep in mind, as I repeat myself: we don't have to do this.'

Phaedra pulled hard on the earth, creating her own forest-green sword.

'Yes, we do,' she said, twirling her own weapon elegantly. I frowned.

Add ax-fighting lessons to the list, I thought wearily.

'Why keep going, Phaedra?' I asked, trying to stall her. While the labrys felt great in my hand, and my body was singing with power, I still didn't want to have to fight the little Alfar. 'The creature's not going to kill for you,' I said. 'What part of "it's not a weapon" are you not understanding?'

Phaedra shook her head. 'It does not matter whether it will kill for us,' she said. 'Merely waking it will destroy that which we most want destroyed: you, the barghest, your baobhan sith, and hopefully all the other traitors still squatting in that compound.'

'How are they traitors?' I asked. 'It's your master who killed the true king.'

'Orin was no king. He was a puppet. The weakness of such leaders is what has brought down my people.'

I pursed my lips. 'Actually, no. Did you guys not get the part about magic and babies?'

Phaedra looked at me, confused. Our subsequent conversation must have been private, even if the creature had shared its memories of that day. Phaedra hadn't the truth about magic and fertility.

'It's your magic that does that. The no-babies thing? It has to do with how strong you are, with the mojos. How much you use it.'

'Again, you lie,' she spat out.

'Do I?' I asked. 'Think about it. Nahuals, magically your weakest people, still manage to procreate. Alfars, magically your strongest, are almost entirely barren. Everyone else gets filled in somewhere on that spectrum.'

Phaedra shook her head, either in denial of my words or denying she'd even heard them. She beefed up her shields and took a step toward me, her sword a blur as she did some fancy ninja moves.

'Besides,' I said, wondering why on earth I had thought 'take the weapon' was a good idea, 'you don't even know how to free the creature. It's already awake, so that can't be the answer.' I was trying to distract her while I thought to the being in question.

Um, a little help here, I thought. *About the whole 'ax-fighting' thing.*

[I am here to help you,] it told me, and I felt a wave of reassurance – both my own and the creature's – wash through me. Phaedra's next words, however, were not so reassuring.

'You little idiot,' Phaedra hissed, as she pointed with her

sword above my head. 'Of course I do. Do you never look up?'

Will you keep an eye on her? I thought. [Yes,] the creature replied, as I beefed up my shields so I could turn around.

Shit, I thought. For sure enough, several feet over where the eye peeked out of the rock, there was one last glyph carved into the stone.

Undoubtedly the glyph that freed the creature from its prison, taking the rest of us with it.

'So you understand why it is that we must, indeed, "do this",' Phaedra said, giving me her favorite cat's-ass smile. 'You are standing in between me and your imminent demise.'

That I am, I thought, even as I realized something. 'But you'll be destroying yourself too, you loon,' I said.

She nodded, her eyes wide and shining. 'But I will die cleansing this world of the lies spread here today.' Then she looked directly at me, beginning her ninja-sword routine again to punctuate her name-calling. 'And you, you annoying . . . little . . . perversion.'

Wow, she's willing to die just to get rid of lil old me, I thought, almost proud. *I must be* super *annoying . . .*

The creature chuckled in my mind. [I think you might want to get ready,] it intoned, just as Phaedra leaped at me.

My shields were strong enough that neither she nor her sword could penetrate them, but I felt the blow. The sword concentrated the Alfar's force, making it harder to deflect than mage balls.

[And your labrys will do the same,] it said. [If you use it . . .]

With that hint, I raised my ax and tentatively began hacking with it. The problem was, to get anywhere with the hacking I had to pull my shields back to behind the ax. Which meant I left myself vulnerable, especially since I was quickly discovering how very little I knew about edged-weapons fighting.

When I'd nearly had my hands whacked off twice, and I'd taken about a dozen hard blows to my shields, the creature intervened.

[May I?] it inquired politely. [If you'd just open your mind . . .]

I did so, and the next thing I knew it felt like I was floating just over my own head. The creature had shoved me out of my own body so it could do its thang. I watched as Jane began her own offensive – much to Phaedra's evident shock – which included some of her own ninja twirlings and a seriously fast series of thrusts and slices that had worn Phaedra's shields down to nubs. The creature kept up the onslaught until Phaedra had retreated to the other side of the room, panting.

[Jane?] asked the creature, politely. [Would you like your body back?]

Yes, please, I thought. While it was fun watching Phaedra getting her ass kicked, I wanted to be doing the kicking, and not just my body.

[You have a plan,] the creature said, as my consciousness floated back down into my skin.

Yes, I thought. It had been obvious, really, once I was floating well above the action.

As soon as I was back in my body – which was panting for breath despite the creature having done the mental lifting – I struck while Phaedra was still vulnerable.

There was water dripping everywhere, and I let the ax dangle at my side as I reached for it. Not as a power source, but as it was – lovely, dripping H_2O.

'What are you doing?' Phaedra asked, trying to build back her shields. But already there was a thin film of water between her feet and the cavern floor. I pulled harder, and the water that had been trickling from the cave walls now gushed, covering the floor. That said, I was careful to keep all of that water's power for myself. It swirled under Phaedra's feet, but just as if she were a magical-Tantalus, it would never quench her power's thirst.

My plan was elegant, and a bit cruel. Unfortunately, it would also take forever to fill the whole space of the cavern, and I didn't know if the creature liked getting its eye wet, so I wove a basket of power around Phaedra.

[Lovely,] the creature complimented me, as I began carefully neutralizing and then funneling all that water in the room, in torrents, into the prison I'd built around Phaedra. Nearly empty as she was of all other elements, and being surrounded only by water magic I wouldn't let her touch, she could only put up a token struggle.

When she cobbled together enough strength that she managed to reach through the water at her feet toward the earth, I lifted the whole orb off the ground. The labrys helped me, cheerfully spitting power at me as I raised it – and the orb – high into the air. Phaedra sloshed about, up to her neck in water, like a goldfish won at a carnival.

'You know who taught me this trick?' I called to her, raising my voice so she could hear me over the sloshing. 'You did,' I answered when she didn't respond. 'In Boston, on that pier, after you let your minions rape and kill those innocent women.'

Phaedra glared at me, clearly unrepentant.

'I should kill you,' I whispered, thinking of all the atrocities she'd committed or commanded or allowed.

[You should kill her,] the creature agreed.

'But I won't,' I said and sighed, lowering the orb so it hovered inches off the floor. She was contained, helpless. I'd wait till Blondie found us, and then we'd figure out how to deal with the Alfar.

[You won't dispose of her?] the creature asked.

No, I thought. *I'm no killer.* Then I thought back to the men who'd lost their lives attacking Anyan and me. *Well, at least not this kind of killer. Not an executioner.*

The creature's mind was warm in mine as it scanned my feelings.

[You really are kind, Jane True,] it murmured, as I felt its power shift. The next thing I knew my shields surrounding Phaedra had burst, spilling water everywhere. The Alfar was free.

But she wasn't going anywhere.

Her expression was frozen in horror, gazing down through lifeless eyes at the tentacle speared through her torso.

Chapter Twenty-Four

'You didn't have to do that,' I whispered, as the tentacle shook Phaedra free. The bald little Alfar fell to the wet floor with a *splat*. There was no reason to check whether she was alive or dead, not with the hole in her chest so big I could have stuck my head through it.

For a second I envisioned myself wearing Phaedra as a necklace, and I shuddered.

[No,] it said, in my mind. [I didn't. But it made things easier.]

I looked at the Alfar's huddled form. 'I had her contained.'

[Yes, you did. But I've seen inside her thoughts. She would never have stopped coming for you. Or for me, for that matter.]

I understand that, I thought. *But to kill her—*

[Was something I took upon myself, so that your people did not have to. There is no place that could guarantee her captivity, and she cannot be allowed free at this juncture. As I said, I saw into her mind . . .] With these words the creature's thoughts trailed off.

'And?' I prompted.

[And you must believe me when I tell you that I am by no means the most dangerous thing either hidden or hiding out there. My prison's crumbling might destroy a corner of the world . . . but there are things out there that will gladly take the whole planet with them.]

'Is this what you saw in Phaedra's mind?'

[She was but a minion; she knew only her own mission. But she had heard rumors, and knew where others had been sent.]

'Are they looking for other creatures? Other artifacts?'

[Both. But this is not a conversation we should have in private . . .]

I felt the creature's power swirl about me, and then I heard a *pop* as Blondie apparated in front of us.

'What the fuck?' she said, throwing up shields and peering madly about. When she saw me, she sprinted over and nearly knocked me down with her hug.

'Hey, girl,' I said, laughing and trying to figure out where to put my arm. It was tough holding someone while also holding an ax. Or a labrys. Whatever.

'Are you all right?' she said, rearing back to scan my face as she held tightly to my upper arms.

'I'm great. Better than Phaedra,' I said, gesturing with my non-ax hand.

'Ugh,' she said. 'Holey-moley.' Then she saw what I was carrying.

'Jane,' she said, her eyes shining. 'You accepted!'

I looked at the labrys. I looked at Blondie. I looked at the labrys again. And then I put two and two together.

'You conned me!' I shouted, turning around to confront the giant eyeball.

Its presence in my mind was smug, amused, and entirely unrepentant.

'I'm your champion now, aren't I?' I asked.

[Yes,] it said. [By accepting the labrys, you've accepted my power.]

'I don't suppose I can exchange it for a pair of socks?'

[No,] it said. [Now let me see my child,] it insisted, and I realized I was standing between the eyeball and Blondie. So I moved out of the way, my brain struggling to compute that I'd just unwittingly made myself the creature's little pet.

[Hello, child,] came the creature's voice in my mind. I saw Blondie gulp, go pale, then turn to the great eyeball. To my surprise, she fell to her knees.

'Sire,' she whispered, tears choking her throat. 'I'm so sorry . . .'

[No need, my child. We are past apologies. It is good to see you with my real sight,] it said.

She sniffled, and then turned to me.

'I'm proud of you, Jane. You did what you had to do.'

'I found the creature,' I said, trying to figure out if I might actually deserve the creature's confidence. 'And I did pass the Alfar tests. Well, sort of.'

'And you defeated your Rival,' she said. I frowned.

'Did you let Phaedra get to me?' I demanded.

Blondie looked guilty.

'I knew it. I knew you could have just kicked her ass. Why did you let her get through to me?'

[Do not blame my child, my child,] the creature said. It needed to expand his pet name vocabulary, for sure. [You had to face your Rival to earn my power. The Alfar set certain rules. I was not able to do away with them, only alter them. One of the Alfar rules was that you had to face a Rival. My child only did as commanded, facilitating your duel.]

'I'm sorry, Jane,' Blondie said. 'I hated keeping all those secrets. Now, however, my mission is complete, so no more lies?'

'There better not be,' I said, admittedly rather petulantly.

'So, why was I brought here?' Blondie asked, uncomfortably.

[I was telling Jane news you must know. What I saw in

Phaedra's mind – there is much to fear, and her people have been busy.]

'Did you see where they're searching? And which things they're looking for?' Blondie asked.

[They are gathering their forces behind two creatures of evil – of darkness. These beings would destroy everyone merely for the joy of creating chaos. Jane must stand in their way.]

'Me?' I squeaked. Blondie gave me a sympathetic look.

[With the weapon you now possess, yes. You must fight, Jane. And you must lead.]

'But what if I can't? What if I'm not good enough?'

[You shall not be coerced, child. I do not write your destiny. I *am* giving you a choice. But the rebellion needs a leader – someone who can be as much figurehead as warrior.]

'A figurehead? Like what . . . Joan of Arc?'

The creature thought over my question. [Yes, that is an adequate analogy.]

'She got burned at the stake,' I reminded it.

[Perhaps not entirely adequate.]

'So that's all I have to do? Exist? Point at things and make speeches? Try not to get set aflame?'

[No, Jane. You *will* have to fight. It's why I gave you my weapon. I meant it when I said you were my champion. It couldn't be the one you call Blondie – she's the cause, in some ways, of all of this, although she can't be blamed. At heart, this is my fault. My fault for interfering, my fault for being naïve. And so I have created this weapon, imbuing it with my own power, for one whom I deemed worthy in both heart and mind. It will give you what you need in body and strength.]

I looked at the labrys, still glowing with power. I let it go ahead and cool off, so I could really see my so-called destiny.

It wasn't much, to be honest. It looked very plain, very rough-hewn. But when I applied my power again it glowed like it was made of crystal.

'I don't know if I can do this,' I admitted, my voice small.

[I know. And that is why you were chosen. Your humanity will bring you victory. I knew you were a candidate when you were younger, but after being in your soul, when you were attacked . . . You are what the rebellion needs.]

'Speaking of being attacked, do you know who did it?' Blondie interrupted.

[Yes, I know who did it. They were humans, hired by the enemy months ago. That was the first chance they had to attack. And before you ask, it was not Jarl, but one very like him. They work for the same forces.] I felt the creature's concentration again focus on me. [You must learn to think bigger than merely Jarl, Jane. Your enemies are not solitary, nor are they without resources beyond the physical.]

So all of the conjecturing I did with Trill and Nell was correct. There is something bigger going on . . . and Jarl is just one face of our enemy.

'Can you tell me who, exactly, ordered that attack?' asked Blondie.

[I will brief you on what you need to know about what I found in Phaedra's mind, including who hired the humans. I will also send you where you need to go for more information. Are you ready? We must move as swiftly as our enemies.]

'Um, sure,' Blondie said. 'How long will this take?'

[Not long. I am sending you to a source that will have much to tell you. He will, however, need to be coerced.]

'Coercion I can do,' she said. 'Jane, take care. I guess I'll see you soon.' Then Blondie turned and nodded at the great eye. 'I'm rea—' she said, only to be apparated away suddenly.

'Will she be all right?' I asked.

[Oh, yes. This mission will be easy for her.]

And then I asked the question I was dreading, in my smallest mental voice. But the creature heard me.

[Are you still unsure she can be trusted?] it demanded.

'Yes,' I replied, my real voice equally small.

[Yes, she can be. She is your ally, and your friend. My child cares for you very much, little Jane.]

I blushed, and then I glanced again at Phaedra's crumpled form. It was difficult to juggle my perception of the creature as wise and gentle with the Swiss-cheese corpse lying on the floor.

It did what it felt was necessary, I told myself. *Phaedra rarely left anyone with many choices . . .*

[And now,] the creature's voice echoed in my head, [you must return to the surface.]

I looked at the eye, watching me. 'What will you do?' I asked.

[I will remain here and return to my slumbers. But first, you must destroy the glyph,] the creature said, as it rolled its eyeball upward toward the now-familiar carving. [I must never be freed.]

'But that means you'll be trapped!' I cried.

[Yes, my physical form will remain here. But do not think me trapped, child.]

Frowning, I stared up at the glyph. The thought of taking away the creature's only form of release was terrifying.

'I don't know,' I said. 'What if you survive an apocalypse, and we're all toast, and it's just you and the cockroaches, and you could be free again? But the sigil's gone? I would feel awful.'

[First of all, you'd be dead and would feel nothing. Second, we all must make our sacrifices. This is mine.]

'But you've already given up so much,' I whispered, knowing its eons trapped under the earth and ocean . . .

[I am the only surviving member of my race. I have been both blessed and cursed, living as long as I have. And that life is my own, to give or to take. Besides, it's really not so bad. I live among your people's thoughts, experiencing far more in their minds than I ever could otherwise. You humans are fascinating creatures.]

'That's kind of you to say, but still . . .'

[Jane, trust me on this. You cannot spare guards to keep my lair safe. And while I have means of protecting myself, I do not want to have to be awake and alert all the time. Can you understand that by keeping that glyph in place, you're also trapping me? I will always have to be awake and watchful. I would rather dream and play.]

I remembered then the creature's memories that I'd experienced while in my coma. They'd been so vivid, and so peaceful, for the most part. No wonder it wanted to return to its sleeping mind.

'I think I understand,' I said.

[So will you help me?] it asked.

'Yes,' I replied. 'How should I do it?'

[Direct magic will not work. It will only set off a trap. Something physical must destroy it.]

I frowned. 'I'm afraid I forgot my chisel, and while this ax looks sharp, it's magic.' Looking around, I tried to find something to use. All I could see was water.

Well, I thought. *Water does erode* . . .

I carefully laid my labrys on the floor and then approached the eye and the sigil lurking above it. 'A little help, please?'

One of the creature's larger tentacles slid across the floor toward me. It wasn't the one that had speared Phaedra, thank the gods. After an awkward few attempts, I managed to slide myself onto the sucker pad of the tentacle, and then the creature lofted me up in the air and toward the sigil.

I *meeped,* clinging to the sucker, which helpfully clung back. When I was at eye level with the sigil, I called to the water floating on the cavern floor.

It snaked up the tentacle like a living thing, till the tip of the thick cord of water rested in the palm of my hand. Then I directed it at the rock face of the sigil, increasing its force until it was successfully drilling at the stone.

It took a long time, and a lot of power, but eventually the stone where the sigil had been was worn down to smooth, bare rock.

'It's done,' I said, sad for the creature even if this had been its choice.

[Thank you,] it intoned. [I may sleep now.]

When the creature set me down on the floor, I swayed wearily on my feet. I pulled power into me from the water still lurking in the air, but it barely took the edge off my sudden exhaustion.

This has been a long day, I thought.

[And it's time for you to go home,] the creature thought back at me. [You need your rest. War is coming.]

War? I thought, muzzily. *Real war?*

[Yes. My child knows what to do. Trust her. Her thoughts for you are strong. She will take care of you.]

War? was my only, disjointed, response as I bent, wearily, to pick up my new ax.

[I will send you home now, Jane. And I want to thank you.]

'Wait,' I asked, finally able to get my thoughts back on track. I knew there was something I wanted to ask. 'What about Anyan? Can you turn him back from being a dog?'

The voice chuckled. [Already done, child. He did not need

to be out of the way anymore. Nor the gnome. They are both
back to normal.]

I breathed an audible sigh of relief. *Anyan!* I thought,
thrilled to know he'd be waiting for me. *And hopefully no
longer applying his own mouth to his junk.*

As that is my job, snickered my libido. Both the creature
and I ignored it.

'Wait,' I said, suddenly realizing what the creature had
just admitted. 'Did you let them get changed on purpose?'

[You needed to do this for yourself, Jane.]

'No wonder Blondie kept telling me there were things I
needed to do alone. You scared the shit out of me, changing
Anyan and Nell like that. And do you know where Anyan's
mouth has now been?'

[It was the only way to remove them from the picture,
short of killing them. You inspire loyalty in your friends.]

I blushed at that, not able to think of a better compliment.

[Now, are you ready?] it asked.

'Yes,' I said, laying a hand on the tentacle still next to me.
'But will I see you again?'

[I will always be there, in your dreams, should you wish
to talk,] the creature responded, and I could feel pleasure
suffusing its thoughts.

'Good. Then I'm ready.'

[Excellent. Oh, just one more thing . . .]

'Yes?'

[When we talked earlier, about feeling out of control . . .]

'Yes,' I said, feeling embarrassed about my outburst.

[Life is never in our control,] said the creature's voice in
its rich tones. [And it's never easy. For most of us, survival
is the only option. But it's *how* we survive that counts. Does
that make sense?]

I smiled, thinking of the choices people around me had made, including poor, dead Phaedra.

Yes, I thought. *That makes sense.*

[Good. Now let us be off . . .]

And with that I felt the creature's immense power wrap around me, and that familiar lurching sensation of apparation.

[Be well, little Jane. And dream of me.]

I will, I promised, knowing it was true.

The town square? I thought. *Really?*

[I wasn't sure where to put you,] the creature replied. [So I looked for people looking for you.]

'Huh?' I said, out loud, just as I heard a shouted 'Jane!'

Peering around our darkened square – I had no idea what time it was, but it was clearly evening – I saw my dad running toward me.

Despite my weariness, and everything that had just happened, I couldn't help but grin like I'd won the lottery.

My dad is running, I thought. *He's really, honest to gods running.*

'Where have you been?' he asked, when he found me. 'I came home to find you gone, and the house was a wreck, like there'd been a party. And no note! I've been looking all over for you. I thought maybe you were doing inventory at the store, or something.' Suddenly, he stopped chiding me as he finally got a good gander of me.

'What on earth have you been doing? You're filthy. Are you all right?' My dad took a step toward me, placing a concerned hand on my shoulder.

I placed my own hand over his. 'I'm so all right, Dad. It's been a long night, but I'm very, very all right. And you were running!' I exclaimed, squeezing his fingers.

He grinned back. 'I know. I ran twice today, without even thinking about it. Once to grab a runaway paper, and just now, to get you. I can run again! Not too fast, but still.'

'It's awesome,' I agreed.

'Now what on earth have you been up to, young lady? Is that an *ax*?'

'Oh, you know . . . just saving the earth and stuff. Well, some of the earth. A corner of the earth. And yes, I now own what's actually a labrys. That's fancy for ax.'

My dad gave me a funny look. He'd been healed by goblins, but I guess he still wasn't ready for some truths.

'I'm just kidding, dad. I was training. We were doing some . . . mud exercises. With axes. Sorry I forgot to leave a note. We were all hanging out, and it seemed like a fun idea to do some night training.'

'Night training, huh? Well, as long as you're safe . . . Although I don't like the idea of you playing with axes. That looks like a serious weapon.'

Definitely safer, I thought, remembering Phaedra, dead.

'Totally. And yeah, I know it's dangerous and I'm careful. But I am *really* tired. Can we get home?'

'You'd better phone or stop by Anyan's, first. He has been freaking out. He's called the house and my cell about forty times in the past hour.'

A chill floated up my spine as I thought of Anyan once again able to make phone calls.

He's got his thumbs back! I thought, ecstatically.

Mmm. Thumbs, sighed my brain, as my libido contemplated everything it could do to with a man who wasn't afraid to engage in a little opposable action . . .

'Can you drop me off over at his place?' I asked, as we walked over to where my dad had parked the car. I got in gingerly, aware of just how caked I was in mud and grit.

'No problem, if it'll get the man to stop calling me. I'm grateful to him and all but it's after three a.m.'

'I'm sorry to keep you up so late,' I said, automatically concerned for my dad's health before I realized I didn't have to be.

'It doesn't matter,' he said. 'And for once I mean that. I feel amazing.'

My dad started the engine as I buckled up my seat belt, carefully balancing the labrys on my knees. It worked well if I let the handle dangle, with the curves of the ax head fitted over my thighs. My dad watched me, staring at the ax like it was a time bomb, and then buckled his own seat belt. After which, he turned to me.

'You know, this changes things, Jane. My being healthy.'

'Of course it does. It's great.'

'No, I mean, not just for me. But for you, too.'

I frowned at him. 'What do you mean?'

'I mean that you don't have to worry about me so much. And you don't have to . . . always be around.'

I tried to keep my voice light, but what he'd said had hurt. 'Trying to get rid of me already?' I asked. 'Don't forget my ax,' I joked. It fell flat.

My father put his hand on my knee, lightly, below the ax blade. 'No, Jane. You know I'd never want to be rid of you. You are, and always will be, my baby girl.'

I felt my eyes prickle with tears, but I held them back.

'But you're also a woman, now. And you've spent too many years held back taking care of me. I know you had your own reasons, and I'll always cherish the time we spent together. But I want you to know that I'll understand, and support you, if you want to do something different now.'

'Something different?' I asked, unable to think of anything else to say.

'Travel, move into your own apartment, move away from Rockabill even.' He paused when he saw the look in my eye, adjusting his tone so it was even softer, gentler. 'I am *not* saying I want you to go. I'd love for you to stay here, and in our home, for as long as you want. But I do want you to know I'll love you just as much if you decide you need your own space.'

'What if I want to join a cult, shave my head, and become adept at making Kool-Aid?'

'Then I'm locking you in the basement.'

I giggled. 'Thanks, Dad.' I thought of what the creature had said, about war coming. 'I might have to leave at some point. And it's good to know you'll understand.'

We sat in silence for a few moments, my dad's hand still on my knee.

'All right, then. Next stop, Anyan's. Will you be coming home at all?' he asked.

'Um,' I said, as he shook his head.

'Never mind. Just because I support your independence doesn't mean I want to know any details.'

Smart man, I thought, as I leaned back in my seat, visions of opposable thumbs dancing in my head.

Chapter Twenty-Five

My dad beat a hasty retreat after he dropped me off at Anyan's cabin, which was blazing with light. I stood for a second in the driveway, looking at the setting that had featured so heavily in my mirror fantasies.

Is this what I want? I thought to myself. Right then, the screen door opened and out stepped Anyan, dressed only, and mouthwateringly, in some trashy-chic ragged jeans and a tight white T-shirt. Surprisingly, it bore an advert for Whiskas.

No, my libido chimed in, addressing my brain's question. My mouth had actually begun watering. *He is what you want.*

I strode toward the barghest, not caring that I was covered in mud, with ripped clothes and hair sticking out in a million directions. Or that I was carrying an ax. And, except for giving my new toy a funny look, Anyan obviously didn't care what I looked like, either. He met me halfway down his wide front steps only to pick me up in those strong arms and hold me, ax and all.

I shuddered and clung to Anyan, the relief I felt at that moment so palpable it was like a tennis ball in my throat.

'I missed you,' I whispered, knotting my dirty hands in his hair.

His only response was to squeeze me tighter against him.

'I wish I could say the same thing,' he said, 'but I remember nothing.'

'Nothing?' I asked.

'Nothing,' he replied. 'I just woke up here, naked, with a half-chewed rawhide toy hanging out of my mouth. Then I wasn't able to get ahold of anyone, at all, except for Iris who said that you'd gone down a hole a while ago, and hadn't been seen since. I was freaking out. Especially since I can't remember anything after a couple of days ago.'

And that's probably for the best, I thought, *what with all the ball licking, peeing on things, and sniffing of the pee.*

'Trill told me I was just a dog, thankfully. It couldn't have been that bad, right?'

I made noncommittal if vaguely soothing noises and squirmed myself even tighter against him.

Not a dog now, my libido cooed, happily, as Anyan stroked a big hand down my back.

He walked up his stairs and into his house, and then he carried me into his lounge to sit with me, still attached to him like a burr, on his sofa. Before we sat down, I threw my labrys on his chair-and-a-half when I had the chance.

'You're filthy,' he said softly, as he arranged us so that I was lying across his lap, my head cradled on his shoulder. It was delightful, and it kept his sofa clean, the practical canine.

'I was spelunking.'

'You found a souvenir?' he asked, gesturing toward the ax.

'It's a long story.'

'And one I want to hear. Tell me what happened,' he said. 'Did you destroy the threat?'

'No,' I said. 'Well, maybe yes, if you mean Phaedra. She's dead.'

Anyan sucked in a breath. 'Dead? Are you sure?'

'Yep. Impaled on a tentacle. It was gross.'

'Wow. You didn't . . .'

'Nope, no tentacles. I did kinda kick her ass, though.'

'Good for you,' he said and grinned. 'And what about the labrys?'

'You know what it is!'

'Of course. And I can teach you to use it.'

I sighed happily, snuggling closer against him. 'Of course you can, clever puppy.'

'May I ask how you acquired it?'

'A magical creature from the dawn of time conned me into taking it, and now I'm its champion.'

'Huh,' the barghest said. 'You are, are you?'

'Yep,' I replied, my voice thick with exhaustion. 'But more like Joan of Arc, I think. Only hopefully without being martyred and all of that.'

'So an ancient creature made you its champion. Why does it need one?'

'Cuz it's trapped, and for good, now. It wanted me to destroy the only sigil that could free it, so it didn't have to worry. It scoots around in our minds, I think, so it doesn't need its body anymore, anyway.'

'Scoots around in our minds?' Anyan asked, clearly uncomfortable with that idea.

'Don't worry,' I said. 'It's not all judgy and human. It just watches.'

'Hmmm,' he grumbled, frowning. 'So it's no longer a threat?'

'It was never really a threat. It is, genuinely, nice. It didn't even need to be imprisoned. The Alfar just did that so—'

'I know,' he interrupted. 'We all saw that part. The creature must have wanted us to know the truth.'

'How far did the visions go?' I asked.

'Just around Rockabill. Caleb called Ryu and a few other contacts, and no one outside the town saw anything.'

'Did the humans?' I asked, horrified, and then I realized how inaccurate that question was.

'If you mean our nonmagical brothers and sisters, then yes. They did. But we've glamoured everyone to think that some addled hipsters from New York came and dumped LSD in the water. We're stretching that story to cover the possessions, too.'

'Who came up with that? It's terrible,' I said.

'Amy,' Anyan responded. 'She likes to blame everything on drugs, ironically enough.'

'And hipsters,' I affirmed. 'Anyway, so you know that we're all just humans? But like mutated or whatever?'

He smiled at me. 'I've always had a hunch.'

And then I remembered that night after my mom was murdered when he told me that I had to stay human, that all of us had to stay human. I thought he'd meant something all philosophical and hippie-dippie, but he was being literal.

'How'd you know?' I asked.

'Well, people like you, for starters. We couldn't be all that different if we could breed together and make little Janes. Plus, I've seen others do what Carl's done.' Carl was Capitola's dad, who'd cut himself off from magic to die with his human wife.

'He's just like a human, isn't he?' I said.

'Exactly. Anyway, I had my theories.'

'And they were right,' I said, nuzzling my nose against that beautiful crooked thing protruding from the center of his face.

I left a big streak of black dirt on his flesh.

'I think I need a shower,' I said. Then I yawned.

'And bed,' he replied.

I raised my eyebrows at him.

'For sleep, little minx,' he said, smiling at me. But I could see the heat in his eyes.

He stood, still cradling me in his arms, and then headed upstairs. To be honest, I was grateful. As soon as we'd sat down together, and the warmth of his body had started to seep into my bones, I'd become unspeakably tired.

I did make sure my ax would be safe on his chair, and that his chair would be safe from my ax, before I let him whisk me away to his bathroom.

To my disappointment, he left me to my own devices to shower after rustling me up some towels and a toothbrush. I cleaned myself up thoroughly, depositing what appeared to be about ten tons of mud down Anyan's drain, and then brushed my teeth and dried my hair as best I could before combing it out with my fingers and one of Anyan's much-too-small combs.

And I was not at all disappointed to find, when I walked out of the shower wrapped in one of Anyan's huge towels, what appeared to be a deliciously naked barghest waiting for me under the sheets. His room was dark, in a dark house, which held no one else.

No one who will need milk, I thought, shifting nervously on my feet.

I gaped at him for a moment or two, trying to resolidify my knees and make my mouth work.

'If this isn't what you want, please tell me,' he said, his voice quiet in the dark room.

I took a deep breath, forcing my lungs to breathe. I hoped to say something elegant and sexy. Instead, I said:

'I want.'

Luckily, it worked. He smiled. I nearly swooned.

'Um, I forgot to borrow a shirt,' I said, not moving from the doorway to the bathroom.

'You don't need a shirt,' he said, his voice low and gentle. 'Come here.'

I walked toward him, feeling like my legs were made of wet noodle. When I was standing next to his side of the bed, he reached out a hand and slid it over my knee, up my thigh, to the edge of the towel. Then he tugged, gently.

'Off,' he commanded. I held on for dear life.

'Off,' he repeated, meeting my black eyes with his iron-gray ones. This time I let him tug the towel away from my body so that it pooled around my feet.

'C'mon in,' he said, scootching over to give me space.

I laid down next to him, but he wouldn't let me pull up the sheet that, unfairly enough, covered the lower half of his body.

'You, my love, are a mess,' he said, as he ran his hand up my rib cage, causing me to wince.

'Huh?' I asked, looking down. Sure enough, he was right. Cleaning all the mud off had revealed a mass of bruises covering my torso, arms, and legs. A particularly livid affair had set up home on the inside of my right thigh. I was so out of it I hadn't even noticed.

'I always have liked the color purple,' I said, as Anyan's gaze raked over my body. He looked at me with that wonderful combination of protective and predatory that only the barghest could get away with.

'Now, whose ass did you kick again?' he asked, meeting my eyes as he lowered his lips – trailing healing warmth – to a large bruise on my shoulder.

'Um, Phaedra's,' I said. 'I think most of these are from the fall.'

'Fall?' he asked, trailing his healing lips down my arm, stopping at every bruise and scrape on the way.

'Mmm-hmm,' I murmured. 'Although there was a lot of

fighting, too. I beat up the harpies, Graeme, and Phaedra.'
Then I realized what I'd said and sat bolt upright. 'I wonder
if Graeme survived the cave-in?'

Anyan pushed me back down beside him, gently.

'No Graeme. Not now. But what cave-in?'

'There was a cave-in, apparently. I wasn't there. Blondie
had sent me ahead.'

'She sent you ahead, did she?' Anyan asked, disapproval
written all over his face as he shifted me around to his other
side so he could have at my left arm. When that was all bruise
free, he moved his dark head over my mottled belly.

'I'm the champion. So, yes,' I said, resisting the urge to
follow that single affirmation up with Molly Bloom's exultant
'Yes! Yes! Yes!' shouted to the cosmos. It's just that he was
using his teeth, on my ribs, making my hurts zing even as
he healed them.

Wicked barghest, my virtue swooned.

And he's not even used his thumbs, yet, my libido marveled,
clearly in awe.

'Those aren't bruises,' I panted, as he latched onto a nipple.

'Hush,' came his muffled reply.

The feel of him against me was surreal. I was so tired,
and we'd been running around like lunatics for what felt like
weeks, and the last time I'd seen Anyan he'd been a dog *and*
slurping away at his own anus. It was hard to believe that
now, here we were, all human (*really human!* I remembered),
naked, and in each other's arms.

Now I can do the slurping! my libido crowed, causing me
to blush. I hated when I blushed at my own sex drive.

And I'm assuming he's brushed his teeth, my virtue butted
in, all finicky.

He shifted, gently nudging my knees apart so he could
move his body between my thighs. His mouth found mine,

a soft kiss that quickly deepened into something much hotter. When he pulled away we were both panting.

'Minx,' he murmured, as he kissed his way down my torso. Then, lying between my legs, he shifted onto his right side so he could run his palms up my left calf and over my thigh, spreading healing warmth as he did so.

I didn't know whether to moan or sigh, torn as I was between sexual excitement and relaxation.

But when he changed sides to run his fingers up my right calf, switching to his lips to trace up my bruised right thigh, I made up my mind.

'Mmm,' I moaned, throatily, as his lips and magic found my aching flesh and healed me. And then those lips kept tracing upward, biting and licking till he paused above my undoubtedly dripping wet sex.

And then he used his thumbs.

Sweet jeebus, I thought, as he spread my lips apart gently to lick up the entire length of my slit.

I cried out, letting pleasure course through me even as I tamped down on any stray thoughts about how Anyan had become such a proficient licker.

All snark waves ceased, however, when he licked upward again, so slowly, before finding my clit with his teeth and tongue.

I was soon writhing, as he quickly stopped teasing. Instead, he worked my clit with his mouth as I felt two wide fingers slide into me.

'Oh, *puppy*,' I moaned, as he stretched me deliciously. When he added a third finger, curling them slightly to rub against my walls in a way that made me feel so very full, I swore again.

'So wet,' he murmured against me. 'I love how wet you are.'

I gabbled something incoherent at him, which I think translated roughly as 'You are the lord of my vagina!' before I came, nearly screaming my pleasure and collapsing in a sweating, sated heap. Anyan extracted his clever fingers, although his tongue was still busy lapping at me.

Whimpering, the sensation too much, I shoved weakly at his head. He let me push him aside, before kissing his way back up my body.

The smell and taste of myself on his lips as he kissed my mouth pushed one last, tired moan out of me. Then I flopped back on the bed, peering up at him through half-lidded eyes.

'Ravish me?' I said, stifling a yawn.

Anyan chuckled. 'I want you wet, begging, and – most important – *awake* when I ravish you, sweet minx.' He settled beside me, drawing me close.

'Sleep now,' he murmured, nuzzling my ear with that nose. 'In the morning you're mine . . .'

He may have gone into more detail, but I wouldn't know. I was already fast asleep.

I awoke to gentle snores in my ear and a police baton pressed into the small of my back.

That's not a police baton! my libido sang gleefully, way too awake, according to the rest of me.

I waited till my brain and body could catch up to my libido, and then I snuggled back in Anyan's arms.

That really isn't a police baton, I thought, wonderingly. *Which might be a problem . . .* I was, after all, part seal. And we had a long and sordid history with things the size and shape of clubs.

The hand that suddenly found my breasts, pinching gently at my nipples, effectively stopped my train of thought and I snuggled back again against the barghest.

'Morning,' he rumbled, kissing sleepily at the nape of my neck.

'Morning,' I purred, happy as a cat lounging in a patch of sun.

'You snore,' Anyan informed me, as he stroked his hand down my belly.

'So do you,' I said, and then moaned as – without wasting any time – his fingers eased between my legs.

'Mmm, still wet,' he said, as he moved his hand from in front of me to behind me, parting my lips as he slid a finger inside my warmth. I moaned, and his other arm, the one he was lying on, moved up so he could wrap his hand around my throat.

Easing my head around so his mouth could find mine, he slid up my body till I felt something other than just his fingers prodding at me from behind. Wanting him so badly, needing this after so long and after so many worries, I arched my back, whimpering for him, as I felt his cock part my lips . . .

And then Blondie apparated into the room, right in front of us.

'No time!' she shouted, flailing her arms. 'No time! There's no time!'

We both lay there, frozen, staring at her in disbelief.

'We have to go *right now*. What are you two doing? Don't you know what's happening?' I'd never seen the Original discomfited, let alone completely panicked. A chill slid down my spine.

'What's going on?' Anyan asked.

She stopped her frenetic movements, really looking at us for the first time. I knew she was serious when she didn't stop to say anything rude. Instead, her eyes were huge with horror.

'There's going to be a war,' she said, her voice ominous.

'And we have to win. You have to pack for a long voyage and chilly weather. Lots of layers. Now!' she shouted, when Anyan and I just stared at her. 'We leave in a few hours!'

And with that she apparated me right back to my own bedroom. I landed with a thud on my twin-sized bed. My clothes, shoes, and the labrys landed with a louder thud on my bedroom floor just a few seconds later.

I lay there, blinking at the ceiling, while I adjusted to the idea that I would *not* be shagging Anyan in the next few minutes but that I *would* be going to war.

Sitting up, I looked around to muster the will to begin packing. Again. Then, overwhelmed, I stared down at my shoes, splayed out against the double-headed ax.

For starters, I mused, eyeballing my now filthy, battered, and holey Converse, *war calls for a new pair of kicks.*

I'm thinking a champion wears red.

Acknowledgments

My family gets first dibs, as always. Thanks to my mom and dad for always being there – up to and including coming all the way to PA to make spinach dip. Thanks to Chris, Lisa, Abby, and Wyatt for always making me feel I have a home.

Thanks to my friends whom I call when I'm lonely: Jana, Loren, Kristin, Ruth, Jimmy, Mary Lois, and Arlene. You've made another big move bearable and I'd be bat-caca crazy without you.

Thanks to my new colleagues and students at Seton Hill University. I'm really enjoying getting to know all of you, and you've made my working life such a pleasure.

Thanks to all the amazing people at Orbit: Devi, you're a marvelous editor and you've made me such a better writer. Jennifer, you get it done, lady, and thanks for all you do. Thanks to Alex and Jack for getting Jane's face out into the wild, and to Lauren and Sharon for making that face so pretty. And thanks to Tim Holman for overseeing it all. I'm so proud to work for a company with Orbit's reputation.

Thanks to my agent, Rebecca Strauss, who has to be the best agent ever in the history of the universe.

Thanks to my secondary readers: James Clawson, Christie Ko, and Mary Lois White, and thanks to Diana Rowland, my critique partner, whose own work always inspires.

Thanks to the League of Reluctant Adults. I don't know what goddess was smiling on me when she sent me all of you, but I know she has a foul mouth and a snarky sensibility. I'm constantly, deliciously shocked by your shenanigans, and I'm honored to be one of you. Viva la League!

Finally, but with every bone in my body, thank you to my fans. The love you show Jane and me is outrageous, and we appreciate it very much. You really *get* her, and that pleases me immensely. Thank you for all the ways you support me: I couldn't ask for cooler fans.

extras

www.orbitbooks.net

about the author

Nicole D. Peeler lives outside of Pittsburgh, where she's a professor of English literature and creative writing in Seton Hill's MFA in popular fiction. Yes, folks, she's mentoring students in writing urban fantasy. Or, as she likes to say, 'infecting them with her madness'. Equally infectious is her love of life, food, travel, and friends. To learn more about the author, visit www.nicolepeeler.com

Find out more about Nicole Peeler and other Orbit authors by registering for the Orbit ezine at www.orbitbooks.net

if you enjoyed
EYE OF THE TEMPEST

look out for

BLOOD RIGHTS

book one of the House of Comarré novels
by

Kristen Painter

Chapter One

Paradise City, New Florida, 2067

The cheap lace and single-sewn seams pressed into Chrysabelle's flesh, weighed down by the uncomfortable tapestry jacket that finished her disguise. Her training kept her from fidgeting with the shirt's tag even as it bit into her skin. She studied those around her. How curious that the kine perceived her world this way. No, *this* was her world, not the one she'd left behind. And she had to stop thinking of humans as kine. She was one of them now. Free. Independent. Owned by no one.

She forced a weak smile as the club's heavy electronic beat ricocheted through her bones. Lights flickered and strobed, casting shadows and angles that paid no compliments to the faces around her. She cringed as a few bodies collided with her in the surrounding crush. Nothing in her years of training had prepared her for immersion in a crowd of mortals. She recognized the warm, earthy smell of them from the human servants her patron and the other nobles had kept, but acclimating to their noise and their boisterous behavior was going to take time. Perhaps humans lived so hard because they had so little of that very thing.

Something she was coming to understand.

The names on the slip of paper in her pocket were memorized, but she pulled it out and read them again. *Jonas Sweets,* and beneath it, *Nyssa,* both written in her aunt's flowery script. Just the sight of the handwriting calmed her a little. She folded the note and tucked it away. If Aunt Maris said Jonas could connect her with help, Chrysabelle would trust that he could, even though the idea of trusting a kine – no, a human – seemed untenable.

She pushed through to the bar, failing in her attempt to avoid more contact but happy at how little attention she attracted. The foundation Maris had applied to her hands, face and neck, the only skin left visible by her clothing, covered her signum perfectly. No longer did the multitude of gold markings she bore identify her as an object to be possessed. She was her own person now, passing easily as human.

The feat split her in two. While part of her thrilled to be free of the stifling propriety that governed her every move and rejoiced that she was no longer property, another part of her felt wholly unprepared for this existence. There was no denying life in Algernon's manor had been one of shelter and privilege.

Enough wallowing. She hadn't the time and there was no going back, even if she could. Which she wouldn't. And it wasn't as if Aunt Maris hadn't provided for her and wouldn't continue to do so, if Chrysabelle could just take care of this one small problem. Finding a space between two bodies, she squeezed in and waited for the bartender's attention.

He nodded at her. 'What can I get you?'

She slid the first plastic fifty across the bar as Maris had instructed. "I need to find Jonas Sweets."

He took the bill, smiling enough to display canines capped into points. Ridiculous. "Haven't seen him in a few days, but he'll show up eventually."

Eventually was too late. She added a second bill. "What time does he usually come in?"

The bartender removed the empty glasses in front of her, snatched up the money, and leaned in. "Midnight. Sometimes sooner. Sometimes later."

It was nearly 1 a.m. now. "How about his assistant, Nyssa? The mute girl?

"She won't show without him." He tapped the bar with damp fingers. "I can give Jonas a message for you, if he turns up. What's your name?"

She shook her head. No names. No clues. No trail. The bartender shrugged and hustled away. She slumped against the bar and rested her hand over her eyes. At least she could get out of here now. Or maybe she should stay. The Nothos wouldn't attempt anything in so public a place, would they?

A bitter laugh stalled in her throat. She knew better. The hellhounds could kill her in a single pass, without a noise or a struggle or her even knowing what had happened until the pain lit every nerve in her body or her heart shuddered to a stop. She'd never seen one of the horrible creatures, but she didn't need to in order to understand what one was capable of.

They could walk among this crowd without detection, hidden by the covenant that protected humans from the other-naturals, the vampires, varcolai, fae, and such that coexisted with them. She would be the only one to see them coming.

The certainty of her death echoed in her marrow. She shoved the thought away and lifted her head, scanning the crowd, inhaling the earthy human aroma in search of the signature reek of brimstone. Were they already here? Had they tracked her this far, this fast? She wouldn't go back to her aunt's if they had. Couldn't risk bringing that danger to her only family. Maris was not the strong young woman she'd once been.

Her gaze skipped from face to face. So many powdered

cheeks and blood-red lips. Mouths full of false fangs. Cultivated widow's peaks. All in an attempt to what? Replicate the very beings who would drain the lifeblood from their mortal bodies before they could utter a single word of sycophantic praise? Poor, misguided fools. She felt sorry for them, really. They worshipped their own deaths, lulled into thinking beauty and perfection were just a bite away. She would never think that. Never fall under the spell of those manufactured lies. No matter how long or how short her new life was.

She knew too much.

Malkolm hated Puncture with every undead fiber of his being. If it weren't for the bloodlust crazing his brain – which kicked the ever-present voices into a frenzy – he'd be home, sipping the single malt he could no longer afford, maybe listening to Fauré or Tchaikovsky while searching his books for a way to empty his head of all thoughts but his own.

Damn Jonas for disappearing without setting up another reliable source. Mal cracked his knuckles, thinking about the beating that idiot was in for when he showed up again. It wasn't like the local Quik-E-Mart carried pints of fresh, clean, human blood. Unfortunately.

The warm, delicious scent of the very thing he craved hit full force as he pushed through the heavy velvet drapes curtaining the VIP section. In here, his real face, the face of the monster he'd been turned into, made him the very best of their pretenders and got him access to any area of the nightclub he wanted. Ironic, considering how showing his real face anywhere else would probably get him locked up as a mental patient. He shuddered and inhaled without thinking. His body tensed with the seductive aroma of thriving, vibrating life. The voices went mad, pounding against his skull. A multitude of heartbeats filled his ears, pulses around him calling out like siren songs. *Bite me, drink me, swallow me whole.*

Damn Sweets.

A petite redhead with a jeweled cross dangling between her breasts stopped dead in front of him. Like an actual vampire could ever tolerate the touch of that sacred symbol. Dumb git. But then how was she to know the origins of creatures she only hoped were real? She appraised him from head to toe, running her tongue over a set of resin fangs. "You're new here, huh? I love your look. Are those contacts? I haven't seen any metallic ones like that. Kinda different, but totally hot."

She reached out to touch the hard ridge of his cheekbone and he snapped back, baring his teeth and growling softly. *Eat her.* She scowled. "Chill, dude." Pouting, she skulked away, muttering "freak" under her breath.

Fine. Let her think what she wanted. A human's touch might push him over the edge. No, he reassured himself, it wouldn't. *Yes.* He wouldn't let it. *Do.* He wouldn't get that far gone. *Go.* But in truth, he balanced on the edge. *Fall.* He needed to feed. *To kill.* To shut the voices up.

With that thought he shoved his way to the bar, disgusted things had gotten this dire. He got the bartender's attention, then pushed some persuasion into his voice. "Hey." It was one of the few powers that hadn't blinked out on him yet. Good old family genes.

His head turned in Mal's direction, eyes slightly glazed. Mal eased off. Humans were so suggestible. "What'll it be?"

"Give me a Vlad." Inwardly, he died a little. Metaphorically speaking. The whole idea of doing this here, in full view of a human audience, made him sick. But not as sick as going without. How fortunate that humans wanted to mimic his kind to the full extent.

"A shot?"

"A pint."

The bartender's brows lifted. "Looking to get laid, huh? A pint should keep you busy all night. These chicks get seriously damp over that action. Not that anyone's managed to drink the pint and keep it down." He hesitated. "You gotta puke, you head for the john, you got me?"

"Not going to happen."

"Yeah, right." The bartender opened a small black fridge and took out a plastic bag fat with red liquid.

Mal swallowed the saliva coating his tongue, unable to focus his gaze elsewhere, despite the fact he preferred his sustenance body temperature and not chilled. A few of the voices wept softly. "That's human, right? And fresh?"

The bartender laughed. "Chickening out?"

"No. Just making sure."

"Yeah, it's fresh and it's human. That's why it's $250 a pop." He squirted the liquid into a pilsner. It oozed down the glass thick and viscous, sending a bittersweet aroma into the air. Even here in the VIP lounge, heads turned. Several women and at least one man radiated hard lust in his direction. The scent of human desire was like dying roses, and right now, Puncture's VIP lounge smelled like a funeral parlor. He hadn't anticipated such a rapt audience, but the ache in his gut stuck up a big middle finger to caring what the humans around him thought. At least there weren't any fringe vamps here tonight. Despite his status as an outcast anathema, the lesser-class vampires only saw him as nobility. He wasn't in the mood to be sucked up to. Ever.

The bartender slid the glass his way. "There you go. Will that be cash?"

"Start a tab."

"I don't think so, buddy."

Mal refocused his power. "I've already paid you."

The man's jaw loosened and the tension lines in his forehead disappeared. "You've already paid."

"That's a good little human," Mal muttered. He grabbed the pilsner and walked toward an empty stretch of railing for a little privacy. The air behind him heated up. He glanced over his shoulder. A set of twins with blue-black hair, jet lips, and matching leather corsets stood waiting.

"Hi," they said in unison.

Eat them. Drain them.

"No." He filled his voice with power, hoping that would be enough.

They stepped forward. Behind them, the bartender watched with obvious interest.

Damn Sweets.

The blood warmed in his grasp, its tang filling his nose, but feeding would have to wait a moment longer. Using charm this time, he spoke. "I am not the one you seek. Pleasure awaits you elsewhere. Leave me now."

They nodded sleepily and moved away.

The effort exhausted him. He was too weak to use so much power in such a short span of time. He gripped the railing, waiting for the dizziness in his head to abate. He stared into the crowd below. Scanned for Nyssa, but he knew better. She only left Sweets' side when she had a delivery. The moving bodies blurred until they were an undulating mass, each one undistinguishable from the next until a muted flash of gold stopped his gaze. His entire being froze. Not here. Couldn't be.

He blinked, then stared harder. The flickering glow remained. It reminded him of a dying firefly. Instinct kicked in. Sparks of need exploded in his gut. His gums ached, causing him to pop his jaw. The small hairs on the back of his neck lifted and the voices went oddly quiet, save an occasional whimper. His world converged down to the soft light emanating from the crowd near the downstairs bar.

He had to find the source, see if it really was what he thought. If it was, he had to get to it before anyone else did. The urge drove him inexplicably forward.

All traces of exhaustion disappeared. The glass in his hand fell to the floor, splattering blood that no longer called to him. He vaulted over the railing and dropped effortlessly to the dance floor below. The crush parted to let him through as he strode toward the gentle beacon.

She stood at the bar, her back to him. The generous fall of sunlight-blonde hair stopped him, but the fabled luminescence brought him back to reality. So beautiful this close. He rubbed at his aching jaw. *You'll scare her like this, you fool. You're all fang and hunger. Show some respect.*

He assumed his human face, then approached. "Looking for someone?"

She tensed, going statue still. Even with the heavy bass, he felt her heartbeat shoot up a notch. He moved closer and leaned forward to speak without human ears hearing. Bad move. Her scent plunged into him dagger sharp, its honeyed perfume nearly doubling him with hunger pains. The whimpering in his head increased. Catching himself, he staggered for the bar behind her and reached out for support.

His hand closed over her wrist. Her pulse thrummed beneath his fingertips. Welcoming heat blazed up his arm. A chorus of fearful voices sang out in his head. *Get away, get away, get away…*

She spun, eyes fear-wide, heart thudding. "You're…" She hesitated then mouthed the words "not human."

Beneath his grip, she trembled. He pulled his hand away and stared. Had he been wrong? No marks adorned her face or hands. Maybe…but no. She had the blonde hair, the glow, the carmine lips. She hid the marks somehow. He wasn't wrong. He knew enough of the history, the lore, the traditions. Besides, he'd seen her kind before. Just the once, but it wasn't something you ever forgot no matter how long you lived. Only one thing caused that glow.

She bent her head. "Master," she whispered.

"Don't. Don't call me that. It's not necessary." She thought him nobility? Why not assume he was fringe? Or worse, anathema? But she'd addressed him with the respect due her better. A noble with all rights and privileges. Which he wasn't. And she'd surely guessed he was here to feed. Which he was.

She nodded. "As you wish, mast—" Visibly flustered, she cut herself off. "As you wish."

He gestured toward the exit. "Outside. You don't belong here." Anyone could get to her here. Like Preacher. It wasn't safe. How she'd ended up here, he couldn't fathom. Finding a live rabbit in a den of lions would have been less surprising.

"I'm sure my patron will be back in just a—"

"We both know I'm the only real vampire here." For now. "Let's go."

Her gaze wandered to the surrounding crowd, then past him. She sucked her lower lip between her teeth and twisted her hands together. Hesitantly, she brushed past, painting a line of hunger across his chest with the curve of her shoulder. *Get away, get away, get away...*

She was not for him. He knew that, and not just because of the voices, but getting his body to agree was a different matter. Her scent numbed him like good whiskey. Made him feel needy. Reckless. Finding some shred of control, he shadowed her out of the club, away from the mob awaiting entrance, and herded her deep into the alley. He scanned in both directions. Nothing. They hadn't been followed. He could get her somewhere safe. Not that he knew where that might be.

"No one saw us leave."

She backed away, hugging herself beneath her coat. Her chest rose and fell as though she'd run a marathon. Fear soured her sweet perfume. She had to be in some kind of trouble. Why else would she be here without an escort? Without her patron?

"Trust me, we're completely alone." He reached awkwardly to put his arm around her, the first attempt at comfort he'd made in years.

Quicker than a human eye could track, her arm snapped from under the coat, something dark and slim clutched in her hand. The side of her fist slammed into his chest. Whatever she held pierced him, missing his heart by inches. The voices shrieked, deafening him. Corrosive pain erupted where she made contact.

He froze, immobilized by hellfire scorching his insides. He fell to his knees and collapsed against the damp pavement. Foul water soaked his clothing as he lay there, her fading footfalls drowned out by the howling in his head.